Front Yard

Books by Norman Draper

Backyard

Front Yard

Published by Kensington Publishing Corporation

Front Yard

Norman Draper

KENSINGTON BOOKS
www.kensingtonbooks.com

KENSINGTON BOOKS are published by

Kensington Publishing Corp.
119 West 40th Street
New York, NY 10018

All Kensington titles, imprints, and distributed lines are available at special quantity discounts for bulk purchases for sales promotion, premiums, fund-raising, educational, or institutional use.

Special book excerpts or customized printings can also be created to fit specific needs. For details, write or phone the office of the Kensington Sales Manager: Kensington Publishing Corp., 119 West 40th Street, New York, NY 10018. Attn. Sales Department. Phone: 1-800-221-2647.

Kensington and the K logo Reg. U.S. Pat. & TM Off.

eISBN-13: 978-1-61773-308-6
eISBN-10: 1-61773-308-3
First Kensington Electronic Edition: October 2015

ISBN-13: 978-1-61773-307-9
ISBN-10: 1-61773-307-5
First Kensington Trade Paperback Printing: October 2015

10 9 8 7 6 5 4 3 2

Printed in the United States of America

For the aunts and uncle I never met:

Norma Ann Draper, 1925–1934
Margaret Eva Zimmerman, 1918–1935
Lt. j.g. Norman Claflin Draper, 1921–1944

1

New Frontier

At first, it was all about the front yard.

That was the part of their corner lot that was so obviously scenic. Spreading out westward from the house, it stayed level for about twenty yards before sloping down thirty feet to Sumac Street.

Beyond Sumac the land dipped more gradually to the thin screen of cottonwoods that bordered Bluegill Pond, the third-biggest *lake* in suburban Livia. The gap in the terrain created by Bluegill Pond opened up the sky. Winter nights would treat them to panoramic displays of stars, meteor showers, and northern lights. On summer days, columns of clouds would billow up in plain view forty miles away.

George and Nan Fremont, on purchasing the hilltop rambler at the corner of Sumac and Payne Avenue, immediately set to work to take advantage of this wonderful setting. They'd make their front yard the showpiece of their new home, and use it to take advantage of Nan's developing skills as a gardener.

They hired a landscaping contractor to build a stone wall that curved upward, following the cement steps rising from the driveway to the stoop, on which were situated a table made of a laminated slice of tree trunk and three plastic chairs.

Their first plantings were the sweet-scented dwarf Korean lilacs, which they placed next to the huge silver maple that shaded the front entrance to the house; a mistake, they soon discovered, since dwarf Korean lilacs are sun worshippers. Somehow, they had managed to bloom adequately.

Then came the pachysandra and purple-flowering ajuga at the base of the stone wall. The rotten wooden railing on the lake side of the steps came down, to be replaced by an elegant, curving, gray-painted iron one.

Nan dreamed of much more: a cedar deck, carpets of ground covers, and swaths of annuals and perennials that would turn their slope into a quilt of bright colors and rich earth tones. But she soon discovered that all this would have to wait; three small children demanded too much of her attention. They'd also require an unobstructed playground of hardy grass that could be trod on and trampled to their hearts' delight. Once they were older, Nan would be able to give her new hobby the attention it deserved. For the time being, she had to make do with some petunias and impatiens, and a ring of irises she planted around the stand of mugho pines that came with the house.

Over the years, though, the front yard's stock nosedived.

It was all about George, who had developed a front yard phobia. That might have come from having to push a lawn mower without a self-propelled mechanism up and down that steep slope. Or maybe it was the need to continually spray a particularly stubborn patch of dandelions and cockleburs that rose halfway from the street to the top of their little hill. Another thing: The slope and sandy soil meant water drained away quickly from the grass's shallow roots. Any week-long stretch of dry heat scratched brown patches across the lawn, even with regular sprinkling.

There was also the front yard's history of violence.

George had once been attacked while mowing by a honking mother goose who must have figured he was going to run over one of her goslings. Her sudden waddling charge caused him to let go of the lawn mower, which trundled down the hill, barely missing a passing minivan as it crossed the street, jumped the curb, and careened down the slope and into the lake. A swift kick to her feathered midriff that left George losing his balance and sprawled on the lawn finally drove the attack goose and the maniacally squabbling goslings away.

It was in the front yard where George made the mistake of spraying a yellow jacket nest in midday. The result of that was an upper lip swollen by stings to three times its normal size and Nan taking photos of it, which she advertised to friends as "George's Homer Simpson look."

All this got Nan to wondering whether her gardening ambitions had been off-target. She began shifting her attention from the front to the loamier and more level back.

This new project started with George renting a chain saw to clear out the volunteer trees that had turned much of the backyard into a junkyard of mismatched vegetation. Then, he built pea-gravel-and-railroad-tie steps into the weed-choked bare patch that separated the driveway from the patio.

Nan took over from there. Her maiden garden effort was to plant lilac bushes and variegated dogwoods next to the fence that separated the Fremonts from the Grunions, their neighbors to the east. That was eight years after they bought the property.

Six years later, they'd transformed the backyard into a suburban paradise of vibrant blooms, trilling songbirds, and hovering hummingbirds that, last summer, had defied the destructive whims of Mother Nature and even some ridiculous efforts to sabotage them by the local gardening nutcases. It had won them first place in the world-famous Burdick's Best Yard Contest, and the unprecedented $200,000 tax-free windfall that came with it.

Now, at last, it was the front yard's turn.

"Lots of work to do here, George," said Nan as they sat on the covered front stoop. George gazed out through the sheets of endless May rain at their blank canvas of a yard. This would be a start-from-scratch job, just as the backyard had been. A flare of pain shot through his knee. Then, another one, this time starting at the small of his back and rocketing all the way up his spinal column. It was his body's reaction to the prospect of hard, painful labor ahead. He flinched.

"Yeow!"

Nan snorted.

"You can't fool me, George. I know those phantom aches and pains of yours. So, buck up, because I'm gonna need you to do most of the heavy lifting here. Dig. Rake. Mix. Haul. And maybe you can sometimes give me a little input as to what we should plant and where. But, mostly, you'll be my good old semi-reliable gardening mule."

George cringed. This was the hyper-caffeinated-morning Nan talking here, and when she started jabbering away about projects that would put the Pyramids of Giza and Hoover Dam to shame, you just had to listen and nod politely. She'd calm down once the day moved into its afternoon stage, and wine-induced relaxation replaced all the let's-build-the-world's-best-garden-in-a-day stuff. What especially worried him was this stark comparison: It had taken them six years to transform the backyard. Nan wanted the front yard planted by the end of the month. George, at a loss for words to express his foreboding, looked stricken. Nan regarded him with a mixture of connubial pity and scorn.

"Oh, don't look so miserable, George. Just think of all the new flower buddies you'll have to talk to. And imagine the magnificence! This front yard project will make us whole. Back-yard *and* front yard. The Fremont *gardens,* not just the Fremont backyard. Won't that be wonderful? If it would only stop rain-ing for a few days."

"What's wrong with resting on our laurels?" George said. "For, say, four or five years, maybe a decade, before moving on to new projects."

"Oh, stop being Mr.-Lazy-Ass-Fussbudget," Nan har-rumphed. "You've got helpers this time, you know. Mary's going to pitch in big-time, and we've got Shirelle as our gar-dening intern all summer. With two strong, motivated young women like that, you won't be overworked. With any luck, you can spend a good amount of your shiftless days just lord-ing it over those of us who'll actually be working."

Yes, that's true, George thought; we've got reinforcements for this project! His mood brightened instantly. And just as in-stantly the clouds returned to darken it. What about the psy-chotic rage unleashed by the local criminal gardening element on the backyard last year? And the freak hailstorm? And all that weird, otherworldly stuff that they didn't dare tell their pastor about? What about the deadly angel's trumpets that would once again sprout their seductive and hallucinogenic flowers?

Are we through with all that, or is this just the beginning? George wondered, involuntarily bouncing the balls of his feet on the cement. Who or what's going to try to deep-six us now?

It was at this point that the caffeine racing through Nan's brain found the appropriate neurons responsible for inventing horticultural riddles and knock-knock jokes.

"George, what flower is like a cartoon character?"

George could only shrug, looking as he did like a mourner who's wound up at the wrong funeral and decided to stick around anyway.

"A *daffy*-dill. Get it? Daffy Duck? Daffodil? Tee-hee-hee . . . Now, let's get a move on, mister. We're off to the Historical Society."

"Waste of time, if you ask me," George said. "I mean, why do we need to encourage Jim and his stupid delusions of buried treasures somewhere underneath us?"

"Because he's one of our dear friends, George, as you may recall. And he happens to be recently bereaved. . . . Quit being so morose and contrary just because you've got one of the Labors of Hercules ahead of you. Besides, I'd have thought the Mr. History Buff in you would jump at the chance of getting a little glimpse back in time of the very place where you eat, tipple, and otherwise fritter away your slothful days. . . . Hey, here's something that'll perk you right up: It's stopped raining. And look over there to the west. That patch of blue's getting bigger by the minute. Let's go; it's time for us to do our annual spring inspection tour anyway."

George and Nan pulled out of the driveway with George's disposition improved. The notion of a front yard makeover, assisted by a mug's worth of French roast coffee, was beginning to appeal to the semi-developed aesthete in him; especially since there were others who would be sharing the toil this time. There was also the fact that the front yard was smaller than the back. Something else to look forward to was picking up the skinny on their property's pedigree. That was long overdue, especially after the scare they had gotten last year about there being an Indian burial ground under the backyard gardens. That had turned out to be a false alarm . . . or so they'd been told.

Besides, what if there *was* something to this buried treasure notion of Jim's?

"Why is this museum we're going to like an overly emotional woman?" George quizzed Nan as he peeled out of the driveway.

"This is a joke?" wondered Nan, pleasantly startled by George's sudden impersonation of a getaway car driver. "If it is, it's sexist, and I'll have no part of it."

"Because they're both *hysterical*. Or, you know, *historical*. Ha-ha!"

2

What Lies Beneath

"You mean to tell me a man was *killed* in our backyard?"

Nan's knees buckled. She propped herself against the front counter and gripped its ledge hard. Having steadied herself, she pivoted away from the woman at the information counter to stare, goggle-eyed, at George.

George was doing his speak-no-evil impression by clamping his hand over his mouth and chin. He did that when he couldn't decide whether to be astonished, scared, or completely indifferent. Nan wished he would stop; it made him look like such a dolt.

But this! It was disturbing enough that their placid and orderly little oasis at one time harbored thickets of weeds, natural grasses gone wild, and shrubs and trees growing and multiplying by nature unchained. To now be told that it was the scene of a violent death, why, it was unthinkable!

"Well, we don't actually know that for a fact," said the historian, a Miss Price.

Miss Price's baleful glare had challenged them to approach her as they sauntered into the Livia Historical Society during one of the few times it was open to visitors: ten a.m. to eleven a.m. on the third Saturday of the month, alternating months, even-numbered years only. "But we are reasonably certain that two men associated with Sieur de La Salle—Messrs. Boyer and Ducharme—departed from La Salle's main group at some point. They might have made their way to Livia and camped out in the vicinity of Bluegill Pond. The best place to camp along Bluegill Pond would have been the east side, on top of the rise on which your house now stands."

"This guy was actually *killed* on *our* property!" George said. "Whoa!"

"Yeah," said Nan. "Who was this 'La' guy?"

"La Salle, the French explorer."

"Oh, *that* La Salle," George said. "Sure. The guy who canoed the Mississippi all the way to the Gulf of Mexico. And that was before they had lightweight Mylar materials. Ha-ha! Of course I've heard of him! And who would have been the victim, Boyer or Ducharme?"

"Very possibly . . . Boyer," said Miss Price. She peered at an old map covered with indecipherable markings, but on which the pear shape of Bluegill Lake was plainly visible. "The murderer, Ducharme, might have buried him out of guilt; they were friends and early business partners in the fur trade with the Indians, after all. Or maybe he wanted to hide the evidence. Well, let's be fair to Ducharme; he might have killed in self-defense. Most likely, Boyer's body was just left there to be consumed by wild animals."

George shuddered.

"And that was a very long time ago, I take it?" said Nan. George caught the hint of a tremor in her voice.

"Of course, Mrs. Fremont. The voyageurs were active in the area from the mid-sixteen hundreds all the way until the early eighteen hundreds. La Salle flourished in the late sixteen hundreds. This would have occurred around then. I would know—I have specialized in the study of the Livia area my entire adult life."

Nan released her hunched-up shoulders.

"Well, I'm really relieved. When you first mentioned it, I thought you were talking about something that happened not all that long ago."

"Why, certainly not!" Miss Price gasped. "Most certainly not! This is a historical society, not the local constabulary. What, do you think French explorers and missionaries and fur traders were mucking around here after World War Two? With maybe hundred-horsepower Evinrude outboard motors on their birchbark canoes, and outfitted with breathable-fabric anoraks and bazookas to ward off the bad old suburbanites?"

Nan jerked back from the counter at this sudden outburst.

"Well, when you first told us about a murder, you didn't say right away when it was. And it's still a little unsettling to know someone might have been killed in your backyard, no matter when. Goodness!"

"Some believe the spirit lives on," said Miss Price. "Perhaps you'd better be mindful of that, hmmm?"

"Actually," said George, clearing his throat and glancing at Nan, whose pursed lips and unflinching stare he knew to be the signal to be resolute. "We wanted to know if you have records of anything else . . . uh . . . buried there."

Miss Price gave a start.

"Some *thing* buried?" she said. Nan and George glanced at each other. A telepathic connection warned them to shift into evasive mode.

"Uh . . . uh . . . some old papers and things like that," George said. Why, oh why can't my husband be a better liar when the need arises? Nan mused to herself disconsolately.

"Buried? Now, let me think . . . Ah, yes. I've heard that one. Yes, indeed, I've heard that one. Yes. Not papers. No, siree. It's the lost treasure of Livia. Ha-ha!"

George and Nan smiled politely as Miss Price continued.

"As the story goes, pirates from the Spanish Main used to

travel fifteen hundred miles inland to bury their doubloons right here." Miss Price stabbed her finger at the point on the map that marked the Fremonts' three-quarter-acre lot. "There could be a dozen chests of pieces of eight buried in your yard. Those pirates would have sailed right up from the Gulf on to the Mississippi, veered on to the Muskmelon River, branched off on the Big Turkey, and found your place on the high ground. Probably ten, twelve feet down, but who knows exactly where."

"You're not serious!" Nan cried.

"Dead serious. You know what else is there? Jesus's bifocals. Dropped off after the Last Supper. So is Captain Kidd's spittoon, and the lost racing bike of the Incas. All right there in your yard waiting to be dug up."

George frowned. Nan frowned. Miss Price coughed up a brittle laugh.

"I'm pulling your legs, Mr. and Mrs. Fremont. There's no buried treasure of Livia. Otherwise, I'd have the complete dossier on it, and it would have been dug up a long, long time ago." She glared at Nan and George with bulging eyes.

"Not about the murder, though," she said, her voice quavering. "I wasn't joking about the murder."

Gwendolyn Price wrung her hands in furious agitation as she watched the Fremonts walk out the front door, tinkling the little bell that signaled the comings and goings of the few visitors who ever passed through the portals of the Livia Historical Society.

She couldn't believe it—4250 Payne Avenue come back to haunt her, and after she had pretty much given up on it! How long had it been since she was forced to sell the place? How many years had she yearned and striven to get it back?

The old farmhouse had been torn down and a new house built that had nothing to do with farming. Two sets of owners came and went. As a teacher subject to continual layoffs and bouncing from school district to school district while caring for a terminally ill mother, she was powerless to do anything about it.

When her mother finally died, Miss Price went back to college for her master's degree and eventually found a place in the history department of the St. Anthony metro's most prestigious private school. Having never married, and with only one true passion—the history and genealogy of Livia—making demands on her time and resources, she was able to amass a large savings over the years. So, when the house, or, more important, the property, came up for sale again, she was ready. But then, she was outbid by these . . . these Fremonts! Why, they had bought the property from right under her nose!

Now who, of all people, should suddenly come waltzing in on a quiet Saturday morning!

"Astonishing!" she blurted to no one in particular since there was no one else in the big museum-styled room at the moment. She had acquired the habit of talking to herself from years of living alone.

Hold on! There were possibilities here. Miss Price's febrile imagination began firing up, but it was moving in too many directions. She was being handed an opportunity, given a sign, but how to proceed? They had heard something. They had heard talk and hearsay, probably nothing more. But even talk and hearsay could be dangerous. They might find it, and after she had searched high and low these many years.

"Who do they think they are?" she mumbled. "They don't *know* anything, do they? But, yes, they must. They know something is buried there. Or maybe just suspect. That's why they came in. They must be up to no good."

At first shocked and confused when the Fremonts had walked up to her counter and presented the address she knew so well, Miss Price had struggled to figure out what to do. Ultimately, she had chosen on the fly to tell them some truths and some falsehoods. Voyageurs could well have visited the site. They might have even camped there. But nobody would know who they were.

The murder was pure fabrication. Why had she made that up? To throw them a red herring. It just wouldn't do to tell them nothing at all had happened there. That would arouse suspicion more than anything. The rest was pure buffoonery, in detail if not in general concept. She had masked the true situation further by laughing off the whole mystery as a joke.

Miss Price's face reddened with solitary mirth. Private jokes were so much better than shared ones, she reflected. But this was no time for levity. Time to stop amusing herself and get back on-task. She gave her cheek a stinging slap.

"Yeow!" she cried. "Not so hard."

Self-mortification was Miss Price's way of keeping her thoughts from wandering. It could be a slap, a pinch, a jab with a just-sharpened pencil. As a teacher, she had thrown erasers and even pieces of chalk at inattentive students. Jarring acts of physical violence, she found, were excellent focusing mechanisms. That practice had stopped when several wealthy board members had threatened to pull their children out of the school and run Miss Price out of town on a rail. But Miss Price had taken that lesson and applied it to herself. She frowned at the memory and found herself beginning to dwell on it. That called for a pinch.

"Ouch!"

Miss Price retrieved a business card from her purse. She picked up the receiver of the Historical Society's circa-1960 Princess phone and dialed the number on the card. After four rings, the voice mail kicked in. The recording startled her. It started with the booming of cannons and clatter of musketry. Then, barely audible above the din, came the sound of a muffled voice.

"Hi, Scroggit Brothers here. Antiquities Sales and Investigations. History is our strategic objective. Can't talk now. The Rebs are coming. Looks like our regiment will be right in the thick of it. Leave your name, number, and a brief message and we'll call you back once we've repulsed the attack. Or you can find our stores on the Web at www.fightyankee.com. Here they come, boys. Aim low."

The Scroggit brothers were borderline criminals with few scruples when it came to ferreting out and scavenging historical rarities. They had, in fact, unearthed such items for her on more than one occasion. Her Indian peace pipe, for instance. And pioneer woman Violet Tagget's diaries. Tales of their extralegal methods had failed to shock her, which was good because it was time to take off the kid gloves and claim what was rightfully hers.

"Gwendolyn Price here," Miss Price barked into the phone after the beep. "I have a mission for you that requires discretion. This demands your immediate attention. I promise a commission based on the finding, which will be significant in both a pecuniary and historical sense. Please respond ASAP."

3

Detours and Delays

"Stupid full-of-herself historian!" sputtered George as he and Nan drove back home. "How can they have somebody like that running the Historical Society and dealing with the public? You'd never know when she was telling the truth and when she was playing her little joke at your expense."

George and Nan decided to make their way home via a slow detour down hidden, winding residential streets in tucked-away neighborhoods, rather than going straight back along the most direct route—34th Avenue West. This was their scenic tour. Now that the Livia gardening season should be in full swing, it was time to see what some of their favorite gardeners were up to. But their mood, which would ordinarily have been bright and expectant—or at least moderately curious, in George's case—was colored by what Nan referred to as the "ugly incident" at the Historical Society.

"The nerve of her!" Nan said. "Getting us going the way she did. I should have known from the moment she started talking about pirates. Who ever heard of pirates in Livia? Or on the Big Turkey River! You can barely get a kayak down that thing. Too bad for Jim. It would have made him so happy to find something really big with his whatchamacallit."

"Metal detector."

"Yah, metal detector."

"Well, we did what he asked," George said. "We checked it out and found *nada*. Jim and his stupid buried-treasure story! What a bunch of baloney! No more digging up the yard to find maybe a few screws and some flattened cans, like he did last year."

"Just hold on, dear," Nan said. "I've been doing some revisionist thinking about this. It's a big yard. I wouldn't be surprised if he missed a few spots, front and back. We're just starting our big front yard gardens, so what's the harm in him rooting around before Mary and Shirelle get planting? Heck, he can still dig around a little in the backyard under where the new angel's trumpets will be."

George's stomach churned at the mention of the angel's trumpets.

"I probably won't get around to planting them for another week or two," Nan continued. "And, speaking of which, I'm still trying to figure out whether we should plant them at all since you get so freaked out every time you look at the ones that are there already. It's a nice sunny spot. Maybe I'll transplant some of those volunteer spirea there."

"I have made my peace with the angel's trumpets," George huffed.

"No, you haven't. I bet you won't come within ten yards of them, even before they bloom. They're really not *that* poisonous, you know. Could they cause some mild hallucinations? Maybe. But you're already hallucinating in your advanced middle age anyway."

"Could we continue on this Jim-digging-up-our-yard line of conversation, Nan-bee? You might recall that Jim said he wanted to dig up our beautiful blue hydrangea, too. Remember how hard we worked at that to make the blasted soil more alkaline? And now we're going to, what, dig it up, plant another hydrangea, and hope that it turns out as blue as the one we've got now?"

"I know."

"Those peonies and astilbe that *finally* started to bloom last year would get dug up, too. They were some of your best cross-cultural communicators, or whatever it is you call your little plant buddies. I guess you'll be getting a real earful once they pop up through the soil and find out what you're thinking about."

"I know, George. I know. I'm willing to say now that's all moot since there's nothing to this buried-treasure talk. I just wanted to find something to get Jim's mind off Alicia. He's so sad these days with her gone and taking the dog and parakeet and his baseball card collection and all."

George chuckled. In doing so, he elicited a brief, icy stare from Nan. As bad as he felt for Jim, he couldn't help but admire Alicia for running off with the baseball cards, especially the Phil Croxton rookie card. Why, that card must be worth a mint!

"I feel sorry for Jim, too, but listen, will you, Nan-bee: Those won't be dinky little pick-and-shovel jobs Jim was proposing, like last year's. He wants to dig down six or seven feet and ten to twelve feet across. That means you bring in the heavy equipment. How long would it take those scars to heal? And how could your little flower friends ever forgive you? You'd be just another flower murderer in their minds."

Nan blanched at the thought of having to break the news to some of her flowers that they were to be sacrificed for the sake of filthy lucre. But, hard as it might be to believe, there were other, more pressing matters to consider.

"Listen here, buddy, a few stray gold coins wouldn't have hurt us any, especially since I'm guessing our current financial situation isn't looking all that rosy. Eh?"

George didn't respond. He bit his lip and tightened his

grip on the steering wheel. He had begun to fret that they'd been burning through their recent first-place Burdick's Best Yard prize earnings at a clip they couldn't keep up. Maybe he should start paying more attention to their bank accounts and mutual fund balances. Hang on—what mutual fund balances? Oh, yeah, he had cashed those out a couple of months ago.

"Did you hear me, George? Huh?"

George jerked the steering wheel violently to the right to turn onto Old DanTroop Drive. The tires squealed and the car tilted a few degrees as the left-side wheels lifted an inch or two above the road. Nan froze in rigid attention as she heard the squeal and felt the lurch, then leaned against the tilt of the car with a leering grin.

Nan was always excited and sometimes transformed when he took that right-angle intersection at forty, actually speeding up into the turn instead of slowing down. George figured it was because it gave her the sort of adrenaline thrill she didn't often feel among the more subtle attractions of their gardens. Could it be that for those few seconds she was actually inhabited by the spirit of some dangerous woman from times gone by? Annie Oakley, for instance? Whatever it was, it would occasionally create in Nan a trance-like state. That would last about fifteen seconds. Then, once she came out of it, she started with a fresh slate, and anything said or seen during the previous five minutes might as well have never happened.

"Whew!" she gasped. "That was rockin', Pops!"

George chuckled. After a few seconds of silence, he knew he had passed the crisis point; there would be no contentious discussion about the family finances on this drive.

They only had a few blocks to go to one of Livia's finest and most extensive stretches of residential gardens. This, along with Waveland Circle and the Billings Lake neighborhood, was where Livia's gardening bluebloods honed their craft. It was a place that was hallowed—like Gettysburg or a Sagelands merlot vineyard—and through which you traveled awestruck: respectfully, quietly, and attentively.

But they weren't quite there yet.

Nan smiled and rocked her head back slightly. She's lost in appreciation of her own ingenuity, thought George. Brace yourself, buddy, 'cause here it comes.

"Knock-knock," Nan said.

"Who's there?" answered George for whom Nan's plant jokes and riddles had all the appeal of a prickly sow thistle–induced skin rash.

"Phlox."

"Phlox who?"

"Phlox of luck getting those marigolds to grow in that shady place next to the rock border."

"You watch, Nan-bee," sputtered George. "You just watch. That spot gets six hours of sun a day."

"No, it doesn't. It gets two and a half hours max. Besides, you were looking at it before the silver maple leafed, and even then it was only getting four hours of sun. Those marigolds will produce no floral display of note. Lord knows, I tried to warn you. Slow down, George."

They had turned onto Cabot Drive.

George lifted his foot off the accelerator and gently applied it to the brake. Their new, gun-metal-gray Toyota Avalon slowed to five miles per hour—Fremont garden cruising speed.

There were signs of the messy, unattractive beginnings of gardening activity everywhere. Husbands and wives were out in their shorts and T-shirts, baseball caps and broad-brimmed straw gardening hats, working the soil in their flower beds, and carefully inserting little blobs of color into them with their gloved hands. Flats of petunias, alyssum, pansies, coleus, and impatiens seemed to be lying around everywhere, as did gardening forks, shovels, hand trowels, and two-cubic-foot bags of pre-fertilized soil.

But so far, only one week short of Memorial Day weekend, there was little to show for it. Everything seemed to be going so slowly this year. That troubled Nan, for whom bloom bursts of lilacs—both of the regular and dwarf Korean variety—ajuga, irises, and bridal wreath spirea typically marked her favorite holiday, which was by common accounting in this neck of the woods to be the first day of summer. She watched in sullen disappointment as the passing front yards slowly slid by.

About halfway down the block on the right was the Knights'. Here was a sign of encouragement: The Knights' dwarf Korean lilacs were leafing nicely!

"I wonder how they'll look in a week or two, after all that extreme pruning they did last year," Nan said. "Bleeding hearts are out, but just barely. Must have been the long winter. I mean, jeez, ours just poked through the ground a week or so ago. They're going to get all covered up by the hosta before they even get going."

Livia's winter had lingered into the first week of May, and it wasn't until late April that the ground finally thawed. The last showers of snowflakes had come in two quick, sloppy bursts just a week and a half earlier. There followed a period of cool, showery weather that had kept everyone indoors. Already it was May 19, and the temperature had just nicked 60 the previous Saturday.

The result of all this was that Livia's gardening season had been set back two to three weeks. Sure, the crocuses and tulips had come out a few weeks ago—bright, shiny medallions of purple, white, red, and yellow punctuating the last watery snowscapes of the season—but not a sign of hosta. There wasn't even any spring phlox yet.

"Okay," Nan said. "Time to go check out Waveland Circle. Let's see what Marta Poppendauber's up to this year, assuming she's even started."

The Burdick's three-foot-by-two-foot wooden sign stood right next to the driveway of the house on Waveland. It trumpeted the news: CONGRATS! MARTA AND HAM P., RUNNERS-UP, BURDICK'S BEST YARD CONTEST!

"Hmmm," said Nan. "How come they haven't put ours back up? *We* won the stupid contest."

George and Nan gazed into the yard that had so dazzled them last June. Everywhere, there were signs of beginning cultivation, with freshly planted annuals dotting the yard and filling numerous flowerpots—both hanging and on pedestals—of all sizes. Gardening tools and bags of fertilizer were everywhere. Clearly, here was a work of art in the making.

A middle-aged couple stood behind their picture window watching them. They waved. George and Nan waved back to Marta and Ham Poppendauber, and pulled out of the cul-de-sac.

"Time to go check on last year's biggest *loser,*" Nan said.

About a mile to the south, Dr. Phyllis Sproot was outside, squatting over a large patch of freshly turned dirt. She was wearing a big woven-straw sun hat encircled with a black leather band that George couldn't help but imagine emblazoned with a skull and crossbones, sunglasses with oversized lenses that made her look as if she were part praying mantis, and a bandanna knotted into strangulation tightness around her neck. She clawed violently at the ground with a hand cultivator.

"Scary," Nan whispered.

"Yeah," George said. "I wonder if she's planning a big comeback this year."

"Even if she does, who cares? There won't be another contest like last year's to get people all riled up. And there won't be another for four more years if my math's correct. Burdick just said they'd have it every five years, correct? With any luck, we'll all just quietly tend our gardens this year and everyone can keep out of the news. Even a proven gardening thug like Phyllis Sproot might have to behave herself this time."

Dr. Sproot looked up briefly as they approached, her eyes turned into big black caverns by the capacious sunglasses, a deep scowl painted on what there was of her face that they could see, then resumed viciously attacking her soil.

"Why couldn't someone have been murdered in *her* yard?" Nan said as they drove off toward home. "Step on it, George, before she comes over and kills us or something."

The drive home continued in its dawdling manner, with occasional short detours to view the beginnings of gardens the Fremonts had only just discovered last year, when they were scoping out the competition for the contest. Not surprisingly, signs of this year's activity were much harder to spot. Livia's fair-weather gardeners had obviously been thwarted by the drawn-out winter and the lack of any high-stakes gardening competition to match last year's.

"Down to the hardcore this year, I guess," said Nan. "Livia's true-blue gardeners, the ones in it for the long haul. Speaking of which, we'd better get crackin' ourselves. We don't want a couple of girls showing us up, do we?"

George didn't respond. He was stewing about someone getting murdered in their yard, however long ago that might have been.

The Fremonts were intermittent Christians belonging to the Please-Redeem-Me Lutheran Church, an offshoot of the Evangelical Lutheran Church in America that allowed a little pagan-flavored nature worship to enter into its doctrine. While that was plenty good enough for Nan, George occasionally entertained extreme spiritual notions more in line with his druidical antecedents. For instance, he thought it was quite possible that malevolent spirits of the unsettled dead rattled around and created mischief in the places where they had died.

Nan, though she had become an accomplished plant whisperer and had petitioned the synod to add an epicurean element to the tenets of their faith, had no doubt that the dead went to abide blissfully with Our Lord and Savior unless they were real creeps. In that case they just turned into the fossil fuels of tomorrow, and were quite incapable of oozing up through the earth.

George turned on the radio. The exuberant babblings of Milo Weavermill and Bernie "Bad Dog" Simpson, the voices of the St. Anthony Muskies, salved his nagging anxieties. So did the fact that the Muskies were hammering the Pelicans, 12–2, and Johnny "Smokestack" Gaines had already jacked two out of the park.

"Turn that down, please," Nan said.

From a block away, they couldn't see daughter Mary and Shirelle, their gardening intern, who were supposed to be hard at work prepping the soil in their front yard for the new gardens that Shirelle had purportedly been designing for them over the winter and spring. No sign of any turned-up soil, the rototiller, or burlap-encased shrubs or bushes. In fact, there was no sign of any activity at all.

But there was something else that caught Nan's attention, something new, big, and artificial sticking out of the yard.

"Look, George, they put it back!" Nan beamed.

On the rounded corner of their lot, at the little grassy spot where their unshaded bluegrass, rye, and fescue tended to cook brown by late July, the Burdick's sign had reappeared. Made of wooden planks and posts sunk deep into the turf, it measured six feet wide by four feet tall. Most important was what the sign said in dark letters branded boldly, yet tastefully, into the knotty pine boards:

CONGRATS, G. AND N. FREMONT, 1ST PLACE PRIZE, BURDICK'S BEST YARD CONTEST. The G. AND N. FREMONT part was on a little raised panel, detachable, so that when the next contest came around in four years it could be replaced by a similar panel with the new winners' names on it. George cringed, then made a manly effort to give Nan some positive support.

"Oh, boy," he said. "It's back."

"Last year's sign was better," said Nan, as she leaned forward, squinting and knitting her brow. "The letters are too big. Gee whiz, they couldn't even make the room to spell out our first names. What's going to happen if Jocelynbower Kerplunkinpoof Wimblybones wins next time? Ha-ha! I mean, hey, they're giving away hundreds of thousands of dollars in prizes, and they're going to skimp on the sign design?"

George didn't answer. He was too busy trying to figure out who had just hit that double while he honed all his senses to be alert for any signs of dead-guy activity.

4

A Spring Prelude

"Mom, Daddy, they put the sign back up!"

Mary bounded down the steps to the garage quivering with excitement as George and Nan got out of the car.

She and Shirelle had been sitting on the front stoop lazily sipping cold lemonades. They had been wishing aloud that they could be in Martinique or Maui pounding down alcohol-fortified coconut milk and scarfing down native chocolate served to them on gold platters by cute guys in tight swimming trunks.

As George and Nan pulled up the driveway at a crawl, they saw that the two girls were engaged in languid conversation, probably not about the horticultural condition of the front yard, and clutching beverages instead of gardening hand tools. The yard looked empty. What happened to their trip to Burdick's?

"They just put it back up about an hour ago!" Mary said. "We watched them. The guys putting it up were real hunks!"

"Yes, dear," said Nan laconically. "How exciting. Too bad we don't have much to show for it yet. Maybe they could have waited until after Memorial Day since it's been such a late season."

Nan found herself wondering whether Mary's newfound gardening jag was all just for show, and if she might turn out to be like George's side of the family, in other words, a little slow to the mark. If that was the case, had they been too quick to stop calling her by her childhood nickname—"Sis"—last summer?

"They did actually say they were going to put it up again this year for a few weeks," said George glumly. "No big surprise there."

"Daddy, don't be such a stick-in-the-mud. Don't you want to be famous some more?"

"No. I do not."

"Oh, George," said Nan, giving George a playful jab to the ribs. "A little more notoriety won't kill us."

"Yeah, Daddy, when someone gets to be your age you gotta go for it while you can."

Nan and George smiled tepidly.

A car stopped at the corner, and a woman poked her head out of the driver's side window. She studied the sign, then craned her neck to see around it and take in the barren slope that was gray-brown with still-dormant grass. After a few seconds, the visitor scowled and drove off.

"Not much to see yet, is there?" said Nan. "I hope she comes back when things look more promising."

"By the time things look good the sign will be gone, Mom," Mary said. "You need to ask them if you can keep the sign up at least through the middle of June. By then, the gardens'll be the *bomb!*"

Nan scanned the front yard for any sign that the girls had actually been doing something that might resemble physical labor.

"So, how are we doing here? The stuff from Burdick's you bought—you dumped it in the backyard, right?"

Mary frowned, then pursed her lips.

"Uh, okay, Mom, here's the deal. You know the plan Shirelle

was drawing up? She wants to tear it up and throw it away. She said it wrecks all the spontaneity that succeeded so well in the backyard. So, we didn't get anything from Burdick's. We didn't even *go* to Burdick's. We're waiting for you and Daddy to have a front yard inspiration."

Nan and George exchanged knowing glances: Here was solid evidence that Mary's newfound passion might be a fleeting one.

"But Shirelle has spent a lot of time working on those plans," Nan said. "And she has so much expertise and training that your father and I don't have. Besides, the backyard took us *six years*. We want to get the front yard into shape now."

"Yeah, but Shirelle said that, from now on, we're throwing all the by-the-book stuff out the window and going with your gut. C'mon, you can do it. Just get inspired."

George smiled in a sort of pained way, as if trying to hide a sudden hemorrhoidal flare-up. Nan snorted derisively.

"As you recall, Miss Mary, we're responsible for continuing the backyard. You and Shirelle were to take on the challenge of new gardens in the front yard. Being amateurs, we wanted to see how the experts did it. In fact, you might recall that we changed our minds about having her work for free and decided to take on Shirelle as a *paid* intern. How's she going to get her college credit if *we* do all the work?"

"But, Mom, Shirelle felt like her efforts were so puny compared to what you and Daddy did in the backyard. She needs your help."

Nan looked sternly up at Shirelle, who smiled guiltily and raised her ice cube–filled glass in salute. Mary laughed.

"Don't worry, Mom; it's just lemonade."

Settling into the new celebrity-endorsed swivel rocking chairs on the back patio, George and Nan gazed out over the expanse of their backyard. They quickly noted how little there was to see.

Well, there were the beginnings of a few things. Pointed hosta tips had emerged to the extent that if you brushed away the vegetative detritus that seemed to be everywhere, and leaned low enough to bring your eyes within about a foot of them, you could make out a couple of centimeters' worth of plant, recognizable only as beads of purple and green.

The columbine was two inches tall. No sign of any clematis, which had a long summer's trip to make, climbing up the trellis and the newly positioned weathered-gray ladder tilted at about a seventy-five-degree angle against the siding. The lovely magenta phlox, such a dependable source of early-season color, was only just showing signs of life, as were the lilac bushes, which ordinarily would have been masses of purple perfuming the lower twelve feet of the backyard atmosphere with their delicious grape scent.

The irises were up, but only barely, and there was no sign of the buds that should soon be shrouding the bridal wreath spirea with clouds of tiny white flowers.

With the exception of the marigolds, which George had ill-advisedly insisted on planting in two spots that would allow only intermittent sunlight once the trees leafed, their annuals were still sitting in their flats. They had bought this first installment of annuals two weeks earlier, but the late-flying snowflakes and persistent rains had made it impossible to plant them. George and Nan had uncharacteristically left them out in the elements, strewn all over the patio. As a result, the cardboard flats had been softened by a continuous bombardment of moisture into soggy cellulose.

Nan gazed at George's weather station, with its rain gauge screwed into the end post of the split-rail fence that divided their backyard into two distinct garden sections. He had emptied it just two days ago, and the floating red ring had since then been raised by countless thousands of collected raindrops to the one-and-a-half-inch yellow marking.

Things were starting to look up, though. The ground had dried some yesterday afternoon. Enough to get planting, as they discovered on their tour. Puffs of refreshing wind from the north careened around the corners of the house and over the roof. Fragments of the cloud scud that had blanketed the sky earlier in the morning were in rapid retreat.

And here was that welcome stranger, the sun! It dappled the yard on and off again for a couple of minutes, then lit it up for good, causing Nan to squint and think about searching for those elusive sunglasses.

Here was something else to cheer her. George was back after a very brief absence, having retrieved a bottle of their house wine—the Sagelands vintage 2007 merlot. He extracted the cork with a gentle suction "pop," then poured them both a half-glass, giving the bottle a little quarter-turn twist that, from Nan's careful observations, had never resulted in so much as one spilled drop anywhere.

A couple of healthy sips later, Nan found herself entering that blissful place called "Merlotland," where you were more than welcome to leave your petty little concerns behind, in the care of the teetotaler. All but one little concern, that is.

"So, where do you think this Sieur guy is buried?"

"You mean, Monsieur Boyer, or Sieur de la Salle?"

"Whomever."

George glugged down the remnants of his wine to fortify him for the unpleasant dead-person speculation he had hoped to avoid. "I hope nowhere," he said. "And besides, who's to say anyone was killed here at all? If that Historical Society lady yanked our chain about the so-called treasure, why wouldn't she yank our chain about that?"

"I don't know, George. I think she could have been telling the truth about that. Another thing: I have a sneaking suspicion she was lying about there not being any treasure. Didn't you notice how freaked out she was when you first mentioned something else buried there? I think she knows something she doesn't want us to know about. Like maybe there *is* a treasure, or *some*thing of value."

"I still think it's all a big bunch of hooey," said George.

"Speaking of a big bunch of hooey, look who's coming."

Jim Graybill charged clumsily up the railroad-tie-and-pea-gravel steps to the patio with the relentless energy of a man determined to do something big that he can't quite put his finger on. He was a loping, disjointed, and careless walker, and Nan, no matter how much her mood had been brightened by a half-glass of Dr. Feelgood, watched with irritation as his clunky work boots scattered her pea gravel everywhere.

"Fremonts!" Jim gasped.

"Graybill!" said the Fremonts.

"May I sit?"

"Of course you can sit," said George. "Glass of merlot? It's a new vintage this year, 2007."

Jim shook his head. He was one of the few neighbors who rarely partook of the Fremonts' Sagelands bounty. That never stopped George from asking. After all, it was darn near an insult to turn down a glass of merlot at the Fremont table.

"Whaddup, Jimmikins?" said Nan.

"Pardon?"

"Whaddup, Jim-bob?"

Jim's face was a blank, a sure sign of the slow-wittedness that had come over him as of late. Nan and George attributed that to a sort of post-traumatic stress resulting from the loss of Alicia, his wife. Alicia had run off six months ago with the guy who came by to fix their dryer.

"Okay, I guess you're asking me how I am."

"Very good, Jim," said Nan.

"I'm fine. So, how'd it go?"

" 'It'? What's 'it'?"

"C'mon, Nan. Your know darn well what 'it' is."

"Okay, no foolin' around," said George, freshening up the wineglasses with the remnants of the Sagelands. "What's 'it'?" Nan laughed.

"You guys know. The Livia Historical Society. You went there this morning, didn't you?"

"Why would you think that?" said Nan in a robotic tone. She had zoned out and was staring off into the gardens, preoccupied by the stunted look of one of their bleeding hearts. Jim sighed.

"Maybe you want a gin and tonic, Jim," George said. "Bombay Sapphire with just the right touch of lime." Jim waved off the offer. George shot up and bolted toward the backdoor anyway.

"How did I know about your visit?" continued Jim. "Because you promised me you'd go. And George and Nan Fremont never go back on a promise." Nan, brought back into the here and now by the loud chirp of the resident male cardinal, smiled in a sweet, perky way. "And the only Saturday they would have been open for weeks was today. So . . . how'd it go?"

Nan had drifted off again. This time, she found herself deep in thought about her proposal to the synod for linking old-fashioned Christianity with something more indulgent to mold a new spirituality. Actually, the deeper she got into it, the more the old-fashioned Christianity part got shoved to the wayside. This was turning into more of a cult, with the pastor playing the part of Bacchus, and offering up some really good merlot—Sagelands preferred—or gin and tonics for the non-wine drinkers, at communion. With unlimited refills. Communion would be followed by some kind of revelry, a hymn or two for appearances' sake, and the selection of designated drivers to make sure everyone got home safely.

Then, Jim choked on something and an old rattletrap belonging to the Stephens boys roared and came sputtering down Payne. That broke the spell. Nan shifted her gaze skyward as the prickly flagellum of Christian guilt whipped her back into shape. She quietly apologized to the one, true God, for entertaining such paganish notions.

I'm sorry, Lord, she said in silent prayer; I've had a bit too much to drink here. Didn't mean to stray. Blame George; he's been plying me with alcohol, which you put on this earth in the first place, didn't you. So, it's you guys' fault if I end up worshipping false idols before the day's over.

Looking back down at the table, she noticed that a tall, ice-filled glass dripping with condensation and topped with a slice of lime perched on the rim had suddenly appeared in front of her.

"I hope this is mixed weakly, world's fastest bartender," she said. "We just had a glass and a half of wine in a matter of about five minutes, you know. And there are young and impressionable folk roaming about the grounds. Don't want to set a bad example."

"Mixed weakly yours, mixed strongly mine," said George with a grin.

"Say," Jim said. "I think I *will* take one of those, if you don't mind terribly."

"I do mind terribly," said George. "But I'll get you one anyway."

"Uh, Nan," he said. "The Historical Society?"

"Oh, yeah. You wouldn't believe the historian we ran into there."

"That so?"

"Oh God, Jim, she was a piece of work and a half. . . . Hey, this drink isn't weak at all. Goldarnit!" Nan clinked her ice cubes and stared at the witch's brew of gin and tonic, then shrugged and took a sip. "Very rude and strange, Jim. She kept telling us all these stories about things that happened here. And by 'here' I mean right here where we're sitting now. One was about murder."

"Murder?

Back came George, who placed a fizzing gin and tonic gingerly on the table in front of Jim.

"Presto!" he said. Nan smiled. She was happy to see George showing off something he was really good at.

"Well, it was a murder that was supposed to have happened, what was it, George, about three hundred years ago?"

"Give or take forty or fifty."

"And that was just the start. She said there were pirates heading up the Big Turkey with gold doubloons."

"Pirates? The Big Turkey? You couldn't even take a kayak. . . ."

"That's *just* what I told George, wasn't it, George?"

"They're the ones that murdered someone?"

"No, that was some French guy. So, get this, she even had Jesus Christ—Our Lord and Savior—burying his bifocals here after the Last Supper."

"That was pretty much the clincher for me," said George. "That made it obvious she was just laying a bunch of baloney on us. I mean, why would Jesus have needed bifocals at his age? Ha-ha!"

"To say nothing of the sacrilege involved. Oh, yeah, the erasers of the Aztecs are supposed to be buried here, too."

"That's the racing bike of the Incas," corrected George.

"Huh? Oh, yeah, the racing bike of the Incas."

"Hmmm," said Jim, sipping his drink, then stroking his chin and gazing pensively up at the sky, as if calculating how much a racing bike of the Incas might be worth.

The pause that followed allowed them to turn their attention to some activity around the bird feeders. They all watched as a blindingly bright yellow goldfinch lighted on a perch at the thistle feeder. Then, another one, this time a drab, greenish female. That caused Nan a momentary pang of sadness. Why did all the girls in the bird family have to fly around decorated so frumpily by Mother Nature?

Something about the two birds' actions injected a note of sobriety into her cottony, fading euphoria.

"Shhhh," Nan whispered, clamping her raised forefinger to her lips. "Don't be too loud, or we'll scare them away. Boy, the males have really brightened up in the past several weeks."

"Looks like a canary to me," said Jim, who turned, twisting clumsily in his chair and screeching its ringed metal skid across the concrete to better view the thistle feeder.

"Goldfinches, Jim," said Nan. "No more jerky movements, please. You almost scared them away. Look how unsettled they are. Just looking around all the time. Barely taking time to eat. They're scared."

A sudden disturbance, announced by a whir of clumsily flapped wings and a little shriek, covered the feeder in a blur of miniature-hurricane-force action. The chaos of the struggle lasted just a few moments, then left the feeder tube swinging wildly. All three jumped up from their seats.

"Goddamn!" said George, jolted into complete sobriety.

"Jesus!" said Jim. "What *was* it? I didn't really see it."

"It was a hawk!" said Nan, panting with excitement. "A hawk just attacked our feeder!" George rose unsteadily, walked over to the gyrating plastic tube, and reached up to still it with his hand.

"Damn," he said. "There's drops of fresh blood on here." He looked down at the chips of graying and decomposing cypress mulch on the ground and saw something bright. Bending over, he noticed they were tufts of yellow-and-black feathers and down.

"Damn again. Looks like the male just turned into dinner. What a rip-off for those guys. They get the bright plumage, which means, what, a hawk can see them from twenty miles away? As usual, the male of the species gets the short end of the stick."

"Poor thing," moaned Jim.

"Part of the cycle of life," Nan said.

"What was it that did this?" Jim barked in a suddenly tremulous, cracking voice.

"Sharp-shinned hawk," George said. "There's a bunch around here. Small hawks. Like suburban yards with lots of trees. They especially like suburban yards with bird feeders. They eat songbirds. That one was probably hiding in the branches, staking out the feeder, and saw the goldfinch. You saw how quickly it got here."

"Jesus." Jim looked around pensively, his lips pursed and eyes narrowed into little squints. For a moment, Nan thought he would start crying. She had never seen him so serious. "I *hate* that that happened."

Nan and George looked at each other, bewildered. They loved what had just happened.

"A wonder of nature, Jim," George said. "One of life's little dramas. You probably won't ever see something like that again."

"Thank God for that," Jim said.

Nan cleared her throat in a manner she used to call attention to the true matter at hand.

"Well, Jim, the long and short of it is there is no hidden treasure of Livia. That hideous historical woman told us that after she played her little joke on us. It's nothing but a village myth." Nan decided it was best for now to withhold her suspicion that the historian might know something she wasn't willing to tell them. She winked at George and hoped he got the hint.

"But, Nan," said Jim. "The beeping was really strong over there near the . . . the . . ."

"Angel's trumpets."

"Yeah, that's where."

"But you already dug there and found nothing, or next to nothing," Nan said. "A few little chunks of metal."

"That's right, but after I dug, I began to think about it some more. I'm not sure I dug down deep enough. And over there."

Jim pointed his drink toward the barren but richly damp flower beds that George and Nan had prepared as additions to the already-extensive backyard gardens, and which they hoped would soon be crowded with hydrangeas, astilbe, peonies, and a lot of annuals. They stared silently past Jim, then at their drinks, which always seemed to offer solace in troubling situations such as the one unfolding before them now.

"There was another thing," said Jim. "I think my power was running down when I did the sweep between the fence and the woods. I might not have been getting accurate readings."

"Oh, sheesh, Jim!"

"George, I would be willing to bet that what we find down there at that spot near the whatever tree next to the woods will make that $200,000 First Place Burdick's Best Yard prize you won last year seem like Monopoly money."

"That being the white oak, our one and only and extremely old white oak?" asked George, pointing his drink in the direction of the massive and stately tree that rose from the neglected northeast corner of the lot, about twenty yards in front of the woods.

"The same," Jim said.

"Why there?" wondered Nan.

"Just a hunch. My battery was dying at that point by the time I got there, but I thought I heard some tiny little beeps around the tree. Besides, I've swept just about every place else. Couldn't pinpoint the exact spot. It might have been under the tree. You woulda had to cut down the tree if there were strong beeps there."

"Wouldn't have done that," George said.

"That's what I figured."

"And you said this treasure chest came from where?" Nan wondered. "And when?"

"Well, it's not a 'treasure chest,' technically."

"What is it, then—a treasure torso?"

"Ha-ha."

"So," Nan said. "You've been a little oblique with us about this so-called treasure buried under our yard other than to say it's huge and will make us all fabulously wealthy, with us getting, what was it, half the take?"

"Yes, that's right, Nan. I'm prepared to offer you half of what I find. Normally, the property owners get more like a third. What's oblique?"

"The information you've given us so far on the treasure."

"I mean what does 'oblique' mean?"

"It means you haven't been giving us much in the way of details of what exactly it is that's supposedly buried here," Nan said. "In fact, you didn't tell us anything at all when you first started digging last year. We just thought you were playing around with your little toy. Then, you kept pushing us to visit the Historical Society, and we have to bully you into coughing up this buried-treasure nonsense. We need you to tell us more. Do we need to go get the thumbscrews?"

Jim pursed his lips.

"Another gin and tonic to loosen your tongue a bit, Jim?" said George. "Then we can forgo the thumbscrews. Ha-ha!"

"Sure, George." Jim raised his empty glass and waggled it. "And not as strong, please? And with a bigger slice of lime?"

"And, dear," Nan said. "While you're at it, a Coke for me, please."

In what seemed like barely enough time for a nuthatch to

make its transit from the thicket of lilac bushes to the forest-green, counterweighted bird feeder, George had placed a fresh gin and tonic on the glass tabletop in front of Jim and an ice-cube-clogged glass of fizzing Coke in front of Nan.

"Now that that's taken care of . . ." said Nan, with a hint of brittleness coloring her tone.

"Spill it," said George.

"Okay," said Jim, who tilted his head back for a long, deep, fortifying draw from his drink, then wiped his lips with the back of his hand and smiled. "Here goes nuttin'."

5

Treasure Quest

Miss Price slurped noisily and repeatedly at her whipped-cream-topped Ovaltine, which Artis and Nimwell Scroggit, who counted themselves among the nation's minority of hot chocolate haters, were forced to endure with a quiet yet squirmy grace. She stared at them in disbelief. So, these were the alleged professionals who had so blithely detoured from the straight and narrow of the law to procure for her some of her most treasured historical artifacts? In the past, her surreptitious dealings with them had been strictly by phone or letter. Deliveries had been left on her doorstep, and cash payments left in the mailbox.

Now that she was actually meeting the Scroggit brothers in person, she began to have second thoughts. Why, these two looked and acted like ne'er-do-well slugs, mere husks of men barely able to summon the energy to tie their shoes in the morning, much less flout the law. Look at them, all hangdog expressions and fumbling hands, weakness etched into every pore of their putty-like faces. Why, they were just wheezing, doddering old fools! But who else was there? They were all she had.

Artis and Nimwell sat quietly on the sofa, daintily drinking their Ovaltine out of scalloped china cups, and thinking that mugs would have done a better job of conveying the offending beverage to their lips. They took care to keep their eyes averted from the steely, unremitting gaze of Miss Price, who finally turned her head in disgust, almost sloshing hot chocolate all over herself in the process before setting the cup on the lampstand next to her.

But the Scroggit brothers brought a sort of bumbling passion to their work as antique hunters that was great enough to sometimes offset their absolute fecklessness. Aware at least subconsciously of their limitations, they often operated in the shadows of their profession, sneaking around on lightly patrolled public lands looking for easy pickings and targeting desperate widows and widowers willing to part with their historical relics for some ready, piddling cash.

Why, it was only last week that they had dug up the steel band fitted around the rim of a Conestoga wagon wheel in western Nebraska. Sure, it was on government property, but Nebraska was in budget-cut mode, slashing the state park budgets. Supervision having been drastically reduced, the Scroggit brothers were able to just waltz up to the site with their tools, probe around with their metal detectors, and dig the thing out without anyone but a few visitors being any the wiser. Besides, they were wearing their gray shirts with official-looking arrowhead-shaped patches stitched onto them to make it look like they were supposed to be there. They knew a collector who would pay $3,000 for that band.

While they were at it, they had detoured west to that vast sandstone megalith, Goliath Rock, where, under the cover of a heavy rain, they chiseled out the carved autographs of a dozen pioneers. That'd be good for a cool $10,000.

The Scroggit brothers, bachelors by both choice and lack of opportunity, did not really like women in general and Miss

Price in particular. She was prissy and domineering. She treated them like children and derided them as oafs.

Still, Miss Price would pay well for what she wanted, and she knew her history. This new job offer sounded intriguing. If they had to skirt the law a bit, that was just an occupational hazard that would jack up their price.

Then again, taking liberties with the law was something they'd have to consider carefully. They could handle mild infractions posing negligible risks. An overt criminal act involving the distinct possibility of getting caught was a whole other matter.

"Miss Price, what you're asking us to do is against the law," said Artis, who gazed distastefully into his cup of Ovaltine, then took a reluctant sip.

"This is justice we're serving here," said Miss Price. "That's a lot bigger than something written down in a statute book. Something that is rightfully mine remains buried on that ridge across from Bluegill Pond. Don't you want to help somebody do the right thing in the name of history? Besides, professionals such as yourselves are supposed to know how to minimize risk. And where's your sense of adventure, huh?"

Artis tugged his ear distractedly and fidgeted in his chair. Nimwell stole a quick glance at his watch. A pocket notebook, pages flapping, sailed by Artis's head. A ballpoint pen, launched with some force, grazed Nimwell's forehead.

"Hey!" they both cried.

"Pay attention!" shouted Miss Price. "Am I boring you, or are you dimwits incapable of showing a prospective employer a little consideration?" She sighed. "I guess good help is hard to find these days in the historic antiquities business."

"Well, Miss Price, we had planned to visit our St. Anthony store, which is on the brink of going out of business. We're already late for an appointment with our accountant."

"It can wait!" Miss Price hissed. "If you do as you're told, you won't care if your whole bloody Civil War empire comes crashing down. What I'm proposing could make you rich in ways you can't imagine."

Artis and Nimwell cringed, both at the thought of their flagging business, and at the notion that, somewhere, just out of reach, there might be a treasure that could set them up in comfort for the rest of their lives. But they were inclined to view stories about buried treasure near where the old Price place used to be as just a bunch of old wives' tales unworthy of investigation, and certainly not worth breaking the law for.

"Miss Price, you can't just go traipsing around in some-body's yard, without permission, looking for some buried trea-sure," Artis said. "You just can't do it."

"It is against the law," Nimwell said. Miss Price sucked in a big breath, then heaved it out with an exasperated gasp.

"Why don't we just explain to the Fremonts what the sit-uation is, and ask if we could please look for it, whatever it is?" wondered Artis.

"Because we don't want them to know what's under their property and get it for themselves, you dingbat! What is on, or under, that property belongs to me and my family. It's just that the law as it is now written doesn't recognize that. So, do you want to help, or do you intend to chicken out? And where did you get the idea that this is a treasure? I never told you about any treasure."

"Old treasure hunter stories," Nimwell said.

"Every treasure hunter worth his salt has heard them," added Artis. "Those stories have been circulating for genera-tions. There's nothing to them."

"Well, I happen to know differently," said Miss Price. "And I'm a historian. I don't traffic in *stories*. I amass evidence and reach conclusions. And my conclusion is that there is some-thing of great value and much significance buried in that back-yard. And the thing is that we have to get moving on it because they suspect it's there. Just you go over there with your watchamacallums—"

"Metal detectors."

"Metal detectors. That's right. They're good ones, too, I take it."

"They'll do in a pinch," Nimwell said. "Mine found a belt buckle, scabbard, and three minie bullets at the Chickamauga battlefield site. That was under a bunch of forest clutter and a foot of soil."

"And you did that on the sly, didn't you!" whooped Miss Price. "You did that on the sly because you weren't supposed to, were you? I remember. That's National Park Service property, and you snooped around and dug up stuff there anyway, now didn't you? See, I remember. You told me so!" The Scroggit brothers looked at each other sheepishly. "So what makes this one any different, huh?"

"That was Civil War stuff," Artis said. "That's different. And it was government property we were digging on, not somebody's own yard. The government has no right to own land in a democracy. We were merely carrying out our commission as private citizens expropriating resources unlawfully locked up by a socialist state."

Nimwell nodded vigorously.

"Don't assault me with any of your right-wing libertarian claptrap! You cowards! You frauds! You unmentionables! If I told you what I almost know beyond any doubt is buried on that ridge, you would jump right off your duffs and hightail it right over there because you wouldn't be able to contain yourselves. That's how big it is! That's how big it is!"

Miss Price jumped up out of her chair in her excitement, knocking over her cup, spilling hot chocolate over her beautifully woven circular rug of many colors, and not even noticing. She shook a balled fist at the Scroggit brothers.

Artis and Nimwell reared back instinctively, holding up

their free hands to ward off whatever Miss Price was prepared to unleash at them.

"This is wha' the hightail that struck mightily in which his was arrears," cried out Nimwell, who had the disconcerting habit of mangling his syntax and vocabulary when faced with a high-stress, threatening situation.

"Huh?" said Miss Price, suddenly taken aback. "What'd he say?"

Artis shrugged and rolled his eyes.

"And now!" roared Miss Price, her voice taking on new fervor, steadiness, and unwavering purpose. "I'm gonna tell you what it is that's buried under 4250 Payne Avenue, and you just try to tell me you're not going to itch to go lookin' there to find it!"

6

Tall Tales

"Jonas Peters? You mean *the* Jonas Peters? The infamous bandit, train robber, second only to Jesse James as a subverter of Midwestern public morals? The guy whose buried loot is supposed to be worth millions, but that no one's been able to find?"

Nan leaned back in her chair, swiveling it a bit to the right, then left, then rocking it back precariously. She drained the dregs of her Coke, then went back to work on a fresh gin and tonic that had appeared without her even asking for it.

"The same. And Beetle Peters and Jimmy Durko and the rest of the Peters Brothers gang," Jim said. "They were probably camped out, um, a hundred and thirty-eight years ago right here where we're sitting."

Jim looked earnestly from Nan to George, then back to Nan again.

"It's known to everyone that they robbed the bank at Millerton, what, thirty miles east of here, and that the townsfolk turned out en masse with guns and shot Jimmy and another gang member, Caleb Westerly. But the rest got away, and did something with $100,000 in Liberty Head gold coins that didn't involve spending them. But that's not all. They got another $250,000 in Liberty Heads from the train robbery near Fountainville, which is . . . uh . . ."

"About twenty miles."

"Yes, thanks, George, about twenty miles west of here."

"Well, it's known by anyone familiar with local history that they were hiding, more or less in plain sight, somewhere in Livia, There were seven or eight farms and homesteads in Livia at the time, and they had kinfolk and friends here. Of course, they couldn't stay long since everyone knew this was one of their stomping grounds where they could rest and refit. They must have lit out after just a few days. As you know, things just didn't work out after that; what was left of the gang were either gunned down or caught in a botched steamboat hijacking on the Missouri, in what was then the Nebraska Territory not two months later. Jonas and Jimmy were the only ones caught. They died in prison. And all that loot was never recovered."

"I didn't know that," said George.

"And you think that's what's under the backyard here?" said Nan.

"I think there is a distinct possibility. Mabel Gleason, Jonas's main squeeze, lived a couple of miles away. There was a little house and store here run by some European immigrant and his Indian wife. They might have known the gang. They might have let them bury the money here until it was safe to come back and dig it up. Consider this: You're on a hill here, and back them, there were hardly any trees, except by the lake. Great place to be able to see for miles around in every direction. Remember, everyone was looking for them then, and, of course, St. Anthony is only fifteen miles away. It wasn't much more than a glorified crossroads back then, but it was crawling with lawmen looking for Jonas. I'm betting they knew the store owner and his wife, got their supplies, and buried the money in the yard before heading out for that one last holdup."

"That's quite a tale," George said. "But you're just playing a hunch, aren't you?"

"Sure, George. All successful treasure hunters work off hunches."

"A little country store here, eh?" said Nan. "I didn't know that. It seems as though our historian could have told us something about that if she hadn't been so busy having a good laugh at our expense, for heaven's sake."

"The store burned down right around that time," Jim said. "Along with the nearby house. That's no hunch, it's historical fact."

"Wow!" said George. Nan shuddered.

"What happened to the store owner and his wife?" she wondered.

"Don't know," Jim said.

"Good grief, this little piece of suburbia has certainly seen its share of history," Nan said. "Still, that's not nearly enough to go tearing through our yard again. Besides, last time you dug, when everything was already ruined, we had nothing to lose. Then, of course, you filled in the holes like a good boy and everything came roaring back. This time, everything's in good shape as far as we know, and primed to burst through to the surface any day now."

"So," said George, "that's a nix on the digging. We don't want a bunch of big holes messing up our gardens. Is that clear?"

"Can't I just do a little more sweeping with the old Treasure-Trove XB 255? Pul-eeeze? I would just bring it over and sweep for any old insignificant stray stuff and we can forget about the buried treasure. And whatever I find is yours! Can't you see, I just *have* to sweep. It's in my blood." Jim started to tremble.

"In other words, you're addicted to it," Nan said.

"I suppose that's one way of putting it," Jim said sheepishly. George laughed. Nan shot him a cold, hard stare.

"Ouch," said George, flinching.

"We don't want to be encouraging your addiction," said Nan.

"Yeah," said George. "Maybe you should kick the habit and try something healthier and less annoying to the neighbors, like maybe using a magnifying glass to set ants on fire or playing the ocarina in your basement, ha-ha."

"How about gardening?" said Nan. "We could help you get started. George, could you please consider shifting to the diet Coke, dear? You're getting a little noisy."

"Well, I'd be the last person who'd want to mess up your wonderful work of art here," Jim said. "Gardening, huh? You know what kind of landscaper I am. Brown thumb."

Even before Jim's wife left, the Graybill property was a disaster. Shrubs and bushes went untrimmed for years. Dandelions were allowed to sprout and spread their noxious seed fluffs unchecked. Jim and Alicia had dabbled in snapdragons, potted palms, and "purple misanthrope," a flower neither George nor Nan had ever heard of, but which looked like several pansies grafted onto a milkweed. But they had watered and cared for their flowers only intermittently.

As a result, the Graybills' flora always had a burned-at-the-edges, gone-to-seed look.

With Alicia went any semblance of order to the yard. Weeds found fallow ground in the topsoil, springing up unhindered and muscling out their tamer brethren weakened by neglect. The lawn was rarely mowed. It was currently flourishing as a knee-high thicket of just about everything the more conscientious homeowners of Livia strove to keep out of their own yards.

Nan was beginning to get bored with all this false-treasure talk, especially now that the good effects of the wine and gin and tonic were being replaced by a wistful sobriety and mild headache.

She became even more wistful as she stared at the little birdhouse that was screwed into the bedroom window frame, under the eaves. No activity at all, even though their hyperactive house wrens should be back by now. The males would be first, making themselves prominent on high branches, fence tops, and telephone wires, burbling away with their territorial warnings, rustling through shrubs and popping in and out on their inspection tours of the three wren houses George and Nan had placed around the backyard.

So, where the hell were they?

Jim's head drooped abruptly to within an inch of the tabletop. When he lifted it up, his eyes were red and moist, and his eyelids flickered spasmodically. He rubbed them shakily with his fists.

"Jim, what's wrong?"

Jim glanced, teary-eyed, at Nan, then George, before turning away, embarrassed, his throat choked with sobs.

"Is it the metal detector thing?" George said. "Heck, you can mess around with that a little if you want to so badly. Just don't count on us getting a backhoe to dig up the yard is all I'm saying."

"It's not that." Jim sniffed. "Who cares about the stupid metal detector? It's the canary. I can't stand that canary dying."

"The what?" said Nan. "Oh, the goldfinch. That wasn't a canary, that was a goldfinch."

"Gee, Jim," said George. "Do you think you could tell the difference between a turkey and a robin? Or maybe . . ." A hard look from Nan stopped George in mid-sentence as Jim cradled his head in his hands and began to sob.

"I really have to go," he said, his voice cracking. "Sorry to be a burden. Why do things have to die? Why do . . . that poor canary!" With that he jumped up and strode awkwardly back down the steps, losing some of Nan's sympathy by kicking the pea gravel all over the place.

"Jeez, talk about sensitive," said George. "You witness one of nature's little dramas, and you want to celebrate it, not start bawlin'."

"You lout!" she spat at him. "You stupid lout! It's not the canary . . . I mean the goldfinch. It's not the goldfinch he's thinking about, it's death. And death means the loss of a spouse, who, okay, maybe she didn't die, but she might as well have died, at least to Jim's way of thinking, by running off with that repair guy."

Chastened, George lapsed into silence. For three seconds, you could have heard the respiratory sighs of a goldenrod. Then, Mary and Shirelle threw open the screen door panting with excitement.

"Mom, Daddy," cried Mary. "We've got a new plan for the front yard. Shirelle just came up with it. It's a stroke of genius!"

7

Stunted Growth

The Scroggit brothers stared dumbfounded at their part-time bookkeeper, Mrs. Tuertle, whom they had just hired to go over their neglected records.

It had been a year since they had been forced to fire Mrs. Monck for hectoring them about unpaid taxes and threats of retribution from various socialist agencies they did not recognize as legitimate institutions empowered to order them about. Once they got notification from the proper elected authority—the county sheriff—then they would listen.

Two weeks ago, state agents appeared at the store and spoke with the manager. They demanded a meeting with the owners, and relayed a threat to shut the store down if back state debts weren't paid. The Internal Revenue Service dropped by two days later.

Feeling powerless to stem this rising tide of government tyranny, the Scroggit brothers decided that perhaps an update on their tax status was advisable. They hired Mrs. Tuertle because she came highly recommended by their aunt Florence, who had met her at an over-eighty croquet tournament.

Mrs. Tuertle, fifteen years their senior and twenty years removed from her last job, that of staff accountant for PeeWee's

Black Forest Pretzels, held a letter in her shaking hands. Her voice quaked as she read to them the order from the State Department of Revenue and Budget Management. It appeared that Scroggit Brothers Enterprises, doing business in three locations as Fightin' Yankee Antiques, had neglected to turn over taxes to the state on sales totaling $6.5 million over the past six years.

Not only that, said Mrs. Tuertle in her barely audible voice, but they had failed to withhold income tax over five years from the wages of all eight of their current employees and fifteen of their former ones.

This was the second threatening letter Mrs. Tuertle had brought to their attention. The first was from the IRS making a similar withholding tax claim, and also daring to accuse them of failing to report and pay taxes on personal income totaling $3.4 million since 2002.

Both letters cited numerous previous warnings, and contained some threatening language about seizures and jail time.

"The nerve of these socialist entities!" thundered Artis. "Abrogating the right of businessmen to make a decent living right here in the U.S. of A. Why . . . why . . . it's un-Christian. It's un-democratic. It's socialism, and I won't have it! Won't have it!"

"Me neither," said Nimwell.

"We need our attorney. Uh, what's-his-name. With Crabshaw, Oates, and Crabshaw. Which one is it?"

"Donaldson," Nimwell said.

"That's right, Donaldson of Crabshaw, Oates, and Crabshaw. Ring him up, please, Mrs. Tuertle. Right this instant."

Mrs. Tuertle just sat there shivering, her head bowed, the letter in her hands still shaking like a brittle leaf caught in a gale.

"Well, what's the matter, Mrs. Tuertle? Got the dt's or something? Ha-ha. Let's get a move on. What's at stake here is nothing less than the right of a couple of small entrepreneurs to prosper in a free capitalist society."

Mrs. Tuertle made a noise akin to a French horn croaking a misplayed note. Then, she whispered something.

"Please speak up, Mrs. Tuertle," said Nimwell. "Just like Mr. Scroggit said, there's no time to lose."

"Can't," said Mrs. Tuertle.

"Can't?" barked Artis. "What do you mean, can't? Don't be afraid, Mrs. Tuertle; all we can do is fire you. Ha-ha."

"Mr. Donaldson no longer works for us."

"What! And why not?"

"We haven't paid him," Mrs. Tuertle gurgled, her voice now broken by sobs. "Haven't paid him in two years. We've already heard from a collection agency. They're taking action. I've got their letter here somewhere."

"This is monstrous!" said Artis.

"Monstrous!" echoed Nimwell. "A monstrosity!"

"And how long have we known about this, Mrs. Tuertle?"

Mrs. Tuertle cringed and seemed to transform in her chair and before their eyes into a very old fetus.

"I just found out. You just hired me."

"Eh?"

"You had no accountant or bookkeeper for years," she whimpered. "Until you hired my predecessor, whom you terminated, nobody knew. You were supposed to know, as the owners."

The ire of the Scroggit brothers, focused up to this point on bloated socialist bureaucracies, now redirected itself onto this miserable lump of humanity, who had been toiling away for them for a mere three weeks, trying desperately to assemble documents, letters, and computer e-mails that had not been filed or dealt with since Mrs. Monck left.

"Get out!" barked Artis. "Get out now. You'll get no severance or reference from us, Mrs. Tuertle. We're firing you on

the spot for incompetence, and maybe even dishonesty. Someone will have to check your books. Have you embezzled anything from us? Oh, stop your blubbering."

"Please, Mr. Scroggit, please . . . Please . . . Need the work.
My husband, Frank. He can't work. Sick. Please."

"I tell you what, Mrs. Tuertle, you can keep that box of
Kleenex over there, but that's it. Now, out you go. You don't
have anything to worry about. Our socialist state specializes in
cases like yours. Once you and your husband go on welfare,
you'll probably be making twice what we're making by not
working at all. Ha-ha!"

Nimwell nodded and pursed his lips in righteous indignation. With that, the Scroggit brothers stalked out of the office
and into their retail showroom.

The showroom of Fightin' Yankee Antiques was a history
nut's dream come true. Civil War muskets and rifles, both real
and replicas, lined the walls. There were cavalry sabers, artillery
sponges, and spiral-coiled worms, flagstaffs, pennant staffs, and
moth-eaten uniforms colored blue, gray, and butternut. The
big showpieces, covering half of the north wall, were bullet-
ripped American and regimental flags captured by the Rebs at
the Battle of Gaines' Mill.

In the center of the floor sat a replica Napoleon six-
pounder, complete with sponging bucket and attached sight.
The replica had been cast in 1934 to exact historical specifications and had been in the hands of rich collectors for years until
the Scroggits bought it at an estate sale in 1981 for $12,000. It
and the flags were for sale only if the price was right.

The glass display cases housed minie bullets dug up from
battlefields, bayonets, uniform blouse buttons, canteens, real
letters from the battlefield, medals, eating utensils (which were
usually bent), decks of playing cards, surgeons' saws and scal-
pels, haversacks, and gum blankets.

The St. Anthony Fightin' Yankee Antiques store was the

flagship of a chain started by the Scroggits in 1974, more as a place to store their sizable and growing collection of artifacts than anything else. Business boomed for a while, and they expanded to another store, in the suburbs, in 1981, and then a third, in the midsized city of Chester, about seventy-five miles to the south, in 1985. The sprawling thirty-three-part Civil War public television epic, *Four Awful Years,* in the mid-nineties, kept interest high and sales brisk. The Scroggits expanded to three more stores in two neighboring states and plowed their profits into what had become the largest Civil War artifacts chain in the nation.

At that point, the Scroggits turned the day-to-day operation of the St. Anthony store over to their staff, and concentrated on beating their competitors to the most highly prized artifacts of American history they could find, by whatever means possible. Their cutthroat methods kept their stores filled with top-flight merchandise and the mail order branch of their business humming, but it alienated other dealers, who began blackballing them from shows and leaving them out of the dealer-to-dealer sales loop.

As mass interest in American history in general and the Civil War in particular waned, the embargo on dealings with the Scroggits by all but the most unscrupulous dealers began to hurt their business. By 2005, they had shut down the three out-of-state stores and scaled down the rest of their operation. By 2010, they had found smaller spaces for the two other in-state stores.

It was now becoming clear, even to the Scroggits, that the market for the kinds of big-ticket artifacts they specialized in—an authentic .58-caliber Springfield rifle-musket and Revolutionary War–era ceremonial sword, for instance—was fading fast. And now, to have to deal with this irksome matter about some unpaid taxes, which were being illegally assessed anyway!

On this particular day, the store was empty except for Matthew, the manager, and a geeky-looking teenager who was looking at the minie bullet collection.

"Hey, kid," barked Artis. "Either buy the merchandise or scram. No loitering in the store. We're a business, not a museum." The teenager stared up at him with owl-like eyes, then slithered silently out.

"Kinda slow today?" said Artis to Matthew, who was standing at the counter, his elbows splayed out languidly over the glass case displaying replica Confederate money and authentic letters home from three officers who served in the Iron Brigade.

"Yeah, boss. As usual. We sold a couple of minies, three uniform buttons, and some old Civil War cards. No big-tickets, though. We got that other battle flag coming in Tuesday. Fair-to-poor condition. A couple possible buyers. We're asking $16,000, but I doubt if we'll get that. The sale's coming up next month. We're advertising in the local papers. I bought a spot cheap on the university radio station."

"We're still losing money, though?" asked Nimwell. "Hand over fist?"

"That would be correct," said Matthew. "But that's nothing new. We've been losing money for the past three years, ever since I've been here. And you were already in the hole when I got here. Unless we can find something unique, like an intact sutler's wagon or a *real* six-pounder Napoleon, we're gonna be shit outta luck."

Artis didn't like his manager's tone. He didn't like his track record either. Besides, why did he seem to be in the dark about the big-government wolves at the door? Artis wondered why they had kept him on as manager so long. There was no reason in the world why genuine relics of American history couldn't sell, and sell for a pretty penny, given competent and enthusiastic sellers. Obviously, the staff that remained were getting jaded. Maybe they needed some fresh blood to get things back on track.

"Are you aware of our little tax problem?" asked Artis.

"Yessir. I've been telling you about it for as long as I can remember. I'm sorry you decided not to pay attention."

"That's not the kind of tone we should have to hear from an employee," said Nimwell, blinking rapidly to fight back the tears of indignation. "Where's the respect these days that employees used to show their employers?"

Matthew shrugged.

"How much are we paying you, Matthew?" Artis asked.

"Sir?"

"You heard the man," said Nimwell. "How much do we *over*-pay you?"

"Uh, hmmm. Maybe sixteen hundred a month. About twenty thousand a year."

"That's too much!" barked Artis.

"Um-hmm," said Nimwell.

"It's not that much," Matthew said. "Especially for someone like me, who has the contacts and knows the market."

"And where is that getting us?" said Artis through clenched teeth. "We should be in a position to be the foremost retailer of Civil War and historic American memorabilia in the nation. Huh? It's Mr. Scroggit and I who have to come up with all the big finds."

"Maybe you should pay your taxes."

"There's some more of that lip," said Nimwell. "Stop it, please, with the lippy backtalk."

"I'd like to suggest a new salary deal for you, Matthew," Artis said. "A hundred dollars a week, plus a ten-percent commission on whatever you sell. Maybe that'll get your ass in gear."

"That seems really fair," Nimwell said.

Matthew stared at them, his mouth agape. "You've got to be kidding me."

"No joke," said Artis. "Take it or leave it." The bell on the door jingled, signaling the third customer in the four hours the store had been open.

"Leave it," said Matthew. "I'll take care of this last customer, then I'm outta here. Maurice comes in at noon."

The Scroggit brothers looked at each other, stunned. They had expected their manager, disheartened by lagging sales and afraid of getting fired, to jump at their new offer. It had never occurred to them that he just might up and walk. And when he did, which it appeared would be in about five minutes, who would run the store?

"One of us has to check in at the store in Gable Oaks," said Artis. "That should probably be me since I'm sort of the brains of the operation. You stay here and man the store for the rest of the day once Matthew takes off. You know how to operate a computerized cash register, right? And run credit cards?"

Nimwell shrugged and forced a wan, tremulous smile.

"Okay, whatever," said Artis. "We're gonna have to sell this place and file for bankruptcy anyway, so don't sweat the customers too much. You'll probably just end up twiddling your thumbs. You know what? That treasure deal Miss Price was talking about is looking better all the time."

Nimwell nodded furiously as Matthew put on his jacket and walked out, barely a minute before the constant jingling of the bell signaled that a busload of foreign tourists had just crossed the threshold.

"Go get 'em, tiger," said Artis as a dozen new prospective customers gawked at the display cases. "Just think, Miss Price is gonna make us millionaires. It's just a matter of figuring out how to get to it."

Nimwell smiled and scampered over to make his first

sale—a bullet-dented canteen that had once belonged to a major who served on the staff of Major General Lew Wallace at the battle of Shiloh.

Ten miles away, slumped over the walnut desk that served as the centerpiece of her cloistered office in the venerable Eamons Hall, Dr. Hilda Brockheimer stared at the foot-high pile of paper stacked in front of her and sighed. It was the sigh of great ambitions thwarted.

God, how she hated teaching! Research, that was what she was born to do, and here she was with no major research grants to her name and a bunch of her students' final papers and internship reports gathering dust and daring her to touch them, to read them, perchance to grade them.

The year was almost over and she would have to deal with these sooner rather than later. Dr. Richlin, the department chair, had just reminded her in no uncertain terms that she was to wrap up her final grades immediately.

"What seems to be the problem, Hilda?" he said. "We have got to get these kids' grades completed. They're leaving in a couple of days. Everyone else has their grades in. So, what's your story?"

"Research," said Dr. Brockheimer severely. "I've got important research to wrap up."

Dr. Richlin rolled his eyes, then smiled condescendingly. He'd heard this before from Dr. Brockheimer, and knew it to be either an exaggeration to hide her distaste for the requirements of teaching, or the futile exercise of a professor who hadn't been responsible for a single bit of important research in at least six years. She was cruising on her reputation, that's what she was doing.

"Okay, Hilda," he said, employing the diplomatic tone he trotted out for stubborn incompetents and malcontents. "Research is important. We all know that. Everyone here does it. But you must teach here to be a professor of horticulture. That is a basic requirement at this institution."

His point made, Dr. Richlin modified his smile to reflect a more pleasant, avuncular persona. He removed his glasses, and leaned toward Dr. Brockheimer, who stood before him as rigid as a post.

"You have been a great credit to this institution, Hilda," Dr. Richlin said. "We all know and respect this. But, quite frankly, you've been coasting on your reputation for quite a while. All of us here have other duties to perform, and that includes you. Will you please make my job easier by getting your grades in by Friday noon at the latest?"

Dr. Brockheimer was one of the top floriculturists in the St. Anthony metro area and, one could argue, the entire state. Dr. Phil Goudette, at Headwaters State University, in Sap City, was really the only one who could give her a run for her money. They had quite an impressive department up there at Headwaters that they coupled successfully with a landscape design division.

Dr. Brockheimer burned with jealousy after reading Dr. Goudette's research paper on the use of bogs to develop exotic new flora that could then be transferred to semi-moist soils without the benefit of intermittent flooding. It had been groundbreaking—and it had been her idea, too. They just hadn't given her the time to work on it, a fact she pointed out when she thundered into Dr. Richlin's office with the news.

The importance of that paper would have been evident to even the most callow of undergraduates, but Dr. Richlin had just brushed it off as if it had been a middling senior thesis, instead of seeing it for the threat it was. Now, Headwaters was going to be getting the research dollars, not them. Didn't the fool see that? Instead of sloughing it all off, he should be freeing her from her teaching responsibilities and giving her carte blanche to do whatever research she saw fit to do.

But that's the way it is around here, thought Dr. Brockheimer. The faculty gravitated toward sloth and the undemanding status quo once they were tenured. They tended to pad their résumés with meaningless journal articles and insignificant board positions, and rest on the laurels of whatever token research they'd accomplished in their younger years. They'd pile up bogus honors while teaching a few classes and serving as consultants to large companies and wealthy homeowners who figured a PhD added to a title had a lot better ring to it than just a plain old bachelor's degree in landscape design.

Dr. Brockheimer was not so inclined. At the age of thirty-nine, she felt she was just hitting her stride as a researcher of national repute. She had been stuck in her associate professorship for five years, watching as other less-talented colleagues vaulted ahead of her. That included that no-brain Dr. Felicia Wellbeng, whose papers on sphagnum peat moss had made her the laughingstock of the discipline, worldwide. And Dr. Powell Pucker, who managed to churn out forty or so scholarly articles a year, all basically saying the same thing. Why couldn't that old fart of a department head see that?

It was Dr. Richlin who made sure the big research money got funneled to his tennis-playing cronies and their inane and spurious projects instead of her own more meaningful and potentially revolutionary initiatives.

So, despite the widespread acknowledgment that she had done revolutionary research in the area of winter-hardy herbaceous perennials' survivability in semi-permafrost conditions and growing southern magnolias on Virginia creeper–like vines in an upper Midwest climate, she was stuck on a middle rung of the ladder that lead to full professorship. That meant making a measly $67,000 a year.

What irked her even more was that her estranged husband, the archaeologist Dr. Ferdinand Lick, had been named a full professor six years ago, despite the fact that he had never unearthed anything more significant than a few crumbling chipping tools.

Dr. Lick's particular ambition was to prove that European explorers had made their way up the Mississippi River to the current site of St. Anthony and environs as long ago as three hundred years prior to Columbus. They might have been Vikings, or Gascons, or wanderlusting Celtic and Anglo-Saxon monks populating the British Isles. Dr. Lick had spent much of the past dozen years researching the subject at the expense of smaller projects that at least would have borne some fruit.

As a result of all this, and despite his rise through the ranks of his department, Ferdinand Lick had virtually no influence in his field, and hadn't published a single book or scholarly article in years. That utter academic fecklessness had been a major contributor to the breakup of their marriage.

And speaking of idiocy, here was Dr. Brockheimer having to put up with this mound of ersatz research from her Neanderthalish undergraduates. What a waste of time! Things had gotten even worse this year when two sections of freshmen were foisted on her! Thank God classes, exams, and all the rest of this malarkey that passed for a college education were ending for the summer.

Dr. Brockheimer took a deep breath, stared malevolently at her stack of unfinished work, and pushed a reluctant hand slowly toward the pile.

8

Transformation

George and Nan leaned over a large sheet of vellum drafting paper spread out on the backyard patio table. Shirelle's design, drawn to scale and displaying the accurate contours of the land, was punctuated with measurements, dimensions, and comments. It laid out for them a front yard the sheer majesty of which garden-by-the-gut naturals such as George and Nan could never have conceived. They silently studied the plan, their eyes open wide and darting across the paper, then narrowing into thin slits as they bowed their heads closer to the paper to try to make out Shirelle's handwriting and draftsman-like renderings of shrubs, bushes, and flowers.

"I can tell you what things are if you're having a hard time reading my notations," said Shirelle. She watched nervously as the Fremonts' expressions veered dangerously toward the quizzical.

What if they hated her plan? She would just die! But if they loved it? A hint of a smile creased Nan's face. Shirelle's heart leaped. Then, Her Munificence, the Grand Goddess of Gardening, spoke.

"My goodness, Shirelle, you've even got the contour lines

on here," she said. "And there they are bunched together to show our slope. Wow!" Shirelle flushed with pride.

"For my floriculture degree, I had to take courses in architectural drawing and basic cartography," she said, trying to sound secure in her knowledge without being boastful. "If you don't have the scale right, or the topography, or the correct location of things, you can really mess up your design, and it won't turn out right."

"Mmm-hmm," said Nan, who went back to her silent study of Shirelle's drawing. What does that "mmm-hmm" mean? wondered Shirelle. It sounded kind of noncommittal. She wondered if Nan had just brought up the contour lines to disguise her intense dislike of everything else. Damning with faint praise. Shirelle could feel her face drooping.

"Shirelle," said Nan. "This is . . . this is . . . amazing."

What was that?

"Why, Shirelle, I don't know what to say. My goodness, this is just amazing, isn't it, George?" George nodded and smiled at Shirelle. "We had been having a tough time figuring out what to do in the front yard, and you've just solved our problem. It's beautiful, Shirelle. Just beautiful. How can we thank you?"

Oh, joy! thought Shirelle. Oh, rapture. I will never, ever, ever have a moment like this. I must capture it, revel in it, take a mental snapshot of this so it will live on forever.

"I told you it was good, didn't I?" said Mary.

"Yes, dear," Nan said. "But I didn't know it was going to be *this* good."

Shirelle had taken a gamble by introducing some flowers and patterns the Fremonts had not used in their backyard gardens. While those gardens were truly magnificent, why just clone them for the front yard? Shirelle thought the Fremonts might want to shift gears a little.

"I recognize a couple of names here," said George. "A

bunch of others I don't. We've never planted these flowers. We'll want to see photos, of course."

"No problem, Mr. Fremont; got them right here on my laptop."

"These are all sun worshippers, right, Shirelle?" asked Nan. "That's mighty sunny territory out there, not a mix like the backyard."

"You can almost see all these flowers wearing sunglasses and putting on the sunscreen; that's how much they like sun," said Shirelle, with a giggle.

"When do we start?"

"We can go to Burdick's this afternoon," Mary said. "We'll have to order what they don't have."

"Knowing Burdick's, I'm not worried," Shirelle said. "It's got to be the most well-supplied gardening store in the state, maybe even the region."

"Okay," George said. "Get to it. Give me the bill when you get back and I'll reimburse you. . . . Uh, how much do you think all this will cost?"

Work on the new front yard gardens began in earnest the next day, with multiple trips to Burdick's and a pop-up thunderstorm having eaten up most of the afternoon.

What Shirelle had mapped out for the Fremonts was nothing short of regal.

She had an entire bed, eighteen feet by six feet, given over to roses. The backyard certainly had its roses, but they were of the climbing variety, smothering two big whitewashed trellises. The front yard bed would have stand-alone hybrid tea roses, lined up at the top of the slope and picked especially for their varied and vivid colors. And Shirelle had some real show-offs in mind. There'd be buttery-white Full Sail roses, lavender Blue Girls, dreamy red Chrysler Imperials, and apricot Bronze Stars.

"I'm still looking for one or two more," said Shirelle during a backyard patio break from the soil preparation work. "But this will give you quite a showcase for folks driving by on Sumac or walking along the lake. The backyard was kind of hidden away, you know. A hidden gem. You had to come up into the yard to really see what was going on. Everybody will see this. With hybrid teas, you'll have to make sure to protect them from the cold. They're finicky, too. We can talk about that more before I leave, around Labor Day."

"Oh, Shirelle, it's so hard to think about you leaving. Isn't it, George?" George nodded a bit too noncommittally for Nan's taste. "You've been so helpful to us, and I almost think of you as one of the family here. You're almost like a sister to Mary."

"Mom!" cried Mary. Shirelle blushed.

"Well, Miss Mary, you've had to grow up with two older boys, which hasn't always been easy. You would have loved to have had a sister like Shirelle when you were little. Anyway, you must move on in the gardening world, I suppose. Of course, we'll be very attentive to your instructions. I have always wanted a hybrid tea rose bed. And just the right place for it, isn't it?"

"It sure is, Mrs. Fremont," said Shirelle, poking a work-gloved finger decisively at her plan. "They'll get nothing but sun here, and the soil is sandy, which means good drainage. I bet you have to water a lot here, though, for the grass and all."

George leaned forward toward Shirelle, a disturbing shade of concern painted across his otherwise blank canvas of a face.

"I hate to be the reality-check guy here, but how much do you figure these beautiful roses will cost, Shirelle?"

Shirelle felt herself draw back involuntarily in shock. The thought of the Fremonts actually being cost-conscious about what they planted had never occurred to her. Since when did garden royalty ever concern itself with such trivialities as pricing? Just as she felt her jaw drop in dismay, Nan came to the rescue.

"Oh, George, this is not really the time, is it? We've got this beautiful plan here that Shirelle prepared for us, and why spoil its magnificence with our petty little money concerns? You go ahead with the hybrid teas, Shirelle, and we'll reimburse you for every penny. Now, walk us through the rest of your wonderful schematic here."

Covering much of the slope would be beds of Walker's Low catmint, with stands of Happy Returns and Rosy Returns daylilies anchoring the left and right flanks. Spotted around the yard, often where some vertical edging was called for, were Magic Fountain delphinium of pink, blue, purple, and white. Shirelle was still working on placement of the ornamental grasses—Karl Foerster and prairie dropseed.

"I'm toying with a couple more ground covers and maybe even a tree or two. I *love* paper birches!"

"I love paper birches, too, Shirelle!" Nan cried. "And I had just been thinking about placing one at the bottom of the slope, where it levels out, next to the intersection. Then, maybe putting a little rock garden around it."

"That's exactly where I was thinking of putting it, Mrs. Fremont! You'll need to give it plenty of TLC, though. Lots of mulch. A rock garden? Hmmm, I don't know. You need to concentrate on moisture collection at the base of paper birches. Very nice, design-wise, though. We'll see. You know, Mrs. Fremont, this would *not* be a paper birch's favorite location. But in terms of letting it stick out in all its glory, yes!"

"Now, Shirelle," said a suddenly stern Nan. "Your plan is wonderful and we're delighted with it. I couldn't have asked for anything better. But . . ."

But? But what? There are reservations? Shirelle felt the color drain out of her florid face.

"What I mean to say, Shirelle, is that I have one teensy-weensy concern."

Nan leaned over the tabletop toward her in a conspiratorial way and began to whisper.

"I've heard through the grapevine that hybrid tea roses are stuck-up prima donnas. Real snobs. Um-hmmm. And that they will cause us nothing but grief."

Wanting to be cooperative and conspiratorial, too, even though she had no idea what Nan was talking about, Shirelle lurched forward instead of leaning slowly, almost knocking heads with Nan. Nan cupped her hands around her mouth to whisper into Shirelle's ear, which Shirelle had obligingly tilted toward her.

"Our backyard friends," she said. "Our flowers. They know these things." Shirelle nodded, then slowly looked around as if to spot any hidden and unwelcome eavesdroppers. She knew Mrs. Fremont was well-versed in the arcane art of plant whispering, but this was taking it to a whole new level. She tingled with excitement.

"Ordinarily, you might chalk this up to pettiness and jealousy," Nan said. "But this is coming from reliable sources, too. You know, the petunias. They're only here for a year. They believe they have to prove themselves during their brief existence by not only making themselves beautiful, but by ratting on the bad influences in the gardens."

Shirelle just nodded. What could you say when someone was passing on such a remarkable confidence?

"Well, let's go ahead with them," said Nan, pulling away from Shirelle and throwing her hands up. "I'm sure we can handle a few difficult characters in the gardens. Not everyone can have the stoicism of the clematis or the equanimity of the daylily."

"Or the humor of the variegated dogwoods," said George, chuckling. "They're such a hoot!"

"Yes, dear, you do have a way with the variegated dogwoods, don't you? You must have tapped into their male persona. Their female persona is too snooty by far for my taste. Well, and I did have that problem with the Dusty Miller."

"Ah, yes," said Shirelle. "I heard about that."

George wrinkled his nose and frowned.

"They wouldn't grow for me, the little albino shits. They were the only ones that never responded to anything I did. All my coaxing, putting them first in line for the Miracle-Gro, singing my favorite songs to them. Lord knows, I tried everything. I'll try them again sometime, though I must have earned a pretty bad reputation, yanking them out of the soil and throwing them in the compost the way I did."

"Massacre," George said. "They might have been mutes. Did you ever stop to consider that?"

"That's putting it a little strong, George. Besides, they weren't wanted. I never heard any of the other plants complaining about it when I did that. It was a 'good riddance' kind of thing."

Shirelle smiled. Wasn't it amazing that Mrs. Fremont could actually talk to her flowers! And Mr. Fremont, too, though Shirelle couldn't help but believe that that was likely on a much more rudimentary level.

"Don't forget the Baltimore oriole feeder and the bluebird houses, Shirelle."

"Huh? I mean, excuse me?" Shirelle placed her fingertips decorously on her lips as if she had just said something untoward and instantly regretted it.

"The oriole feeder."

Birds. Shirelle knew nothing about birds.

"And, while we're at it, the bluebird houses. We already have them, so you don't have to worry about making them."

Shirelle bent over her drawing, looking for the best place to put these new additions to the front yard gardens. She stroked her chin, erased something, then drew something in. Nan leaned over to try to get a peek.

"Simple," said Shirelle. "I've got the bluebird houses at either end of the highest part of the slope, then the oriole feeder smack in the middle, among the hybrid tea roses. The symmetry should work out just fine. It's good to have a few manmade items sticking out of all the natural stuff."

Mary, meanwhile, had gotten up and was inspecting the backyard gardens, which were poised to spring to life once the temperatures rose, now that the rains had stopped and a bright, direct May sun was shining down on them.

"Any day now," Mary said, sitting back down at the patio. "God knows we've had plenty of rain. I can see the tips of hosta, there are buds on the creeping phlox, and the bleeding hearts are three inches tall. Hope they shoot up before getting covered by hosta leaves. Nothing wrong with the columbine. Another couple of days and they'll be bursting out. Silver maples, ash, locust, and sugar maple just starting to leaf."

A white sedan of uncertain make, but which looked vaguely familiar, pulled into the driveway.

"Who might *that* be?" wondered George.

A lanky middle-aged woman wearing oversized sunglasses got out of the front passenger side of the car, followed by the driver, a shorter, stouter woman, also wearing sunglasses.

"My God!" cried George.

"My God?" said Nan. "What are you 'my God-ing' about?"

"Keep looking. Because you will soon recognize Marta Poppendauber, accompanied by one Dr. Phyllis Sproot."

"My God!" cried Nan.

9

Reunion and Reparation

"Mary, Shirelle, you girls go ahead and scoot. Go around to the front yard and continue staking out your plots, or whatever it is you're doing now. Go on, shoo. George, a couple of gin and tonics for us, please. Mixed strongly. I think I'm going to need to fortify my constitution for this. Chop-chop!"

"So that's the infamous Dr. Phyllis Sproot," said Mary. "Ha-ha! I guess I better go fetch the shotgun and shells, huh, Ma?"

"You got a shotgun?" said Shirelle, who had grown up in the western part of the state, where you had to have bagged a minimum of four Canada geese and three mergansers before you could attend high school or get your driver's license. "What kind? At this range, I'd say a twelve-gauge pump action. Five-shell magazine capacity. Yep, that should do the job just fine."

"Scat, I said!" yipped Nan, and the two girls scurried off toward the back, then around the corner.

"George, are you armed?"

"Sure am," said George, setting two freshened gin and tonics on the table. Nan took a quick sip, then puckered up her lips.

"Whoa, George, are you loaded for bear or what!"

The two women had been making their way deliberately up the steps from the driveway to the patio. Halfway up the steps, the tall, lanky woman stopped, seemingly oblivious to the two seated persons anxiously awaiting her arrival, and made a slight pivot to her right, turning her head to take in the full panorama of the still-dormant backyard.

"The season's late this year," she said, either addressing everyone or no one. The shorter woman smiled up at the Fremonts, then grabbed her companion by the crook of her arm and moved on slowly up the steps.

"Nan and George," she said. "Long time, no see. How are you? How's everything progressing this year?"

"Slow, Marta," said Nan. "Slow. As you can see. I'm afraid we don't have much to show you yet. Dr. Sproot, I presume." The taller woman nodded, her face largely shielded by her sunglasses. "And to what do we owe the pleasure of this visit?"

Nan noticed that Dr. Sproot was carrying what appeared to be a miniature house; not a dollhouse or a birdhouse, but something in between. It looked a bit like an A-frame cabin open on one side and made of twigs and bark with flooring fashioned from stained popsicle sticks. Sphagnum peat moss and grass clippings had been stuffed into the corners of the structure, which was about a foot tall and wide, and seven inches or so deep. It smelled of pine sap, even at this distance.

"A little house for your rats, Dr. Sproot? Or your tarantulas maybe?"

"Nan!" said George.

Dr. Sproot's hands trembled. Her lips curled into a sneer that she meant as a smile. George chuckled and took a long draw from his gin and tonic. Marta squinched her face in sadness.

"Gin and tonic?" chirped George.

"Thanks, George," Marta said. "But maybe some other time for me. Right now, we're here to ask a favor, and my friend, Phyllis, comes here as a supplicant."

"What, you can't speak for yourself, Sproot?" scolded Nan, emboldened by the gin with its hint of tonic she had just guzzled. She turned to Marta, addressing her as if Dr. Sproot wasn't even there. "She's got a lot of nerve, asking us for a favor."

Marta turned to Dr. Sproot and nodded. Dr. Sproot cleared her throat in a disgusting, phlegmy way.

"This is a fairy house," she said in that gravelly contralto Nan and George remembered so well from last year. "I was wondering if I could put my fairy house in your garden this year. It attracts fairies, you know, and from everything I've heard fairies are very good for gardens. I brought it as a gift for you. Since I've never really properly made up to you for what I did last year. I made it myself."

"Nice craftsmanship," said George upon taking another emboldening draw from his drink. "And it's comforting to know that you actually eat Popsicles. The moss, I assume, is kind of a fairy bed."

"Yes, that's right, Mr. Fremont."

"George."

"George." Nan turned to frown at George. This was a bit too much familiarity, especially after what had happened last year. Dr. Sproot placed the fairy house carefully on the glass tabletop.

"I'm also paying tribute to your gardens," she said, a tremor modulating her voice. "This, I think, is where the fairies will truly come."

Nan didn't believe in fairies, and was astonished that such a force of naked empiricism as Dr. Sproot would. Or maybe this was some kind of elaborate joke. That, on reflection, would be unlikely since Marta was here. Marta, after all, was the former close Dr. Sproot ally who had turned against her when Dr. Sproot tried to wreak havoc among their gardens in order to win the Burdick's Best Yard first prize.

Nan chuckled at the thought of that night in July last year, when, at the same ungodly hour, Dr. Sproot and her unwitting confederates had arrived in their backyard to create mayhem. And in the middle of that terrible thunderstorm! They had scared the living bejesus out of her and George. Dr. Sproot had carried a hatchet in one hand and a tomahawk in the other and was wearing a gas mask to ward off what she was afraid would be debilitating poisonous fumes coming out of the angel's trumpets.

Her inhibitions pretty well put to flight by the gin, Nan erupted in a kind of hee-haw laughter that she would normally allow to escape only during the most intimate of family occasions. George, telepathically privy to Nan's thoughts, began to laugh. Marta looked amused. Dr. Sproot, suspecting herself to be the object of all the mirth, sighed and frowned.

"Oh, oh!" said Nan, gulping back a guffaw and stopping to catch her breath. "I can't get over it. You with that gas mask! All because you were afraid the angel's trumpet fumes would start you hallucinating! It's just too much!"

George stopped laughing and frowned. Mention of the angel's trumpets awakened his own fears that those wretched plants, known for their toxic and hallucinogenic poisons, would eventually bring them to grief.

Nan laughed again, this time with such force that she almost keeled over the chair's armrest. George had to reach over to stabilize the chair as she pitched back against the mesh fabric backing, causing it to skid noisily across the patio concrete.

"And George thought you were a zombie. A *zombie!* And you, Marta, in that ridiculous cowl that made you look like a monk. George thought you were, what, an angel of the Lord? Ha-ha! Ha-ha!"

Marta blushed. The hint of a smile crept across Dr. Sproot's face. She nervously grabbed the fairy house off the tabletop and pretended to study it.

"Maybe that's enough alcohol for you, dear," said George, patting the hand of his wife, who was still shaking with unrestrained mirth.

"So now," gasped Nan, struggling to regain her composure and relishing Dr. Sproot's discomfort. "So now, we have this, we have this fairy house as a, what, peace offering?"

Dr. Sproot nodded.

"It's made exact to specifications of fairies' size and demands for creature comforts," she said, her voice oozing earnestness. "You can place it next to a tree, or in the middle of one of your gardens if you prefer."

"What, the fairies don't appreciate the . . . what was that blend of flowers you used to advocate? The coreopsis . . . Help me out here. . . ."

"The coreopsis-salvia-hollyhock blend."

"That's it. So you can't attract your own fairies with this special blend of yours?" Dr. Sproot and Marta looked at each other knowingly.

"Actually, I've abandoned the coreopsis-salvia-hollyhock blend."

"No!" said George.

"Yes, Mr. Fremont."

"George."

"George. I've decided, especially after all of the trouble I got into last year, and all the hardships I created for you, that I would free myself to plant something that's not so dogmatic. I just want to plant a regular garden that I can nourish and love."

Nan guffawed, once again threatening her balance.

Dr. Sproot bowed her head. "Yes, Nan."

"That's 'Mrs. Fremont' to you," Nan sputtered.

"Yes, Mrs. Fremont, it's true. I'm really trying to put my

heart into my gardens this year. And Marta, who I'm very thankful to say is once again my friend, is going to be my adviser and help me out. She's a special consultant to Burdick's now, you know."

George and Nan nodded approvingly at Marta.

"But I am a work in progress. It will take time to show my flowers the love I need to show them. Fairies can sense that. Until they feel the garden ambiance is right, they won't come. That's why I've brought my fairy house to you. If anybody can attract fairies, it's the Fremonts."

"What a nice thing to say," George said.

"Why would we want fairies in our gardens in the first place?" Nan wondered. "That's assuming they exist, of course, which I don't, although after what happened last year, Lord knows I'm prepared to be open-minded about it. It's also assuming that, if they exist, we'd want them to come anyway. I imagine their little nighttime frolics among the buttercups can be quite noisy. Ha-ha! Ha-ha!"

"Fairies can protect your gardens and help them flourish."

Nan shook her head disjointedly in utter bewilderment. It absolutely defied logic that she was listening to the same person who only a year ago had been such a shining example of what happens when you cross a pedant with a hatchet murderer. Part of her couldn't help but think that Dr. Sproot was still out to get them, and that there was some flower-destroying scent or spraying device built into this little fairy house.

"I know it seems strange to you, Mr. and Mrs. Fremont, but Marta can vouch for the fact that I'm a changed woman. Or, at least, I'm trying to change."

George and Nan looked at Marta, who shrugged in what could magnanimously be described as an indecisive way.

"She's definitely putting forth the effort," said Marta. "And, yes, she has been humbled by the events of last year. You heard about Earlene McGillicuddy and the chain saw?"

This time it was George who guffawed. Dr. Sproot bowed her head and pursed her lips in a way she hoped would look like someone who's been martyred a dozen or so times. On the day of the contest judging last year, Earlene, who'd feuded with Dr. Sproot in a dramatic fashion, had chain-sawed her way through most of Dr. Sproot's flowers before the police finally arrived.

Dr. Sproot turned toward Marta, and both Nan and George thought they detected the beginnings of a snarl.

"Well, I think even you will admit, Marta, that *that* was going too far."

"Yes, I do admit that, Phyllis." Dr. Sproot smiled at the Fremonts.

"There. You see?"

"See what?" said Nan.

"Evidence that I've changed. I no longer insist that everybody call me *Doc-tor* Sproot. Now, with the new me emerging, it's okay to just call me Phyllis."

"I actually prefer Dr. Sproot," Nan said. "Don't you, George?"

"Why, yes," said George. "It has that, that gravitas to it. I like it."

Marta chuckled. "Oh, you Fremonts," she said.

"One last thing about the fairy house," Dr. Sproot said. "Fairies like sweets, or so I've heard. A few M&M's or Hershey's Kisses placed strategically inside your fairy house or in the form of a trail leading up to the house from the nearest wooded area wouldn't hurt. You can space these treats one to two feet apart. Do these things and the fairies should start appearing once things start really blooming. Fairies can sense the positive energy emanating from these blooms. So don't be disappointed if they don't come right away."

"We'll try our best not to be," Nan said.

"With your natural gardening abilities, and especially considering that you can apparently communicate with your plants . . ." Here, Dr. Sproot paused, wrinkled her nose, and sniffed, as if smelling something pungently unpleasant. "Then, I'd say your chances of having at least the first scouting parties of fairies arrive in the next, say, two weeks, are really good."

"And how," said Nan, "shall we know we're being visited by these tiny supernatural fiends . . . I mean, friends?"

"A little glow, bluish-white, deep in the night, barely discernible. Gardens healthier than you can imagine. If you wake up in the middle of the night, you might think you're hearing voices. Sort of like what you might imagine if you can hear the movements of a brook or river, or the whispering of the wind. Don't try too hard to understand because you won't be able to. Also, you will see no physical signs of a fairy's presence. Your candy won't appear to be eaten. Your fairy house will never appear to be disturbed. They operate on a plane that leaves no physical evidence."

"That's convenient," said George.

"It is true, George. It is most certainly true. I believe it."

"What do you have to say about this, Marta?"

Marta offered up another noncommittal shrug.

"Anything that helps Dr. Sproot . . . uh, I mean, Phyllis . . . turn over a new leaf works for me. Besides, who am I to say such forces don't exist? Your own gardens are testimony to that. Their remarkable recovery. Phyllis knows what I'm talking about. So do you. It wasn't by chance."

"You mean that so-called spell?" cried Nan. "What nonsense!"

"I don't know, Nan," said George. "That was awfully weird. Along with the super-localized hailstorm."

"Bad spell followed by good spell?" said Marta. "But who am I to say? Coincidence, perhaps. Divine intervention?"

"We'll take care of the fairies for you," said George, who was secretly planning to treat them to little saucersful of merlot. Nan made a big show of looking at her watch. She was getting tired of all this fairy talk, and had concluded that this new, reincarnated Dr. Sproot was probably a fraud and definitely a bore.

"Gosh, we have to get to work, don't we, George?"

"We do?" said George, slouched into his chair, deep in contemplation about these new fairy findings.

"Yes! We do!"

"Well," Marta said. "We have to go, anyway. But thank you for taking on the fairies. And I must say this was entirely Phyllis's idea. She's hoping to be reconciled with you. Then, we can all be gardening buddies."

"We will take that under consideration," Nan said curtly. "But you're just about the last person we'd want to reconnect with, Sproot."

"I understand that," said Dr. Sproot. "But try to be open-minded about me. I have changed. I'm trying to change some more. I'm trying so hard to undo the bad things I did to you last year." Marta tugged at Dr. Sproot's elbow. Dr. Sproot, as rigid as a tomato plant stake, turned silently and walked, with Marta in tow, slowly back down the steps. Nan was forced to note, approvingly, that neither she nor Marta disturbed the pea gravel.

"Strange," George said.

"Strange?"

"Didn't you notice anything strange about Dr. Sproot?"

"Everything is strange about Dr. Sproot, George."

"Something in particular I noticed. Marta took her sunglasses off when she was up here on the patio with us. Dr. Sproot never did."

"So?"

"I think there's something in that. I can't help but think that Dr. Sproot hasn't really changed at all, but is just going through the motions. Something's going on behind those Foster Grants that we don't want to know about. We need to treat her with care, or, better yet, not at all."

"No argument from me," said Nan, who was feeling too good from the gin and tonics to be too concerned about how Dr. Sproot, whom she had humbled with so much ease, might somehow threaten them in the misty, uncertain future. She made a note to file this in her mental "George's paranoid observations" folder for possible future consideration.

Something completely off the subject and infinitely more pressing suddenly occurred to her.

"Here's a treat for you, George. A new plant joke."

George groaned.

"How many Joe-Pye weeds does it take to move a pressure-treated railroad tie? Ponder that while you go freshen my drink, please."

10

The True Nature of Things

A year ago, Dr. Sproot would have scoffed at the notion of supernatural powers at the beck and call of those who knew how to summon them. There had been a dramatic turnaround in her thinking since then.

For one thing, there was that blight on her garden that had no horticultural explanation. That was Edith Merton's doing; that bitch of a witch casting her gardening spells hither and yon, and Dr. Sproot knew it was so because she had seen the dire results herself.

Edith had been rejected for membership in the Rose Maidens, and had not taken rejection sitting down. She had punished each and every voting officer by visiting a gardening plague of biblical proportions upon their gardens. Including Dr. Sproot's.

Dr. Sproot had thus been the victim of supernatural extortion, having to pay Edith to undo the curse on her own yard. While she was at it, she figured she might as well pay Edith to take down her archrivals, the Fremonts, big-time. That freak-of-nature hailstorm couldn't have happened without some supernatural intercession. Then—drat that Edith!—she must have cast a good spell that revitalized the Fremonts' gardens—

and in August, no less!—after everyone got caught on that awful night, and Marta got Edith to turn over a new leaf and play nice.

Dr. Sproot surveyed the expanse of her five new garden plots, which she had staked out, churned up, fertilized, and aerated in the hopes of turning them into her new, revolutionary creations. Yes, she thought; maybe there are things that happen that no amount of gardening erudition and wisdom—such as her own—can explain. Maybe that means that the Fremonts really could talk to their plants, and that gardening spirits await only the proper medium for unleashing their cosmic influences, for good or evil.

Dr. Sproot frowned. A Christian of sorts, she wondered how all this could be reconciled with the tenets of organized religion. Maybe she was destined to go pagan.

The night she spent in the clink following her Fremont backyard escapade had also made a profound impression. Even such a hard case as Dr. Sproot could give some serious thought to reforming after spending time with a couple of mucus-smeared drunks, a middle-aged prostitute who chomped on about ten pieces of gum while leering at her through sparkling Day-Glo lips, and three loquacious teenagers who kept taking off their shorts and waving them around until the prostitute threatened to "scrotum-kick" them.

Besides, there were a few chromosomes of good in Dr. Sproot that occasionally exerted a teensy bit of influence on her behavior. She decided that it was time to give those chromosomes full rein, and to become the new "Phyllis."

The new Phyllis would be kind, engaging, and encouraging to any and all gardeners who would flatter her enough to seek her advice. Gone were her old rigid formulas that dictated to the percentage point the amount and types of flowers you had to have in your garden for it to truly achieve a measured magnificence. She would garden from her heart now, letting pure instinct tell her what to do. She would be plain old Phyllis-the-Gardener, and drop any pretense of being Livia's ruling gardening savant.

This new attitude made it easier for Dr. Sproot to concede that there were other gardeners in Livia far more accomplished than she. True peace of mind was now within reach. All she had to do was step out of the gardening limelight and let the dictates of her soul steer her toward a fruitful, contented anonymity.

How heartening it was for her to see that this new Phyllis thing was getting results. Her few friends and many acquaintances were back on speaking terms with her. The Rose Maidens announced they would consider her for readmittance to their ranks. Dr. Sproot had even thought about calling Edith. A contrite Edith had allegedly given up her dark practices, though Dr. Sproot knew she was keeping her hand in because would you look at her gardens! She was the rankest of amateurs, yet her meager little blooms, once so bedraggled and puny-looking, shone out like guiding beacons of the gardener's craft. Well, bless her little heart anyway.

Mostly, it was poor Marta who had worked so hard to change her. Good old self-effacing Marta. It was Marta who had come by to visit her after she was branded a pariah, a marked woman expelled from the Rose Maidens, and whose name was nutrient-deprived mud in every gardening circle for miles around. It was Marta who had worked hard to extract the tiniest nugget of pure good that was buried deep down inside her. Marta said she had that little wavering flicker of saintliness that made her want to love and cherish her flowers, and not to treat them so callously as *things*.

And, speaking of the little saint maker, here she was now, coming through the fence gate to get her first long look at Dr. Sproot's straight-from-the-heart creations.

"Morning, Marta."

"Hi, Phyllis. Lovely day . . . finally!"

"Isn't it, though?" said Dr. Sproot, proudly scanning the panorama of her new flower beds. "So, what do you think, Marta?"

In the past, Dr. Sproot's gardens would have been crowded with her coreopsis-salvia-hollyhock blend, yuccas, and a smattering of dahlias and roses. Marta had always thought it a weird combination, especially based as it was on Dr. Sproot's insistence on assigning a precise percentage of the whole to each particular flower grouping. It had been her pedantic way of doing things, and for that reason it had always had a sort of artificial, mathematical look to it.

What we had here now was so different Marta didn't know quite what to make of it. Dr. Sproot had kept it a secret from her and implored her to stay away until she could properly unveil her new gardens. It appeared Dr. Sproot had completely given herself over to geraniums and spikes, which gave her yard the appearance of a bristling red, pink, and white torture chamber. Marta had to stifle a gag impulse. In small doses, geraniums and spikes were just fine, though not to her particular taste. When planted solely and over such a broad expanse, it would make any experienced gardener want to run to the nearest weed patch for shelter. It screamed out obsession of the absolutely worst kind.

"It's quite impressive, Phyllis," she said. "It truly is." She had not lied. It would also be telling the truth for Marta to call a giant sanitary landfill impressive. Dr. Sproot's geranium-spike extravaganza was impressive in that it was one of the most ridiculous horticultural displays she had ever seen.

Marta wiggled her nose in a subtle show of disgust. My gosh, she thought, I'll never be able to come over here again. It will make me nauseous. She reflected with some sadness that in trying to let her spirit take over from her old, coldly pedantic ways, Dr. Sproot had shown that her passion was woefully misguided. It was now plain that gardening from the heart was not going to be her forte, and that, in essence, she had no gardening soul at all. In fact, it would have been much better had she kept her gardens the way they were before, though Marta had no desire for the old, rampaging-nutcase version of Dr. Sproot to reassert herself.

"This is something else," said Marta again, trying desperately to sound enthused in order to encourage Dr. Sproot's personal transformation.

"These gardens are from the heart, Marta," said Dr. Sproot. "From the heart, I tell you. All my fabulously impressive knowledge and revolutionary approaches to gardening innovation mean nothing to me anymore. I don't care what anybody says about what I'm doing here. I'm doing this to please myself. And I've found that I am obsessed with geraniums and spikes."

Marta cringed.

"I'm so proud of my geraniums and spikes, and, Marta, I don't go by the book anymore. I go by my gut. I water when the spirit moves me. Same with fertilizing. I figure my inner gardening being will tell me when it's time."

And your inner being better start telling you to come up with a new plan, thought Marta, because there's way too many geraniums and spikes here. Ecch!

"I'm so happy with the way I've changed," Dr. Sproot said. "It's so much more spiritually fulfilling. In time, I feel I'll be able to be one with my flowers—see how they seem to be bending toward us as I talk about them; it's almost as if they can hear what we're saying and want in on the conversation."

Marta saw no such thing. She couldn't imagine Dr. Sproot talking to her flowers. As happy as she was to behold over the winter and spring what seemed to be a truly contrite Dr. Sproot seeking forgiveness and redemption for all the bad things she did last year, there was a ring of artificiality in what she was saying and doing. It was as if Dr. Sproot was reading from a script, and once the pages of the script ran out, the imperious, cruel, manipulative bitch the whole world knew to be Dr. Phyllis Sproot would come roaring back in ways that would be too awful to imagine.

What was the story with that fairy house?

Marta was skeptical, to say the least. Still, she had witnessed so many strange things last year that she couldn't completely discount the notion that gardening fairies went gallivanting around in the gardens of people whose green thumbs sent out powerful signals of nurturing and kindness.

In reality, Dr. Sproot had come up with the fairy house idea after reading an article about them in the St. Anthony *Inquirer*. What better way to cement a new beginning with the Fremonts than by giving them a gift of one?

Marta had to admit it was nice of Dr. Sproot to make such a gesture of atonement. And a handmade fairy house at that. A really ugly and jerry-rigged one to be sure, and one that no self-respecting fairy would use even as an outhouse, but still . . . What the Fremonts would make of it she had no idea. She stifled a chuckle as she imagined them drinking their merlot and horsing around with a bunch of naughty, besotted fairies. She pictured Dr. Sproot as Tinkerbell with a little Tinkerbell wand, waving it around and sprinkling fairy dust all over her stupid geraniums and spikes. Dr. Sproot still had a pretty good figure, Marta thought, but she'd have to put on a few more pounds in the right places to look good in that Tinkerbell costume.

"Tee-hee, tee-hee."

"Why, Marta," said Dr. Sproot, the icy sting returning to her voice. "What is it you find so funny? Eh? Is it my flowers? Do you find my geraniums and spikes amusing? So maybe they're not good enough for Miss-Second-Place-Contest-Winner, huh?"

Marta stepped back, stunned, from Dr. Sproot. This was

more like the Dr. Sproot she used to know, not the newly reincarnated Phyllis.

"I was just chuckling at a funny thought that entered my
head, Dr. Sproot . . . er, Phyllis."

"Well, how about sharing your little funny thought with
us, missy?" said Dr. Sproot. Marta imagined undersized gossamer wings sprouting from either side of her and making dainty
flicking motions.

"Ha-ha! Ha-ha! Oh, Phyllis," Marta cried, "I was imagining you dressed up like Tinkerbell in a little fairy suit, with
that super-short skirt, low-cut to show whatever cleavage you
can muster, and you waving a little fairy wand around. Ha-ha-
ha-ha!"

Dr. Sproot seethed with fury. How dare a little pipsqueak
like Marta make fun of her in such a mortifying way! And
right on top of the humiliation she had suffered at the hands of
that Nan Fremont. Why, she could only turn the other cheek
so many times. Maybe it was time to start hitting back.

Dr. Sproot trembled. She could feel her "nice Phyllis"
chromosomes shrivel into nothingness. A meek, halting voice
from somewhere deep down pleaded with them to come back,
but it was time to silence that inner milquetoast. It was time to
call forth the real, the dominant, the merciless Dr. Sproot. And
what better time than now to cast off her Little-Miss-Priss ve-
neer and start sowing some havoc and discord.

Her gardening-gloved hands pressed against her bony hips,
and her arms rigidly akimbo, Dr. Sproot lurched forward, using
her five-eleven height to dominate the much smaller Marta,
and trying to bore laser holes through her with those piercing
gray eyes.

My God, what have I done? thought Marta. It's the old Dr.
Sproot back from the depths of poor Phyllis's blackened soul. I
could be in mortal danger!

More terrified than saddened, Marta, nevertheless, stood

her ground resolutely. For Phyllis's sake, for Livia's sake, for humanity's sake, she had to stand tall, at least figuratively speaking, in the face of this new threat.

"Don't you dare try to come back, you awful Dr. Sproot!"

"What! I am back, you little turd! Do you dare to presume that you could transform me into one of your namby-pamby little flower-slut friends? Huh? Not on your life! And to turn me into your circus-sideshow laughingstock? Huh? Well, look here, little Marta, and look good; the real Dr. Sproot is here now, live and kicking, and she's got some scores to settle."

Without quite realizing what she was doing, and aware that she had to take immediate action to ward off this incarnation of evil, Marta crossed the forefingers of her hands into a crucifix configuration and thrust them up and out toward Dr. Sproot's contorted face. It wasn't much, but it was the best she could do under trying circumstances.

"What in the name of Hades-on-fire are you doing, Marta? I don't believe it. What, you think I'm some kind of *demon?* How insulting! Or maybe I should say how flattering. Ha-ha!"

Marta opened her eyes to see Dr. Sproot still looming in her threatening manner, still shaking with all the pent-up evil that had been boiling up, unvented, for so long. Okay, she thought, so the crucifix thing doesn't work. What now?

"I know how to deal with little pests like you!" screeched Dr. Sproot, a thread of spittle hanging from her trembling lower lip.

Dr. Sproot turned away from her and sprinted toward her deck. She didn't bother to detour around a bed of geraniums and spikes, and tromped right through them, even stopping for a few seconds to gleefully smush the drooping, barely semi-erect spikes beneath the grinding heels of her work boots. Marta watched her scramble up the steps to her deck, then reach for a long stick-type object propped against the back of the house.

She wouldn't do that, thought Marta. No, she wouldn't dare do that. But then she saw Dr. Sproot aim the BB gun at her and heard a soft, distant poof.

"Ouch!" A BB grazed her wrist. Dr. Sproot worked the BB gun's lever and aimed it again. This time, Marta didn't wait to be shot. She turned and ran. As she turned the corner of the house, opened the door to the fence, and raced to her car, she could hear Dr. Sproot's demonic cackle. Afraid that Dr. Sproot would run through the house to the front and start taking pot-shots at her windshield, Marta turned on the ignition and peeled out without even putting on her seat belt or looking back.

11

Seeds of Envy

Shirelle was in the office of Dr. Brockheimer, who was her faculty adviser, delivering her final internship oral report, which was also her senior project final report. She clutched her portfolio close to her body. She was making her report right on deadline. To be precise, thirty-five minutes *before* deadline. What was bad about that was Dr. Brockheimer had already listened to about thirty similar reports and was sick and tired of hearing them. In fact, she wasn't even pretending to listen. It looked like she was about a million miles away.

Still, Shirelle made her presentation with swagger and verve. She was certain the magnificent results she, Mary, and Mr. and Mrs. Fremont had achieved would win her plaudits, and assure her graduation with magna cum laude honors.

Dr. Brockheimer stared, glassy-eyed, past Shirelle and into a future that had already doomed her to insignificance. When would this interminable report ever end? What was this chirpy and rather rustic and unsophisticated student droning on about? Dr. Brockheimer toyed with the notion of telling her she had wasted a lot of time in college, that she had no future, and that she should go back to the farm out in Hicksville and specialize in cleaning out the chicken coops. That last thought struck

Dr. Brockheimer as especially funny. She laughed. Shirelle stopped talking.

"Go on, please, go on," said Dr. Brockheimer, waving a hand at Shirelle dismissively. "I just had a silly thought about something I ate last night, that's all."

All Dr. Brockheimer could think about now was the research she could be doing and the fame and position she would attain if only she could secure the funds for a couple of her pet projects. Even that grew tiresome as Shirelle droned on. Dr. Brockheimer made no effort to stifle a yawn.

"Am I keeping you awake, Dr. Brockheimer?" Shirelle barked. The tone and volume startled Dr. Brockheimer out of her somnolence. What was that she'd said? Why, the very effrontery! She'd never had a student speak to her in such a manner.

"Earth to Dr. Brockheimer," Shirelle said, snorting derisively.

"What did you say to me, Ms. Ediston?" said Dr. Brockheimer, suddenly alert and focused.

Shirelle fought the urge to squirm. She was not going to be intimidated by this uninspired loser of a teacher and alleged flower expert.

"That's Ms. *Eadkins,* Dr. Brockheimer. I said, 'Am I keeping you awake?' Here I am making my report, and you seem to be lost in a daydream or something. How can I get your attention?"

Dr. Brockheimer smiled indulgently. Her thoughts drifted toward her dream research project—tomatoes so frost-resistant that they could be planted outdoors and harvested in January! Why, only the seedlings would need water! Wasn't that amazing! Then, there was her idea of cultivating a type of sugar maple that flamed fuchsia, lavender, battleship gray, and honey gold in the fall, and—

"Dr. Brockheimer? Dr. Brockheimer?"

Dr. Brockheimer snapped to attention once more and sneered at Shirelle.

"Yes, well, Ms. Eadkins," she said, taking a long look at her wristwatch. "You've got about seven minutes left, so let's make it snappy."

Shirelle started over again, condensing what it had taken fifteen minutes to recite into a shorthand version of how she and Mary had worked with the Fremonts last summer, and now again this spring, to create a new paradise on earth. Dr. Brockheimer wrinkled her nose and frowned when Shirelle actually said "a paradise on earth." No major root systems to worry about in the current front yard project. Soil a nice cross between acidic and alkaline, pH of 6.7. They had staked out five basic plots, none of which was square or rectangular shaped, Shirelle liking a much more meandering and curving style that might resemble a teardrop or one of those squiggly designs on paisley ties.

"Hmmm," said Dr. Brockheimer. "Soil type?"

"Sandy, so good drainage, and an easily accessible faucet for the hose."

"Go on."

Shirelle proceeded to list the flowers and grasses she'd planted. With thirty seconds remaining in her time, Shirelle told Dr. Brockheimer how Nan had worried about the hybrid tea roses being prima donnas and not able to get along well with their neighbor flowers. Dr. Brockheimer, attentive to this new comedy angle of Shirelle's report, laughed.

"Oh, yes, this is our plant whisperer, is it?"

"Yes, she really does talk to plants, Dr. Brockheimer. I've seen her do it."

"Um-hmmm." Dr. Brockheimer leaned forward, tapping a mechanical pencil against her lips.

"Ms. Eadkins, are these people . . . uh, Mr. and Mrs. Fremont . . . are they . . . how shall I say it . . . uh . . ."

"Whacko?"

"Well, for lack of a better word, yes."

"No, they are perfectly sane."

"But they do drink, you say?"

"Oh, yes, merlot . . . and . . . and . . . what is it . . . gin and tonics."

"To excess?"

"No, not that I've ever noticed. They just get a little jolly and silly sometimes."

"That plant whispering's just old-wives'-tale stuff," Dr. Brockheimer said. "It's along the line of the idea that plants flourish when they're listening to classical music. That's just poppycock. The plants flourish because the type of person who listens to classical music is probably the type of person who appreciates beauty and is responsible enough to take proper care of her plants. The person who listens to rock 'n' roll or rap or heavy metal is probably nowhere near as responsible. That type of person probably won't have flowers anyway, much less know their names or the kind of care they require. There has been no empirical evidence that I've run across that shows that flowers respond to music or noise of any kind for that matter. There's no empirical evidence that they respond to any outward manifestations of love or concern. They do well because the kind of person who shows them love and concern will also know how to care for them and will be assiduous in their constant upkeep. That's why."

"They listen to Jethro Tull. Or at least Mr. Fremont does," Shirelle said. "And baseball games."

Dr. Brockheimer smiled.

"Who's Jethro Tull?"

"A rock band from a long time ago. With a flute player. The Fremonts are almost sixty, I think."

Dr. Brockheimer chuckled.

"Well, Shirelle," she said. "It doesn't matter what kind of

music someone plays, or what kind of noise they create. If they're as committed to gardening as you say they are, then that's what makes a difference. Gardeners who know what to do and take the time to do it consistently will most likely create good gardens; though, without the proper training, it's hard to imagine that they could come up with anything that has the right mix or design scheme to it."

"They have the most beautiful gardens in the world, Dr. Brockheimer. If you go there, I promise you will be transformed. It's like you're entering another world. And a lot's coming out now. Already!"

"Maybe someday I will, Ms. Eadkins, but getting back to all this malarkey about plant whispering—do you actually talk to these flowers yourself?"

"It's not exactly 'talking,' Dr. Brockheimer. It's almost a sort of . . . um . . . um . . ."

"Brain wave communication?"

"No, not that, just a sense of harmony, a sense of knowing what they're trying to tell you. Mrs. Fremont says they're always trying to tell her something, except for the Dusty Miller, which she tore out by the roots and threw in the compost. She said she actually hears sort of whisperings, which she has learned to translate."

"Shirelle, you know this is just the stuff of old gardening lore, and isn't true at all."

"No, Dr. Brockheimer, it *is* true."

"It is *not!* Scientists with nothing better to do have attached all manner of electrodes to plants to see if there are reactions to various stimuli. This, I might add, is on the fringe of the field, and not taken seriously by most of us."

"I know what I see," Shirelle said, getting up from her chair. "What I see are gardens that would surpass your wildest dreams, Dr. Brockheimer. You should see the hybrid tea roses.

They have a lushness, a purity, a brilliance, a depth I wouldn't have thought—"

"Time's up. Your portfolio, Ms. Eadkins."

"Oh, yeah." Shirelle handed her thick portfolio of photographs, plans, and notes to Dr. Brockheimer, who would review them and hand them back in a couple of days with suggestions before Shirelle's project committee graded it. As Shirelle bolted out through the office door, glad to be freed of her adviser's unwavering pedantic doubts, Dr. Brockheimer flipped through a few pages of photos Shirelle had assembled for her.

My God, would you look at that! Page after page of flower power exploded out at her. Amazing. Even the ag school's meticulously maintained gardens couldn't approach this. Every flower so lustrous, even making allowances for photo quality and lighting!

There was a knock on the door. Dr. Brockheimer looked up to see a pimply, moon-faced teenager peeking around the door at her.

"Hi, Dr. Brockheimer. I hope I'm not disturbing you."

"In fact, you are."

"Uh, well, I guess I had an appointment."

"Something urgent has come up. Call back to reschedule."

She shooed her former appointment away and got up to shut and lock the door. Then she sat back down and eagerly began to plow through Shirelle Eadkins's suddenly fascinating final internship-and-senior-project report.

12

Noxious Weed

Dr. Sproot was a gardener possessed. She slashed, dug, and extracted, driven by a sense of purpose she hadn't known since last year. Her muscles ached and her palms blistered. Sweat stung her eyes and so soaked her shirt that it clung to her like sticky body paint. But Dr. Phyllis Sproot was never one to let a little discomfort stand in the way of the mission at hand. By Sunday evening, after two days of work interrupted only by a few hours of sleep, seventeen coffee breaks, and thirty-two trips to the bathroom, her job was done: Every trace of geranium and spike was out of the ground and piled into eight giant mounds around the yard.

Discarding her sopping shirt and brassiere onto the nearest mound of dead and dying flowers, she stood on her deck, her hands braced on the railing. Ingloriously topless, Dr. Sproot imperiously scanned her yard. What was once a paean to gardening monotony had now been reduced to churned-up and empty brown garden plots and piles of color-blotched, spiky green beside them. A wonderful sense of confidence and well-being surged up in her. No geranium or spike would ever blot her gardens again. Never! They seemed like abortions to her. But, oh, what a joy it was to be the abortionist!

Someone was opening the fence and entering her back-yard inner sanctum. Out of the corner of her eye she saw several figures walking toward her. Only a few besides Marta would ever dream of taking such liberties, and Marta would obviously never do so again after the BB-gun incident of three weeks ago. It could only be an official delegation of Rose Maidens, the bitches!

Dr. Sproot turned to watch their tentative and halting approach. Livia's premier women's gardening club had cut all ties with her after last summer's garden rampage fiasco. The Rose Maidens stopped halfway between the backyard fence gate and the deck, where Dr. Sproot stood, immobile, gazing down at them. They stared, open-mouthed in shock, at the destruction around them and at Dr. Sproot's naked torso.

"Why, Phyllis, what in heaven's name have you got going on here?" said Dawn Fisher, the club's outgoing president. "Who did this to your gardens? And . . . and would you please put on a shirt?"

"I did it," said Dr. Sproot, folding her arms proudly across her sagging, smallish breasts. "I did this to my gardens. I also have no intention of putting on a shirt. I have no need of it. If you're going to be squeamish about it, you can just leave."

"My gosh," said Muffy McGonigle, the former president who now served as secretary-treasurer. "Those are piles of geraniums and spikes, aren't they?" Dr. Sproot nodded. "What got into you, Phyllis?"

"Nothing got into me," said Dr. Sproot sternly. "I'm just piling up the rubbish. Then, I'm going to burn it!" A collective shudder rippled through the Rose Maidens.

"What a travesty," said Muffy. "And shameful!"

Muffy and her fellow Rose Maiden officers were trying to choke down their disgust at what they were seeing. But they were also afraid. Dr. Sproot's transformation back to gardening gorgon was obviously nearing completion. What might that portend?

"Phyllis . . ." began Muffy.

"That's Dr. Sproot to you, Muffy. I am no longer Phyllis, so don't call me that. I'm a Ph.D. who deserves the title she's gained by dint of hard work and unstinting devotion to a plan of action no one else could even dream of accomplishing."

"We're actually here to do an intervention," said Sarah Feingold, the club's vice president.

"An *intervention?*" said Dr. Sproot. "What kind of intervention?"

"Marta told us you were changing back to your old self. We want to stop that from happening. It looks like we're too late for your gardens, but maybe not too late to help you. Keep being Phyllis—don't go back to being Dr. Sproot. We will give you some time to go inside and make yourself presentable. Or do you plan to continue going around like that in public?"

Dr. Sproot cackled.

"You want to help me! You were the first ones to turn your backs on me after last year's little trouble!"

"Little!" cried Carla Kitchener, the sergeant-at-arms. "You call that *little?*" She moved toward Dr. Sproot in a threatening sergeant-at-arms-like way. Displaying the reflexes of a cheetah, Dr. Sproot turned suddenly toward the back of the house.

"Phyllis! Phyllis!" cried Dawn. "Don't run away. Stay and talk to us. Maybe we can all sit on your deck and have some coffee."

Seconds later, the Rose Maidens were running, shrieking, for the fence gate. Dr. Sproot had her BB gun at eye level and was firing one pellet after another at them. The first one hit Dawn's purse with a whack. The second hit Carla in the thigh, which she clutched in agony.

"What are you doing, Phyllis!" they screeched. "We're your friends!"

"We're all going to die!" gurgled club president-elect Wanda Sperling between sobs, as she struggled to release the latch that would open the door in the fence.

"Damn you, Phyllis Sproot!" shouted Dawn, the bravest of the five officers, who, after the initial panic, turned to stand her ground and shake her fist. BB after BB whistled past her ear. Finally, one nicked her earlobe.

"Yeeeoow!" she howled. "We'll call the cops!!"

When another BB nicked her wrist, she turned and walked calmly toward the fence, one BB after another popping against her jeans, the coarse fabric of which was thick enough to protect her bottom from anything more than tiny stinging sensations.

"Pests!" shouted Dr. Sproot. "And don't come back, Rose Hags!"

That night, Phyllis Sproot's neighbors watched as the flames from her bonfire momentarily rose higher than the eight-foot fence separating their property. They considered calling the fire department, but settled instead for just keeping a careful watch on the fire, which soon subsided, having quickly ingested all of Dr. Sproot's geraniums and spikes, plus whatever other scattered yard detritus she could find lying around that would act as tinder. Had the neighbors been in a position to see what was going on, they would have found it unsettling. After piling all her flowers on their funeral pyre, Dr. Sproot lit the fire, then just watched impassively, the flames flickering spurts of light across her emotionless face, which only toward the end, as the flames subsided into glowing embers, tightened into a smile of grim satisfaction.

The police never came, just as Dr. Sproot figured. The Rose Maidens were, at heart, timid souls not wanting to draw attention to themselves and more than willing to accept a few little stings and some low-grade humiliation as the price they had to pay for trespassing, and still perhaps were stricken by guilt at abandoning one of their former officers in her time of peril.

Three days later, a Federal Express truck pulled up into Dr. Sproot's driveway and delivered a dozen large boxes to the front porch. An hour later, she was already unpacking scores of seedlings and planting them in ground she had already turned and fertilized. By nine p.m. Sunday, the last seedling was in.

Over the next few days, their rate of growth astonished her. Why, it would only take a few more weeks for them to reach their full maturity! This was where her legacy lay, she reflected. The coreopsis-salvia-hollyhock blend. From tried-and-true methods passed down through the generations, and her own studies, she knew that the perfect flower-garden combination melded those three lovely flowers into one geometrically pure, properly-spaced-to-the-centimeter display. How wonderful to have released herself from that ill-conceived masquerade. A malevolent sense of freedom mingled with entitlement and a violent spirituality surged through her. Just let Earlene try to come back through with her chain saw again, she thought. Why, she'd BB the chain right off its guidebar. Then, with Earlene at her mercy, she'd put a BB right smack in the middle of her forehead. Whoo-hoo!

Speaking of which, not only had Earlene served some time in the workhouse for that chain-saw incident, but Dr. Sproot has successfully sued her for damages, making quite enough out of the settlement to leave her job at Cloud's department store and devote herself full-time to gardening.

She beheld her creation with the satisfaction of a general inspecting her ranks on review, and, upon calling them to ramrod attention, found them to be straight as arrows and unblemished.

"We're back!" shouted Dr. Sproot. "And this time, we're going to kick some Livia gardening butt!"

13

Paradise Reborn

With the bountiful and cool spring rains finally giving way to warm sunshine, the Fremont backyard gardens sprang to life with a sudden spurt of enthusiasm that surprised even George and Nan. It was as if they were making up for lost time.

The columbines threw out their purple-and-white flowers. The hostas and jack-in-the pulpits that had been mixed in around the edges of the hosta beds were several inches tall and already leafing. So were the pink, white, and blue hydrangeas.

The creeping phlox was out. Good old dependable phlox. And, of course, there were the lilac bushes, which seemed to make up for a late start by being especially lustrous and fragrant this year. Their grape aroma stayed with you like the aftertaste of a good wine.

And, oh, the hibiscus! Last year's hibiscus had lent a carnival gaudiness to the backyard gardens. Big and florid and bright, they pushed out lurid, concupiscent blooms that caught your eye from wherever you were standing or sitting in the backyard.

Like everything else, the hibiscus had engineered wonderful recoveries after being thrashed about by last July's freak hailstorm. But no matter how much mulch the Fremonts piled on them, they could see there was no way these tropical natives could survive even the mildest of Livian winters. So, they dug them up and put them in big pots, which they placed under artificial light in the utility room downstairs. All of the plants had made it through the winter, and were now flourishing in their garish way, flaunting their flowers unapologetically like the extroverts they were.

"Show-offs," George called them affectionately.

The irises were still up; they were the early season's vertical white-and-lavender beacons. The bridal wreath spirea were big masses of jubilant white. That would last a few more days.

Who knew when the climbing roses would be out? Nan could see the beginnings of buds, but, good Lord, it could be July before they burst out in their full glory. Most of the later-blooming perennials were just now breaking through the ground. Still, at the rate things were going, they'd be bursting out way ahead of schedule.

As for the annuals, my goodness! The backyard was crowded with scores of them, all planted a mere three weeks ago, and going great guns.

There was alyssum, sprouting from among the rocks in one of the sunny spots, and the impatiens, shade lovers that could tolerate dappled sunlight. There was coleus, with its red-and-purple-veined leaves.

The petunias were ever-dependable and vibrant blobs of color, sometimes a bit too vivid for Nan's taste, but certainly better than velvet-textured pansies.

In the far back, halfway between the split-rail fence that bisected the backyard and the thirty-yard strip of woods that formed their border with Jeri and Tom Fletcher's property, was the little flagstone arbor, its small and rustic bench, and a surrounding border of crab apples, a few alpine currants, and paper birches.

The arbor was significant in that they had made it nine

years ago, a good two years before their full-bore backyard efforts began. The paper birches and crab apples had grown nicely, all of them well above the height of a tall basketball player by now, though the cement bonding the flagstones in the little path from the fence gate to the arbor was beginning to chip and show hairline fractures. They'd have to call Jerry, their favorite neighborhood handyman, to fix that.

Nan had decided, with George's unenthusiastic blessing, to plant more angel's trumpets. They were already pushing out their trumpet-shaped and seductively scented white flowers. Those flowers seemed to George to be blowguns aiming hallucinogenic darts at him every time he passed within fifty feet of them. Nan cared for them just as lovingly as she did all the other flowers, though George noticed that she always did so with gloves on.

There were some new neighbors back here. Nan prepared a large bed for liatris and rudbeckia in the big, sunny spot between George's rarely turned compost pile and the arbor. But, gosh, didn't the liatris need a lot of water! Heavens, you would have thought you were trying to grow them in Death Valley. George added a bed of his own favorite annual, coleus, to one of the shady areas. He planted at least twenty coleus, and lined the bed with white-flowered browallia, which Nan thought would look odd, but was actually taking on the appearance of a gardening inspiration.

The bleeding hearts arrived late, but still produced their customary profusion of heart-shaped blooms. The clematis were also late, which had George and Nan especially worried since it had been so hard to get them going in the first place. The problem was all a matter of location—keeping the roots of their three clematis in the shade while the tentacle-like vines were allowed to climb the whitewashed trellis in long-lasting sunlight. Last year, their rate of entwining themselves in vertical spirals around the interstices of the trellis was almost magic-beanstalk-like. George had once measured their growth at three inches a day.

Even though they had broken through late this year, the clematis were spreading and climbing so rapidly that George claimed he could actually see them growing.

"Why can't I see it?" wondered Nan, who peered, squinting, at the clematis for ten minutes straight in the hopes of detecting growth in motion. Surely another glass of Sagelands would improve her vision.

It was too early to try to communicate with the clematis, or any of the other perennials, for that matter. They were putting too much energy into breaking through the surface, photosynthesizing, and growing like gangbusters. Try to schmooze with them now and you got what amounted to an earful of gasps and wheezings.

"Here's a riddle for you, George," said Nan after another glass of merlot did nothing to improve her visual acuity. "How is an approaching storm like a certain climbing flower?"

George grimaced.

"You have five minutes. If you don't come up with the correct answer in the allotted time, I'll subject you to four more riddles."

George pondered the question, though not very much. Many of Nan's stupid riddles were impossible to answer because a) he was bad at solving riddles and b) the riddles themselves were awful. The exception would be those riddles and jokes she repeated over and over again, which she did fairly often. This one, though, didn't carry the stench of something stale and overused.

"Well, it has something to do with the clematis," George said.

"You need to answer the riddle, George, not just say what it's about."

"Hmmm. Okay, is it because a storm is *inclematis* weather; technically, *inclement* weather? That's the best I can do."

Nan's jaw dropped. For a moment, she just sat there gaping at him.

"Well?"

"How did you know that?"

"It just popped into my head. Maybe the fairies are helping me out. Ha-ha-ha."

"Well, as promised, you get a reprieve from plant riddles and jokes. At least for now."

Mary and Shirelle were now in front yard maintenance mode.

While smaller in total area than the backyard gardens, the front yard could be counted as every bit as magnificent as a result of the concentration of its stunning beauty into a more compact space.

The hybrid teas were in full bloom. They hadn't turned out to be nearly as snotty as Nan feared, and lent the front yard the sort of lustrous and creamy depth that only a hybrid tea can provide.

"Maybe they were hybridized with something a bit more humble," Nan joked to Shirelle.

The feathery purple catmint thrust out hundreds of violet flower-covered spikes, and blanketed the sandy-soiled slope all the way from its summit, where the hybrid teas resided, to the curb. The bordering daylilies weren't out yet; it would be another month before they burst out, and probably a few more weeks for the delphinium.

Shirelle and Mary had decided to pull back some on the ornamental grasses, which, though they would provide a nice vertical and wild-looking element to the front yard gardens, would also interrupt the massive display of color. All of this would contrast with a lushly green lawn of rye and fescue, which was already there, and which Mary and Shirelle liberally reseeded and fertilized.

"We'll have to be watering out here quite a lot, more than the backyard," Shirelle said. "It's so much sunnier, and the soil's so sandy. We can do all the flowers, no sweat, but there's plenty of lawn now, too, that'll need watering." So, they watered as a dry spell, broken only by widely spaced and gentle showers, stubbornly persisted into late June.

"Can I ask something that might seem stupid to you?" Shirelle asked Nan as they headed toward the patio after a hard day's worth of inspecting and watering, and even a bit of soil amending needed to accommodate a couple of late-addition flowers.

"Sure," said Nan, wiping her sweating brow with the back of her gloved hand and shooting a few glances at the clematis blossoms, which, though blanketing the trellis, didn't seem to be blanketing it enough. "I'm sure it's not a stupid question, Shirelle. Ask away."

"What is that a wood carving of? It looks like it got carved out of a tree trunk."

Nan chuckled. "Oh, are you sure you want to know about that?"

She stole a glance at the beady, sunken eyes of Miguel de Cervantes, the Spanish novelist whose creation *Don Quixote* was a favorite of George's. She hated tree trunk art, and, in a moment of weakness, had let George hire an acquaintance of his to carve up the lower five feet of the old, dying silver maple when they'd cut it down.

Miguel was so creepy-looking with his quill pen and what must have been intended as his manuscript in his hands. That was a lot of detail to get carved into a tree, and Lord knows it hadn't been cheap. Nan scowled at the tree sculpture, which was about eight inches shorter than she was, at least giving her a height advantage. And then he had to have it painted, for crying out loud. Whenever she was sitting on the patio it looked like he was staring directly at her.

"I hate the stupid thing," said Nan. "Hate it. I wish I had never let George do it, and let the tree guys just cut that old maple down to the ground and grind its stump!"

She made a face, then stuck out her tongue at Miguel. Shirelle snickered. She actually kind of liked the carving. And the new fairy house, too, for that matter. They lent the backyard just the right amount of weirdness. They were so *Fremont*.

"Hmmm," she said, unable to reconcile her fascination with the carving and her desire to please her mentor. "Well, it certainly is unique."

"That it is. Maybe when the fairies move in, they'll bring old Miguel to life and we can all work on our Spanish."

14

The Tree

"Who do we have here?" George said as he lifted the cork out of a fresh bottle of Sagelands.

Nan twisted in her chair to see an unfamiliar car inching its way into their driveway. It was a new American model. Standard sedan with no frills. Spic-and-span and humming along quietly. All in all, a nice, marginally attractive, unremarkable car.

A similarly unremarkable woman, middle-aged and primly dressed, emerged from the driver's side, glanced up in their direction, and made her way quickly up the pea gravel steps.

Nan was pleased to note that, despite the apparent swiftness of her movements, she barely disturbed the pea gravel.

"Welcome!" said George, whose conviviality was heightened by a just-finished glassful of merlot. "Won't you join us? And can I get you a drink? Merlot and gin are the house beverages. We also have Diet Coke, water, and skim milk."

Their visitor waved off George's offer and, without asking permission, plopped down into one of their patio chairs.

"Hey!" cried Nan. "I know you. You're the woman from the Historical Society!"

"Oh, yeah!" said George, the sudden recognition coloring his face with the flush of remembered anger and resentment.

"That I am," said Miss Price.

"Well, what brings you here for a visit? Here to play some more jokes on us, Ms. . . . Ms. . . . ?"

"Price."

"Ms. Price."

Miss Price turned and twisted several times in her chair, jerking her head this way and that to what seemed like every point of the compass.

"*Miss* works fine," she said in a distracted way. "I'm kind of old-fashioned about things like that. And, no, I'm not here to play any jokes. Excuse me, please. Do you mind if I walk around a bit?" George and Nan looked at each other and shrugged.

"Why would you want to do that, Miss Price?" Nan wondered.

"This is my old home. I grew up here when it was a farm, before the house right here next to us was built, or any of the other houses around here, for that matter." Miss Price stood up and indicated with a regal sweep of her hand the surrounding neighborhood.

"That was back in the fifties and sixties," she said. "We grew vegetables, mostly, a couple dozen acres or so, and trucked them in to St. Anthony for sale. We had three vegetable stands. We did okay. In fact, we always had bumper crops, even in times of drought and deluge. We had a henhouse, some sheep, another five acres planted in sweet corn, a little pasture for my pony. Our little barn was where the third house down is now. Our land stretched all the way over to the interstate."

Nan and George turned to gaze toward the interstate to get a sense of the scale Miss Price was talking about.

"But it wasn't enough to pay the bills after Father died and

Mother got sick. We didn't have much in the way of insurance then, see. And Mother, bless her heart, lingered and lingered. She just couldn't let go."

She stopped to look at them. They nodded, more out of politeness than anything else.

"We had some pigs and ducks, too. Back then, you know, Bluegill Pond wasn't much more than a slough. An intermittent lake when it rained a lot and when the snow melted. They have that well in it now to keep it filled up."

Nan and George nodded. They were getting tired of nodding. They were also getting tired of Miss Price's little peroration. What exactly was she getting at?

"This is all very interesting, Miss Price," Nan said. "But why didn't you tell us that before? Too busy pulling our legs, I guess." Miss Price laughed.

"Oh, I don't know why," she said, smiling and waving her hand dismissively. "But I'm telling you now. That's the important thing, isn't it?"

"I suppose it's okay for you to look around, don't you think, George?"

George nodded. Miss Price ambled off into the yard in a sprightly fashion, stopping occasionally to marvel at how the property had been transformed from a working garden to a recreational one.

"My goodness, your gardens are lovely," she said, turning to address the Fremonts.

"Thank you," George said.

"Yes," said Nan. "We've done quite a lot of work over the last seven years. In fact, all of what you're looking at now is our handiwork. When we bought it, it was all dirt and weeds and overgrown shrubs."

Miss Price smiled, turned, and walked out of easy conversation distance. Yes, she thought, they truly had worked a miraculous transformation on the property. Although Miss Price grew up a farm girl, more sensitive to the productivity of what came out of the earth, she did have an appreciation for beauty. And that was what she beheld here, beauty in one of its showiest and most stunning manifestations. But who was really responsible for all this glorious change, eh? Miss Price walked on. Besides, beauty wasn't really what she was here for.

After walking through the fence gate and toward the edge of the tree-lined arbor, she stopped to look at the strip of woods beyond the backyard. Back then, she thought, this was prairie, that is, prairie with the sod broken and turned for the planting of crops. This whole area would have been open, except for around the farmhouse and the neighboring ones on the horizon, and the lake. Now that she had the lay of the land pictured, she tried to extrapolate even farther back, all the way to the 1800s. That first house and its little store, she figured, stood on the site of the farmhouse that came later and the current house. There was some evidence of that, but nothing certain.

Now, where would they have buried that? And where would he have buried *them?* Though a historian by training and by instinct, Miss Price could always depend on her native intuition to guide her in deciding how human nature often asserted itself. That was tricky, the vicissitudes of the human psyche being what they were, but, more often than not, she was right when she played out her hunches.

Right now, she had her hunch. But what if her hunch was merely a close one? "Close" didn't win the cigar. What if it was under the property next door, or a little ways down the street? All the signs pointed to 4250, but signs could be wrong.

Miss Price kneaded her throbbing forehead. Her joy upon setting foot on her old home ground had vanished, and that rare smile she had worn on greeting the Fremonts was gone. Was the key to the lock she'd never been able to pick being handed to her, or being hidden somewhere in all these beautiful flowers surrounding her?

Her father thought he knew. With his daughter's help, he had searched and searched. He had combed through old archives and documents. What was it that he had found? Tidbits. Tantalizing tidbits, sure, but they were solid clues and nothing more. Lucius Price went to his grave a disappointed man, wringing from her a heartfelt pledge to continue the search.

An only child, Miss Price had taken over the house when her mother's physical and mental health had faltered and she had to go to a nursing home. The St. Anthony suburban boom was by now in full swing. When land prices soared, Miss Price stopped the farm operation, released the manager and other men she had been hiring to plant and harvest, and sold all but the house itself and three-quarters acre of land. Houses connected by new roads began to spring up around her. So did lots of new trees planted by the developers.

Miss Price had continued to live in the home alone to continue her father's research. She read every scrap of paper in every rolltop desk nook and stuffed in every file cabinet. She did three thorough searches of the attic and cellar. She had found nothing. Her mother had never been any help; she had considered her husband's and daughter's quest to be a fool's errand.

Miss Price felt her eyes moisten and her hands tremble. She had been forced to sell the house when her mother lingered so much longer than expected and the bills mounted. She bided her time, writing treatises and teaching snot-nosed idiot high school kids who couldn't care less about the illustrious past.

She made it her second job to bury herself in the lore and legacy of those early Livians, and even those who came before there was a Livia at all. At school, her obsession made her lax in her duties, impatient of the demands of friendship, and abrupt in her dealings with colleagues. Tiring of department politics and rich-kid Ivy League aspirations anyway, she retired from her position four years ago, and took this post with the Historical Society.

Along the way, there had been the occasional, short-lived romance. Miss Price was a not-unattractive, well-presented woman of a regal carriage and prone to sudden and silky passions. She allowed these liaisons to last as long as they didn't interfere with the overriding ambition of her life. The average length of her several affairs was two months.

Over the years, she combed through the real estate listings, hoping to see the old address up for sale again. It never was. She considered making an offer anyway, but backed off. That would have tipped them off, especially if she offered them more than the property was worth. So, she waited. And watched. And waited some more.

These days, it was tougher to stay focused on what few documents there remained to unearth and study. It was also growing too tiresome to nurture the barely flickering hope that she might someday get her old lot back. So, the all-consuming urge had softened into a peaceful dormancy. Miss Price sighed.

It was only last year, however, that, as an armchair connoisseur of zinnias and violets, she was drawn to the story of the Burdick's Best Yard Contest in the *Inquirer*. It was no shock to her to discover that the owners of her old property won the contest, but then suffered through a series of misfortunes. Neither was it any big surprise to discover that they had risen triumphant out of the ashes of destruction.

It was a harrowing yet wonderful story. But a big part of it was left out. The cause of everything that had happened was missing, and only one person in the world—Gwendolyn Price—knew what that was. But she was so tired after so many years of trying. She had wasted so many years of her life. What was the point anymore?

So, Miss Price had reconciled herself to the prospect that she would carry the secret of 4250 Payne Avenue to the grave. Not only her secret, but likely the secret for all. The other branches of the family had ended as withered twigs, then broken off. Accidents. Barrenness. Wars. Disappointments or disinterest in love. They had all taken their toll. She was all that was left.

And then, *they* came in! Inquiring about some . . . *thing* buried there!

"Whap!"

A self-inflicted slap signaled that it was time for action, not all this dwelling on the past.

Miss Price found herself staring at a massive tree thrust out a short way from the edge of the woods. A white oak, no doubt. She walked over to it. It was the same tree she remembered. Back then, it stood almost alone at the boundary between the little farmhouse area and the endless fields. Her father had told her that it was old, maybe more than a century when she was a young teenager. Planted, most likely, by their descendants to remind them of more verdant climes. A good choice in that white oaks can adapt to a number of habitats to which they aren't native.

And what was the other reason for planting the tree? As a windbreak? No, it would have been useless as a windbreak. You planted *rows* of trees for windbreaks, evergreens mainly. As a marker, perhaps? Yes, as a marker! If you buried something, and had to remember where you put it, you'd want to mark the spot with something permanent, wouldn't you? Especially since there were just a few other trees around it, or maybe no other trees at all. What better way than to plant a tree on top of it? What better way indeed! And if you had to dig it up, chances are the tree wouldn't have grown that much yet. Easy to cut down.

"I found it!" Miss Price cried. "I've found where it is! Isn't that wonderful, isn't that wonderful?"

"What's so wonderful?" Miss Price turned to find Nan and George standing next to her.

"That tree, Mr. and Mrs. Fremont! That tree! It's so wonderful, isn't it? Why, back when this area was first settled, this was one of the only trees out here on the windswept prairie. My gosh! That was before those woods over there. There were no woods. Everything had to be planted. Then, the seeds spread and the procreation of trees began. Then, the towns and cities sprang up and trees were planted everywhere. Back then, before we were there, they used trees for markers. It was how they remembered where things were buried without signaling it to strangers who might be out to rob them. That meant valuables and dead people and special pets. This was before cemeteries and safe deposit boxes, you know. It was also a way to get the tree population started. So, you see, they killed two birds with one stone."

Miss Price placed her hand on the bark of the tree and stroked it.

"This was one of the anchors of our clothesline. Mother tied it between the two trees." She looked over toward the house.

"Oh, dear, the other one's gone, I guess. Cut down or died, I suppose. You've just got those crab apples and paper birches over there now. I remember all those wet clothes flapping in the wind. Ninety feet of line it took to go from one tree to the next. I remember her saying that. 'Ninety feet of line. I don't need ninety feet of line. But where else am I going to put it?' I remember her saying that for some reason. Daddy had to screw iron hooks into each tree to hold the line. And, goodness, where's that hook? It must have broken off or something. Oh, well . . . later, there were more trees. And, now, of course, look at it. There are even woods."

Miss Price clucked her tongue, and looked up toward the spreading crown of the white oak. She stroked the bark again.

"This is a wonderful tree," she cooed. "Wonderful. But it has to go now, doesn't it? Its time has finally come."

"Wonderful?" said George. "Yes, I suppose. We've just never paid that much attention to this corner of the lot. It's shady over here and close to the woods. . . . What the *heck* happened to this tree?"

"No kidding!" said Nan. "Sheesh! Look at it!"

The white oak had apparently suffered a traumatic injury of some sort. Its leaves were crinkled and brown. In fact, dozens of them were falling, sprinkling the ground around them with detritus. The tree itself looked suddenly decayed and wilting.

"How can that be?" said Nan. "There was no sign of anything wrong. And, now all of a sudden . . ."

"I was just sitting out here yesterday in the arbor, looking at it, and it looked fine," said George. "And, yes, someone did tell us it could be at least 150 years old. Now, it's just a blot on our beautiful backyard. We're going to have to call the tree guys to cut it down. How could this happen?"

"Lightning," said Nan, walking around to the other side of the tree.

"Huh?" said George.

"Here's a huge scar running down the back of the tree. Crown to roots, it looks like. Lightning must have killed it . . . but instantly?"

"Impossible," said George. "The other problem with that theory is we haven't had a thunderstorm in weeks. And that last one was a weeny one. Hardly any thunder or lightning at all."

"Maybe its time has just come," Miss Price said. "Maybe it has to die to make way for something better. This tree must come down."

Nan and George stared at Miss Price.

"What are you talking about, Miss Price?" Nan asked.

"What I mean is that maybe this is a sign that it is time to cut down the tree and to search further."

"For what?" wondered George.

"It's making it easy for us," Miss Price said, appearing to be in the clutches of a rapture. "It's saying, 'Cut me down to learn what you should learn.'"

"Okay," said George. "I think it's time to go now. Nan and I have a lot to do, and I'm sure you've seen quite enough, Miss Price." Nan gently took hold of Miss Price's arm.

"We must talk some more," said Miss Price as Nan led her gently down the steps. "Please, let's talk some more. Don't cut that tree down until you talk to me. Don't do it! Please! Something awful may happen if you do!"

"And a good day to you, Miss Price," said Nan with a sarcastic wave as Miss Price got into her car. "No need to talk anymore, I'm sure." Nan was shaking her head as she climbed back up the steps to the patio.

"What could that weirdo have possibly meant?" she said as George met her at the top of the steps with a glass of Sagelands.

"No more than what she meant that day at the Historical Society," George said. "She's got a screw loose somewhere."

"But you must admit that some very strange things have happened around here. What is *with* this place?"

"Here, drink this," said George, handing Nan her refilled wineglass. The real magic was how a glass of Sagelands 2007 merlot could disperse even the most unsettling thoughts and premonitions. By the time Nan had drained her last drop, Miss Price had been reduced to the status of a fleeting whimsy.

"George?"

"Nan-bee?"

"Heard the one about the aphid and the Ukrainian vegetable gardener?"

15

Settling In

The combination of the new gardens and the Burdick's sign that still stood on the corner of Sumac and Payne attracted a steady stream of gawkers and visitors through June.

One Saturday morning, from eight thirty a.m. until noon, George counted twenty-three cars either slowing down to a crawl or flat-out stopping at the sign. These cars often disgorged drivers and passengers who would read the sign, then move a few steps toward the gardens for a better view. Sometimes they'd take pictures and wave to the Fremonts, if they happened to be either sitting on the front stoop or puttering around among the new flowers, which were in full, fresh, show-off mode.

The grass, for a change, was thick and green. Plus, it was now being regularly mowed by their yard-care reinforcements, sons Cullen and Ellis having meandered their way home from college several weeks earlier. Neither of them demonstrated the slightest interest in any gardening that went beyond the rudiments of operating the new self-propelled whiz of a Toro wide-swathed lawn mower. Both landed summer jobs in the ready-made-food-preparation-and-delivery field.

"I'm sick of planting flowers," said Ellis, even as George

and Nan pointed out that he had never had to plant one. "My dream is to own a chain of fast-food outlets specializing in some kind of upscale confection. I haven't decided which one yet."

George and Nan, being supportive parents, encouraged Ellis in his ambition, and made sure to patronize Yukkum's Creamery, where he worked scooping out thirty-seven flavors of hand-churned ice cream.

"I'm going to start my own fresh-veggie delivery business at Dartmouth," said Cullen. "I can make a mint, especially around exam time. What better way to serve an apprenticeship than by making pizzas at Curbside?"

Nan and George had to concede that the logic of that decision was hard to dispute. Plus, they especially liked the "veggie blaster" thin-crust pizzas Curbside made, and looked forward to the discounts Cullen could presumably now get for them.

So, the boys were left to their own devices, as long as they chipped in toward the general care of the household, which involved doing their own laundry as well as those onerous mowing duties. The real challenge lay in getting them to abandon the notion that they could blast iPod music through their headphones while mowing, special care being needed to avoid cutting off all the blooms bursting out right up to the very edges of the mow-able turf.

"The grass likes getting haircuts," George said. "Not the flowers. Leave that to us. Pay attention when you mow; don't rock out!"

Speaking of decapitating flowers, it was time for George and Nan to start deadheading the hybrid teas. It stood to reason that haggard blooms past their prime needed to be cut off for the health and well-being of the entire plant. It was to their credit that the hybrid teas understood that. Plenty of other flowers needed the same treatment. Deadheading ensured that the energy of the plant would be redirected toward shooting out fresh new blooms, besides lengthening the lifetime of the annuals. Of course, fresh blooms in their prime could also be cut for decorative purposes, such as filling indoor vases. Roses, lilacs, and daylilies were especially good for that.

"George, it's about time to move the sprinklers," Nan said. "Then, we need to switch over to the soaker hose for the hybrid teas."

George, entranced by the front yard scene laid out before him in the perfect definition of a late-morning's light, looked over from the stoop at the misting yard and listened to the hypnotic snip, snip, snipping of the two sprinklers that were currently spewing their water over the lawn. The daylilies would be blooming within the next week or so, and George and Nan couldn't wait to see how the Happy Returns and Rosy Returns varieties would perform. From what they were picking up from the other flowers, both varieties would be outgoing, exuberant in their beauty, and fully cooperative in any gardening plans George and Nan might have for them.

A male oriole emerged from the hidden lower reaches of the slope, and attached itself to the shepherd's crook pole from which the oriole feeder was suspended. For an entire minute, it jerked its head one direction, then another, then darted to the feeder jar to gorge itself on grape jelly and live mealworms. Having sated itself, it perched on top of the feeder, scanned its surroundings again, then took off in a blur of orange and black. It disappeared momentarily, then reappeared on the other side of the street, and soared into the upper reaches of one of the tall cottonwoods that grew on the near shore of Bluegill Pond.

"Earth to George-dear," came a voice from out of the watery sprinkler haze. "Looks like you're getting ready for the switchover to wine, so I thought I'd better catch you now. Detach the left sprinkler and attach to the soaker hose for the hybrid teas. They really get thirsty."

"No kiddin'," said George, who had picked up the parched-stamen vibes. "Every time you walk past them, they're letting you know. Kinda used to being the queen bees of the garden, aren't they?"

"They're not so bad," Nan said. "They like to show off, and they need constant watering to always be at their best. Don't worry; once the daylilies bloom, they'll keep them in their place."

George nodded. The daylilies. The enforcers of gardening discipline and equity. You could really count on those guys to keep everyone in line. But they weren't out yet, so they had to depend on the delphinium to keep order.

"Sprinkler on the right goes farther to the right, George, and a bit down the slope. We don't need to water the street, though."

George really hoped it would rain soon: a big, long, soaking rain, because the way they were pumping out water, it was only a matter of time before they'd be lowering the water levels of a half-dozen major rivers and a good fourteen tributaries. After turning off the water and moving the sprinkler coming out of the right spigot, he turned his attention to the left one, from which a hose already snaked toward the hybrid tea roses. He connected the male end of the hose to the female end of the black soaker, manufactured from super-porous material to drip water from a thousand points along its length on to the plants among which it had been strategically placed. That was the best way to water plants, right at dirt level and down directly to the roots at slow-motion optimum soaker speed. A horn beeped from the corner.

"Hiiiii!" George heard Nan yell in her shrill long-distance-greeting voice. He looked up to see the Winthrops walking up the slope toward them.

"So, this must be the true source of the Mississippi," said

Steve Winthrop, chuckling, as the sprinklers twirled water everywhere.

"I see the Winthrops are here," said George, coaxing his knees into slowly lifting him upright. "It must be time for alcoholic beverages." He lifted his left wrist to look at an imaginary watch. "It's two fifteen, which means it is absolutely cocktail hour in Halifax, Nova Scotia."

"Well," Nan said. "Let's all convene in the backyard for a little burgundy delight."

Juanita Winthrop rubbed her hands expectantly. "Yummy, can't wait!" she cried. "Oh, and I've been meaning to ask, where do you guys get your wine . . . that . . . that . . ."

"Sagelands 2007 vintage merlot," chirped George.

"Yes," Juanita said. "But we can't get it any more at Lubbock's. We were only able to get it there once. Three bottles. Then, next time, poof, gone."

"Of course," Nan said. "Lubbock's stopped carrying it. Distributor stopped bringing it around. We had to start going to Frey's in St. Anthony, then *they* stopped carrying it. We can't understand. We tried to get Frey's to order it for us, but they said they can't get it. Now, what kind of a liquor store is that? We have to special order it now right from the company. Costs a pretty penny, I'll tell you, but worth every cent."

"Maybe we can go in with you," Steve said. "We love that wine, and you could maybe save on shipping. I bet the McCandlesses'll go in, too, if you can wean them off their chardonnay."

"Sounds like a deal," Nan said. "Though you're welcome to continue leeching off our supply. Hey, speaking of leeches, it's the McCandlesses. They look lost. Yoo-hoo! Yoo-hoo! Over here!"

The McCandlesses had just branched off from the driveway and were starting to head up the steps toward the backyard patio. They turned to face the familiar welcoming voice.

"We really don't know where to go anymore," said Jane McCandless. "Now that you've got your front yard going like gangbusters and started hanging out on the front stoop there. So, we just put ourselves on automatic pilot and head where it feels familiar."

"That's all right," cried Nan. "We've had enough quality time with the front yard for the time being. We'll be headed over there in just a minute with the wine and some glasses. We haven't forgotten the chardonnay, since I'm guessing you're still drinking that swill."

Alex McCandless balled a fist and shook it in triumph.

"George! George!" he cried. "Get the radio. We're headed out back. Muskies playing afternoon game today?"

"Yep," shouted George, who was just passing out of sight around the north side of the house. "Home against the Deer-ticks. God-Awful pitching."

George's voice trailed off as he continued walking around the house, mumbling doubts about Kurt Gottaufal—chris-tened "God-Awful" by Muskie fans because of his perfor-mance to date. He stopped briefly at the edge of the arbor and gazed again with disbelief at the white oak, whose leaves were now all crinkled and brown. Many of them had broken loose and were drifting through the still air toward the ground.

"Amazing!" he muttered.

As the game headed into the fifth inning, the Muskies were getting walloped, 14–3. God-Awful had fully justified his moniker, giving up nine earned runs in four innings before the bullpen came in to try to stop the hemorrhaging. They were only partially successful, and the men gathered on the patio wondered aloud whether last year's run at the playoffs was just a fluke.

"Well, at least Smokestack'll hit number 500 soon," Steve said.

"Yeah," said Alex. "He's at, what, George, 487?"

"He just hit 491," said George, who spent a fair amount of
his indoor spring and summer time watching baseball games
and poring over the game's voluminous statistics. "But he'll be
coming off the bench more from now on. They're already pla-
tooning him with Goodhue. It'll be September before he notches
number 500."

The women paid a little polite attention to all this baseball
gab, which the wine had heightened into a thin patina of genuine interest, then went on to talk about the subjects they were
really interested in: their children, most of whom were now
matriculating at various colleges and universities throughout the
land; the new antique store on Robertson Drive, where Bayle's
supermarket used to be; and the sudden drop-off in activity
next door.

"You know, George . . . George!"

Encumbered with baseball-loving husbands, the women
sometimes found it difficult to break into conversations when
their spouses were locked in discussions with like-minded
friends about who held the record for most wild pitches
thrown, who played shortstop for the Marmots back in their
inaugural season—which was 1962, for those who have to be
reminded—and how many ways there are for a pitcher to
commit a balk. It got even harder when "Bad Dog" Simpson
launched into his customary off-key rendition of "Yonder
Comes That Mud Dauber Special," as was customary after the
seventh-inning stretch. When that happened, fans throughout
the St. Anthony metro—at home, in bars, or at the ballpark—
sang along, usually mimicking Bad Dog's execrable delivery.

This backyard rendition, fueled by enough alcohol to
make it particularly boisterous, constructed what amounted to
a sound barrier as impenetrable as a cinder-block wall encased
on both sides with a foot of insulation and sprayed with a film
of clear soundproofing epoxy that hasn't even been invented yet.

But Nan was well versed in methods of interrupting male-bonding rites. She stuck the forefingers of both hands into her puckered mouth, and, as both Juanita and Jane covered their ears and opened their mouths to equalize the air pressure, let loose with a shrill whistle that left Livia residents as far as six blocks away scanning the clear skies for any signs of approaching tornados.

The three men jumped out of their chairs. Miraculously, they didn't spill a drop of their wine.

"Attention! Attention!" barked Nan. "George, what's going on next door? We've been so busy with our garden preparations, and spending so much time now creating the front yard, that we haven't noticed that there are no cars in the Grunions' driveway. And when was the last time you saw or heard any sign of activity over there?"

"They're old people," said George, still stunned from the effects of Nan's aural blitzkrieg. "They don't do much. How often do we see them anyway?"

"Well, their kids and grandkids are usually over there once a month, aren't they? When was the last time you remember seeing them?"

"Come to think of it . . ."

"Maybe the old guy croaked. He wasn't faring so well, you know."

"We heard the Grunions were in some serious financial trouble," Juanita said. "Made those big improvements to the house, then couldn't foot the bill. We heard they carried three mortgages on their house."

"At their age!" cried Nan.

"Gambling debts," said Jane knowingly. "I've heard, and this is only fourth-hand, mind you, that Marva Grunion piled up hundreds of thousands of dollars in gambling debts at the Little Rabbit Casino, and that Ben loses money at the track every week."

"No!" said everyone in unison.

"Which means, what, they're getting foreclosed on?" said Nan.

"Precisely," Jane said.

"Couldn't happen to a nicer couple," said Nan. "They were the sourest, rudest, slowest, most un-neighborly people in the neighborhood."

"Isn't that the truth," said Jane. "When we went to the door last year campaigning for Pete Beinderschmidt, they just stood in front of the window staring out at us like that couple in the *American Gothic* painting. Then, unlike the couple in the *American Gothic* painting, old Grunion flipped us the bird. Can you believe it!"

The women tittered as the men almost instantly lost interest in the Grunions' problems and resumed their baseball chatter.

"I can believe it," Juanita said. "When the kids went trick-or-treating there once, they'd posted a sign on the door. It said, 'Trick-or-Treaters: Go to Hell!' Ha-ha!"

"And you know, now that I think of it, I haven't seen any lights on over there in weeks," Nan said. "Just hadn't really noticed, we've been so busy with our yardwork."

What followed was the typical detour into gardening talk that always happened around this time of year. Mostly, that involved Jane and Juanita fawning all over the Fremonts' latest efforts, which they could only hope to reproduce as poor facsimiles on a much smaller scale. George opened another bottle of Sagelands, which he duly poured out with that little twist of the wrist. Smokestack Gaines came off the bench to deliver a three-run, eighth-inning jack in a losing effort.

As the postgame analysis droned on, Nan brought out the ice water, and the men settled into their semi-silent disgust at having to digest another galling Muskies loss. The midsummer dusk began to settle over the backyard in its dawdling way. A

few lightning bugs flickered. A cardinal perched on the telephone wire, delivered a few loud chirps, then settled in at the
backyard feeder for a late-evening snack. Then, came the hems
and exchanged glances that signaled it was time to go.

"Before everyone leaves and before we lose our light, we
want to show you something," said Nan. "This is truly weird."

Never averse to seeing something truly weird before heading home for a late dinner and early bedtime, the McCandlesses and Winthrops rose slowly to follow Nan and George,
who were striding purposefully toward their white oak.

"Oh, what's this?" said Jane, stooping over to examine the
new fairy house as they approached the gate through the fence,
and, in doing so, bringing the whole procession to a standstill.

"Why, yes," said Juanita, kneeling to study the model structure. "Isn't that precious! A little bit of gardening potpourri
you just added this year?"

The men, afflicted by various knee and back ailments, and
generally unwilling to test out their muscular flexibility to indulge the odd points of interest so beguiling to the feminine
eye, remained standing, silently shifting their weight from one
leg to the other.

"Oh, ha-ha, that's our new fairy house," Nan said. "Yes, a
fairy house."

"These are quite the trend these days," said Jane. "I read an
article on them in the *Inquirer*'s variety section a month or so
ago. Where'd you get it?"

"It was a gift from Dr. Phyllis Sproot," said Nan tartly.
"You might remember her as the fomenter of some of our
troubles last year."

Jane and Juanita laughed. "You're hoping to attract fairies
this year?" Jane said.

"Yes, to keep your talking flowers company?" Juanita added.

Nan chuckled. "For the record, I do not believe in fairies,
or any similar superstitions. We are good Lutherans, and don't

subscribe to most pagan beliefs. Flowers and other plants, however, are living, sentient beings. Making contact with them is nothing more than trying to communicate with any other non-English speaking organism . . . somebody from Portugal, for instance."

Juanita and Jane smiled. They supposed someone as adept at the craft of gardening as Nan Fremont was allowed some idiosyncrasies, even as they wondered whether it might be a sign of incipient mental illness. They had both pledged to watch Nan carefully for any telltale signs of any further deterioration.

"Well, if it's from that Dr. Sproot, you'd better watch out," Juanita said. "It might be put here to collect little midget demons instead of fairies."

Now standing at the foot of the white oak, the Fremonts, McCandlesses, and Winthrops stared up into a blizzard of falling, swirling, crinkled brown leaves.

"Musta been hit by lightning," Steve said. "One strike is all it takes. You might not have even heard the storm. Man, that's a huge scar. Good thing you guys weren't standing here when *that* happened."

"Well, then, that would have been the quietest thunderstorm in recorded history," Nan said. "I always wake up to thunderstorms."

"Me too," said George. "Only thing I can think of is it happened last year. We've only had showers and gentle rains this year. Or maybe even the year before. But I would have noticed that a long time ago."

"Yes, George notices things like that," said Nan. "Well, we'll have to cut it down. Can't be letting a dead tree spoil all our gardening efforts. Look at it this way: It's going to let a little more light in on the grass back here. Though I hope it won't let too much light in on the astilbes and Virginia bluebells. I just planted those this year. They like the shade."

As they walked back toward the patio, George was worrying about the cost of cutting down a tree, dragging it down to the street, and disposing of it. Why, for a big tree like that so far from the street, it would probably cost $2,000, conservatively. And where would he come up with that kind of money? George glanced at Nan nervously. Too bad she didn't have the acumen to handle the family budget. About the only skill she had with money was spending it. And once he filled her in on the latest dire straits they were in, she would light into him like a lacewing larvae into a mealybug.

The ugly fact of the matter was that the Burdick's first-prize money was running out fast and the Fremont family finances had once again turned precarious.

George and Nan still had a few unreliable sources of income. George authored greeting card doggerel, with a special emphasis on deaths, terminal illnesses, and the loss of favorite pets. His work tended to rise and fall with the mortality rate. That would be supplemented on occasion by the need for something fresh and contemporary for the busy holiday seasons.

He was also an occasional inventor. His once-in-a-lifetime success was the Whirl-a-Gig Bubble Blower, which had a brief fling with fame in the last decade before being recalled because of a defective part that could painfully pinch a child's pinkie. No problem for George; he had already been paid $350,000 by Dum-de-Dum Novelties for the rights to the toy, which made a minor comeback once the defective part got glued on better.

That bonanza had allowed Nan and George to quit their jobs as an assistant librarian and suburban shopper editor, respectively, to concentrate on their gardening. That money was now gone.

As for Nan, she was a knitter of some note when she wasn't

coaxing her little darlings up through the earth and into displays of floral magnificence. She knitted her own handbags,
mostly in the winter as the gardens slept under a blanket of
snow. She sold them through two major department stores—
Cloud's and Deevers—which paid her a commission of 10
percent of their profit on the handbags. As Nan readily admitted, it was more a labor of love than anything else.

That $200,000 Burdick's first prize that was sustaining
them now wouldn't last forever. In fact, it was in peril of barely
lasting through another year.

The problem was the absence of anything approaching
thrift in the Fremont family. There were the shopping expedi-
tions immediately following the presentation of their check
right there in the backyard by gardening mogul Jasper Burdick
himself. Nan had considered their purchases to be restrained,
but that word had a particularly subjective meaning when employed by the Fremonts.

There had been Nan's new blouses, skirts, pants, pantsuits,
and shoes. This sudden interest in fashion baffled George, seeing as how he and Nan mostly dressed in an informal way
suited for garden toil and patio lollygagging.

Then, there was the new garage, a real necessity considering they only had a one-car tuck-under. That had meant three
cars had to be parked on the curb or on the little concrete slip
that angled out from the driveway; not the sort of setup that
was ideal when you had fabulous gardens to display. The new
garage meant they could now hide Cullen's sunset-orange Ca-
maro and Ellis's corroded Duster.

Mary now had to have transportation. George and Nan
bought her a Ford 4x4 after she successfully argued that her
newfound interest in gardening required a certain amount of
hauling capacity. Then, they had splurged and bought the
Avalon—brand new—for themselves.

Paying off their mortgage and its late-payment penalties cost another $30,000, but that almost didn't count because it saved them money in the long run.

There were college tuition payments for their eldest, Ellis, at Augustus-of-the-Prairies, which, though a nice college of a slightly-better-than-average reputation, still cost a bundle.

Now, there were Cullen's Dartmouth expenses. Another daunting financial prospect was on the horizon: Mary was headed to Stanford at the end of the summer.

Nan set Shirelle's stipend at $200 a week, which had made George cringe, but, heavens, wasn't she worth it?

Not counting forthcoming college payments, which generous scholarships had whittled down somewhat, that left them about $20,000 out of their original prize winnings.

There had been some extra money that George sometimes forgot to add to his haphazard and often inaccurate calculations. That was the $25,000 they had just earned for two garden-product endorsements. That lifted their total to $45,000, good enough for a year, George figured, especially with the mortgage paid off. Best case scenario: maybe even a year and a half.

Then what?

"One week till FremontFest," said Juanita, as the two visiting couples began their descent down the pea gravel steps toward the driveway, then the street. "Can't wait!"

"We wouldn't miss it for the world," Jane said.

"Yeah, what is this, George, the fifth year?" said Alex.

"Something like that," said George, without enthusiasm, as he and Nan waved the Winthrops and McCandlesses into the gathering twilight.

"You *have* made all the arrangements for next week, haven't you, George? I mean, everything'll be ready, right? I'd kind of lost track of it. You sent out the invitations, didn't you? Ordered all the food? Root-beer-float fixin's? Extra chairs and all?"

"Of course," said George, who was now adding the cost of the Fremonts' annual neighborhood bash to that of cutting down a dead tree and pumping the equivalent of the Caspian Sea on to their flowers and lawn over the course of the summer. "That's not the problem. The problem is, how the hell are we going to pay for it?"

"Oh, no," moaned Nan, her shoulders sinking into a deep slouch. "Not again."

"Yes, I'm afraid so, Nan-bee. We might actually start having to look for real jobs again sometime soon. . . . Oh, and Nan-bee?"

"George?"

"Next time you're by the tree, look about twenty feet up the trunk. There's a little protrusion there that kind of blends in. It's not part of the tree. It's the old, rusted clothesline hook Miss Price assumed broke off when she didn't see it lower down. She forgot to take about forty years of vertical growth into account."

16

FremontFest

There's nothing like a good root beer float to perk you right up. Or to take your mind off an approaching insolvency crisis. George and Nan were never quite sure what it was that set Peter Sunset's Brew apart from so many other plenty-tasty root beers.

There were three varieties—Honey Calm, Greased Wheels, and Yellow Jacket. George and Nan stocked up on all three, though their personal favorite was Yellow Jacket. It had that bite that left you shaking your head and extremities involuntarily after each quaffed draft. Toss in a couple of gobs of Sandytown coffee/vanilla ice cream, and the buttery-rich semi-soft chocolate chunks mixed with nuts made locally by the Wasserman sisters, and you had a confectionary delight that would send you soaring heavenward.

George and Nan made their first floats. Why stand on politeness and wait for the first guests to arrive? They then toasted each other on the successful preparations for the fifth annual FremontFest, their neighborhood fete held on whatever Saturday coincided with Nan's or George's birthday—July 1 and 7, respectively—or, barring that, on the Saturday that came between those two dates.

Guests were arriving. Here came those wonderful contrarians, Mitzi and Howard "Frip" Rodard. George and Nan chuckled watching them walk up the steps toward the patio, chattering away, contradicting each other, no doubt, at every step. They rose from their chairs to meet their first guests and lifted their frothy-topped plastic cups to them in salute.

"Root beer floats again, no doubt," said Frip. "Don't you folks ever change your routine?"

"What routine?" said Mitzi. "There's no root beer routine. The routine around this place is wine, wine, and more wine, and gin, gin, and more gin. Root beer's non-alcoholic the last I heard. And at least it gives them a chance to steer away from incipient alcoholism." George and Nan smiled as they gestured to the tapped kegs of root beer and ice-packed cartons of ice cream.

"What!" said Frip. "Are you implying that George and Nan are alcoholics? Well, that's not a very gracious way of greeting your hosts."

"I'm implying nothing of the sort," Mitzi said. "I'm saying it outright." George and Nan drained their root beer floats with moans of satisfaction. "See what I mean? Listen to that. We're consorting with people who are instant-gratification, pleasure-seeking malachites."

"Malachites?" said Frip.

"Malachites."

"Ha-ha. I don't think that's the word you intended to use. You mean sybarites."

"It is *exactly* the word I intended to use," said Mitzi, turning for support to George and Nan, who just shrugged as they headed back to the kegs for refills. "What's so funny?"

"You are," said Frip. "You're what's so funny with your malapropisms."

"My *what?*"

"Your *mal-a-prop-isms*. Usage of the wrong words, usually with comic effect."

"How dare you hold me up for ridicule! How dare you! My own husband! And in front of our dearest friends!" Here came George and Nan charging to the rescue, handing Frip and Mitzi root beer floats smoking and bubbling with foamy goodness.

"Ah, just what the doctor ordered," said Frip after a long, head-tipping draft. "Do your stuff, magic brew!"

"What magic?" said Mitzi. "No such thing as magic."

George and Nan sighed contentedly. They were accustomed to this Rodard routine, and, in the presence of the right crowd, it was quite harmless. Frip and Mitzi had been married as long as they had—twenty-three years. They had been married on exactly the same day, in the same year, in the same city, at churches two blocks apart, and had never even come close to divorcing as far as George and Nan could tell. Indeed, each one's contradictory nature seemed to complement the other's, strengthening the bonds of their union. Had one of them been cooing, agreeable, and ceaselessly pleasant and deferential, the marriage wouldn't have lasted three months.

"It's just an expression, dear," Frip said. "A manner of speaking."

Mitzi shook with contrarian ire, then knocked down a big slug of root beer.

"Ah," she went, wiping the foam off her mouth with the back of her hand. "This has got to be the best root beer float I've ever tasted."

"I would suppose," said Frip. "Considering how this is the only place you've ever tasted root beer floats, and the last time you would have tasted one was right here, almost exactly a year ago, which is to say at this same FremontFest celebration."

At this point, George and Nan were laughing out loud. Mitzi and Frip, baffled, stared at them. Then, in unison, they took long, Adam's-apple-bouncing draws from their cups. A couple of car doors slammed shut. George and Nan could see new cars parked along the Payne Avenue curb. Figures were making their way toward the patio. Some of them were approaching in a civilized manner up the pea gravel steps. Others baldly traipsed up the slope of the yard itself. Mitzi and Frip would have to find a new audience for their contrariness now. Within an hour, they would be stomping back down the steps toward home, having offended at least a dozen people and making their continued presence at FremontFest untenable.

Here were the Mikkelsons, warily ascending the steps. Their faces were etched with concerns that trickled up from some deep, unfathomable well of inexplicable woe. Deanne was carrying their ten-month-old, Sievert, Jr., as if he were a bundle of jeweled Fabergé eggs.

The Mikkelsons, modest and quiet folk even in the most engaging of circumstances, approached with solemn deliberation.

"How nice of you to come! And here's little baby Sievert. How are you, little baby?" Nan cooed and played with baby Sievert's wrinkled fingers as he did nothing but look down forlornly at the cement patio. A true Mikkelson, thought Nan; no need to worry about true parentage here.

"How's it going there, Sievert?" said George, pounding Sievert's shoulder in a show of excessive camaraderie he always thought necessary to bring the shy chap out of his shell.

"Okay, doing okay," said Sievert with a meek smile.

"Well, that's great, Sievert, just great. Gee whiz, this is you guys' first time here at FremontFest, isn't it? Well, there's pulled pork sandwiches and lots of chips, and snacks, and some fruit over there. We've also got our patented root beer floats, and you're welcome to indulge yourself. Right over there are the kegs and taps. Plastic cups, spoons, and napkins on the table, and there's the ice cream. We had to pack it hard in ice on a warm day like this. It'll stay cold and hard for a couple more hours."

Sievert nodded, and tried hard to smile. He leaned close to George.

"You don't happen to have some of that special wine of yours lying around, do you?"

George squinted and knitted his brow. "Special wine? Now what special wine is that?"

Sievert looked distressed. "Don't you remember?" he whispered. "That special wine made from coast-of-Oregon grapes? So strong that you don't really notice how strong it is? And the amazing thing, it doesn't make you sick or act like a complete drunken fool?"

George couldn't remember how long it had been since the Mikkelsons had asked for their "special wine," though no one could forget their introduction to it. He smiled at the recollection of that first encounter. The introverted Mikkelsons had become alarmingly drunk, boisterous, and, even threatening on that day he and Nan had invited them up to the patio for a glass of Sagelands. After they'd glugged down three filled-to-the-brim servings, then demanded—yes, demanded!—more, George had been forced to improvise for the sake of everyone's safety. He had switched them over to Cranberry Power-PressPlus, Cullen's power drink, and pretended it was wine so potent that it didn't even taste like ordinary wine. Advertised as having "three times the caffeine and twice the sugar of a regular Coke," it had made the Mikkelsons rambunctious, but saved them from what could have been an ugly scene that day.

"Hmmm, well, we might have some left. But you know, Sievert, this is a non-alcoholic event. We don't want you and Deanne running naked through the woods and leaving little Sievert Junior to be eaten by raccoons and opossums. Ha-ha!"

Sievert blushed and looked down at his sneakers, which

George noticed were decorated with pictures of babies in cowboy and astronaut outfits.

"You know that wine doesn't make you do that," Sievert said shyly. "Otherwise, we wouldn't dream of taking so much as a sip. What it does is make you more sociable. Don't you remember? That's such a good thing for us in a setting like this. And we'd like to get to know some of our neighbors a little better."

George stroked his chin and pretended to give the matter careful consideration.

"Well, okay, I'll see if we have some. I'll just put it in regular cups for you so the other guests don't come asking for it. Okay?"

Luckily, there was plenty of PowerPressPlus in the refrigerator. George emerged from the back door with two brimming cups.

"Oh, wonderful!" gushed Sievert. "You have some!"

"Yes, we do," George said. "But this is all you get. Be very careful about mixing this with the root beer floats. I'd say limit yourself to one each. Otherwise, I'm not responsible for your behavior. And, if people ask, tell them we gave you some grape juice."

"Yes, George, will do, though that would be telling a lie, and we're not very good at that. In fact we're awful at telling lies."

"A couple sips of that and you'll get much better. Trust me."

Sievert marched off with the sloshing cups to Deanne, who was talking very quietly to Nan as Nan played with an unresponsive baby Sievert.

"Our special beverage," said Sievert, holding up the cup for Deanne to inspect as if it were a gemstone of incalculable value. "You know, the one we liked so much when we used to come here. . . . Sorry to interrupt, Nan."

"Oh, no," said Nan, whose exchanges with Deanne were falling well short of anything you'd worry about interrupting. "Not at all, Sievert."

Deanne's eyes lit up.

"Oh, yes," she cried. "Oh, heavens yes. Would you please hold Sievert, Jr., for me for a minute, Nan, while I take a couple of sips of your wonderful drink?"

What wonderful drink? thought Nan. She took the baby, who looked at her with a witless, uncomprehending expression, and turned toward George, who winked and smiled at her. It took ten seconds for the Mikkelsons to glug down their drinks and sigh almost orgasmically. They looked at George pleadingly.

"Oh, okay, but just one more. Our supplies aren't limitless, you know." The refills went down in five seconds flat.

"Watch it now," George warned.

"Don't worry about us," Deanne said. "We can hold our booze, can't we, dear?"

"Of course, sweetest. Well, newly fortified as we are, shall we go and mingle?"

"Let's go mingle till the cows come home," said Deanne, yanking baby Sievert back from Nan. Then, off they went, accosting everyone they came across with a surfeit of bonhomie that had the neighbors talking about them for months.

"Cranberry PowerPressPlus," said George to Nan once the Mikkelsons had gotten out of earshot. "Turns the meek into the mighty. They needed a booster shot to be able to function here."

Nan laughed.

"Ah, yes," she said. "Our special Mikkelson drink. Maybe they ought to start giving that to baby Sievert."

The yard was starting to fill up with guests. Here were the Winthrops and the McCandlesses, and such lesser, though still considerable, friends as the Davieses, the MacDonalds, the Brittles, and the LeBlancs. Some folks new to the neighborhood—the Spinozas, Jon Warneke and Geoff Beadle, the Rodriguezes, and the Singhs—were here, mostly oohing and aahing over the gardens. Jon and Geoff were showing signs of being future, though smaller-scale, competitors if they expanded what they had growing in their yard. What was there now was already beautiful—especially the resurgent peonies, which had been left in a rather dire state by the previous homeowners—though they used too much Dusty Miller in their borders. And here were the Fletchers, plowing straight through the thick underbrush tangling up the strip of woods. There was the usual complement of neighbors, barely known acquaintances from the world of education, politics, religion, and the Livia Athletic Association, and the occasional complete stranger drawn by the now-well-known glories of the Fremont gardens. In fact, the Burdick's sign was still up, with one week left before it was to be taken down. Probably as a result of that, the number of strangers in attendance seemed to be greater this year than last.

"Some people must figure this is a public tour-the-Fremont-garden day," Nan said to George. "I've picked out at least a dozen people here I've never seen before. Mostly in the front yard."

"Me too," said George. "And after what happened last year, I can't help but get a little nervous about it."

Nan snorted.

"Oh, don't sweat it, George. There's no contest this year. No reason for gardening saboteurs to be casing the grounds like they did last year. I just hope they don't all discover the root beer floats, or we're gonna run out pretty quick."

Nan sauntered off to greet the Boozers, who would stay for one quick root beer float only, then leave. She was soon back at George's shoulder, surveying the crowded yard to make sure the children weren't trampling through the flowers, and to spot newcomers who might merit a personalized greeting.

"There's that idiot, Merle Pressman, on the school board," said Nan, pointing her float toward a clot of visitors who were standing in one of the hosta beds. "Amazing how people feel that they can just stand right on top of somebody's hosta as if it were some kind of rubber plant that can spring right back up after you grind it down good. Of course that's where the stupid politicians are, since that's where they can do the most damage. I see Richard Mellon and Lucia Everett. Aren't they running for their House and Senate seats again?"

George shrugged.

"And there's our idiot mayor. What's he doing here? Slumming among the middle-class voters, I suppose. George, please go tell them to kindly get off the hosta. Or we won't vote for them in November. Ha-ha!"

George, fortified by another root beer float, strode off to take on Livia's political machine while Nan took in the rest of the scene.

There must have been a hundred and fifty people in the backyard now. The crowd took up almost every square inch of lawn, which was probably why some were standing in the hosta beds. Here came another procession of visitors up the steps toward Nan. The Goodriches offered their customary cold, formal greetings. The Buckwalds were perfunctory. The Hoosenfoots and Mitchells were absolutely gaga over how the gardens looked this year. All moved on quickly to the feeding stations. Then came Marta Poppendauber, all by herself and smiling in the subtle, unself-conscious way that suggested she was basking in the glories of the Fremont gardens. Nan and Marta hugged unabashedly.

"Marta!" gushed Nan. "How nice of you to come!"

"I must say I felt like I'd be intruding," Marta said. "Especially after what happened last year. I was even reluctant to bring over Dr. Sproot last month to do her penance. But she *insisted* on having a chaperone. Ha! Imagine that."

"If we thought you'd be an intruder we wouldn't have sent you an invitation," said Nan, ignoring the reference to Dr. Sproot. "You're always welcome here, Marta, and so is . . . oh, my . . . what is your husband's name?"

Marta smiled. "It's Hamilton, but I call him Ham," she said, giggling. "He really is not very interested in gardening and things like that. Just kind of leaves it to me to tell him what to do and where to put things. It must be nice to have a husband like George, who takes such an active interest in gardening."

"Ah, yes," said Nan. She cast her gaze over to where George was lost in conversation with the politicians, who were still standing on the hosta. "Uh, George needs to be told things sometimes, too, but he's picked up a lot over the last seven years. You know, Marta, Ham doesn't have to talk about gardening when he comes over. George is always looking for someone to talk Muskie baseball with."

"Ham is a huge fan," Marta said. "I'll tell him that. My gosh, Nan, your front yard is divine. I went over to look at it before coming back here. I know most of what's there, but not everything. Will you tell me?"

"Of course I will," Nan said. "Anything you want to know. There are no gardening secrets here."

"Maybe not," Marta said admiringly. "But there is gardening talent that puts all the rest of us to shame . . . Uh, Nan?"

"Yes?"

"This might be nothing. It might be nothing at all. In fact, I almost hesitate to bring it up."

"Yes?"

"Dr. Sproot might be back on the warpath again."

Nan gulped down a cold lump of ice cream that almost choked her, suffered through a brief bout of constricted esophagus pain, then forced out a brittle, defiant laugh.

"What!"

"She's changed back into her old self."

"What's that to us? She can gag on all her spite and hatred for all we care."

"She seems to be out to extract some vengeance. We're all on the lookout. No one feels safe."

"After almost going to prison last year for all the havoc she wreaked?"

"Yes. She's really out of her mind."

"Marta," Nan said. "You can tell that woman, if you are still on speaking terms with her, that if she comes over and threatens our property the way she did last year, I will call the police and press charges. Or, if I'm mad enough, take George's baseball bat and smash her little pea brain in."

Nan stared at Marta, then spooned another glob of ice cream into her mouth and worked it slowly around.

Marta smiled, remembering how brave the Fremonts were last year, George with his baseball bat and Nan with her butcher knife triumphing during that terrible storm.

"I don't talk to her anymore, Nan," she said with a sigh. "I've given up on rehabilitating Dr. Sproot. I really hope she doesn't mean us harm."

"That stupid old harpy!" cried Nan. "Let her just show her face around here. And she can have her dumb old fairy house back, for that matter. It's just sitting over there taking up space and acting as an unfortunate conversation piece for our friends, who somehow equate my horticultural communications with a belief in fairies. Oh, Marta, you wouldn't believe it!"

"Yes, I would," Marta said. "But I think you should keep the fairy house, Nan. You never know when it might come in handy. Well, I'll leave you to your other guests." With that, she slipped away into the crowd.

Nan shivered with a strange, murderous impulse. Tremors of unfamiliar rage shot out through her extremities, threatening her balance and forcing her to clasp her root beer float with both hands. How dare that awful woman so much as think about coming back here to do harm! She began to entertain images of Dr. Sproot entwined and constricted to death by the clematis, or torn to shreds by serrated saws whose teeth were made of hybrid tea rose thorns.

"Nan-bee." George was back, having failed to move the politicians off the hosta bed. "Look who's here." It was Shirelle and a guest. Shirelle beamed. Her guest stretched her curled, sneering lips into a faint smile.

"Mrs. Fremont, I'd like you to meet Dr. Brockheimer, from the horticultural department at the university. She's my academic adviser and one of my teachers."

Nan thrust out a shaking hand, as her float sloshed wildly in the other.

"Excuse my shakes," she said as George and Shirelle jerked back, startled, from the spilling root beer froth. "I've just had a bit of a shock. Nothing serious."

"I've heard so much about you, Nan," said Dr. Brockheimer, grasping her proffered hand firmly. "And your husband, too. May I call you Nan? Shirelle speaks so highly of you."

George smiled. "Shirelle's our secret weapon," he said. "She really helped us design our front yard this year."

"That's true," said Nan, becalmed to the point of displaying only an occasional facial tic. "Without Shirelle, we would have been hopeless trying to figure out a new design."

"I really doubt that," Shirelle said, blushing. "Anyone who's taken the right classes can design a garden. It takes true genius to make what's on paper come alive the way you have. The front yard is unbelievable. I never dreamed even you guys could make it so good. And the backyard? Same old story. Amazing!"

"Shirelle's being too humble," Nan said. "She and our daughter, Mary, actually did most of the front yard work."

Dr. Brockheimer smiled in a way Nan interpreted as patronizing.

"They do look good," she said. "There are some things I would change, but, yes, not bad for neighborhood gardeners."

Nan blinked rapidly, and swallowed back a rude remark before it could get past her gullet.

"We have sandwiches, chips, and root beer floats over there, Dr. Brockheimer, if you'd care to avail yourself." Dr. Brockheimer stared at Nan with eyes intent on shrinking her down to plant size.

"No, thank you, Nan; I ate a big lunch. I'm here because Shirelle tells me you talk to plants. I'd like to learn more about it."

Nan shook her head, then smiled.

"This is not something easily explained to strangers," she said. "I consider it a form of cross-cultural communication."

Dr. Brockheimer tilted her head in a quizzically condescending manner.

"But you can probably imagine why it's so hard to talk about. To our friends, yes. But even they're skeptical and think we're off our rockers. We aren't off our rockers, are we, George?"

"Certainly not," said George, having tossed back the remnants of his float with a massive and, Nan thought, rather indelicate, sigh. "But two floats from now, I certainly might be."

"Well," Dr. Brockheimer said. "It sounds like I'd better sample one of these concoctions. Then, Nan, can we talk some more about your efforts at 'cross-cultural communication'?"

Nan didn't like this Dr. Brockheimer's attitude or tone, but figured maybe after a root beer float worked its magic on her they could have a nice little off-the-record chat about what it was like to be a plant whisperer.

By this time, most of the visitors had settled into their little clots of conversation, broken only by return visits to the food and beverage tables. Here and there, and where the crowds would allow, individuals or groups of two or three walked the entire backyard inspecting the Fremonts' new summer bounty.

A respectable number had even wandered around the north

and south ends of the house to the front yard. A few strangers attracted by the Burdick's sign had parked their cars right there in the intersection and walked up the slope to take photos. Nan and George briefly worried that the front yard gardens might be in danger from all these visitors, either through malevolence or unintended carelessness. Cullen, Ellis, and a few of their friends were out front, but a fat lot of good they would do. At least, Mary, Shirelle, and that Dr. Brockheimer were out there. Weren't they?

Just to be sure, and with her third root beer float in hand, Nan marched off to the front yard. Clearing the northwest corner of the house, she was amazed to see thirty to forty people—most of them, strangers—scattered around, and, Lord help her, a couple of children rolling around in the Walker's Low catmint. Nan was just about to spring into action when a figure emerged as a running blur out of her peripheral vision. This figure, now identifiable as a slender and youngish woman, carefully picked its way through the catmint and its bordering lilies, grabbed the offending children firmly, and guided them out of the flower beds.

"Whose offspring are these?" barked Dr. Brockheimer. A young couple who had been taking pictures of the hybrid teas responded to the summons, and stood before her at meek attention.

"These brats have been ruining these beautiful flowers," said Dr. Brockheimer. "Either keep them under control or *get out!*"

The couple quickly herded their children back down the slope toward their parked car as Dr. Brockheimer watched them go, her chest heaving and her face reddened with ire.

Nan walked over to Dr. Brockheimer, who, with her arms akimbo, still seemed poised for confrontation. Gazing down across the expanse of the catmint, Nan couldn't see much to worry about. A few plants beaten down; they'd probably bounce back within a day. No real damage done.

"Well, Dr. Brockheimer."

Dr. Brockheimer wheeled around to face this new threat.

"Thanks for helping us police our gardens. I'm sure the children meant no harm. I doubt there'll be any lasting damage."

Dr. Brockheimer huffed.

"Nan, you must take more care of your gardens if you want them to truly flourish. For a gathering such as this, I would have posted a guard."

"That's usually not necessary for FremontFest."

"With children running around it is. And Shirelle has told me all about what happened last year. I'd have thought you'd have learned a lesson as a result."

"I'm sorry, Dr. Brockheimer, but we can't afford a guard. Neither would we want one. FremontFest is open to all comers. We haven't really had any problems before. Besides, this an open and welcoming event, not a museum tour. Still, we do appreciate you protecting our flower beds. We might even need you to help out with the hosta in the backyard. Those politicians just don't seem to think about where they're standing. And George . . ."

"He's pretty worthless, isn't he?"

"I beg your pardon!"

"He's not much help with the gardening, is he? I can tell. Just another feckless male. I know. I'm married to one. Soon to be my ex, I might add. Ha-ha!" Nan felt her jaw tighten and the hand clutching the root beer float cup quiver.

"How dare you talk about my husband in that manner!" she said. "George has been my true partner for seven years of hard gardening toil, much more actual work than you've ever done, Miss-Fancy-Pants PhD. I've dealt with people like you before, Dr. Brockheimer, and one thing I've discovered is that you don't know what the hell you're talking about and you've got corncobs shoved so far up your rear ends that no implement or machine yet invented could extract them. If you don't like George, or me, or what we're doing here, then either shut up about it, or take your little snot-nosed gardening high fa-lutin' rectitude and get off my . . . *our* . . . property!"

Nan chugged the dregs of her root beer float and threw the plastic cup at Dr. Brockheimer's feet.

"If you don't mind, Dr. Brockheimer, could you please pick that up and throw it away for us. The garbage is in the back, right next to the patio."

Both women were shaking as Nan stalked off in a rage, ig-noring first a greeting from the Hausers, and then the Mar-tensens. Another root beer float was exactly what she needed now, she thought, her head held high as triumph and regret mingled together and vied for dominance of her emotions. As she plopped a couple of scoops of the softening ice cream into a new cup, a disquieting thought suddenly intruded itself upon the welcome return of her equanimity.

Oh, my gosh, she thought, I hope this doesn't damage Shi-relle's academic standing!

At the nearby float stand, George scooped himself out three giant hunks of coffee/vanilla ice cream, then kept lather-ing them with root beer until the foam started cascading over the side of his cup. He opted for the Honey Calm flavor in the hopes it would ease his troubled mind. What was especially troubling George lately were the latest tuition hike notices from both Cullen's and Ellis's expensive colleges. Then, there were the credit card bills, the prohibitive cost of insurance, and the small matter of keeping the family fed and clothed.

At least the mortgage was paid, but that was just the first mortgage. George had taken out a second, and thank God Nan was such a trusting soul and had signed off on it. Borrowing money was such a mystery to her. It was almost as if she saw it as a gift to be paid back at leisure, or maybe even not at all. And, as always, God would provide.

Banish these thoughts! And these thoughts were now being

rather easily banished by the root beer float, which had a Novocain-like power of deadening his every trouble.

George moved through the gate, then toward the fence so he could keep a discrete watch on the angel's trumpets. It simply would not do to have children wandering around back there, testing out the pretty flowers and seeds and ending up wandering around in psychotropic trances. Of course, he had forgotten to post DO NOT TOUCH signs on the plants.

What's this? he thought, his attention drawn to activity far beyond the angel's trumpets and at the very edge of the woods. Who the heck was that checking out the white oak? Why, what an unpleasant surprise; it was Miss Price. What was it with that tree that seemed to attract her like iron filings to a magnet?

As George approached the tree, he noticed, shocked, that it had taken a dramatic turn for the worse. Not a single crinkled leaf remained on its branches, which now had appeared to wither and blacken. Even the trunk itself appeared charred black, as if it had just been cooked in a forest fire.

"My God!" cried George, his eyes lifted to behold the spectacle of a tree dying before his eyes. "Look at it! Ah, and look who's here. It's Miss Price. You decided to come back for some more tree gazing. Why is that, Miss Price?"

"The tree must come down," Miss Price said portentously.

"Huh?"

"I said you must have this tree cut down."

"Well, yes, Miss Price, but you've already told us that. What business is it of yours?"

"The welfare of all trees in this community is my business, Mr. Fremont. As I've told you, I grew up right here, almost exactly on this spot. I knew this tree quite well. I do not want to see it in misery. Put it out of its misery, Mr. Fremont."

"Uh, sure, sure. I'm sure Nan and I plan to do that. It's just that I didn't realize its condition was so far advanced. I mean, wow, look at it!"

"So far advanced that in the matter of weeks, maybe even days, it will fall. When it falls, it will probably wreck either this nice privacy fence, or worse, as far as your wife is concerned, her beautiful flower beds over there, to say nothing of your little shed."

George gulped. He certainly didn't want that. But the cost! Where would they get the money to do that?

"You're thinking about the cost, aren't you, Mr. Fremont?"

George stared at Miss Price, astonished.

"How'd you know that? Well, I'm not sure my thoughts are a matter for you to concern yourself with, Miss Price."

"I know how you can get that tree cut down, get the stump taken care of, and the site cleaned up, and have it carted away, dirt cheap," Miss Price said. "I know someone who's just getting into the business and needs to get the word out. What better place to start but here?"

George frowned. He was torn between the appealing prospect of paying virtually nothing to clear up a backyard problem and the nagging suspicion that there was a huge catch lurking somewhere in Miss Price's offer.

"Well, we'd want references," he said. "We don't want just anybody learning on the job with a big tree like this. We'd want somebody who's experienced, with references."

"Sure," Miss Price said. "And those kinds of people cost a lot. But I must repeat myself. You must cut down this tree, Mr. Fremont. Don't let the poor thing suffer."

George bit his lip. He fought back an urge to throttle Miss Price.

"Can I help you to your car, Miss Price? Or you're certainly welcome to stay for a root beer float. But you'd better hurry because the ice cream's melting fast."

"Thank you, Mr. Fremont, but I'm quite capable of making it back to my car on my own. . . . And, please, don't do anything to that tree without contacting me first."

Before George could warn her never to return, Miss Price bounded across the north end of the yard and down the hill with an agility that would have put him to shame.

"George!" It was Nan, whose voice he could barely hear above the cacophony of the root beer–enlivened crowd. "George! What are you doing over there?"

George sauntered back toward the patio as Nan threaded her way toward him through the knots of guests. She regarded him with concern.

"Why are you being so antisocial, George? And could that have possibly been Miss Price you were talking to?"

"It was. She wants us to cut the tree down."

"What is the deal with her anyway? I want to cut the tree down, too. But what's her big stake in all this is what I want to know."

George shrugged.

"She knows the tree from when she lived here," he said. "She wants it put out of its misery. She said she knows someone who'll cut down the tree, remove the stump, the whole kit and caboodle for dirt cheap."

"That so?" said Nan. "Well, I'm getting sick and tired of all these busybodies trying to tell us what to do with our property. Why, you should have seen that awful Dr. Brockheimer! George, she—"

George made bug eyes at Nan and gestured with a quick nod to a point over her right shoulder. She turned to see Shirelle and Dr. Brockheimer standing rigidly behind her. Shirelle looked pale and sheepish. Dr. Brockheimer had obviously been crying; she daubed at her eyes and puffy cheeks with a wadded-up Kleenex.

"Time for us to go, Nan and George," Shirelle said. "Dr.

Brockheimer wanted to say something to you first. Dr. Brockheimer?"

After some more daubing and a few false starts at making what was obviously a little mini-speech she had been preparing, Dr. Brockheimer finally spoke.

"Nan, I can't tell you how sorry I am to have treated you and your gardens so cavalierly." Here, Dr. Brockheimer paused to sniffle and apply the Kleenex to her misting eyes. "I was very rude to you and to your husband." She turned to face George with a meek, solicitous smile. George smiled forgivingly while having no idea what she was talking about. "In absentia, of course. I hope you both will forgive me. No one's ever stood up to me like that, Nan . . . and . . . I admire that. I truly do. I'd like to consider you my friend."

Dr. Brockheimer stretched out her arms toward Nan. Nan, moved to tears herself, opened her arms to enfold the smaller woman.

Watching this act of repentance and forgiveness unfold, Shirelle found herself transformed. An hour ago, she was a shame-faced apologist for Dr. Brockheimer, seeking to ingratiate her with the Fremonts, yet mortified by her arrogant and boorish behavior. Watching the two women embrace, she became a cherubic angel of hope. The sun appeared to have gotten the message. It chose that very moment to peek out of the clouds and cast a beam directly onto her rosy, freckled cheeks. She started to cry.

George was taken aback by this showy manifestation of womanly emotions. His first impulse was to about-face and hightail it back to the root beer stand, or maybe it was time for another pulled pork sandwich. But George was bigger than his base prejudices. In a burst of genuinely inspired yet artificial goodwill he, too, thrust out his arms for a hug from Dr. Brockheimer. By then, though, Dr. Brockheimer and Nan had unclasped, and Dr. Brockheimer had turned to head down the steps to the driveway. That left George embracing millions of air molecules that had come within the range of his grasp. He sheepishly drew his arms back in and dropped them limply to his sides. Dr. Brockheimer wheeled around to face Nan.

"I'm sorry we had our differences today," she said, her voice having lost its tremor and regained its bite. "Maybe I came on a little strong. I do that sometimes. I still want to talk to you about plant whispering. I also want to see you in action. This could be big for me *and* for you! When can we do it?"

Nan recoiled briefly, then perched her fingertips delicately on her sternum, a sign of what everyone there except Dr. Brockheimer knew to be of temporary confusion and speech-lessness.

"Well," said Dr. Brockheimer, "you'll hear from me later, probably through Shirelle."

Dr. Brockheimer wheeled to her right with military preci-sion, then loped clumsily down the steps, kicking up pea gravel with every footfall. Shirelle, still misty-eyed, hugged George and Nan.

"Thanks for the wonderful time, Mr. and Mrs. Fremont," she said. "The food was great and the floats were dreamy. See you next week."

She had to quick-step it to catch up with Dr. Brock-heimer, who was already striding purposefully down the drive-way and toward the street.

"Well, that woman is quite the enigma," Nan said. "One minute she's coming on like a freight train and the next she's a blubbering puddle of helplessness. Then, back again. How am I supposed to teach her how to *talk* to flowers? Or why should I even try?"

"We don't need to worry about that now," said George, extending his arms to embrace her. "Our guests are leaving. Let's be good hosts and bid them all adieu with smiles on our faces and laughter in our hearts. . . . By the way, what hap-

pened to you right before Shirelle and Dr. Brockheimer arrived? You had the shakes pretty bad there for a minute."

"That? Oh, it was Marta talking about Dr. Sproot. She said
to watch out because she's on the warpath again. I guess I got
a little mad."

George chuckled. "Hmmm," he said. "Maybe Shirelle ought
to go get her shotgun after all."

Clinging to each other like two strands of a clematis vine,
George and Nan toured the yard and made as many stops as it
took to say thanks and good-bye to their guests, even waving
to the Jerlicks, who, as usual, dropped their napkins and empty
cups right on the lawn, as unabashedly as if they had just deposited them in the garbage can.

After another fifteen minutes, all that remained were the
McCandlesses and the Winthrops—who stood looking at
George, awaiting his annual post-party announcement. George
cleared his throat and broke free of Nan's embrace—a little too
abruptly, she thought.

"Your attention, please," he said. "It appears all the riffraff
have blown away. Time to break out the hard stuff."

As the sun dipped into its summer evening zone, and the
Muskies wrapped up their 12–3 laugher over the Starlings, the
Winthrops and McCandlesses got up listlessly from their chairs
and began to move toward the steps. The McCandlesses were
already halfway to the driveway, with Steve Winthrop right behind them, when the slowpoke of the group, Juanita, finally
rose from her wine-induced semi-stupor, turned toward the
back, and stopped abruptly, staring at the woods.

"What is it?" wondered Nan, gaping. Her third glass of merlot had apparently unhinged her jaw.

George laughed. "Better close up," he said. "The male wrens
are looking for homes again, and your mouth is just about the
right size."

"My gosh! Your tree! It's like the Leaning Tower of Pisa."

All heads turned toward the back, and there was the dying white oak, only not nearly as vertical as it was when George stood next to it with Miss Price. Now, it had tipped precipitously toward the west, part of its root system unearthed, and leaning at a sixty-degree angle like an arboreal sword of Damocles over the shed and Nan's new bed of brilliantly flowering liatris and rudbeckia. Only the bracing effect of its massive branches had apparently prevented it from toppling over, and several of them had cracked and broken.

"Good Lord!" cried George. "When did *that* happen?"

"Must have been in the past, what, fifteen minutes?" said Nan, whose mouth opening had returned to its customary aperture. "We must have been too besotted by wine to notice."

"Well, good grief," said Steve, who was now standing there, along with the Winthrops, staring at the tree. "You'd think it would have creaked or groaned. The lowest branches look like they snapped. Wouldn't we have heard that?"

"I heard a groan," said Jane. "I thought it was just Alex. Tee-hee-hee."

"Why do weird things always happen in your yard?" Jane said. "You poor Fremonts. Haven't you had enough drama in your backyard to last you a lifetime?"

"Apparently not," said Nan with a sigh. The couples exchanged another round of hugs and farewells, then the Winthrops and McCandlesses picked their way down the steps, careful even after three glasses of wine not to disturb Nan's pea gravel.

"George, on to the Internet, chop-chop. There's gotta be a twenty-four-hour-a-day, seven-day-a-week tree service around here somewhere. That tree has to come down, and I mean right now."

George disappeared into the house and emerged, down-cast, a few minutes later. He pretended to watch the unsteady clot of Winthrops and McCandlesses passing out of view in the course of their stop-and-start transit down Payne toward their homes.

"George?"

"Okay, Nan-bee, but there's one little problem. It's called family finances. We can't afford it. We're either going to have to get Jerry over here with his chain saw, or we're going to have to take Miss Price up on her offer."

Nan shuddered, then picked the last wine bottle up off the table, put it to her lips, and glugged down the remaining contents.

"I'm not sure I trust Jerry with a project that big. Besides, he'd charge us, of course, and I'm guessing more than we'd want to pay. Looks like Miss P.'s our only option."

"There's only one problem with that," said George. Nan hiccupped, then sighed.

"Spill it," she said. She hiccupped again. "Not literally, of course. Ha-ha."

"I just checked; both she *and* the Historical Society are un-listed. I have no idea how to reach her. She'll have to come back."

"Given her recent track record," said Nan between more hiccups, "that shouldn't be a problem."

17

Tree Disposal Done Cheap

Two hours later, George and Nan were on their second cup of lite coffee, having determined that the amount of alcohol they'd consumed over the course of a late afternoon would be of little help in solving their stricken-tree crisis.

George was on the brink of volunteering to rent a chain saw and take on the dangerous job himself when a sputtering and clanking noise announced the appearance of a European-looking car in the driveway.

"Wow!" cried Nan. "Look at that! It's a Rolls-Royce!"

George rolled his eyes.

"That is a Citroën, Nan-bee. An *old* Citroën. A Citroën is about as far removed from a Rolls-Royce as a sixties Volkswagen bug."

For all her breadth of knowledge on many subjects, Nan could be ill-informed when it came to certain important matters. For instance, though she often joined with George in rooting for the Muskies, especially if they were winning, she would have been at a loss to identify Smokestack Gaines with his position—first base—on the team. Finances, bills, and investments baffled her. Money, she figured, was for spending, especially as it related to gardening, furnishings, and numerous items of clothing and footwear that would reside in her closet unworn. She let George take care of all that accounting stuff.

When it came to cars, she was similarly at a loss. If aliens from the Andromeda galaxy were to drop down for a visit, join the Fremonts for a civilized glass of wine, then ask to be shown what a Corvette Stingray looked like, she might well point to the Oldsmobile Cutlass parked in the driveway across the street.

"A what?"

"A Citroën. French-made. Jeez, I haven't seen one of those since . . ."

"And who do we know that drives a . . . whaddayacallit?"

"A Citroën."

"Sit-ron."

"No one. This is somebody new. And it could sure be someone unusual 'cause, I mean, how many people around here drive Citroëns?"

Two men they didn't know emerged from the car. They smiled up at George and Nan as they trod gingerly on the pea gravel, which made a good first impression on Nan.

"Greetings," said the first man, lifting his hand up in the pantomime of a windshield-wiper-pattern wave.

"Hello," said Nan.

"What can we do for you?" said George, who had already lost any enthusiasm he might have had for entertaining Citroën-driving visitors.

Both men were now standing on the patio, studiously looking around and upward.

"Most of these look okay," said one to the other.

"Mmm-hmm," said the other. "These trees are in good shape."

"That's nice to know," Nan said. "Who are you and what do you want?"

One of the men cleared his throat and looked at the other.

"We are the Scroggit brothers," said the taller, less stupid-looking of the two. "Artis and Nimwell Scroggit. That's us. I'm Artis, he's Nimwell." Nimwell nodded, then did some more looking around at the treetops.

"Nice, healthy-looking trees you've got here," he said.

"Yes," said Artis. "We are in the tree care business. Chickamauga Tree Service. Maybe you've heard of us?"

"No," said Nan curtly. "We haven't."

"Hmmm," said George. "You named your tree service after a Civil War battle? One that was fought twelve hundred miles or so away?"

Artis and Nimwell looked at each other, stunned.

"You are familiar with the battles of the great Civil War, sir?" said Artis, his voice trembling with the historical profundity of it all.

"George is a Civil War buff," Nan said. "In fact, we visited Chickamauga, Chattanooga, Murfreesboro, Shiloh, Forts Donelson and Henry. What else, dear?"

"The great cyclorama of the Battle of Atlanta."

"The great cyclorama of the Battle of Atlanta . . . uh . . ."

"Nashville, Franklin, and Perryville."

"Nashville, Franklin, and Perryville. We visited all those places right after we were married. It was what some people might call a honeymoon."

"My goodness!" Nimwell cried. "Would you be interested in buying some artifacts we just happen—"

Artis clamped his hand over Nimwell's mouth.

"That's a secret, brother," he said. "Don't you remember, those are not for sale?" He winked at the Fremonts.

"Precious family heirlooms. We've been instructed not to sell them, or even tell anyone about them. Now, can we behave?"

Nimwell nodded. Artis removed his hand from Nimwell's mouth, and turned to the Fremonts. "Gee whiz, I can't take him anywhere."

"I can sympathize," Nan said.

"Well, it's just a matter of one side of the family wanting to sell these particular heirlooms and one side not. It's unfortunate that we have to air out these family differences in front of prospective customers. Isn't it, Nim, you dimwit?"

"Yes," said the fawning Nimwell. "Yes. I don't know what got into me. Please accept my most fulsome apologies."

George and Nan frowned at this display of familial scorn. Mostly, they were wondering when this brother comedy routine was going to get around to telling them about their connection to Miss Price.

"Well," said Artis. "Now it's time to get down to brass tacks. Our business, as you can undoubtedly tell from our company name, is trees."

"Trees," Nimwell said. "Yessir."

"So, you just decided to stop by and tell us our trees look fine?" Nan wondered.

"Why, no," Artis said as Nimwell shook his head violently. "There is a tree we noticed back near your woods that isn't fine at all. In fact, oh, my goodness, look at it—it's almost fallen down!"

"Yes, it has, hasn't it?" said George. "We figure that to have happened in the past one half hour or so, though we were entertaining at the time and didn't notice it."

"That tree must come down," said Artis.

"That tree must come down," repeated Nimwell.

"Jeez, that sounds familiar," said George, chuckling. Artis frowned.

"It does? How so?"

"Never mind," said Nan, wanting to enjoy the rest of the performance. "Continue, please."

"We can get rid of it for you, lock, stock, and barrel, for a price no one can beat. Say, $450?"

"That's a good price," said Nimwell. "No one can beat that."

"And that includes what?" asked Nan.

"That includes cutting the tree down, removing the stump, filling up the hole, and carting everything away. We, or our field crew I should say, could be here tomorrow."

"We usually like to see references for that kind of work," George said. "And there's another matter. It's a good price, but we're running a little short right now." He cast a guilty and forlorn look at Nan. "We can't afford it."

Nan pitched back in her chair. She had expected as much, but George's bald announcement right here, in front of strangers, had come as a shock nonetheless.

"Payment plan?" offered Nimwell.

"Nope," said George.

"No problem," Artis said. "We'll do it for free. Then we'd just ask you to tell your neighbors about us. Consider it a promotional special."

"Free?" asked Nan.

"Free?" asked George.

"Just tell your friends and neighbors to think of our name—Scroggit Brothers Tree Care—when they've having trouble with their trees," said Nimwell.

"I thought your name was Chickamauga Tree Service," said Nan.

"Of course, of course it is," Artis said. "My brother just can't seem to break free from our old name. We just changed it."

"Yesterday," said Nimwell, nodding violently. "And since the vireos have departed, weather-wise, as to like our own dearest departed ones."

"Yesterday, yes. We haven't even changed our business cards or repainted our trucks yet."

"We haven't even changed what is our thankfully, and in the fullness of the recipe for hot apple fruity cobbler we have prepared," Nimwell burbled. Artis pretended to chuckle as he jabbed Nimwell violently three times in the shoulder, then twirled his forefinger next to his head to indicate there were a few lose connections in his brother's brain wiring.

"That's right, we did move, didn't we, Nim? Thanks for reminding me. Now, where was I? Oh, yes, we will take care of your tree removal for free. No charge at all. Is it a deal?"

"What do we have to lose?" George said.

"They could cut it down the wrong way and wreck the shed and my new flower beds," Nan said. "The branches are already pushing down on the shed's roof, and have probably dented it beyond repair."

"Good point," said George. "That's a concern."

"If that happens, we pay for the damages," countered Artis quickly. "Guaranteed. Now how about it. Should we have a crew here tomorrow?"

"Sure," said Nan. George nodded.

"Okay," said Artis, as he and Nimwell turned to walk back down the steps. "Tomorrow around eight a.m. You don't have to be here. In fact, we encourage you to either sleep in or go out and have some breakfast or something while we're working. The noise really bothers some people. Thanks, folks."

"Hang on," said George. "Don't you want us to sign a contract?"

"Heck, no," Artis said. "You look like trustworthy folks. We'll take your word for it."

"Okay, but remember, it's free," Nan said. "No charge."

"That's our deal," said Artis. "And a deal's a deal. Just spread the word about us throughout your neighborhood."

The Scroggit brothers scampered down to the driveway

and drove off in the clanking Citroën, which was burning oil and blowing out a greasy blue cloud of smoke from its exhaust pipe. George and Nan shook their heads.

"Well, those are the world's worst liars," Nan said. George laughed.

"The connection with that Miss Price is so patently obvious," he said. "I mean, what kind of rubes do they take us for?"

"But what's the deal with the tree?" Nan wondered. "Why do they want so badly to cut it down? It's obviously important for them to get to the tree quickly, as in before we hired someone else to cut it down."

"Maybe it's the body of that dead guy," said George with a snort. "Remember the one she talked to us about when we went into the Historical Society?"

"It's got to be something bigger than that. Why would they want the moldering bones of an old dead guy?"

"My brain's starting to hurt trying to figure this all out," said George. "I think a glass of Sagelands might help. You?"

"Of course."

It was almost dark, and they'd lighted the citronella candles ringing the patio to keep the emboldened mosquito population at bay. Here and there, a stray lightning bug shone in a brief point of luminescence. The earlier heat had subsided into a heavy, humid warmth that lacked the day's occasional breezy freshness and would soon send them into the house for their nighttime dose of central air. Nan moved in her chair, and the motion-sensor light turned on.

"George, dear, please go turn that off," she said. "I don't want to sit here in the spotlight."

A cardinal broke the evening stillness with its simple, loud, and solitary chirp.

First to the feeder was the brown, red-smudged female. She cracked open one sunflower seed, then another, for her last evening snack. Then came the male, magnificent in its red plumage and dignified wariness, always turning to watch for predators as it extracted the sunflower seeds from their shells.

From out of the woods came a noisy, deranged chatter that had no discernible pattern, always loud, but varying, the most anarchic animal sound they had heard except for the death throes of some rodent that they figured had been punctured by a great horned owl's talons at around one a.m. a couple of weeks earlier.

"What is that?" George wondered. "What kind of bird was THAT?"

"Mockingbird," Nan said. "I believe that is a mockingbird."

She reached behind her chair to a small wooden crate sheltered under the overhanging eave of the house, and plucked out the *Peterson Field Guide to Eastern Birds,* which had been carelessly left outside after they I.D.'d a brown-headed cowbird strutting across the lawn.

Nan flipped through the pages as George watched the dark, abrupt form of a bat zigzag across the sky. He heard the buzz and noticed the slight movement on the hair of the forearm currently in use as his drink appendage, then swatted the mosquito with his left hand. He flicked it off, and raised his glass to the bat, which was still swerving drunkenly on its evening flight as it chowed down on one mosquito after another.

Back came the racket from the woods, a solitary noise now that the cardinal had quieted. "That is one partying bird who's going to have a hell of a headache tomorrow," George said. Nan cackled as she read from the bird book.

"It *is* a mockingbird," she said. "I'm almost sure of it. Listen: 'Song, a varied, prolonged succession of notes and phrases, each repeated a half-dozen times or more before changing. Often heard at night.' I think we've made an identification."

"I don't," George said. "I think we've identified a new species. *Birdicus crazicus*."

Nan smiled and shut the bird book, then gazed longingly at the empty wren house under the eaves. "Wouldn't it be wonderful if the wrens came back for their second brood? Wouldn't that be just grand? What a treasure our wrens are for us."

George almost jumped out of his chair, knocking over his wineglass, which survived intact, but emptying what was left of its contents onto the glass tabletop.

"Clumsy oaf!" cried Nan, laughing. "And, hey, you just ended your streak of never having spilled a drop of wine!"

"Clumsy oaf nothing!" said George. "Brilliant detective, more likely. I've got the answer!"

"The answer," repeated Nan woozily. "To what? The meaning of life?"

"To our mystery, you silly Nan-bee. You said *treasure,* as in wrens. What about treasure as in the real McCoy? It's the lost treasure of Livia they're looking for. It's here!"

Nan sat up straight in her chair.

"George, please get me a tall glass of ice water. And one for you, too, while you're at it. This is the sort of thing that's going to require a little more attention on my part than I can give it at this point."

George moved briskly, and, before Nan knew it—before it seemed that she had so much as blinked—the glass of ice water was sitting on the tabletop in front of her.

"Glug it down," he said. They both knocked down the cold drafts in a few seconds.

"Now, where were you?" Nan asked.

"The treasure of Livia. It exists. It's right here in our backyard. It's under the white oak. Think of what Jim's been telling us all along. Think about our first meeting with Miss Price and all her ridiculous stories. She was just trying to trip us up.

And all this interest in a tree, especially now that it's dying and needs to be cut down. And for what?"

"Because Miss Price remembers it as a child, from growing up on the farm," Nan said. "Maybe she wants to preserve some of it, just like you did with that stupid carving of Miguel when we had to cut down the silver maple."

"I doubt that. I seriously doubt that. We . . . I . . . might do weird things like that with a tree, but other, more normal people don't."

"Oh, and she's normal?"

"No, definitely not. But someone either knows or suspects that the lost treasure of Livia is buried under that tree. I mean, why the sudden appearance of those guys pretending to be some tree care company who probably don't know the difference between a dogwood and a Douglas fir?"

"They want the tree for Miss Price?"

"No, they don't. Think about it, Nan-bee. What the heck would you want with eighty feet of dead white oak?"

"Make a bunch of barrels, maybe. Ha-ha! Okay, so maybe she wanted to put it out of its misery. Isn't that what she told you? That's not so far-fetched. Or, maybe she's stocking up on firewood for the winter."

"Unlikely. Most unlikely. She doesn't want the tree. Doesn't give a hoot about it. She wants what's buried *underneath* the tree."

"That kinda brings us back to the dead guy. Maybe that dead guy is some kind of big deal."

"She doesn't want what's left of some old French guy. That story was probably just a load of bs. That tree's a marker for something a lot more recent. Remember her saying that? So, the question now is what to do."

"Well, we have to cut the tree down. That's a no-brainer. I won't have a dead tree crashing down on our flowers and tool-shed, to say nothing of ruining the aesthetics of the backyard."

"Okay, but when the dimwit brothers show up, we're going to be sitting on this patio watching them."

"And explain to me, dear, why we have to do that?"

"Isn't it obvious? We have to make sure they don't go carting off something that's rightfully ours as the owners of this property. Something that could solve all our money problems once and for all."

18

The Scammer's Guide to Tree Removal

The tree service crew showed up the next morning as advertised, at eight a.m. Only the name of the service wasn't "Chickamauga." The painted cursive script on the side of the truck parked on the Payne Avenue curb read CURLY'S TREE CARE.

"I guess there must have been another name change," said Nan as she and George sat on the patio with their first steaming cups of coffee.

A parade of heavy vehicles pulled up alongside the curb. A dump truck. A pickup towing a flatbed trailer on which stood a chained-down swinger with a clam grip to move the logs. A crane. Another truck hauling a chipper. Nan and George watched as the tree pruners walked by with their chain saws and climbing gear.

"How long?" Nan asked.

"Oh, about three and a half hours," said the one crew member who was barking orders to the others, and whom they figured was probably the foreman. "That's cuttin' 'er down, taking out the stump, removing everything. Takin' that stump out's gonna take time and effort. Kinda weird, diggin' out that stump, then haulin' it somewheres. Don't worry about us, though; we're addin' it to the bill. Our crane's gonna have to come up the lawn some. Gosh, they've got some beautiful gardens here. Awesome!"

"*Our* gardens," Nan said.

"Yours?" said the man. "Well, whatever. We should be able to move the crane up through here without squishing your flowers. It'll put a few dents in your lawn, though. We'll put particleboard down under the track to limit the impact. Say, you folks are okay where you are, but just don't get no closer. For safety reasons, you understand."

At about eight thirty the Scroggit brothers showed up in their Citroën, parked on the other side of the street, and stayed in the car, shielded by tinted windows. Forty-five minutes later, the major branches of the white oak were down, getting churned up into sawdust by Curly's chipper. But the Scroggit brothers remained in their car.

"What are they doing in there?" wondered Nan.

"What they're doing in there is probably slurping coffee, eating doughnuts, and waiting for the tree to come down and the stump to come out," George said. "After that, they'll come out, inspect the hole, and do some more digging. I'm betting they've got three things in the trunk of that car: picks, shovels, and metal detectors. Then, they'll whisk off whatever goodies they find down there."

"So, our job is to prevent them digging."

"That would be correct."

Nan noticed the foreman-like guy talking on his cell phone, probably to the Scroggits.

"One thing it would probably be good to do is make sure we're squared away with that guy in charge," she said. "Make sure he knows what's what."

The whir of saws was continuous now. The man they

identified as the guy in charge was walking back from the tree and toward the curb, probably to consult with the hidden Scroggit brothers, George and Nan figured.

"Uh, sir, sir," said Nan, motioning him over. The man smiled and walked over to the patio. "How about a nice, strong, rich cup of coffee? And a Danish pastry to go along with it? Cream-filled."

The man—much younger than they would have expected, and a pleasant-looking chap, with tangled, curly hair sticking out from under his hard hat—hesitated for a moment, then grinned.

"Well, I shouldn't stop for more than a couple minutes," he said. "But I won't say no. Thanks a bunch!" Nan jumped up and darted through the backdoor.

"I didn't have time but for a half-cup on the drive over," the man told George. "And it's that cheap swill they serve at Pecker's."

"Pecker's?" wondered George, chuckling. The man blushed and chuckled right back as he looked down, embarrassed, at his scratched-up Red Wing work boots.

"It's what we call Packer's," he said. "We stop off there to gas up and get our industrial-strength sludge before the first job of the day. Pardon the language."

George smiled.

"You must be Curly," said Nan, who returned with a cup of steaming special Fremont blend and a warmed-up pastry.

"That's right," said the man. "How'd you guess? Ha-ha!"

As Curly slurped his coffee and munched on his pastry with evident relish, George and Nan pumped him for information, which he readily furnished. They'd been hired by the Scroggits to cut down this tree. He figured the Scroggits were the property owners, and that perhaps the Fremonts were renting from them or something. No, he said, the Scroggits had no connection with the company whatsoever. Curly seemed confused, then irritated, when George and Nan told him that the Scroggits had made out that they owned the tree company, and that they had no connection with the property whatsoever.

"We're the property owners here, Curly," said Nan. "And we can prove it. Those guys sitting in that Rolls-Royce over there think there's something in the ground under the tree that they want. The problem, of course, is that it's our property."

George rolled his eyes. Curly squinted and furrowed his brow, wondering where the heck around here a Rolls-Royce was parked. He said they were to haul the stump over to a location specified by the Scroggits, and that when they'd finished the job, and the site was cleared, the Scroggits were planning to do some digging at the site.

"I figured, 'Hey, that's fine with me, you can dig all you want on your own property.' What that meant was we wouldn't fill in the cavity the way we ordinarily do when removing the stump."

"They're not going to do any digging at all," George said. "It's *our* property, and those guys are a couple of crooks trying to mess with us. If worse comes to worst, we'll call the police and see what they have to say about it. And if you see anything in that hole after you pull out the stump, you need to tell us about it first."

Curly looked puzzled; this clearly was not the kind of complicated situation he was anticipating when he climbed into his truck for the first job of the morning.

"What I'm saying is the guys who hired you are working for us. They're sort of middlemen, I guess you'd say. But they're secretly trying to rip us off."

Curly placed his empty mug on the tabletop and slapped his hands together to brush off the pastry crumbs. Frowning, he took off his hard hat, scratched his head, then tried to smooth out his uncooperative curls before putting his hat back on.

"Look, folks," he said. "I don't know what's going on here.

All I know is I'm getting paid for a job—actually, already got paid, and I got paid a big bonus to clear my schedule and do it first thing this morning. Everything's on the up-and-up as far as I'm concerned. We're a licensed and bonded service, and we're fully aware of what all the regs are for cutting down and disposing of trees. My intentions are to do what I got paid to do and clear out." He paused, looking suddenly panic-stricken.

"Say," he said. "Seein' as how you folks are the actual property owners, you're okay with cuttin' down the tree, right? And removin' the stump? I don't want to get into no trouble here."

Nan and George chuckled.

"Sure," Nan said. "We're fine with that. The tree and stump have to go. Look, go ahead and do the job you're getting paid to do. Once you leave, we'll take care of those two guys. You don't have to get involved one way or another. How's that sound?"

"That sounds just fine," said Curly. "I just don't want to get involved in no property dispute here. But I will say this, I've got a bone to pick with those two if they're going around pretending to be running my company. This is *my* outfit, and ain't nobody gonna say otherwise. I worked fourteen years in the tree business before bein' able to start my own company five years ago. So, just who do *they* think they are? Well, hey, I gotta get back to the crew. Looks like they're getting' close to wrappin' up the job. Thanks for the coffee and pastry. That really hit the spot. And sorry for any misunderstanding. Once we finish the job, we'll be on our way. Say, you don't mind if we leave the stump hole and don't fill it in? That's what those guys told us to do . . . or told us *not* to do."

"We're fine with that," Nan said. "And, hey, thank your guys for taking such care to protect my flower beds. From what I can see, they're still intact."

"When we take a tree down, nothing gets damaged in the

process," Curly said proudly. "That's our guarantee. One other thing. Those guys in the car want us to deliver the stump to somebody. That okay with you? I mean, they're paying for it."

George and Nan looked at each other and frowned.

"I guess that's okay," Nan said.

"Stump's already partially out of the ground due to the tree tipping over," Curly said. "Usually, we grind it into sawdust. Unusual, to say the least, that somebody actually wants to keep the stump. We might end up using the swinger over there to yank 'er out and haul her 'er down to the street."

"I wonder what the heck it is they want with the stump," Nan said.

Curly tipped the bill of his hard hat, then strode off toward the tree and his four-man crew, who were busy cutting up chunks of the downed tree. A half hour later, the swinger with its clam grip had hauled everything down to the dump truck, and the tree service crew silently departed. Before they had reached the truck, Curly knocked on the passenger-side window of the Citroën, which silently rolled down.

"Wonder what he's telling those two?" George wondered.

"He could just be telling them that the job's done," said Nan. "Then again, he could be chewing them out for misrepresenting themselves. He strikes me as that kind of guy."

Once all the tree service vehicles departed, the Scroggit brothers got out of the Citroën and popped open its trunk, which groaned loudly enough to be heard all the way to St. Anthony.

"Needs a little WD-40 there," George said.

The Scroggits strode brazenly up the slope, one carrying a shovel and pick, and the other a metal detector slung over his shoulder. Panting from their loads as they got to the part of the yard level with the patio, they stopped for a breather, and turned to look at George and Nan.

"My, aren't we up early," said Nimwell.

"Yeah," said Artis. "We figured you'd either still be sleeping, or maybe off to work by now."

"You figured wrong," said George. "We work at home."

"I see," said Artis. "Well, I hope our service so far has been satisfactory." He made a big show of examining the scene from afar. "Everything appears to have been cleaned up nicely."

"Just a little more cleanup work to do," said Nimwell.

"Yes, no need for you to sit around here and wait for us. You're welcome to go about your daily business. Go out and get some breakfast. Get some shopping done. Don't feel like you have to stick around on account of us."

"Yes, this is just routine stuff. And you're not being charged, so there's no payment to make and nothing to sign once we're done."

"We figure an hour, maybe an hour and a half at most."

"I think we'll just sit here and watch you guys," Nan said.

"Oh," said Nimwell.

"Well," said Artis. "If that's the case, you should probably go inside, just for safety's sake. We all have to follow safety rules, you know. You don't want to be breaking the law by staying outside here and risking injury, or possibly even death, do you?"

"We'll take our chances," George said.

"What's that thing you're carrying?" asked Nan, knowing full well what it was.

"This? Oh, this is a shovel," said Nimwell. "And this is a pick."

Nan snorted.

"I know what those are. What's that thing slung over your brother's shoulder?"

"Oh, *this!*" Artis said. "Of course. Not too many people know what this is. This is . . . uh . . . this is a detector of tree gases. Sometimes, trees that have died give off gases. Poisonous, noxious gases." Nimwell wrinkled his nose in mock disgust.

"This . . . uh . . . gas detector will let us know if your tree is passing . . . uh . . . releasing gas. If that's the case, we'll have to have our gas people come by and get rid of it; the gas, that is, since we already got rid of your tree. But I'm guessing there won't be any gas. This seems to have been a clean, gas-free job, wouldn't you say, Nim?"

Nimwell nodded.

"Still, we have to be diligent about these things and take the proper precautions. You wouldn't want poison tree gas infiltrating your walls and killing you in your sleep, would you?"

Nan and George stared at them silently. Nimwell fidgeted.

"Well," said Artis, making a show of looking at his wristwatch. "Gosh, will you look at the time! We've got another appointment in an hour and a half. Let's get a move on, Nim, so we can get our customers' work done for them."

"Hold on!" barked George as the two men and their clanking loads began to trudge toward the stump hole. "Because you're not going anywhere but back to your stupid French car."

The Scroggits turned and sighed.

"What's the problem?" asked Artis. "Is it noise? Well, I promise you we'll work quietly. If you go inside, close the blinds, and draw all the curtains, you won't hear anything at all."

"I think you two had better head back to your car and make tracks out of here," said an icy-toned Nan. "And then, never come back. We know what your game is. You don't have anything to do with the running of that tree company. You just want our tree, or whatever's under it, eh?" The Scroggit brothers smiled meekly.

"You can go peacefully or choose from two options," George said. "Option one, we call the cops on you as trespassers and God knows what else for pretending to be door-to-door tree removal guys. Two, I will go get my genuine Smokestack Gaines baseball bat and Nan here will get her butcher knife and you can take your chances with your pick and shovel."

"You have a genuine Smokestack Gaines bat?" cried Nimwell. "We'll buy it from you. Just name your—" Artis slapped his hand over Nimwell's mouth.

"Don't call the cops, please," Artis said. "We'll leave. We didn't mean any harm. Really, we didn't. Yes, you're right; this is a metal detector. We just heard there might be a few knick-knacks under the tree. We would have immediately notified you and offered to share."

"And now you'll go back to report to Miss Price," Nan said. "Correct?"

"Miss who?" Artis said. "Price? Never heard of her."

"Yes," said Nimwell. "This was her idea, not ours. We're going. We're going right now. Please don't report us to the police. There are outstanding warrants on us in three states. Theft of federal property. Sales of stolen property . . . And, and . . . let's go sending the covered wagons via the villages and Hopi Indians of America. Et cetera and off to the woods we go, fait accompli."

Artis smacked Nimwell on the head with a *thwack*.

"The jokester of the family," he said sternly. "Ha-ha! Ha-ha! Aren't you, Nim? Well, we'll be taking our leave now."

The Scroggit brothers trundled down the slope, quickly threw their tools and metal detector in the trunk of the Citroën, and drove off, the Citroën's tailpipe spewing greasy blue smoke.

Nan turned to George and patted his hand. "Now that we've gotten our caffeine boost for the morning, let's get over there to see what all this fuss was about."

Removal of the trunk had left a sizable hole, about four feet deep and ten feet across.

"Dang!" said George. "It looks like a bomb crater. I sure don't see anything that looks like a treasure chest." Nan was looking up to where the oak's canopy used to cover the sky.

"My gosh, will you look at all that open space up there. This is going to be a sunny spot now. Great place for another bed, mostly annuals with a couple of perennials thrown in for good measure."

She looked around gravely at the other beds. "We'll have to see how it affects the other new beds," she said. "Those over there used to be in complete shade. Now, maybe it's going to be more of a dappled effect. They can probably stand that, but they might not do as well."

"Mmmm-hmmm," went George.

"Okay, buddy," said Nan with a clap. "Now that we've seen our bomb crater, shall we do the morning rounds? Uh, George, where are you going?"

"Pick and shovel," said George, who was already twirling the combination lock on the toolshed door. "Maybe you forgot, but I didn't—there could be a treasure under there somewhere."

"Oh, I suppose," said a resigned Nan, who hated any-thing—even the prospect of finding a buried treasure—that interfered with the morning rounds of their gardens. "Just don't hit a utility line with that pick, please, George. Good Lord, look at the roof of that poor shed! Talk about dented!"

An hour and what seemed like a gallon of perspiration later, George and Nan had deepened the tree stump crater by two feet and widened its diameter by another four with noth-ing to show for it.

"Okay, so where's the dang treasure?" said a panting and exhausted George. "I'm not going to dig all the way to China, for crying out loud."

"You can stop right now, dear," said Nan, who had refilled her coffee mug twice, and was enjoying watching George dig for the last half hour while she just stood there wondering if this would be a good place to plant her volunteer spirea. "You know, this might be the perfect place to give Dusty Miller another chance."

"Whoa!" said George.

"Yes," said Nan, her eyes glazing over with a trance-like vision of floral creativity in action. "The one flower that's failed to respond to my gardener's Midas touch. Here's the spot where it will flourish. . . . George? George!" George wasn't paying any attention. He'd gone back to digging.

"George, stop it! Stop it right now! There's no treasure under there. Never was. It's just a myth created for people who don't have anything better to do in their lives but chase phantom riches. George! Stop!"

"Okay," said George, panting and covered with a glistening sheen of perspiration. "But only because I can't dig anymore. There's something under here, Nan-bee, and what's under here belongs to *us*. Not to the con artists who are trying to rip us off."

Nan stamped her foot in irritation.

"George! You're just as bad as Miss Price and those Scroggit brothers. Can't you see, the real treasure is going to be what we'll plant here and nurture to a Fremont-worthy magnificence? Add that to the existing backyard and our wonderful new front yard, and we will have created our own heaven on earth. What more do we need? Things aren't *that* bad. We'll get by somehow."

"Money," said George, his voice croaking from despair and exertion. "Money's what we need. I haven't told you this, Nan-bee, but I might as well tell you now; I can no longer make the payments on our second mortgage."

"The what?"

"I took out a second mortgage on the house. You signed it. Don't you remember?"

"Vaguely. But you said we could make those payments. And now you're saying we can't? I sort of leave these things to you, you know. I guess I should know better by now, shouldn't I?"

"Don't act so shocked!" George snapped. "It's not as if you've ever taken an interest in family finances. In fact, the only interest you've ever really taken in bills is how many you can accumulate with all your purchases. So, don't you be looking at me like that, as if it's all my fault."

Nan bit her lip, and tried hard to fight back the tears. In all their years of marriage, George had never talked to her like that. And now, once again, they were teetering on the brink of financial ruin. When would it ever end?

On the surface, Nan seldom admitted to any fault, oversight, or weakness. Deep inside, though, where all living things derive their nourishment and capacity to grow, she knew better. She realized she'd been the big spendthrift in the family, burning up money like it would never end, and treating bills like junk mail when she paid any attention to them at all. She knew George was right, and that she was making the poor slob her scapegoat.

Nan staunched the flow of moisture to her eyes and took a deep breath. She spread her feet to straddle the good earth that had been so kind to them, and braced her hands firmly against her hips.

"Okay, mister; there's only one thing left to do."

Shamed by his outburst, George looked up at Nan and beheld a startling vision. Nan appeared to him as the avenging Gaia-earth-deity woman brought to life, even though she wasn't really dressed for the part. Instinctively, he threw down his shovel and bowed his head in a gesture of abject surrender.

"George!" said Nan. "You doof! What are you doing? We need to call that idiot Jim and get him over here pronto with his . . . his . . ."

"Metal detector."

"Yeah, metal detector. If it shows there's something down there, we'll dig all the way down to the molten core of the earth if we have to. Now, go make yourself useful, will you? And put on another pot of coffee. Full strength."

"There's nothing here," said Jim, his headphones clamped to his ears as he slowly and methodically waved his wand over every square inch of the stump crater. "I know I said I thought I heard something around here last year, but there's not even the tiniest beep now. Must have been the low-battery warning." It was mid-afternoon, and Nan and George had switched from coffee to merlot mode. They stood a few feet from the edge of the stump hole and gazed at Jim vacantly.

"Impossible," George said. "All the signs point to it. Okay, granted, some of those signs are pretty weird."

"Keep sweeping, Jim," Nan said. "George's right; there's gotta be something down there."

Jim shrugged.

"Sorry, the TreasureTrove XB 255 never lies. If it's not beeping, that means there's nothing there. Battery's fully charged this time, too."

"Maybe it's deeper," said Nan.

"Could be," Jim said. "If it's down too deep, this won't pick it up. Say, more than seven or eight feet. Do you think it's that deep?"

"Who knows?" said George after a healthy sip of Sagelands. "It could be a mile down, but this has got to be the spot."

"And what if it doesn't have any metal on it? What if it's a plain wooden chest with leather hinges wrapped up in burlap or something like that?"

"Hmmmm," said Nan. "We hadn't really thought about that."

"Also, why does this have to be the spot?"

"Jim," said Nan. "Come sit down and join us for a glass of merlot . . . or hang on, you're a gin-and-tonic guy, aren't you? You look like you need one. And we've got a lot to tell you."

19

Giving the Gift of Stump

"What do you mean, it's not there?"

Artis and Nimwell wrung their hands and looked down at the floor.

"We mean it's not there, Miss Price," Artis said.

"And you actually went to the hole itself and looked in, and used your treasure detectors, and dug around some?"

"Well," said Nimwell. "Not exactly, Miss Price."

"What do you mean by 'not exactly'?"

Artis tried steal a glance at his brother, and gave his head a tiny shake, which would have been barely perceptible to most people.

"I saw that!" screeched Miss Price. "I saw that. It's a signal, isn't it? It means 'Don't tell Miss Price the truth,' doesn't it? Huh?" Locking her jaw into a steely smirk, Miss Price gazed first at Artis, then at Nimwell, in a manner that reminded them of the judge passing down the sentence—a $15,000 fine and one year in jail, suspended—for trespassing on public property and theft of same. That was at Vicksburg.

"What happened?"

Artis and Nimwell looked at each other.

"No more signals, now," Miss Price barked. "As you've seen I can detect your little secret signals. Fess up!"

"Well, we really didn't get to look at the hole," said Nimwell, who was usually the brother delegated to making incriminating confessions when they were warranted, mainly because hardly anyone could understand what he was saying once his nerves got the better of him. "Is often accountable and found out through discovery, and, I must say, of a threatening nature, is the sot which out is through and back again."

"What in the name of God are you saying? You didn't get to the hole? Well, I thought that was the whole idea behind the tree-removal ruse!"

"The Fremonts found us out," Artis said. "They figured out what was up and threatened to call the cops if we didn't leave. We can't afford any more law enforcement encounters, Miss Price. We've got two convictions on our records, and there are outstanding warrants on us in three . . ."

"Four."

"Four states."

Miss Price sighed.

"Incompetents *and* criminals, that's who I've hired," she moaned. "What in the name of God have I done to deserve this?"

"We brought you back the stump," said Artis.

"Just as you asked," said Nimwell. "And it's got quite a large and tangled root system."

Miss Price instantly broke free of her mournful reverie and leaned forward toward the Scroggit brothers, causing them instinctively to flinch and draw back ever so slightly.

"That's good," she said. "That's very good. And you had it delivered to the Historical Society parking lot, as I directed you to do?" Both nodded their heads furiously.

"Okay. Let's head over there right this instant. I'm driving.

We want to get over there pronto in case somebody might get it into his head to steal it."

Artis chuckled. Nimwell smiled.

"Miss Price," Artis said. "Who in the world would want to steal a tree stump?"

"Who's to say the Fremonts won't come charging in to reclaim their lost property, eh?" said Miss Price. "Now, get up. We're going to head straight over there. Give me your keys. I'm driving your car, and you're not getting a dime of mileage out of me. You got your pick and shovel to dig the dirt out of those roots?"

Artis shook his head.

"Those are back at our store, Miss Price."

"Okay, never mind. We'll dig it out with our bare hands if we have to."

Billowing their oil cloud behind them, they made the four miles to the Historical Society in three minutes flat, running two red lights and three stop signs, barely avoiding a collision with a Jim's Sanitation Service truck, and miraculously avoiding detection by the Livia police. When they skidded to a stop in the Historical Society parking lot, Artis and Nimwell were quivering mounds of jelly, marveling that they had survived, and wondering, based on the fog-thick cloud trailing them, how long it would take for their engine to blow up.

"All ashore that's going ashore!" shouted Miss Price. She jumped out of the car and found herself face-to-face with the turned-over stump, which sprouted a Medusa head of roots, turf, and clotted dirt covering at least seventy square feet.

"Let's get digging!" she shouted. "Hey, what's wrong with you two? Or should that be a big surprise to me?" As Miss Price ran her hands over the roots and began to claw away at the dirt trapped within their tangled network, Artis and Nimwell hung back, standing silently by the car.

"What is it you want us to do?" wondered Artis meekly.

"Well, what do you think I want you to do?" barked Miss Price. "Drop your trousers and do your business right here in the parking lot? My God, you would've thought I was asking you to jump through hoops of fire. We're going to dig through this mess to find out if our treasure's tangled up in it. If it's not down in the hole somewhere, it just could be all knotted up deep in these roots. There's no telling what could be locked up in here. Now, go to the back of the building, and look for a couple of big plastic buckets under the eaves. You should find some trowels and gardening forks in them. I use them in my groundskeeping. We can claw through all this stuff in no time."

One hour later, Miss Price and the Scroggit brothers were soaked in sweat. A big pile of dirt and gravel lay at their feet. Coiling out from the trunk was a fibrous network of roots and rootlets still caked with thick hunks of damp subsoil. It looked impenetrable.

"Okay," said Artis. "It's obvious that there's nothing here. And I personally have my doubts that even a tangled mess this thick can hold up a heavy chest full of treasure."

"Who said it was a heavy chest?" said Miss Price. "Haven't you ever heard the saying that good things come in small packages? This could be a small chest. Who knows, it might not even be a chest at all."

Artis and Nimwell looked at Miss Price, puzzled.

"Uh, how could you fit a lot of coins, or gold, or whatever it is into a little chest?" wondered Artis.

"You'll see," said Miss Price. She kept stabbing at the clot of dirt and roots, trying to tear away the web of smaller roots to free the spaces between the bigger ones. "You must take my word for it; this is a treasure that will make you wealthy men, wealthy beyond your wildest dreams."

As their thoughts drifted back to the tens of thousands of

dollars they owed various autocratic government agencies, and their dream of someday recapturing the glory days of their artifacts business, the Scroggit brothers attacked the tangle of roots with a fresh energy.

"Hey!" said Nimwell with uncharacteristic excitement as he pulled back from the stump. "I just hit something hard. What on earth . . . or I guess *in* earth, I should say, is that?"

Artis and Miss Price crowded in for a look. Deep within the fibers of stringy roots was something that looked like a bleached rock.

"Is it a fungus of some kind?" wondered Artis.

"Too hard for a fungus," said Nimwell. "I think I chipped it with my trowel. It's more like a rock."

"That's no rock," Miss Price said ominously. "I'm not paying you to sightsee. Dig!"

Artis and Nimwell furiously attacked the roots surrounding the yellow-gray object, which appeared unnaturally smooth. Once they had cleared the dirt away from it, it dangled there, an orb suspended in place by the roots still attached to it.

"What is it?" gasped Artis.

Miss Price tittered.

"Give it a good pull and you will soon find out."

Artis began to tug at the object, at first without using much force, afraid it might be something of great value that could be broken unless a delicate touch was employed.

"Pull hard, yet steadily and carefully," said Miss Price. "Dig your fingers in at the sides a little and jiggle it. But, careful! It should come out now without too much more work."

Artis hesitated, placed his hand firmly around the hard object, and yanked with all his might. With a crackle of roots, the object broke free, more easily than he expected, causing him to fall backward and drop the object on the parking lot pavement, where it shattered into a dozen pieces. Miss Price and

Nimwell yelped. Nursing his wrist, which had been bruised by the fall, Artis got up slowly and looked down at the object, which the other two stared at in silent awe.

"My God!" he cried. "It's . . . it's . . . what is it?"

"You know damn well what it is," Miss Price cried. "It's a human skull! Or pieces of a skull, you oaf, thanks to your clumsy incompetence. Now, keep digging."

20

Roots

The Scroggit brothers stood stunned and petrified as Miss Price jabbed at the shrinking stump. Human bones—or pieces of bones, to be more precise—were littering their dirt pile, and more pieces of varying sizes were still falling out of the tangle of roots that had now been largely cleared of caked dirt, gravel, and sod. Miss Price was wielding her gardening trowel like a woman half her age, her energy never flagging as she stabbed, chopped, and pried things loose. Brittle bone fragments dropped onto the pavement or the other bones. Mainly, they fell in small and hard-to-distinguish parts, broken and severed by time, the absence of coffins or any other protective receptacles, and the violent actions of expanding roots and the oak's final death throes.

"Miss Price," said Artis softly. Miss Price was too caught up in her task to pay any attention. Artis and Nimwell looked at each other.

"Miss Price!" Artis shouted. Miss Price stopped her digging and turned to look at the inert Scroggit brothers.

"No need to raise your voice, Scroggit. What is it? And why are you two just standing their passively like bumps on a log? Gonna let me do all the work for you, eh? Well, if that's the case, I'm going to deduct it from what I owe you, that's for sure."

"Miss Price," said Artis deferentially. "Is it too much for us to ask what is going on here? We've got human bones falling at our feet. It's not exactly what we were given to expect. This is very macabre."

"*Very* macabre," added Nimwell.

It should be noted that the sight of human remains being unearthed was not, per se, a shocking one for the Scroggit brothers. They had, on a number of occasions, back before their obsession with Civil War relics and other Americana took hold, exhumed skeletons, mummified remains, and even shrunken heads from the jungles of Indonesia. But, on all of those occasions, they knew what they were looking for, and were to be well paid for their efforts. Here was the unanticipated spectacle of remains falling out of the crumbling root system of a suburban American oak tree and this weird Miss Price gleefully probing for more. What was also disquieting for the Scroggit brothers was the uncertainty about the legality of all this. They conducted their previous exhumations with full knowledge that what they were doing was either legal or not, and acted accordingly. Here, they had no clue. The fact that a busy city street was within sight no more than a hundred yards away added to their discomfort.

Miss Price ignored Artis's question and went back to her digging. Ten more minutes passed, and the Scroggit brothers found themselves increasingly acting like guards, looking around continuously to see if anyone was coming, or for any car pulling into the parking lot. How the hell were they going to explain the pile of bones and the savagely active Miss Price should someone have the effrontery to ask?

"Eureka!" shouted Miss Price.

Artis and Nimwell perked up. Could this be the treasure Miss Price had promised them? The Scroggit brothers leaned forward expectantly. What they saw was another dirty-white, smooth, rounded object around which Miss Price was plunging her trowel. Gasping for breath, she dropped the trowel with a clang onto the pavement, and pulled out a second skull. Exultant, she turned and held it out for them to inspect.

"Here's number two!" she cried. "Here's number two! Say hello, skull number two, to a couple of boobs, the Scroggit brothers. This one's in excellent condition. Probably because I'm not an incompetent who's always dropping things. Here, make yourself useful, dodo; hold on to it." She thrust the skull toward Nimwell. He accepted it with shaking hands.

"Don't drop it, fool! Now, we need to find something to put these remains in. A box will do. But don't you boys have something in your trunk you can put all this stuff in without damaging them further?"

Yes, they did. Relic hunters such as the Scroggit brothers were always prepared for any chance discoveries that needed to be carefully handled and stored. Artis retrieved a special felt-lined and compartmentalized case from the trunk of the Citroën. The bones were soon safe in the case, and out of view of the general public.

"Okay," said Miss Price. "Those will have to stay in your trunk for the time being." Artis and Nimwell shuddered. "Yes, you're disappointed that there was no treasure. I am, too. I thought maybe, just maybe, it was buried shallow enough to be fastened tight to the stump by the roots. It must be deeper in that hole, deeper down. We must dig deeper down."

"But how, Miss Price?" Artis asked. "We can't just go traipsing on to the site with our metal detectors and shovels. They'll call the police at the first sign of us anywhere near that property."

"That's right," said Miss Price. "You two have bungled that approach completely. But I've got some other ideas. Now, let's get back to my place. We can have a hot cup of Ovaltine while

I tell you what our strategy is. Maybe that'll put a little more sizzle in your pizzles."

Dr. Ferdinand Lick heard the squeal of un-oiled hinges in motion. He looked up from his desk, where he had been studying the symmetrical construction of *Manhood* magazine's June "cozy creature," to see the head of a modestly attractive and seemingly disembodied woman sprouting from his door, which was slightly ajar.

"Dr. Ferdinand Lick, I presume," said the head. At first startled by the appearance of an unfamiliar head craning around his doorjamb, Dr. Lick recovered quickly and began to speculate on the feminine wonders currently hidden from view. He then began to appreciate the absurdity of what he was looking at. He chuckled at the thought of a woman's head flying around the department to spy on professors looking at men's magazines, though why that was particularly funny he couldn't quite say. He quickly placed the copy of *Manhood* back in his top-right-hand drawer.

"Yes, I am," he said. "But my office hours are for appointments only, and my schedule doesn't show that I have an appointment now. In fact, I don't have one for another hour, and I believe it's one of my male students, which is obviously not you."

He smiled. Dr. Lick was not without his winning ways. The disembodied head pushed open the door and became a full-bodied and rather-well-put-together woman whom he struggled to place. Dr. Lick knitted his brow, and successfully pushed aside any carnal thoughts that had begun to insinuate themselves in that realm of the brain where carnal thoughts abide.

"Mother?"

Miss Price chortled.

"Of course I'm not your mother. I'm not nearly old enough

to be your mother. Good Lord above, Dr. Lick, don't you know what your own mother looks like?"

Dr. Lick blushed at being upbraided in such a manner.

"You'll have to excuse the case of mistaken identity," he said. "My mother had me at a very young age. She disowned me for all intents and purposes when I was a teenager. It had to do with some disagreements about my entering the family business. She has lived abroad for the past thirty years, and I've never visited her. I have no earthly idea what she looks like now. But then, I won't bore you with all the sordid details of my family life. What is it you want with me? I'm very busy, and, as I said, you don't have an appointment."

Miss Price plopped right down in the comfy guest chair and leaned forward alluringly across his desk, showing off her décolletage to the best possible effect. Dr. Lick, at first uncertain as to whether he should lean forward or hold his ground in the face of this attempted confidence, ended up lurching so far back in his office chair that he almost tipped it over.

"I've read your work on the early European discovery of America, and how Europeans were actually here three hundred years before Columbus," Miss Price purred. "It is brilliant. I know it has been dismissed as sheer nonsense by the academic establishment. But I also know how you can find the evidence to back up your thesis. In fact, I know exactly where it is. Actual, tangible artifacts that will prove everything you say beyond a reasonable doubt."

Dr. Lick sprang forward in his chair.

"What!" he cried.

"Did you know those artifacts are buried somewhere very close by?"

Dr. Lick, flabbergasted into a mute numbness by Miss Price's stunning announcement, could only shake his head. He began to pant with excitement.

"I can show you where they are. They are right here in the

St. Anthony metro. In Livia, to be specific. A few hours, maybe less, of digging, and they're yours. Not only that, but you'll have the evidence to refute your critics and become the nation's—no, the world's—most famous archaeologist. Academically, you'll be able to write your own ticket. You'll have your pick of any department or any university in the country. To say nothing of the riches you'll find." Miss Price pulled away from the desk, settled herself back into the chair, and smirked.

"Now, what do you say to that?"

Dr. Lick was salivating so hard that he had to consciously shut his mouth to prevent the pool of saliva forming around his teeth from spilling out over his thrust-out lower lip and onto his desk.

"I say, that's amazing, that's wonderful. I will need some more evidence of course, but probably not too much more since you are obviously very learned in this field. Actually, I don't need any more evidence at all. I can assemble a crew and the appropriate equipment in a matter of a few days. You won't tell anyone else, will you, Ms., Ms. . . . ?"

"*Miss* Price. No, of course I won't. This is for your ears only, Dr. Lick."

"Wonderful! That's just wonderful! Now, if you can tell me the location of this particular find, and some other salient details, I'll get the process rolling here."

"Two things," said Miss Price.

"Uh, what's that?"

"First, I must be present when you do your excavation work."

Dr. Lick frowned and tapped a pen against his forehead.

"Our workplace safety rules prohibit that," he said. "Liability issues, you know."

"Take it or leave it, doc."

"I'm sure we can find a way to circumvent the red tape."

"Two . . ."

"Yes?"

"Two, you can't just go waltzing over to the site and start your work."

"And why is that?"

"It's on private property."

Dr. Lick smiled. "We can talk to the homeowners," he said. "I've dealt with reluctant property owners before. Usually, they can be persuaded to let us dig, especially if we offer some kind of pecuniary inducement. They're usually flattered that something so important has been discovered on their property."

"That probably won't work here."

Dr. Lick frowned. "And why won't it?"

"The property owners know there's something there. They know it could make them very rich. You're probably going to be the last person they want showing up at their place with picks and shovels."

Dr. Lick, his mind swimming with visions of wealth and glory, leaned back in his chair, folded his arms, and gazed at Miss Price with glimmering, dream-sparkled eyes.

"We sometimes run into difficult property owners," he said. "Never fear, Miss Price. We have our ways."

"Actually, there's another thing."

"Yeeesss?"

"I must have some of the credit for the discovery."

"Well, certainly you would get *some* credit. Mention in whatever press coverage there would be, for instance."

"I would want more than that," said Miss Price. "I would also want the rights to some of the artifacts you unearth."

"Well, technically . . ."

"No technically about it, bub. You play by my rules or I will never tell you where the site is. Then, someone else can worry about all the trappings that go with the greatest archaeological find of the past century."

"Ah . . . well . . . we can certainly discuss terms, Miss Price."

Miss Price got up to leave.

"I'll have a document delivered to you that I'm sure we can both agree to," she said. "I'll be back Friday to sign it. Just be sure there's a notary available. Those are my terms. And I'd hurry if I were you. Who knows how quickly others might move to beat us to the punch, eh?"

Miss Price's Plan A was proceeding nicely. Dr. Lick signed off on her stipulations, and she was preparing a map with an address and even an X-marks-the-spot drawn on it for delivery to his office. Now, for Plan B. She picked up the phone and dialed Artis.

A voice weighted down with useless torpor answered.

"Wake up!"

"Wha . . . huh? . . . Miss Price? . . . Wha . . . wha time is it?"

"What time is it? What time is it! How should I know what time it is! The only time I know is it's time for action!" There was silence at the other end.

"I said *action!* It's time for you and your brother to put Plan B into effect." The silence gave way to a prolonged groan.

"Drat it all, Miss Price, it's, uh, two forty-five in the morning."

"So! Wake up, you useless kumquat! I'm not paying you to sleep."

"Plan B," repeated Artis groggily. "Is it legal?"

"Perfectly. At least up to a point. Do you know anyone who can operate heavy machinery? Something that can dig a really deep hole, for instance? And maybe even dig a tunnel?"

"Of course. All professional treasure hunters have proven and discreet heavy equipment crews they depend on. We're no different. We know and use the best."

"Good. Call him up and tell him you've got a job for him. And, yes, one that requires discretion. Oh, and I've got a property I want you to take over. In fact, it was cheap. A foreclosure property. I've already signed the papers on it. I'll give it to you and your useless brother."

"I've already got a really nice home, Miss Price."

"Not to live in, nincompoop. To use as a staging area. The property right next door to the Fremonts. And no more than a few piddling yards to one very large stump hole on the other side of a fence. Get my drift?"

There was a groan and some mumbling. It was soft and distant, as if Artis was holding the phone away from his mouth so he could vent his frustration in private.

"I heard that, Mr. Worthless-Lazy-Bones. Now, if you have a better suggestion, I would like to hear it. Otherwise, Plan B. Come over to my apartment with your pathetic slip of a brother tomorrow—or I guess, technically, today—and we'll discuss Plan B."

"Why so soon?"

"So soon! So soon! You worthless so-and-so's couldn't open a frozen slushie stand in hell. You have a wonder of the New World awaiting your grasp, and you want to wait! Waiting is for saps and losers. You will come over in the morning, the earlier the better, for your briefing. Then, you will put Plan B into effect with all possible dispatch. Otherwise, I will look elsewhere for men of action and you will get no share and no recognition from what will inevitably follow."

"Miss Price!"

"Don't you 'Miss Price' me. Remember, one of the greatest treasures of the New World lies at your feet. Don't let it slip through your fingers!"

21

Drive-by

Dr. Sproot pulled into her driveway shaking so hard she could barely keep a grip on the steering wheel. How she had managed to get home she had no idea. Her eyes were twitching so rapidly that it seemed as if she was watching a strobe light show.

In fact, she was caught in a violent upheaval. The forces of good and evil were locked in combat for possession of her soul. When a soul possession battle happens, there's a certain amount of discomfort and disorientation, the degree of which depends on how badly good and evil want the soul in question. In the case of Dr. Sproot, they wanted it in the worst way. It looked like she was having a seizure. Her head throbbed. Her pulse raced. Her stomach churned like a cement mixer ready to disgorge its contents. Her legs and feet suffered from such tremors that she could barely step down on the accelerator or brake.

"Oh, poor me," she moaned. "Poor, poor me." Even speaking to herself, she couldn't keep her voice from quaking.

This was all the fault of those Fremonts. Dr. Sproot had just been out for a drive down Sumac Street, paying particular attention to the sloping side of the Fremont property. She wanted to see for herself if the rumors about the front yard were true.

And were they ever! My God, what happened to the scabrous desert of cockleburs, dandelions, and barren earth? Here was . . . well . . . an earthly paradise!

Of course, Dr. Sproot recognized everything they had planted. There was nothing there she couldn't have nurtured herself to a certain degree of brilliance. But not to THAT degree of brilliance! She could not have devised as perfect a symmetry or combination of annuals and perennials in a million years.

Goodness, they were dabbling in hybrid teas! Though to call what they did "dabbling" would do a terrible injustice to the magnificent creations that shone along the top of the slope so iridescent in the afternoon sun.

The skilled cultivator in Dr. Sproot couldn't help but appreciate such a rare accomplishment. She herself had tried growing hybrid teas once in her younger days. That experiment had failed dismally.

Dr. Sproot mostly poked along, her car barely moving, as she drank in the wonders of these new front yard gardens. Then, she'd speed up and slow down again. Back up, then drive forward. She'd swerve from one side of the street to the other, then do a U-turn to drive back across the length of the property.

A loud honk signaled that she'd barely missed getting broadsided by a UPS truck.

There, what was that? An orange-and-black blob shot past the front of the car, and skimmed the contours of the slope, then rose to perch in one of the lower branches of the big silver maple. From there, it dropped down to land on the little structure suspended on the shepherd's crook pole a short way to the side of the hybrid teas. Ah, she thought, that must be a Baltimore oriole. Isn't it lovely?

The gardening ogre that had reemerged as *Doc-tor* Phyllis Sproot a month ago was still fully evident to anyone careless enough to cross paths with her. But alone, Dr. Sproot was a conflicted and miserable soul. As dominant as the dictatorial, scornful, and destructive Dr. Sproot persona was, it had never completely subdued the patient, appreciative, and at least marginally humble Phyllis, who could still be lost in admiration for a garden other than her own, even if it defied her own rigid floricultural formulas. Such a garden was a rare find indeed, but this was truly one of them. Dr. Sproot pulled over to the curb, stopped the car, and sighed.

That nagging inner voice was back. It whispered that this was the apex of the gardener's craft, and that her own efforts were no more than a shadow of what was happening here. But that was okay, it said; make your peace with it, Phyllis.

Dr. Sproot whimpered. She knew the inner voice spoke the truth. And that truth had a certain allure. To recognize true beauty and let it suffuse your very being is one of the greatest joys this world has to offer, even for the blackest of hearts. Stories abound of dictators drinking the finest Scotch, dining on Caspian Sea caviar, and whiling away evenings listening to Mozart as they gazed upon the uncovered charms of their mistresses. Nero played a mean fiddle. Attila the Hun was a connoisseur of horseflesh and fermented goat's milk. Who knows whether such monsters would have tempered their behavior had they given full rein to such epicurisms?

So it was with Dr. Sproot, whose road to salvation lay in her discriminating eye for gardening magic and the soothing pleasure on succumbing to its spell.

That salvation, however, would have to wait.

Another voice piped up loud and clear. It was the bleating, hateful voice of a dipshit. It called Dr. Sproot a weenie, and repeated many of the insulting things the Fremonts had said to her. It suggested that if championship-level gardening was too demanding for her delicate sensibilities then maybe she should try something less taxing: juggling two tennis balls, for instance.

"Zip it," Dr. Sproot commanded the voice. "Zip it now, and leave me in peace."

The new voice would not be zipped. In fact, it cackled as Dr. Sproot strove to call back the good voice—the voice of a peaceful, harmonious nature.

"I said shut up, asshole!" Dr. Sproot screeched. "Shut the hell up and leave me alone, or I'll . . . I'll . . ."

That's more like it, said the voice. *That's the Dr. Sproot I want to see. The one we all love to hate. Ha-ha!*

Dr. Sproot pleaded for the good voice to come back. She called up visions of beautiful flowers and extravagant gardens, only to watch them wither and crinkle, then disintegrate in gale-force winds. She cursed at the bad voice, employing a language so profane that it cannot be repeated here. All that did was drive the good voice deeper into her subconscious. She grasped at it, but it was elusive, reduced now to incomprehensible babbling. Then, a barely audible murmur.

At that point, Dr. Sproot caught a glimpse in her rearview mirror of a Livia police cruiser, lights flashing, as it pulled up behind her. Trembling with mingled fear and rage, she lowered the driver's side window and looked up at the police officer, who asked to see her license and proof of insurance.

"Are you okay, ma'am?" the officer asked as she handed him her license and insurance card. "We got a call saying someone was driving erratically on this block. The description we got matches this car. The caller also said that the driver seemed to be flailing her arms around after she stopped, in a no-parking zone, I might add. Are you having a problem, uh, Ms. Sproot?"

"Flailing?"

"Flailing. Someone said it appeared you were waving your hands around while sitting in the car, then grabbing your head and twisting it from one side to the other. And that all this was going on for, oh, fifteen minutes or so."

"I was?"

"That's what was reported to us, ma'am."

"I didn't know that I was flailing," said Dr. Sproot, her voice rising. "Even if I was, what business is that of anyone's?"

"It's not illegal per se," said the officer. "It is, however, highly unusual behavior, and is definitely our business if you're posing a threat to yourself or to others."

"I'm not a threat," said Dr. Sproot. "I wasn't even aware I was flailing."

"Have you been drinking, Ms. Sproot?"

Dr. Sproot drew back from the window, indignant.

"I certainly have *not!*" she said.

"Have you been using drugs, or do you have any drugs in the car?"

"Of course not! And how dare you address these impertinent and mortifying questions to me. Do you know who I am, officer?"

"I do," the officer said. "You're Ms. Phyllis Sproot. At least that's what it says on the driver's license you just handed me."

Dr. Sproot snorted.

"I mean, do you know who I *am?*"

"I do not, and, for that matter, I don't care who you are."

"Well, you should!" Dr. Sproot barked. "I am *Doc-tor* Phyllis Sproot, the preeminent gardener in Livia. I am the person who invented the coreopsis-salvia-hollyhock blend. You probably heard something about that, eh? Or maybe your wife has? I am the person who calculated precise percentages of gardening composition, even for dahlias and roses and yucca. . . . Do you grow yuccas, officer?"

"I'm going to ask you to step out of the car, Ms. Sproot. With your permission, I will administer a Breathalyzer and do a quick search of your vehicle. Please, as you exit the car, make no sudden motions, as if you're going for a weapon of some sort. Do you have weapons on you, Ms. Sproot?"

The trembling stopped. Dr. Sproot grabbed the steering wheel with a renewed resolution of such force and steadiness that her knuckles whitened and cracked. The little voice—the so-called *good* one—had finally responded to her pleas and was making its case in its prissy little hesitant way. But Dr. Sproot now recognized it for what it really represented—weakness! *Lie down and let yourself get trampled on,* is what it was telling her. *Let others hog the limelight while you retreat into the shadows.*

Dr. Sproot willed the little voice back into a silence she hoped would be eternal, got out of her car, and slammed the door so hard the window rattled.

22

A Gardening Hiatus

A nervous and downcast George reported for his first day at work.

This was a milestone of sorts, but not one that either George or Nan would consider to be a mark of progress. How many years ago was it that he had actually driven somewhere with regularity to earn a biweekly paycheck? Back when he was editing the shopper, that's when. That was nine years ago, before his dabbling in creative toys for children led to the big Whirl-a-Gig Bubble Blower payday.

George's reentry into the workforce followed a long conversation with Nan over a bottle of Sagelands. They began on a positive note, weighing their prospects for instantly coming up with tens of thousands of dollars, and not having to find real jobs after all. Cracking open another bottle, they realized, led to the danger of a wine-induced euphoria that would cast their cares to the wind. They opened the bottle anyway and found to no surprise that their situation didn't really look that bad.

"I'm sure you've got another one of your inventions hiding there up your sleeve, don't you, dear?" said Nan.

"Yes," said George, puckering his lips resolutely. "As a matter of fact, I do, Nan-bee." There was a pause.

"And?"

"The talking hose."

"The talking hose."

"Yes. A hose that can actually talk to you."

"How can a hose talk when it's got water coming out of its mouth?"

Nan filled her mouth with wine, then made an effort to talk as an illustration. She gulped it down and laughed.

"And what would a hose talk about? 'Oh, looks like rain; won't need to turn me on today.' Or, maybe, 'Screw me in to that slutty little oscillating number over there, then stand back!' Tee-hee-hee."

"The hose itself wouldn't actually talk," said George stonily. "It would be a simulated kind of talk. More like a beeping. Or I suppose you could substitute some very rudimentary words. It would need some kind of computer chip."

"Ah."

"The computer chip would let you know after a predetermined amount of time that the hose is still on. So, no more leaving the hose on overnight!"

"Okay. Where's that brilliant invention stand now?"

"It hasn't gotten beyond the concept stage."

"Ah-ha. So we can scratch that one off the list. Whatever happened to that beeping greeting card that could read your writing and tell you when you've misspelled a word? I thought that had some real promise. Besides, you've got an in with the greeting card business, don't you?"

"Well, yes I do, considering that they're still asking me for my special-occasion doggerel. I do have that going for me. That's still good for a couple thou a year. The greeting card idea was good, but it still faces a major hurdle."

"Which is?"

"Reading cursive handwriting. Even block print. Everyone writes differently. If everyone typed out their greetings, then we'd have a standardized format that the computer chip could respond to. At least that's my theory, based on a limited knowledge of how artificial intelligences work."

"One big problem there, slick: If you send a greeting card to someone, you're probably not going to type out a note on your computer and stick it in there. You're going to write it longhand. It's what they call the personal touch. You knew that, didn't you?"

"I had sort of an inkling. But I got kind of caught up in the eureka moment, I guess."

"And how is the computer chip going to work?"

"Don't know. I'll have to connect with someone who knows something about computer chips."

"Okay, well, that's probably a ways off then."

"Yes, a good ways." George solemnly refilled their glasses.

"And how's the handbag business going?"

"Have you seen me knitting any handbags lately?"

"Come to think of it, no."

"Well, then, that's how it's going."

"Ah."

"There's been so much to do with our expanded gardens that I haven't even given it much thought. Besides, Cloud's and Deevers dropped my line."

"They didn't!"

"Yes, they did. Cloud's, just last week; and Deevers, about a month ago. I didn't think it was worth telling you. They weren't selling enough of them. Apparently, the fad for custom, great-aunt-inspired handbags has come and gone."

"But you had a great little tag on each one with that wonderful photo of your great-Aunt Lily."

"Yes, I thought that was a nice touch, too. But it wasn't enough."

Nan sighed and slumped over the tabletop. She felt she could hear the murmurings of her many living creations, but they were sad and confused murmurings that would not contribute to healthy growth patterns and brilliance of blooms. George felt he could hear them, too, though to a less sophisticated degree, and as more of a disorganized babel that he could only understand in snippets, as if he were talking over a bad cell phone connection.

Couldn't we muddle through? thought Nan. Couldn't they just wait for another blessed event, like the one last year that saved them from insolvency? There was obviously something about this property that invited good fortune coming hard and fast on the heels of bad.

The flowers were sighing. To the untutored sensibility, it might sound like a rustling or the rise and fall of the wind. It might not be any sound at all, and more like the whiff of a fragrance. To Nan, though, these were all signals. Today, there were a lot of them. Every genus within a hundred-yard radius seemed to be giving voice to its own flowering energy. The signals told her uniformly to stick to the plan. They pleaded with her not to leave them to the whims of nature, which could be wild and cruel.

George's messages were more fundamental. They left quite a bit of room for interpretation. Were they wishing him new luck in his endeavors, or warning that a nibbling rabbit was in the vicinity? There were the hybrid tea roses. They were interrupting in their loud, arrogant way, to demand water. Sometimes, they did that even after he watered them, just to be prima donnas. Ha! There were his buddies, the irises. They were done for the year, their blooms having already crinkled and fallen off. Here they were, with what energy remained to them, telling the hybrids to go screw themselves.

George laughed.

"Don't tell me," Nan said. "It's your buddies, the irises. This is no time for joking, George. The flowers are very upset."

George pondered that for a while. Then, he concentrated on the noise of the nearby interstate to block out all the floral chatter that was rising to the level of a cacophony.

"George," said Nan. "You're blocking them out. You're not listening."

George stiffened.

"That's right," he said. "Because this is the time to turn off the plant world and do what's right, Nan-bee. We won't have any of this without one of us giving it up, at least for the time being, and taking on a full-time job."

The humming of sentient flowers rose to the level of the sound of a hummingbird slurping nectar if you were standing within one centimeter of it.

"There are times when you have to ignore what your little flower beings are telling you, and decide what's right on your own. We can't wait for another miracle to happen. We've got to make money."

The gentle murmurings quieted, then subsided altogether. George and Nan were entering the practical realm of animal conversation, which can be cerebral and confusing during the course of cross-cultural communications. At times such as these, flowers tend to clam up.

"Okay," said Nan, bolting up ramrod straight. "Let's draw straws. I'll cut one to be shorter. The short straw has to go find a real job."

George grimaced.

"There's got to be a better way to do this," he said. "And I have it. Forget your short-straw idea, Nan-bee. I'll be the one who goes job hunting. I'm the obvious choice. Without you, I'd be a complete muddle in the gardens. Without me, you can still make everything flourish. And you've got Mary and Shirelle to help you out. Who needs me, except to finally be the family breadwinner I always should have been?"

Nan stared at George. Her eyes began to mist up.

"Oh, George!" She felt herself going all weak and swoony. Here was the man of her dreams, the man who would conquer the world for her, or maybe do something else a little more reasonable but which was still sort of a sacrifice. This was the George who could rise to any occasion, especially after he had had a couple of glasses of Sagelands. Speaking of which, Nan wondered how long this mood of self-sacrifice would last. If she let things hang there in suspense for too long the good effect of the wine would wear off, and George might start having second thoughts about voluntarily throwing himself on the altar of humdrum, wage-earning existence. Besides, that swoony mood that had come on her so suddenly was dissipating. She had to act quickly. George was pursing his lips and tapping his fingertips on the glass tabletop. It was the sign of a faltering resolve.

"Maybe the short straw idea . . ." he began. Nan quickly grabbed his hand and yanked it to her lips for a kiss.

"I'm so proud of you, George! To have offered yourself up like that. How gallant! Now, go make a pot of decaf and get on the computer classifieds. I've got another garden plot to plan. Go on! Chop-chop. Time's a-wasting. I think you look under Help Wanted—isn't that it?"

The job at Li'l Tweeters bird store wasn't really so tough. George, being an affable fellow with a ready smile, was an instant hit with the staff and customers. He came armed with a solid knowledge of backyard and migratory birds, their habitats, and their feeding habits. Always ready to learn, he quickly became familiar with the twelve different kinds of feed offered in barrels for the customers to scoop up, bag, and weigh, as well as birdcalls. He was given a spiffy blue denim shirt with *Li'l Tweeters* embroidered in yellow cursive lettering on the breast pocket, and even a Li'l Tweeters baseball cap, which he was instructed not to wear inside the store.

The pay wasn't very generous—$12 an hour. For six hours a day, five days a week, that amounted to $360 a week, enough to pay the mortgage, but virtually nothing else, which left him wondering how the heck they would be able to handle three semiannual college-tuition-and-room-and-board payments.

"Oh, well," said Nan, sighing. "It's going to have to be 'Welcome to the real world, kids; you're going to have to take out loans and help pay your own way.'"

As George pulled into the driveway at five thirty p.m. on a Friday, having finished his first week at Li'l Tweeters, he mused proudly about what he had accomplished over the course of the past five days. He had personally sold three squirrel baffles, two wren houses, four bird guides, four tubular finch feeders, one humongous Old Hickory Crafts bird-feeding station, twelve Styrofoam cups of mealworms, twelve cakes of suet, two bird-song CDs, and 340 pounds of birdfeed, with a special emphasis on the store's own "Feast for All" blend designed to attract the biggest possible variety of birds to your feeder.

He had signed up four customers to annual memberships in the Tweeters Club. He was able to offer advice on attracting orioles and hummingbirds.

All this earned him a pat on the back from the store manager, who was impressed enough with his knowledge that he had put George in charge of the bird log, where the sightings of various species were typed into a computer logbook and marked with colored pushpins on a big map of Livia spread out on the wall. Two pileated woodpecker sightings alone in the past week!

As George pulled into the driveway, he had begun to entertain daydreams of success in the bird-business world. Promotion would follow promotion as his talents came to the attention of the bird-store moguls. Before long, he would branch out on his own, starting a chain of high-end stores, appearing on television commercials, and doling out huge donations to the charitable causes and political candidates of his choosing.

Why, he would become to bird stores what Jasper Burdick was to gardening centers.

A sharp rap on the passenger-side window interrupted his reverie. He looked over to see Nan signaling for him to roll down the window. She had her sun hat, sunglasses, and work gloves on, and was sweating to beat the band. Ah, poor Nanbee. Doomed to slave away in the outdoor heat while her husband, the bird supplies wunderkind, gets to soar through the corporate ranks in air-conditioned comfort.

"Fall asleep after your hard day at the office?" Nan said. "Get up here and do your wine thing. It's cocktail hour, you know. And, say, remember how the Grunions' house went into foreclosure? Well, someone must have bought it, because there's a big backhoe making one heck of a lot of noise in their backyard right now."

"There, that should do very nicely," said Nan, standing up to regard her new creation. "And it'll give us a nice swath of color back here close to the woods. My gosh, would you look at all the sunlight coming in now! Seven hours' worth maybe before the sun goes behind the house."

George nodded.

"I suppose it's a nice consolation prize," he said.

"Oh, stop being Mr. Downer, will you? There is no treasure. *Nada. Nunca.* Nix. *Nein. Nyet. Comprendes?* And now that you've got your job, no worries, correct-o?"

"Well, as I told you, we'll be able to pay the mortgage. We should be able to eat reasonably well. New clothes are kinda out of the picture there, Nan-bee."

"What! Shoes?"

"No."

"What kind of new life is this if I can't buy six new pairs of shoes a year?"

"It's called the Year of Living Frugally, that's what it's called. Deal with it, Imelda Marcos. And, of course, the children take on college debt big-time. Why the hell couldn't they go to their state universities, like we did?"

"Ah, well, the Lord will provide. As always."

"Sure, but do you really want to come face-to-face with utter destruction, the way we did last year, before the Almighty decides to come down off His cushy cloud and do something about it?"

Nan decided to ignore George's nagging pessimism, and to resume gazing appreciatively upon her new flowers.

Once Jim's sweep had come up negative, George and Nan ordered three cubic feet of nutrient-loaded soil, which George hauled up from the driveway and dumped into the stump hole. Nan filled the center of the site with pink and white cleome, careful to space them widely since the plants would get much bigger; midnight-purple violets; and yellow Dahlberg daisies, which would brighten and vary the color field, but which probably wouldn't bloom for several weeks, at least. For good measure, she had thrown in the perennials: a couple of peonies, lovely flowers that would last for years and years. And, of course, the volunteer spirea. Three of those.

Around the border, she had planted one of her favorites, alyssum, that hardy, drought-resistant wonder that thrived in direct, hot sun, and exploded into massive clumps of pinkie-sized blossoms. This was also where the Dusty Miller would get its second and final chance to shine.

"Hey, George, let's take a look at the hole they're making next door."

On the preceding Friday, after George came home from

work, he hoisted Nan up to look over the eight-foot slatted-wood privacy fence. There, she saw the backhoe chugging away right in front of her, its bucket shovel ripping up huge chunks of turf, then swiveling to deposit them on a growing mound that was already five feet high. Inside the cab was the operator, a man so intent on his work that he didn't even see her waving. She could see him smoking a cigarette, then flick the still-smoldering butt into the hole.

"That's one daggone big hole," she said once George let her down. "And it's right next to the fence, then stretches a good twelve feet toward the center of the yard. What in heaven's name are they up to over there?"

"Whoa!" said Nan now as George boosted her up. He secretly wished she would shed a few pounds if this hoisting thing was going to become one of his regular duties. "The hole's a lot bigger and deeper. Hey, there's the operator."

A man was leaning against the backhoe, munching on a sandwich half-wrapped in wax paper and drinking from a thermos. The man looked up at Nan, and smiled.

"Hey," he said through a mouthful of sandwich.

"Hey," said Nan. "Whatcha' workin' on here?" The man gulped down his bite of sandwich, then took a swig from the thermos and wiped his mouth with his shirtsleeve.

"Um, some sort of pond garden," he said. "You know, a big Oriental-type thing with lots of landscaping and a pool full of exotic fish."

Nan frowned.

"Why are you digging it right next to the fence?" she asked. "Wouldn't it be better to have it over toward the back of the yard? Putting it here, you won't be able to see it very well from the deck."

The man shrugged. "Hey, lady, I just do what I'm told, and I was told to dig a big hole right here."

"Who is it who told you to do that?"

The man finished his sandwich, tossed the wax paper on the ground, and screwed the cap back onto his thermos.

"The guy who bought the house," he said, putting the thermos into a metal lunchbox and climbing back into the backhoe's cab. "Now, if you'll excuse me, I gotta get back to work. Nice to meet you. Sorry about the noise."

The backhoe started up with a whine, and soon, the big shovel was clawing away at the subsoil and another cigarette was dangling from the operator's lower lip.

"I don't get why whoever bought the house is making a garden right there next to the fence," Nan said. "When you look at it, it's hidden around the corner of the house. There's a nice deck on the back of the house. I can tell by the part I can see jutting out. Gosh, I never knew that was there, but then it's not as if the Grunions ever invited us over. Anyway, you wouldn't be able to see this garden from the deck. Strange."

"Not really. Maybe they want a hidden arbor. And what's to prevent them and their guests from taking a short walk to look at it?"

"I guess," Nan said. "But I tell you, George, there's something fishy going on over there."

"Great. Can I put you down now, please?"

23

Lies and Moles

Miss Price's blood boiled. Her enzymes roiled. Her nerve ends sparked and sputtered. Right here in the Livia *Lollygag* was the greatest lie and scandal ever perpetrated on Livia. The Scroggit brothers watched her with growing dread as they pretended to sip their Ovaltine.

Staring up at her from the front page of the *Lollygag* was the smiling face of Marvelle Olson. She was accepting a plaque from Livia Historical Society board president Kurt Scheinblum, honoring her as a direct descendent of the first known family to permanently inhabit what is now known as Livia.

Why, it was monstrous! It was calumny! It was Miss Price's family that was the first here. That was a fact. The problem was that it was a fact that could not be established by hard evidence. What she had was woefully circumstantial. There were some anecdotes about a couple and their children who lived on top of the rise overlooking the lake and mile upon mile of rolling prairie. There were a few stray papers that bore no official stamp. Unauthenticated letters and diaries. That was about it.

Marvelle had a stack of documents. Land claim, purchase agreements, records of births and christenings, receipts for crop sales. There could be little doubt about who would get the "Livia's First Family" honor.

"So sorry, Gwendolyn," said Mr. Scheinblum on rejecting her claim. "But we have to go with hard evidence, not rumor and conjecture. Real, hard evidence is what we need. Barring that, we have to turn you down. I'm sorry. You've been an excellent director for us, and I know how hard you've worked on this. I hope you'll see fit to congratulate Marvelle at our little ceremony and presentation. Actually, as director of the society, it is your duty to be there and make the presentation."

"I will do no such thing, you old twit!" Miss Price snapped. "This is all a lie! A big lie! And I will have nothing, not one thing, to do with it. So you can take your goddamn first-family plaque and shove it where the sun don't shine! D'ya hear me! And if it won't fit, I'm just the one who can carve you out a big enough hole to make it fit."

Mr. Scheinblum fainted right there in the society museum. As luck would have it, he collapsed unobstructed onto the thickly carpeted floor, which soon revived him with its pungent odor of dander, dust, and any other detritus that had accumulated over thirty years of never having been washed or cleaned.

Miss Price's resignation as director of the Livia Historical Society was accepted unanimously by the board despite her never having submitted it. She held on to the keys, despite the board's repeated requests that she turn them in. She continued to report to work at the appointed times, and thanks to a clerical oversight, kept getting paid.

But now to be blindsided by this article and the photograph! There she was, that stupid, mummified old Marvelle Olson, playing the Norwegian card to the hilt, inflecting her speech with that idiotic, singsongy cadence that everyone from somewhere else and recent arrivals seemed to find so *authentic*.

Well, her family wasn't the first one here by a long shot. It wasn't some bunch of Norwegians that beat her people to the punch.

"Goddamn it!" she shouted. Suddenly realizing that she was wearing a short skirt and sitting in a raised chair, she clamped her legs together and tugged at the hemline. She stared hard at Artis and Nimwell, scouring their faces for signs of any wanton thoughts and glances. Not those two. They were too busy looking stupid to have gotten sidetracked by any carnally motivated sightseeing. It looked like they were pouting, striving halfheartedly to play the part of indignant employees. That was a hard part for them to play, and they couldn't have been less convincing. Frankly, they could have given a hoot about whose family settled Livia first, or whether they were Norwegians, Zulus, or Martians.

Miss Price regarded the Scroggit brothers with barely disguised contempt. Mere boys these were she was sending out to do a man's work. And just look at them, sulkily dreaming away, imagining themselves making love to a musket, no doubt. Miss Price inspected her forearm. Catching a little flap of skin in the tweezer-like grip of her thumb and forefinger, she squeezed hard enough to make herself yelp in pain. Artis and Nimwell looked at each other, baffled.

"Okay, time for work," Miss Price said. "What is the status of the excavation? Eh?"

Artis cleared his throat.

"We're proceeding as planned," he said. "The hole is almost dug. In a couple of days we'll be able to push a big auger bit through to the other side of the fence and under the current depth of the stump hole. Once that's done, we can insert a probe that will be able to detect any metal within seven feet of it. If the treasure's there, the probe should be able to locate it. Then, once it's located, comes the tricky part."

"What tricky part is that, Scroggit?"

"Digging the blasted thing out without the Fremonts being any the wiser for it. We haven't figured out that part yet."

"Well, how about tunneling?"

"Yes," Artis said. "We're looking for a retrieval tool we can poke through while we operate it from the excavation. The hole'll be plenty big enough so we can lie down there and maybe even camouflage ourselves with some kind of coverlet stretched over the hole. Then, we use the retrieval tool to grab or latch onto whatever it is we find, and pull it back through the augered tunnel hole. Trouble is, we haven't been able to find such a tool yet."

"Retrieval tool? Who said anything about a retrieval tool? One of you is going to have to mole through to the other side and do the retrieval himself."

"What!" cried Artis and Nimwell in unison.

"Dig a hole big enough so one of you—probably you, little Scroggit, since you're the runt of the litter—can crawl through and get the treasure from below."

"Miss Price, you've got to be kidding!" Artis said, with Nimwell nodding furiously in assent. "We couldn't do that. For one thing, you'd need special tools. For another, you'd have to brace the ground above you to prevent cave-ins and keep from getting smothered. Besides, we're claustrophobic, aren't we, Nim?"

"Yes, yes, claustrophobic," said Nimwell, shivering from a bout of pretend claustrophobia. Miss Price kicked out her foot and a pointy-toe flat whipped past Nimwell's head.

"Wimps! It's only, what, thirty-five or forty feet to the stump hole. You burrow your way across to the bottom of the hole, then you just lie down and use your hand tools to dig out the chest. Don't you dimwits recall me saying this could be a smaller chest than you think? Easy maybe to slip it back through the hole."

"What if the Fremonts walk by and see us—I mean, see Nim? They're always mucking around back there. And Dave says they've been spying on us. They know about the hole."

"Dave?"

"The backhoe operator. He said that Mrs. Fremont has been watching from over the top of the fence."

"Well, God knows, why shouldn't she? Aren't you making a racket over there? Just make sure Mr. Backhoe sticks to the story. It's our property anyway. We can do what we want over there. Besides, I've put my own Plan A in action."

Artis and Nimwell listened, unbelieving, as Miss Price told them of her deal with the noted archaeologist Dr. Ferdinand Lick.

"This is my trump card in case you two fail, which I accept as a distinct possibility."

"Hold on here a minute," Artis said. "What if this Dr. Lick gets there first? And even if we get there first, does this mean that he gets a cut? Just for the record, our understanding was we were only to share whatever we find with you, not some professor. Somebody here's going to get shafted in this treasure hunt, and somebody's not going to like it."

"What do I care if someone doesn't like it? I could give a rat's ass whether our Dr. Lick gets screwed. He's got to get past the private property problem first, anyway, so I doubt that will happen. If you get there first, I'll just shrug my shoulders and pretend to know nothing about it. And if he gets there first, that's not my problem. I get a big share of the spoils anyway. You two get nothing."

"What . . . what . . . ?"

"Spit it out, little Scroggit," Miss Price barked.

"What if the Fremonts beat all of us to the treasure?"

Miss Price frowned, then drained her cup of Ovaltine.

"Well, then we're all pretty much up the creek without a paddle, aren't we?"

* * *

Nimwell raised his head just high enough over the fence to look into the Fremonts' backyard. The noise of the backhoe made it easy enough for him to climb the ladder without fear of being heard. At Artis's urging, he had donned a wig and sunglasses; no point taking any chances of being identified should he be seen. Peering just over the fence, he admired a bed of flowers that looked freshly planted. How lovely! he thought. I must compliment them once all this treasure business is finished.

Now, where was that stump hole? Why, it was nowhere. No stump hole! Was he imagining things? He took off his sunglasses and squinted. No doubt about it, the stump hole was gone. But where was it? Then, it dawned on him. That new flower bed. The Fremonts had filled up the stump hole and planted flowers over it. How could they! Why, that wrecked everything! A part of Nimwell fought against this sense of indignation. It told him to think on the bright side: He now wouldn't have to go crawling through some wormhole, digging away on his hands and knees, and risking arrest for trespassing while his brother scampered off.

The fence suddenly shook. Thinking that the backhoe operator had accidentally swiveled its shovel into the fence, he turned to see that the shovel was nowhere nearby. When he turned back he found himself face-to-face with Nan Fremont. Both of them screamed. Nimwell tumbled back down the ladder, and rolled into the hole, bruising his shoulder and badly twisting an ankle in the process. He tried to get up, but couldn't. He noticed that the backhoe had been turned off, and saw the dark form of his brother looming over him. But what was that awful hissing sound? And that smell! Like rotten eggs! All of a sudden, hands were reaching for him and the backhoe operator was screaming.

"We hit a gas line! Everyone out! Everyone out! It's gonna blow! Gas line break! Gas line break!"

Unable to move Nimwell without further injuring him and risking their own lives as well, the backhoe operator and Artis decided it was better to at least save themselves. They took off, sprinting, toward Payne Avenue.

Nimwell groaned in pain. There was a rumble underneath him, followed by a shaking. Then, he felt like he was getting swallowed up by the earth and vomited out again. He vaulted skyward and somewhat laterally. Giggling uncontrollably, he passed in what seemed like a slow-motion transit over the Fremonts' backyard and house, Sumac Street, and, just barely as his descent began, the tops of the trees that bordered Bluegill Pond. He landed in the lake itself with a sickening *thwack,* deposited flat on his rear end in three feet of water. His landing had been further blunted by a two-foot-long catfish and a foot of soft, mucky lake bottom beneath it. Nimwell lost consciousness on impact. When he regained it, he saw a bunch of yelling, funny beings dressed in red helmets and garish yellow coats running toward him. With his ability to think rationally severely impaired, his head throbbing, and his rear end hurting like crazy, Nimwell began to prepare himself for the worst.

Uh-oh, firefighters, he thought groggily. I must have died and gone to hell. But at least they're trying to put out the fire with this big lake here.

Hearing the warning shouts from next door, George and Nan had untangled themselves from the heap created by Nan's fall. They quickly calculated that all the children and Shirelle were away from home. Then, they ran toward the slope leading to Sumac Street, and threw themselves on the ground halfway down the slope. Seconds later came the explosion. It seemed to rip the sky apart, and shook the earth beneath them. George and Nan continued to hug the ground until they heard the emergency vehicle sirens and saw the fire trucks go by on Sumac, then turn onto Payne.

"Safe to look now?" wondered Nan.

"I think so," said George. "There doesn't seem to be any fire. As soon as you feel a blast of hot air, though, hightail it toward the lake." But there was no hot air blast. Unknown to George and Nan, and the rest of the neighborhood, an automatic shutoff valve had staunched the flow of gas to the leak within seconds. There would be no fireball. No one would have to be evacuated.

But there would certainly need to be a cleanup. As George and Nan got up and walked slowly toward the scene of the explosion, they noticed branches down, their trellises ripped in two, with the top halves flopped over and dangling by slender slivers of wood. The climbing roses and clematis had been torn to shreds. There was broken glass everywhere from the house's shattered windows. Two of their bird feeders had disappeared. A third one had been hurled onto the top of the gutter. Ten yards of the fence separating their yard from the Grunions' no longer existed. Its planks were strewn everywhere. One was even lodged in the crown of a white pine back in the woods. Then, suddenly, it wasn't; knocked loose by a gust of wind, it fell from its perch to another resting place, wedged between the branches of a mulberry tree.

The smoking hole, which was now swarming with workers and emergency personnel, wasn't all that impressive. In fact, it didn't appear to be any bigger than the hole they were already digging. But the wall on the west-facing side of the Grunion house was no more, giving them an unprecedented view into the interior. George and Nan were amazed that the house was still standing at all. Perhaps the most amazing sight was their new flower bed, or, rather, what it had sprouted. Sitting on top of the bed, upright, and looking none the worse for the wear was the backhoe, which they calculated had been moved forty-plus feet from its original position.

"Damn!" said George. "It looks like someone just parked it there."

"Thank goodness we were the only ones here," Nan said. "Oh, please God, see that no one got killed or hurt." A middle-aged man wearing a hard hat, goggles, and emergency gear strode nonchalantly toward them, a two-way radio hidden somewhere on his person squawking away.

"You two folks the homeowners?" he said.

"Of this house," George said. "Not that one."

"Well, we were lucky this time," the man said. "The house next door was unoccupied. Early indications are that no one anywhere else got seriously hurt, even some guy who got blown all the way into the lake."

"Whoa!" went George and Nan.

"The water and mud saved him. And the catfish he landed on. The catfish got flattened, though. Ha-ha!"

"Who was it?" wondered Nan.

"Not really at liberty to tell you that, ma'am."

"I bet it was one of those Scroggit brothers, George," said Nan. "The stupid, timid one that scared the bejesus out of me when I climbed up on your shoulders for a peek. He was wearing a disguise."

The man from the fire department smiled indulgently.

"Apart from the house next door being pretty much destroyed, there's a heck of a lot of minor damage," he said. "But a pretty small explosion as these things go, really. There's no evacuation, so you folks are free to stay and get to your cleanup work. Someone'll be coming by to ask you some questions." The man followed their gaze toward the backhoe.

"Ah-ha, the culprit," he said. "Funny how these explosions work. They're like tornadoes. You never know. I mean, for cryin' out loud, looks like you folks just had superficial damage. Windows and the like. Well, we're probably going to be making a little bit of a mess over the next few days, repairing that line. I'll leave you alone now. You're probably going to be wanting to call your insurance carrier, and, I'm thinking, maybe a lawyer, too."

The man walked back toward the site of the explosion, stopping briefly for a close-up look at the backhoe.

"George," said Nan, her voice sounding tiny and brittle. "We do still have our homeowner's insurance, don't we? Please say yes, George."

"Yes," said George. "Made the payment a couple of weeks ago. Phew! And you know what I'm thinking, Nan-bee. Just like the man said, it might be time to get ourselves a lawyer. I'm sick and tired of having to put up with all this bullshit."

24

Status Report

The crews came quickly. They finished their repairs to the house and cleaned up the debris in a couple of days. The backhoe had been driven off under its own power, much to the Fremonts' amazement. The garden plot onto which the explosion had so neatly deposited it had miraculously survived. So perfectly had the backhoe landed that only those few flowers directly under the wheels and bucket had been smushed. A few more were run over when it was driven off. But, amazingly, none of those flowers had been pulverized or even mortally damaged. All sprang back to vertical life within two days.

"I can't believe it," said Nan. "All the hurt flowers have bounced back. We won't have to replace a single one."

"It's the magic of the Fremont gardens," George said. "Subjected to devastation no other garden could withstand, they bounce back even better than before."

Jerry built and painted new trellises for them, and, though a number of rose and clematis blooms had been severed from their canes and vines, the canes and vines themselves were back in business and thriving again within the week.

The rest of the Fremont backyard gardens survived the explosion virtually intact. Nan figured it was because the modest shock wave from the explosion was either mostly directed to-ward the house next door or passed over everything close to the ground. George wondered whether something else might have helped them, and hinted strongly at supernatural influences.

"Will you knock it off with that," Nan chided. "Everything has a scientific explanation, unless, of course, the hand of God is involved here."

"I wasn't counting out the Big Guy," George said. "I'm just trying to be open-minded about it."

What was certain was that the Fremont gardens, front and back, were going great guns. This was a summer when the weather was at its nurturing best. Hot spells gave way to cool ones with regularity, and the well-timed rains came gently, steadily, and plentifully.

This was when the backyard's monarda, daylilies, Asiatic lilies, purple coneflowers, and balloon flowers were in all their glory, with the black-eyed Susans just starting to brighten the color schemes up with their luminescent yellow petals and black eyes. The blue hydrangea had erupted in the most vivid deep blue they had ever seen or would have ever thought existed.

In the front yard, Mary and Shirelle were doing ye-owomen's work, but this was the easy part; it was mainly maintenance mode at this point, and not even that much of that, the weather having cooperated so wonderfully.

With that in mind, Shirelle had found a job at Burdick's, where she worked part-time to allow her a couple of days reserved exclusively for the Fremonts. Mary, having gotten the word from Nan that, sorry, her parents would foot the bill for only one semester of college, was working at one of Livia's three smaller nurseries, the Root and Stem. That was a full-time job, but it was the day shift, meaning there was plenty of time left for gardening when she got home from work.

Everything they planted two months earlier had flourished or was flourishing.

The big wave of lavender Walker's Low catmint blooms had come and gone, giving way to lesser and more sporadic displays. Shirelle had lately been using her Fremont time to deadhead the spent blooms, hoping against the odds for a big comeback in August.

On the catmint's northern and southern flanks, the Happy Returns and Rosy Returns daylilies were just now hitting their stride. They were throwing out short-lived flowers daily, and it was Mary's job to deadhead those during her free time in the evening and on weekends. More muted than the catmint and brilliant yellow Happy Returns, the Rosy Returns featured curled-back, frilled-edged petals that were a bronzed pink, funneling down to a vivid yellow-green deep inside the throat of the bloom.

Providing some further edging were the delphinium. They looked like miniature spires or even church steeples of densely packed purple, pink, and white flowers, and were blooming like crazy. They were finicky, though, needing mulch at their base, and had water needs that even the summer's regular rainfall couldn't quite satisfy. Shirelle felt the delphinium gave the front yard crucial narrow and vertical accents.

Waving in the slightest breeze were the clumps of ornamental grasses, which had grown to two-to-three-feet tall. Shirelle had planted just the right amount to break up the riotous colors and provide a more natural-looking contrast. She was glad to see that the Karl Foerster and prairie dropseed were quite enough, and that her change of heart about planting more varieties had saved the gardens from ornamental grass overkill.

How would it be possible to describe the hybrid teas!

Like Crater Lake, or the first swirl of Sagelands '07 merlot on the palate, they beggared description. Crowning the front yard's ridge, their luscious, curling petals and vibrant illuminating colors, one hue giving way to another from the tip of each petal to its base, gave them a three-dimensional luster that none of their other flowers could match. Certainly they were arrogant, thought Nan. But the other flowers didn't seem to mind, and who was she to question the presence of that essence of prima donna in something that could so readily flaunt its perfection.

Her own favorites, which she was careful not to show, were the four Full Sails, which looked to her like a cross between whole-bean vanilla ice cream and an untouched tub of margarine, and had a scent that was stronger than honeysuckle.

Shirelle had cast her usual concerns about overly gaudy color combinations aside when planning for the hybrid teas. She had added a couple of pink Tiffanys to a mix that already included the Full Sails, Blue Girls, Chrysler Imperials, and Bronze Stars.

Shirelle and Mary had also supervised the planting of two paper birches to fill up the bare space at the corner of the lot. They had them sunk into the turf behind the Burdick's sign, which in response to their entreaties, the Burdick's folks had consented to let stand through mid-August; and had decorated the site with a few boulders delivered by Burdick's and set in place precisely to Shirelle's specifications. They then added golden-brown cypress mulch, which they were continually freshening, and plenty of petunias to brighten up the base.

The paper birches bore careful watching and constant care, as prone to disease and sensitive to scorching sun as they were.

Anyone with an hour or two to spend looking at flowers would have spotted a ruby-throated hummingbird hovering around the daylilies and delphinium, and the two hummingbird feeders dangling from shepherd's crook rods. Even the most casual observers would have noticed levitating honeybees everywhere. Shirelle told Nan and Mary that you could even pet honeybees when they were slurping their nectar, so intent were they on their task. She had demonstrated with a honeybee gorging itself on monarda nectar.

"Try it yourself," she said. "It won't sting you." Both Mary and Nan had giggled and declined.

"Some other time," said Nan. "After I've had my two glasses of wine."

For the most part, the butterflies hadn't arrived yet, though they had all noted a few orange-and-black monarchs in the vanguard of the migration that made them eternal travelers. They would always be on the lookout for red admirals, which had swarmed around the gardens four years earlier in late August through mid-September. They had watched, fascinated, as those butterflies would rest in the direct sunlight, soaking up the diminishing solar energy that strengthened their orange-banded and white-splotched brown-and-black wings and powered their flight.

"Why do they call it a red admiral, when the closest color to red on it is orange?" wondered Mary. Shirelle shrugged.

"It was probably the same idiot who named the red-bellied woodpecker," she said. "I defy you to find more than a tiny bit of red on those belly feathers. On the head yes, but the red-*headed* woodpecker name was already taken."

Whatever it was that contributed to that influx of red admirals had apparently not happened again; they had not returned.

As for the Burdick's sign, it was still attracting interest, though that had dropped off considerably since most of the people within a two-mile radius had already seen it and had no need of further study.

Still, the front yard had become an amazing quilt of color, which took on a wondrous waving effect when the breeze moved through the flowers. It was common for motorists driving along Sumac Street to slow down and even stop right there in the middle of the road to gawk. Same with pedestrians strolling along the sidewalk on the other side of Sumac. They'd start with the lake, especially if its mating pair of bald eagles were circling overhead, or its great blue herons wading across its reedy shallows, looking for bluegills or frogs to spear for lunch, then turn to take in the wonders of Fremontland.

Isn't there some way we could charge all those people whose lives we've enriched so much? thought George, being only partly facetious.

"Well, at least it's better than those gawkers who showed up after the gas line explosion," he said to Nan, as two elderly couples crossed the street to get a close-up look at the daylilies.

"That's exactly the way to look at it, dear," said Nan, allowing George to fill her wineglass to midway up the snowy pattern of trees etched into its bulging center. "They are stopping to appreciate beauty, not mayhem."

25

The Black Art of Gardening

Dr. Phyllis Sproot gazed out on what any properly trained gardener in her right mind would deem a nirvana of gardens right here on earth. Spectacular, wasn't it? So well ordered and perfectly in synch with the canons of gardening, as amended and augmented by herself. Perfect little rectangular, oval, and half-circle plots covered most of her one-acre lot. From them rose legions of flowers—mostly comprising the coreopsis-salvia-hollyhock blend, which Dr. Sproot herself had pioneered in Livia, and even in the rest of the world for all she knew.

Here and there were some other flowers and plants. Yucca, for instance, played a strong supporting role.

Dr. Sproot's careful calculations showed that her gardens were 87-percent coreopsis-salvia-hollyhock blend and yuccas, the precise proportion, she had concluded, needed to create nirvana on earth. The remaining 13 percent, of course, were reserved for her token roses and dahlias. There was no need of any others.

Dr. Sproot snorted. What a joke those geraniums and spikes had been! She chortled at the thought of the Rose Maidens scurrying for the gate, their dignity in tatters, as she pep-

pered them with BBs. And, now, she was back on track to becoming the preeminent gardener in Livia.

But there was a rather large bump in that track that needed
smoothing out. And a rather large score that could be settled
in the smoothing-out process. Dr. Sproot laughed, lifted up her
hands, and turned them over to study her trembling fingertips.
Trembling with terrible power! Little had she known that it
was through these slender, insignificant extremities that she
could create so much mischief.

A tingling shot through her hands and settled in those magic
fingertips, causing them to spasmodically flutter as if they had a
life of their own. Reload, thought Dr. Sproot. Reload with the
power of pests long gone. Pests eaten by birds and snakes and
frogs. Pests asphyxiated by pesticides, squished under the soles
of shoes, flicked off leaves, and ravaged by those terrible and
mercenary allies of man: praying mantises and ladybugs. Power
such as this had to be channeled. Unfettered, it could lead to
her laying waste to her own gardens. Even now, something was
lifting her hands and pointing them at the nearest bed of coreopsis-salvia-hollyhock blend. Her arms stretched out, straight
as ramrods, and she felt the discharge, a sort of tickling sensation that shot out of her fingers with a pop, them left them
limp and useless, unable to grasp anything or even move until
the lifeblood surged back into them.

Dr. Sproot shuddered and leaned over to look at the flowers she had, theoretically, just zapped. Nothing. What kind of
quackery is this? thought Dr. Sproot. She waited. Minutes
passed. A half hour. Then, an hour and still nothing. That particular stand of coreopsis-salvia-hollyhock looked no different
from the way it had before she had cast her alleged little
"fingerspell," as that charlatan of a gardening witch, Edith
Merton, had called it.

Dr. Sproot frowned and wondered if she was being had by

Edith. She looked at her fingers and scowled. Nothing there to indicate that the reincarnated souls of thousands of slugs, snails, aphids, cutworms, and Japanese beetles had just passed through her electrically charged extremities.

Maybe it's just a touch of arthritis, thought Dr. Sproot forlornly. She waited some more. It's a delayed reaction spell, she thought hopefully. Spells take time, after all, don't they? When Edith had cast that spell on her yard, and then on the Fremonts,' that had taken a day in her case, and, what, almost a week, for that hailstorm to lay waste to the Fremonts' yard? Even Dr. Sproot shivered at the prospect of someone having such evil powers at her beck and call. Especially when it was someone else.

She looked down at her allegedly zapped flowers, which appeared to be none the worse for wear, and suddenly felt silly. The whole thing was a hoax. Even what had happened last year could probably be explained. Some quick-acting blight had afflicted her garden and the gardens of the Rose Maidens. It had nothing to do with Edith and her little retribution spells. As for the storm, hey, weather during a thunderstorm could be very localized in these parts. That, of course, didn't explain how the Fremonts' gardens had then sprung back to life. In mid-August, no less! Dr. Sproot was still trying to work that one out.

Her fingertips tingled again with energy. Only this time, it felt more like pain. Arthritis, for sure, Dr. Sproot thought. And pretty bad. It was the worst health news a gardener in her prime could possibly get. Arthritis meant no more grasping of shovels, rakes, and hand tools. It meant even prying a seedling out of its little plastic housing would now be a chore. Bending over to plant something? Forget it. It was only a matter of time before her knees got calcified. She tried a couple of deep knee bends and thought she could feel old muscles and ligaments stretched to the breaking point and dried-up bones grinding against one another. Only a matter of time, and then what would she do?

One thing she knew for sure she would do was to teach that Edith Merton a lesson she would not soon forget. Gardening witch, indeed!

It had been a week ago that she had rendezvoused with Edith at the Hi-Lo Doughnut Shoppe, her favorite stop for cream-filled Bismarcks and unlimited coffee refills. At first, when Dr. Sproot had called her to suggest such a meeting, Edith had demurred. Actually, that was putting it mildly. Edith had wondered aloud how Dr. Sproot could possibly work up the nerve to ever speak to her again, and had hung up on her in mid-sentence. So much for diplomacy. More extreme measures would obviously be called for here. The next step involved something that Dr. Sproot excelled at—*threats!*

Lately, business had been tough for Edith and her husband, Felix, who owned Mertons' Liquors and Mertons' TV and Appliance Mart. Livians were spending less on booze, and running their washing machines and refrigerators longer before replacing them. There was also the fact that Edith's sideline business—running séances for youngsters who had lost their hamsters, guinea pigs, goldfish, parakeets, and other smallish pets and wanted to commune with them—had also hit the skids. Livia's parents were cutting back on Christmas and birthday gifts. They had also been counseled by their pastors, who had heard disquieting rumors about this resurgence of paganism in Livia, that communing with dead organisms, even if it was all in fun, was not in the best interest of their spiritual lives.

All this had come to Dr. Sproot's attention. That was mainly through a network of shirttail relatives who operated two of the leading lending and mortgage institutions in Livia and did clerical work at one of the Lutheran Church synod offices in downtown St. Anthony, and usually in return for some gardening consultation work.

It was through this network that Dr. Sproot discovered that Edith and Felix Merton had fallen behind in their business loans, and were in debt up to their eyeballs. That seemed to her to present itself as an excellent investment opportunity. Dr. Sproot's lawsuit judgment against Earlene McGillicuddy and her $1-million life insurance benefit, awarded to her on the death of her cross-dressing drunkard of a husband, Mort, had in the past year alone ballooned to three times its original amount due to some highly lucrative and somewhat shady investments. And all that money was just itching to be put to work in some new ventures.

Dr. Sproot's lender relatives, not really all that excited about the prospects of foreclosing on the Mertons' appliance and liquor stores, were happy to sell her the loans at a premium price.

The next time Dr. Sproot called, she was able to make Edith an offer she couldn't refuse.

"Hi, Edith," she told the answering machine at the hardware store. "Dr. Sproot here. I suggest you reconsider my earlier proposal for a get-together, or maybe you didn't hear it since you so rudely cut me off in mid-sentence. Well, the proposal still stands, so why don't you call back and we can make arrangements for a little tête-à-tête."

The answering machine cut off with a beep. Furious, Dr. Sproot called back, her voice now quaking with rage.

"Dr. Sproot again, dearie," she continued. "There's something else you might be interested to know. I am now the official owner of both Mertons' Liquors and Mertons' TV and Appliance Mart, having bought the loans. Jeez, those were risky loans! I never realized you were such a poor candidate for business loans, Edith. Why, I would have charged you fifty-percent interest, minimum. Why would I have ever wanted to take them on? Call back to find out why. Ta-ta."

The meeting with Edith at the Hi-Lo was everything Dr. Sproot could have hoped for. Edith positively oozed politeness and a desire to please. Dr. Sproot acted the part of the magnanimous landlady, assuring the scared-stiff Edith that, no, she had no desire to foreclose on their properties as long as she was certain she and Felix were making good-faith efforts to meet their loan obligations.

"Yes, Edith, times are tough, I know," said Dr. Sproot as she scarfed down her third Bismarck and inhaled her fourth cup of dark-roast Hi-Lo brew. "And I want to assure you that it is my mission in life to support our struggling small businesses."

Edith was fairly panting with joy and gratitude.

"You and Felix are pillars of the community," Dr. Sproot said sententiously. "Without you, commerce crumbles into dust. I'm here for you, Edith. Consider me to be your lending source of strength and resilience. Lean on me, Edith. Rest assured I don't want to throw you out on the street."

Edith was now positively giddy. She reached across the table to grasp Dr. Sproot's hand, now sticky with Bismarck residue, and shook it violently.

"Thank you so much," said Edith, her voice shaking with unanticipated relief. "I never could have imagined in my wildest dreams that you'd be calling me here to tell me that. My goodness, that's wonderful news. You have no idea what Felix and I have been going through, trying to pay these loans and working these things out. Those lenders, Dr. Sproot, they have no heart, no heart at all!"

Dr. Sproot looked at the cringingly humbled Edith and smiled. Here, under her thumb like a helpless, semi-microscopic bug about to be squashed into nothingness, sat the author of so many of her woes. And the nerve of her, acting as if nothing untoward had ever happened between them!

It was last year, after that horrible, stormy night in July, when Edith had fingered Dr. Sproot as the ringleader of the aborted garden sabotage mission targeting the Fremonts' backyard. Then, she had claimed that Dr. Sproot had black-mailed her into helping because of an affair she had with Mort. And then came that article in the St. Anthony *Inquirer*! Why, it had humiliated Dr. Sproot beyond all reckoning.

"Yes, well, so glad to help, Edith. But you do realize that, as a businesswoman, I expect a return on my investment at some point? I'm not just doing this out of the goodness of my heart."

"Ye-e-e-s-s-s," said Edith, stuttering. "I do realize that. Felix and I are doing the best we can. But, but . . . ah . . . you know, times are tough and business has dropped off. It's going to be hard to make these next few payments."

Dr. Sproot stared at Edith and let a long pause crumple her into a trembling mass of insignificance. Putty in her hands.

"You know what they say, Edith: Adapt or die. You haven't adapted very well. Either make your payments or I will shut you down! You're behind four months' worth of payments on one business, and six months—*six months!*—on the other! How did they let you go this long being a deadbeat? Huh?"

"But you said . . ."

"I said I didn't *want* to foreclose on you, or something to that effect. But you know, Edith, sometimes you're forced to do things you'd rather not. That's the story of life, isn't it?"

Dr. Sproot could see the furiously twitching lips and the eyes filming over, then pooling, with tears. The first one trickled out over Edith's eyelid and streaked slowly down her cheek.

"Oh, please! Please don't foreclose on us! We'll do better! I'm sure we will. Just give us another chance. We'll . . ." Edith's sobs were choking off her words. Dr. Sproot held up her hand to signal Edith to stop all this caterwauling nonsense. She smiled in a gentle way meant to look consoling.

"Stop that crying, Edith. Stop it right now. I think I have a solution to your problem. At least a temporary solution."

Edith dabbed at her eyes with a Kleenex.

"What?" she said. "What can we do?"

"I need to learn some witchcraft. And I want you to teach me."

Edith jerked away from Dr. Sproot. "What!"

"You heard me. Teach me some of your black arts! I've got some unfinished business to take care of, and I need some help from down below."

Edith slouched over the table and cast darting and stealthy glances around the doughnut shop to make sure no one was within hearing range. Then, she leaned over toward Dr. Sproot.

"I can't do that!" she whispered hoarsely. "I gave that up after last year's fiasco. I even threw away my own dead mother's old-fogey spell-casting outfit. I've sworn to never practice witch-craft again."

"*You* wouldn't have to practice it. You'd just pass along a few pointers to me, and I'd do the rest. Then, I'd be willing to put off your payments for a few more months, with late-payment interest accruing, of course."

"But, Dr. Sproot, *please!* I only do my small pet séances now, and that's harmless. To go back to evil plant spells, I just couldn't. Marta's right; it's immoral."

Dr. Sproot cackled. Immediately, despite her reservations, the professional necromancer in Edith saw talent and potential in Dr. Sproot as a witch.

"Don't pay any attention to what Little-Miss-Goody-Two-Shoes says," Dr. Sproot said. "She betrayed me and you. It was in part because of her that our mission failed last year, putting us both in the position we're in now."

"What if I get caught?"

"Are you kidding? Nobody believes in witches. That's how you got off the hook last year, putting all the blame on me, didn't you, you Judas Iscariot, you? Everyone thought I was bonkers when I tried to tell them the truth about you. You sold me down the river, and got off scot-free. Yes, you owe me big-time, Sarah the Witch. Ha-ha!"

Edith whimpered.

"Whaddaya say, Edith? Or should I say *debtor?* Make up your mind now. I'm already thinking of what I'm going to rename my new appliance and liquor stores. Ha-ha! Ha-ha! How about Eye-of-Newt Appliances? Or Magic Wand Liquors? Ha-ha! Ha-ha!"

"Please, Dr. Sproot," Edith moaned. "Please show us some mercy."

Dr. Sproot glugged down the dregs of her fifth cup of coffee and fixed Edith with a cold, hard stare.

"I *am* showing you mercy, Edith. I could foreclose on you right now. Today, in fact. I've given you an out. What's more, it's an out that allows you to stick to your pledge. And, remember this, Edith Merton: I know you've still got the power to take down my gardens. So, now, I've got something to hang over your head, don't I? If I see so much as one little burned tip on my yucca, or a single drooping hollyhock, your businesses are toast. You get me?"

"Okay," said Edith with an exasperated sigh. "When do we begin? I'm picking up a bad vibe from you. A very bad vibe. That's good for what you're planning. I think you're going to be a natural."

"No time like the present," said Dr. Sproot. "Witchcraft 101. Ha-ha! Ha-ha!"

Over the next two weeks, they had met at Dr. Sproot's house, on her deck. The training—which Edith devised on the fly since she'd never been to a witch college or even taken a correspondence course—was intense, but Dr. Sproot was so obviously born to it. Her soul was so dark and malevolent that it created a powerful magnetism for the forces of evil. These weren't *human* forces of evil. That would have been far beyond the ken of Edith, and was reserved for those witches who made what Edith was doing look like a preschool exercise. But, Edith figured, Dr. Sproot had it well within her power to do a bit of localized weather tampering or call forth a plague of something rather minor league, such as that old standby, the plant wilt.

"Tempting, but not dramatic enough," said Dr. Sproot. "Give me something that will truly bring those wretched Fremonts to their knees in frustration. Something big! A calling card with my special signature!"

"Well," said Edith. "I can't do invading armies, or convicted felons with blowtorches. Can't do stampeding elephants or rhinoceroses. Hmmm. Hail and lightning are the best I can do on the weather front."

"You already did that," Dr. Sproot said. "And that doesn't make it explicitly clear that an evil force is at work. Like I said, give me something I can put my special stamp on. My little 'Dr. Sproot-the-Witch-Was-Here' memento."

The two women thought for a few moments.

"I know!" said Dr. Sproot, jumping up from her chair. "Pests! Gross pests that will make a gardener's skin crawl. Slugs, snails, aphids, that kind of thing."

Edith thought for a moment, then nodded.

"Yes, I believe that's possible. You couldn't call forth millions of them, but thousands, maybe even tens of thousands. Yes, you could do that."

It had not been hard to get Dr. Sproot locked in on visions of plant-destroying insects. Having fought them for the better part of her adult life, she could see them up close in her mind.

The electrical circuitry of Dr. Sproot's brain was easily directed toward evil and destruction, Edith discovered. It was only a matter of putting out the call for matter that was dead and gone and to direct it to the intended target.

"Think of bugs that have died violently," Edith instructed her. "Slugs squashed. Aphids gobbled up by ladybugs. Japanese beetles dying slowly after a drenching of bug spray. These are the ones to be summoned back."

One look at Dr. Sproot's spindly, twitching fingers told her that here was the medium.

"This is how you transmit the evil electrical impulses fouling up your mind," said an impressed Edith as she held Dr. Sproot's hand and studied her gnarled fingers. "These look like the shriveled-up twigs on a dying tree. Just what you want. Now, go and call forth the multitudes. Just leave me out of it, okay?"

So, here was Dr. Sproot attempting her first spell, and nothing seemed to be happening. She pointed and fluttered, and pointed and fluttered again. *Nada.* That quack, fumed Dr. Sproot! I'll show her! First thing tomorrow morning it's off to my attorney to start foreclosure proceedings.

The next morning, she followed her usual schedule: downing three mugs of coffee while it was still dark outside, and, once the dawn was advanced enough to provide sufficient light, doing her initial rounds of the gardens.

But what was this! Gazing down from where she was perched at the deck railing, Dr. Sproot instantly noticed that something was amiss. It was in the closest bed of coreopsis-salvia-hollyhock blend. The flowers were twitching. Odd, thought Dr. Sproot, there's not even a whisper of a breeze this morning. And what was there about the color? All the flowers looked so different. Dr. Sproot squinted. My God, they're crawling with insects; the flowers are alive with them!

Her first impulse was to run for the bug spray and douse

the little shits with streams of lethal insecticide. Just as she turned to head inside for the garden products pantry, she stopped and turned to look back at the plants. Then, she looked at her fingers, puffy and twitching with power. It felt as if a surge of blood had just fattened them.

Dr. Sproot laughed. She lifted her arms, and pointed her fingers out and up toward the sky. Then, she thought incredibly evil thoughts, and wiggled them. Halfway expecting lightning bolts to shoot out of her fingertips toward the little cumulus cloud that was chugging away overhead, she was disappointed to see that nothing was happening. Ah, well, she thought, my powers are limited. But just strong enough to do the job at hand.

"It's time to show those Fremonts who's boss in this burg!" she shouted at the thousands of insects that were in the final stages of laying waste to her bed of coreopsis, salvia, and hollyhock. "Destroy! Destroy! Destroy! Ha-ha! Ha-ha!"

26

Fairy Tales

Marta Poppendauber was cutting some brown-and-orange tiger lilies to be placed in a vase on her dining table when she sensed something strange. It was if all plant suspiration had stopped. Not gradually. Suddenly.

Is this some kind of weird dormancy? she wondered. Then came a disturbance she could readily recognize: the sound of footsteps treading the redbrick pathway that threaded its way through her gardens. And here came her visitor, stepping briskly from behind the spirea bushes. Why, it was Edith Merton! Marta dropped her hand clippers clattering onto the brick walkway. What could Edith Merton possibly want of me? she thought. I really don't want anything to do with her.

Edith approached Marta meekly, but out of breath and obviously in a panic about something.

"Why, Edith, so interesting to see you! Is there something I can do for you?"

"Marta, please help! Please!"

Marta was dumbfounded. What could she possibly do to help a gardening witch?

"Calm down, please, Edith. What's happened?"

"Dr. Sproot's on the warpath again!"

Edith paused, heaving for breath. She had run all the way from her home three blocks away, Felix and their son, Merlin, having taken the family cars to a convenience store and beer bong contest, respectively. "Fremonts. She's going to wreck the Fremonts again. I had to teach her. No choice."

Marta frowned.

"This *does* sound desperate. Well, come inside, Edith, and we'll have some tea, and you can tell me all about it. No sense in running around half-cocked."

It was a clear night illuminated by a full moon. That, Dr. Sproot had been lead to believe, wasn't the best time for casting spells. It had something to do with spirits not favoring placid conditions and being more apt to awaken when the weather was really crappy. And, in fact, the weather forecast had called for a 60-percent chance of thunderstorms, the best such opportunity for a week.

Dr. Sproot fumed about the blown forecast. If it messed up her spells she'd sue, that's what she'd do.

But at least I can see what I'm doing, she figured, which is a pretty good trade-off. So, here she was in the wee hours, mucking around the Fremonts' property and preparing to wreak havoc among their gardens. Just like old times.

There were some welcome differences between this time and that night last July. For one thing, there was no torrential downpour. For another, she wasn't carrying sharp-edged tools, or wearing a gas mask to protect herself from the hallucinogenic fumes of the angel's trumpets, which, this time, would be far enough away from her field of endeavor to pose little danger. For yet another, she was starting in the front yard. The fact that she was working the front yard this year posed more of a risk, as she would be visible, albeit as a shadowy form, to anyone driving by on Sumac. It was a risk she was willing to take. Besides, she would be mostly hunched over, keeping close to the ground, for the task at hand.

This job should be over quickly. Point and shoot was pretty much all there was to it. And think really bad, insect-pest-infested thoughts. It only took her forty-five minutes to cover the front yard; now to the back.

What's this? There were some new beds over there next to the woods. She walked over and zapped them. The arbor birches and crab apples? Too strong for her spells, she figured. She zapped them anyway. There, over next to the fence, were the perilous angel's trumpets. Holding her nose, she shot them a long-distance spell with only one hand, then scurried out of range to work her mayhem on the rest of the Fremont gardens.

But what in the name of Lucifer's lighter was this? A blue glow emanated from somewhere in the center of the yard. It came from the base of the ash tree that dominated the otherwise open area of flower beds and lawn. The light wavered, then steadied. Its flickering cast eerie shadows against the fence, the lilac bushes, and the variegated dogwoods. Dr. Sproot suddenly realized that the glow was coming from the fairy house. And what was that? Tiny squeaks. Little mouse-scurrying sounds.

"My God," Dr. Sproot whispered. "It's the fairies. There are actually fairies in the fairy house. What are they doing there? They're plotting against me. They mean to do me harm."

Dr. Sproot listened harder. They weren't speaking English, that was for sure. They were talking so fast. What was *that?* Other voices. These were coming from behind her. Before long, they were coming from everywhere, hundreds of unrecognizable voices that were actually more like murmurings and hissings than talking. What were they saying? She jumped. What was that wriggling around, tickling her toes? She looked down. The purple bloom of a clematis stared up at her and smiled in an anthropomorphic way. It had a nose. It had teeth. It had eyes. It had . . . a mustache?

Rapidly, the clematis spiraled around her bare legs, constricting her like a python wrapping itself around a feral pig. Dr. Sproot screamed, wondering if her scream would carry above the voices. She aimed her fingers at the monster flower, but felt no energy in them. Her powers seemed drained. The clematis understood. It grinned up at her. Then, she ran, yanking the constricting clematis out by its horrible roots. Not seeing the split-rail fence until it was too late, she slammed into it, causing her to fold up at the midriff, then somersault over, landing on her back. It knocked the wind out of her.

What was that hissing? Looking up and over to the right, she beheld her worst nightmare: An angel's trumpet had pushed its white, trumpet-like bloom to within four inches of her face and was exhaling a mist directly at her. The little droplets coated her cheeks and forehead. Close your eyes, thought Dr. Sproot, lying there, aching, and feeling the still-living clematis tighten its hold on her leg. She held her breath to keep the brain-scrambling exhalations of the angel's trumpets from entering her lungs and causing her to hallucinate. She thought that and keeping her eyes closed should keep the poisons at bay; they wouldn't be able to get into her nervous system through the pores of her skin.

Suddenly, the clematis began to move again. It was past her knee, working its way up her leg and toward her shorts. She lifted her head to see it leering at her. Dr. Sproot screamed and scrambled to her feet. She sat up, grabbed the clematis, and clasped it hard at the closest bloom's throat until it drooped and its lolling tongue stuck out of its very reasonable facsimile of a human mouth. The angel's trumpet was still there, hissing at her like a coiled snake. The mist had by now worked its way into the membrane of her eyes. In a gasp for air, she had inhaled it, too. It was only a matter of time before she'd go hop-scotching through psychedelic fruitcake land. What was that? Next to the fairy house, which was still emanating its blue light, a great hulking mass of green trundled down the steps and into the Fremonts' driveway.

"Human sod!" Dr. Sproot moaned. "A giant chunk of human sod! Oh, my God!" Fighting hard against the addling process that was turning her brain into a mush of non-existent colors and Strawberry Alarm Clock songs, Dr. Sproot forced her aching body into a jog toward the woods. Branches and twigs swatted at her and scratched her limbs. She tripped over a root and got a mouthful of forest clutter that began moving and talking inside her mouth.

"Blaaaght!" went Dr. Sproot, spitting out the leaves, and moss, and twigs that then scurried away, chattering.

Using every ounce of strength that remained in her, she pulled herself up, and banged her head against an overhanging branch. She stumbled on, moaning and crying, for what seemed like an hour before finally emerging into the open, and onto the Fletchers' driveway. There were steps under her feet now. If she could only climb she could work her way into thinning air, which would clear her head, wouldn't it? Climb. Climb. Climb.

More flowers were talking to her. Where did they come from? They were urgent, pulling and pushing her. They were assaulting her! She punched at them, pulled them, and reached with both hands to throttle them into unconsciousness. Then, something acrid and horrible splashed into her face and she found herself clawing at it, then clawing at her face to get the horrible liquid off. It was tearing at her eyes. Blinding her.

When she woke up the plants were gone. They weren't babbling at her anymore. But her eyes stung like hell. She was strapped to something and being rolled somewhere. Then, she was inside a warm, restful place that was moving. It felt like a womb. Comforting. And, most important, there were no flowers bent on exploring her private parts. But her eyes . . .

Marta and Edith brushed off the green blanket they had used to camouflage themselves, rolled it up, and threw it in the backseat of Marta's car. They were tittering like a couple of teenagers.

"You make an excellent fairy, Edith," Marta whispered. "Better than a witch."

"I'd give anything to have been able to record that scene," Edith whispered back. "I just hope Dr. Sproot's all right."

"Don't waste your sympathy on her, Edith. She got a little shock to her system, that's all. One thing's for sure—the Fremonts probably won't have to worry about her bothering them again."

"I wouldn't be so sure," Edith said. "The bile in her is strong and resilient. And I'm afraid we didn't catch her in time to stop most of her spells. I wouldn't count her out of the picture by any means."

"Hmmmm," said Marta. "Well, I dropped them a little warning note on the patio. And you think your spell can counteract hers?"

"Yes, but it might have a delayed effect. I tried to stop hers first. Then, in case the stop-spell doesn't work, I tried another. But since this was a rush job, and I had to do it from the street while she was still working the front yard, I'm not sure how effective it'll be. I didn't get to do my little twirling thing, too, where I turn to face all directions of the compass. To say nothing of the weather not cooperating."

Marta shrugged, then stiffened and cocked her ear; she thought she could hear the distant squeal of hinges.

"Well, look at it this way," she said. "The good weather made it a lot easier to get up to the fairy house and light that candle. Though how we managed to get up there without Dr. Sproot hearing us I'll never know. Too absorbed in her spell casting, I guess. And this job was one heck of a lot less miserable than last year's."

"No lie," Edith said. "That gives me the shivers just thinking about it."

Over at the Fremonts', through the network of their flowers, vines, and shrubs, they could see the white points of the motion-detector lights illuminating the patio. Then, a form emerged, carrying what looked like a tapered and remarkably smooth branch.

"George Fremont," whispered Marta as she and Edith crouched close to the car. "With his baseball bat. If Dr. Sproot comes back, she's going to get whacked." Edith shuddered with suppressed laughter.

"So what was your excuse?" asked Marta.

"Uh . . . ?"

"For being out so late."

"Oh," Edith said. "Out with the girls. At Charlene's house. Really late. Taking along a couple of fifths of vodka from the store supply. Yours?"

"None needed. Ham sleeps like a log."

Sirens sounded in the distance.

"Uh-oh," Marta said. "We'd better make tracks, pronto."

Nan met George as he came through the back door, Smokestack Gaines bat in one hand and a piece of paper in the other.

"What in God's name is going on out there!" she barked. "I guess every loony within a twenty-mile radius feels she can go caterwauling through our backyard at all hours of the morning, eh? Who was it? Did you take her down?"

"It was that idiot Dr. Sproot."

"No surprise there. Back for more fun, eh? No more Mr. and Mrs. Nice Guy for us, George. Our days of turning the other cheek are over. Did you smack her with your bat?"

"No."

"No? Got away from you, eh? What's the point of having a bat if you can't whack somebody with it? What's that you're holding?"

"Found it on the patio."

Nan grabbed it out of George's hands, pulled a handwritten note out of the envelope, and read it.

"It says, 'Dear George and Nan, pay close attention to your flowers. Dr. Phyllis Sproot is up to no good. Hope we can help. Two friends.' What friends, huh? That's what I want to know. Everyone we know who gardens is a certifiable nutcase. Okay, I'm going to go get me a weapon and we're going to go out there and track down Dr. Phyllis Sproot. Once we find her, I'm not responsible for my actions."

"No need for that, Nan-bee."

"Don't try to stop me, George!" said Nan from the kitchen as she studied her cutlery for their attributes in the realm of cutting, thrusting, and stabbing.

"I mean, Dr. Sproot is gone. Apparently, she ran screaming up to the Fletchers' door and Jeri Fletcher gave her a face full of Mace. When I got there, an ambulance and the police were already there. They had Dr. Sproot strapped to a gurney and were rolling her into the ambulance. She was babbling something about fairies."

"George," said Nan, looking out the kitchen window. "What's that blue glow out there?"

"The what?"

"The blue glow. There's a blue light coming out of the fairy house. Isn't that the color fairies are supposed to like? Could you go check that out, please?"

"Uh, maybe if they're fairies, we should leave them alone. I doubt that fairies like people poking around their homes with baseball bats."

"Get out there, George!"

There was the rustle of feet coming down the hallway behind them.

"What's all the racket?" said Mary, with Cullen and Ellis crowding in behind her.

"Oh, nothing, kids. Some wacko went running through the yard, and the police hauled her away. And I guess we've got some fairies partying out there in the fairy house. I'm trying to steel your father to go out there and check them out."

"Fairies?" said Mary. "Sweet!"

"There's no such thing as fairies," said Cullen. "Crisis over. I'm going back to bed."

"Me too," said Ellis. "Hey, Dad, don't go hitting anything with that bat, okay? That thing's gotta be worth a thousand bucks now." Cullen and Ellis slogged back to their bedrooms.

"I'll go with you, Daddy," said Mary. "Let's go introduce ourselves to the fairies. If you can talk to flowers, I bet you can speak fairy language, too." Mary bolted noisily out the door, with George tagging sheepishly behind her.

"Pssst, fairies," Mary whispered as she tiptoed toward the center of the yard. "Hello there, fairies. Can you hear me, fairies?"

"Tell them we mean them no harm," whispered George, also tiptoeing, and trailing a few feet behind her. Mary turned to look at him.

"Daddy!" she said. "Daddy! Better lose the bat. They might think you want to knock their little fairy house out of the park."

"What? Okay, sure." George knelt down slowly and gingerly laid the bat on the ground as Mary arrived at the ash tree and leaned slowly over the fairy house. Then, she started giggling.

"What?" said George.

"It's just a candle, Daddy. Somebody put a blue candle jar inside the fairy house. That's what's causing the blue glow, not fairy stuff. Darn it, I wanted to meet some fairies. Nice job, Dad. You really got me goin' there. Fess up."

"Huh?" said George, who was now standing next to Mary and staring down groggily at the blue candle, which had been placed expertly inside the miniature house. "Whaddya mean, 'nice touch'?"

"The candle. You and Mom put it there, didn't you?"

"I certainly did not. And neither did your mother, as far as I know . . . Yikes!"

"Yikes what?"

"If we didn't put it there, and you didn't put it there, and I'm reasonably sure Cullen and Ellis wouldn't have put it there, then who did?"

"Well, I sure didn't put that candle there," blurted Nan in her normal voice. George and Mary jumped.

"Nan-bee!" said George.

"Mom!" said Mary, pressing her hands over her breastbone and panting for breath. "You just about scared me out of my britches!"

"Good thing I didn't have old Smokestack in my hand," said George. "Otherwise, I would have popped you good. Whack first, ask questions later."

"So," said Mary, "who put the candle there, then? Sheeesh! If it wasn't any of us, maybe it's fairies who put it here. Big honkin' fairies."

"It's probably the same person who left us the warning note on the patio," Nan said.

"What warning note?" asked Mary.

"A note telling us our flowers are in danger."

George, his attention having been drawn to a rectangular

pale object that he could barely see on the ground, leaned over to pick it up.

"Maybe this is a calling card from our fairy friends," he said. "Hey, it's a business card." George moved onto the patio so he could read what was written on it. "It says, 'Small-pet séances. Bring your beloved pet back to life. First consultation free.' Then, there's a phone number. It's signed 'Sarah Twiddle.' Sarah Twiddle?"

"Also known as Sarah the Witch," Nan said. "Remember, George? From last year?"

"Oh, yes, our nefarious gardening witch. Also known in liquor-and-appliance-store circles as Edith Merton. The same Edith Merton who dressed up in her dead mother's clothes and who you almost cut to shreds in the hosta bed."

"With the butcher knife."

"Yeah. Too bad you didn't use it when you had the chance."

All three gazed skyward as if they might catch a glimpse of Sarah the Witch doing loop-de-loops on her broomstick.

"Gardening witch!" Mary cried. "Sweet! Can I meet her? That'd be almost as good as meeting up with a bunch of fairies."

27

Archaeology

A familiar-looking car pulled into the driveway. Following close behind was a red sports car with the top down. Just as they expected, it was Miss Price who got out of the first car. A dapper-looking chap dawdled behind the steering wheel of the red sports car, then got out after Miss Price leaned over to have a few words with him. There was something weird about that car; Nan couldn't quite put her finger on it.

"Hmmm," she said. "Now *that's* a Rolls-Royce, right, George?"

George shook his head in amused disbelief.

"That, Nan-bee, is a vintage Triumph. British sports car. You can tell it's British because the driver's side is where the passenger side is in our American cars. See? That's how the Brits do it."

"Ohhhh. I knew there was something odd about it."

"I'm guessing that's probably Miss Price's lawyer."

Miss Price led the way up the steps, clomping purposefully toward the Fremonts at a pace her companion could barely keep up with. Once on the top step, she waggled a hand in their direction. The Fremonts figured it to be her weird form of greeting, one meant solely as an announcement and to convey no warmth at all.

"Miss Price," said Nan. "What a pleasant surprise. What brings you to this neck of the woods?'

"Pleasant surprise?" Miss Price snapped. "I wouldn't have guessed a visit of mine would be a pleasant surprise in any way after what we've been through."

"You clearly don't recognize sarcasm when you hear it, Miss Price," Nan retorted.

"What *we've* been through, Miss Price?" said George. "How exactly is it you've been inconvenienced? Oh, and while we're at it, our attorney has cautioned us not to say anything to you that might have the slightest connection to our case. We're suing you. Or haven't you heard?"

"So, mum's the word," added Nan with a short, brittle cackle.

"Yes, I got served the other day," said Miss Price. "Incomprehensible. I have no idea what it says. Just for the record, what exactly is it you're suing me for?"

"We're seeking an injunction to keep you off our property once and for all," George said. "And damages for our little explosion."

"Hmmm," said Miss Price. "And what have I done to deserve this?"

"Well, the explosion part is pretty self-evident, isn't it?"

"You can see that we've patched up the fence," Miss Price said. "I've already made arrangements to repair the neighbor house. That takes time, though. It's a big job. Our insurance companies are handling the damages to your house."

"Aha," said Dr. Lick. "I was wondering . . . Gee whiz, the whole side of the house is gone."

"This is a matter between the Fremonts and myself," Miss

Price snapped. "It need be of no concern to you and doesn't affect our current mutual interest."

Dr. Lick smiled meekly, and raised his arms in a sign of resigned agreement.

"There's also your constant poking around in our property," Nan said. "That includes sending that pair of idiots to cut down our tree. They were looking for something."

"Ah. Wonder what that was."

"You know darned well what it was," said George.

"Well, I'm certain we can settle all these issues to everyone's satisfaction. But that's not what I'm here to talk about, I've brought an acquaintance by I want you to meet. This is Dr. Lick. Dr. Ferdinand Lick. The noted archaeologist from the university."

Dr. Lick, who followed the exchange between Miss Price and the Fremonts with some trepidation, quickly shifted to charm-offensive mode. All smiles and dignified yet exuberant body language, he thrust out his hand. Both Nan and George shook it limply. Dr. Lick chuckled at the implied slight.

"Dr. Lick, you have the floor," Miss Price said.

"Just so you know, Dr. Lick, because of your evident involvement with Miss Price here, we might not be able to talk to you," George said.

"I understand," Dr. Lick said. "Let's just give it a try and see what happens. Then, you can cut me off if I'm straying into your legal territory."

"Okay, Doc," said George, who made a big show of looking at his watch. "But keep it short. You're disrupting our cocktail hour."

Dr. Lick cleared his throat and smiled. He has a nice smile, thought Nan. Good-lookin' fella, that's for sure. Maybe we could talk to him after all. Who listens to lawyers anyway? Jeez, they'd tell you never to get out of bed in the morning 'cause you might die deadheading an iris. Screw the stupid lawyer and his efforts to muzzle us.

He's a scoundrel and probably a liar, thought George. Anyone brought here by Miss Price has got to have some kind of con he wants to put over on us. And look at the way he plays to Nan, bless her impressionable little heart.

Clearly, Dr. Lick was poised to make a presentation on a matter of some importance, thought Nan. His hair was thinning, yet impeccably groomed, and his khaki slacks were smartly pressed. His light-pink oxford-cloth shirt made a nice match with a navy-blue JoS. A. Bank sport coat. All in all, pleasantly and professorially casual, tennis-club neat and sharp without forcing it, and without looking too official. Yet, he had obviously gone to the trouble to look good, which so few seemed to do these days. As Nan locked eyes with Dr. Lick and took in his craggy, lightly tanned features, she tried to stop herself from falling in love.

You might think you look nice, thought George, but, guess what? I've got a Jethro Tull 2005 American tour T-shirt with its *Broadsword and the Beast* motif. Beat that, Mr. Professor!

"I understand from Miss Price here that you might have a significant archaeological find beneath your feet. Do you know what I'm talking about?"

"No!" said George, squirming in his chair. Nan dismissed him with a fluttering hand.

"Oh, George is a little upset. We *all* are, after some of the things that have happened over the last couple of weeks." She noticed that Dr. Lick seemed to be admiring her bare legs through the translucent tabletop, and crossed them demurely.

"Please sit down, Dr. Lick," she purred. "And would you like a glass of merlot?"

"By all means," said Dr. Lick brightly as he sat down next to Nan and nodded at George, who frowned at him. "Thank you."

"Oh, and Miss Price, you can sit down, too, if you want to," Nan said perfunctorily.

"I will have a glass of wine, too," she said.

"George," said Nan, motioning toward the bottle. George picked up the bottle of Sagelands, inspected it, and emptied what was left of its contents into his glass.

"Shoot," he said. "All gone. Tough luck for you guys. Maybe you'd like some water straight out of the tap."

"Go get another bottle, please, dear," Nan said. "Make that two bottles, actually." George got up grumpily and disappeared behind the back door.

"I really must compliment you and Mr. Fremont on your wonderful gardens," gushed Dr. Lick. "They are truly exquisite."

"Thank you," Nan said. "We try."

"I'll have to tell my soon-to-be-ex-wife about these and bring her over here once we've settled our situation amicably. If that ever happens. We're not really on speaking terms at this point."

His soon-to-be-ex-wife? Nan felt her pulse quicken.

"You're welcome to bring her by. That is, once you're on good terms with her. Of course, with situations like these, you never know, do you? Is she a gardener?"

Dr. Lick chuckled.

"Very much so," he said. "Being gardeners, you may have even heard of her. She's a professor of floriculture at the university. Hilda Brockheimer. *Dr.* Hilda Brockheimer."

A mouthful of Sagelands spewed out of Nan's mouth as if it were grapeshot fired from a cannon. Luckily, most of it wound up on the tabletop and Miss Price's white ruffled blouse and cinnamon blazer.

"Good grief!" Miss Price shouted as Nan sat there choking violently. "Look what you've done to my blouse and blazer. Damnation!"

Dr. Lick recoiled at the eruption, then, regaining his composure, cast his concerned gaze upon Nan, whose spasm of coughing continued. He reached out a hand, ineffectually, to help.

"Are you all right, Mrs. Fremont?" he said. "Heavens!"

"Of course she's all right!" Miss Price cried. "But I'm all splotched over with red wine. Can't someone get me some wet napkins at least?"

"Sorry," said George, who had reappeared with a bottle of wine and two paper cups. "No damp napkins available. I do have some wine for you, however, Miss Price, and would be glad to pour you a cup. Sorry, we only have Dixie cups available."

Nan was flapping her hands around, still coughing.

"Attend to your wife, please, Mr. Fremont," said Dr. Lick, his hand still stretched out impotently toward Nan.

"Right you are, sir," said George. He poured some more wine into Nan's empty glass. She grasped it eagerly and, perching her fingertips delicately on her sternum, downed half the glass in one big glug. Miss Price and Dr. Lick instinctively pulled back in anticipation of another eruption.

"Ah," went Nan, who was able to swallow the wine without feeling so much as a throat tickle. "Just what the doctor ordered. Thank you, dear."

"Now, who did you say your soon-to-be-ex-wife was, Dr. Lick?"

"Dr. Brockheimer," Dr. Lick said. "Dr. Hilda Brockheimer."

Nan frowned and gritted her teeth.

"I have met your soon-to-be-ex-wife. Yes, we know each other. She has a student named Shirelle Eadkins, who works for me as an intern." Nan's view of Dr. Lick underwent an instant transformation. How could anyone marry that supercilious sack of emotional instability? But at least he was apparently divorcing her. That certainly showed a modicum of good taste.

"Ah," said Dr. Lick.

"Yes," said Nan. "She has already seen my gardens."

Dr. Lick nodded, then sat up, ramrod straight.

"I think she wants to learn cross-cultural communication," continued Nan.

"Pardon?"

"Talking to plants."

"Hmmm. Well, we'll have to compare notes. I, as it turns out, would like to see what's *underneath* your gardens."

"I thought that we had dispensed with this whole notion of a treasure, Miss Price," said George, who placed half-full Dixie cups in front of her and Dr. Lick. "And this is getting perilously close to talking about things we're not supposed to talk about."

"This has nothing to do with your pending legal action against Miss Price for whatever reason that has happened," Dr. Lick said. "And the truth of the matter is I know nothing of your grievances. What I have learned from Miss Price is that there may be artifacts of huge significance under your back-yard here, and we would like to see what they are. You will be paid for the use of your property, I can assure you."

"We don't need your money, Dr. Lick," George said. "And we don't want anyone rooting around in our gardens. We've already gone over the spot where Miss Price here figured the treasure was buried. With a TreasureTrove XB 255."

"That's a top-of-the line instrument!" cried Dr. Lick. "For amateurs, at least. There's more sophisticated gear people such as myself can use. Still, sounds like you mean business."

"You already checked the stump hole?" blurted Miss Price. "Why didn't you tell me that?"

"You didn't ask," Nan said. "You tried to get what you wanted by subterfuge and skullduggery. Which is what this whole lawsuit business is about. So, just for the record, there's nothing there. *Nada.*"

"Ah," said Miss Price. "Maybe not what some were look-ing for, but there were skeletons there."

"There were *what?*"

"Skeletons," said Miss Price. "Two of them, tangled in the roots of your instantly dead white oak. We dug them out back at the Historical Society. And you know what they say: Where there's smoke, there's fire. What we're looking for might not have been under that tree, but I'd be willing to wager every penny I own that it's close by."

"Ah!" cried Nan. "The dead guy you told us about that day back in May at the Historical Society. Does he have any-thing to do with this?"

Miss Price sighed.

"Alas," she said, wringing her hands in a show of mock contrition. "That, if I remember correctly, was a lie. A lie meant to confuse you and throw you off the track."

"Hmmm," said Nan. "Just as I thought."

"Could I have some more wine, please?" Miss Price asked.

George, whose indignation had been supplanted by anxi-ety on hearing this news of skeletons in the backyard, poured her some more wine, and waggled the bottle in front of Dr. Lick, who covered his cup with his hand and waved him off.

"Still, we've got *two* dead people who got buried in our backyard," said Nan with some alarm.

"But it was very long ago, Mrs. Fremont. I don't believe you have cause for concern."

Dr. Lick laughed.

"This just gets juicier by the moment," he said. "Miss Price, you told me nothing about these skeletons. My God! I must see them!"

"Afraid that's impossible," Miss Price said.

"Impossible? How so?"

"I've already disposed of them."

"You what! How could you do that?"

George quickly filled his and Nan's wineglasses.

"They scared me. I didn't exactly want them hanging around the apartment waiting for you to figure out what you wanted to do with them."

Dr. Lick sighed. He slumped over and enfolded his face in his hands. Now that he looked more vulnerable, he wasn't nearly as attractive, thought a half-sotted Nan. Hell with him! Betcha can't pour wine like my guy. Naah, naah, naah.

"Well, that's a loss," said Dr. Lick, disentangling his face from the clutches of his fingertips, which had left white marks on his semi-bronzed cheeks. "Oh, well, we move on. I want to make it perfectly clear that what's buried under here, or at least what we have cause to believe is buried under here, is not a treasure in the usual sense of the word. It is an *archaeological* treasure of use to people such as myself and historians. It would have little monetary value in the conventional sense. I doubt that you'd be able to actually *sell* what we found for ready cash and without any familiarity with the museum and antiquities markets."

The Fremonts listened with feigned indifference, made easier by the effect of the wine.

"On the other hand, we're perfectly willing to purchase the rights to dig on your land. I don't think, say, $10,000 would be out of line for such an arrangement. In return, you'd grant us the rights to do whatever exploratory and excavation work we needed to do, and grant us rights to whatever we'd dig up. Then, we'd fill up the holes, clean up our mess, and leave. And you'd have the satisfaction of knowing that you've contributed to filling in a very big hole—ha, if you don't mind me saying it that way—in the recorded history of this country. Oh, yes, if we come up empty handed, you still get the money."

"Hmmm," said Nan.

"Hmmm," said George. "And what if we say no, Dr. Lick? Seems to me like you're lowballing us on that price."

Dr. Lick smiled.

"The price I mentioned is negotiable. I think I can speak for the university in saying we'd probably jack that up to $15,000. Maybe even $20,000. But that's the absolute limit. As a public institution, we are funded by the taxpayers, you know."

"What evidence do you have that there's something here anyway?" said George, who loved the way the Sagelands made him feel like he was the one calling the shots. Dr. Lick and Miss Price looked at each other.

"Now you have the floor, Miss Price."

"Well, there are the skeletons, for one thing, even though, I'll admit, it was silly of me to have disposed of them. And, by the way, Dr. Lick, there's no way to recover them; they emptied the Historical Society Dumpster Tuesday. For another, artifacts were found here when my great-grandfather dug his root cellar. Oh, gosh, that would have been back in the 1880s. They are very, very old. They are not Indian. They . . ."

Dr. Lick turned to Miss Price and touched her hand. Then, he pressed his finger against his lips. He turned back toward the Fremonts, smiled wistfully, and shrugged.

"Sorry, folks, this falls within the realm of unfinished research that is not yet ready for public consumption. We'll have to leave it at that. I should say that there is plenty of anecdotal and circumstantial evidence that has also lead us to this conclusion."

"And if we say no?" said George. Dr. Lick continued to smile as he glanced at his wristwatch.

"Oh, my, I have a class in forty-five minutes, so we'll have to be wrapping this up. If you decline our offer, then we might have to move for a condemnation, an eminent domain proceeding. In that case, we could take your entire property and you would have no choice." He nodded at Miss Price and both stood up.

"You know, Miss Price," Nan said, "you've never told us

exactly what this 'treasure' is you're looking for. What is it you expect to find?" Miss Price and Dr. Lick exchanged furtive looks.

"Ah-hem," said Dr. Lick.

"We'd rather not say at this point," Miss Price said. "Let's leave it as a surprise. You like surprises, don't you? I don't believe I've ever referred to it as a *treasure,* have I? In fact, I don't believe I've referred to it as anything at all. I *can* say that it's something of immense historical significance that will amaze and enrich you."

"Hmmm," said George.

"One last thing," said Nan. "Do you have any identification, Dr. Lick?"

Dr. Lick looked puzzled.

"We had an odd situation a year ago where a Realtor purporting to represent an archaeologist tried to relieve us of our property."

"Under somewhat similar circumstances," George said.

"Yes, the situation was almost identical," Nan said. "There was also the threat of an eminent domain proceeding. In that case, it was an alleged Indian burial ground under our property."

Dr. Lick laughed. Miss Price cackled. George and Nan smiled indulgently.

"She turned out to be a fraud and a nutcase," Nan said. "You wouldn't happen to know her, would you? A Dr. Phyllis Sproot?"

"No, never heard of her. But then I wouldn't have if she was a fraud misrepresenting herself as an archaeologist."

With that, he retrieved a billfold out of his jacket pocket, plucked out a card, and handed it to Nan. "Here's my card. But anyone can print up a card, eh? I suggest you look up the university directory on your own. You'll find me listed in the archaeology department. I assure you I'm no fraud, though some of my competitors at other universities might beg to differ with that. Ha-ha! Good day to you both."

George and Nan nodded as Miss Price and Dr. Lick got up and, with a slow and stately dignity, walked down the steps. Nan watched closely to see if either one mussed up her pea gravel.

"That eminent domain threat is just a bluff," George said gruffly. "And they don't *know* anything's buried here. Besides, haven't we had enough of this mucking around on our property? Good Lord!"

"I don't know, George," said Nan. "You've got a job now, sure, but $20,000 would be a nice cushion, and we could give the kids a little help with their college expenses instead of loading them down with so much debt."

"We should make more money from the lawsuit."

"That'll be months away. It's also assuming we win, or get a decent settlement. Then, the lawyers get their take, and what are we left with?"

"I guess we could bring back Jim for another sweep," George said. "Then dig it up ourselves. But he's already swept the entire property, front and back. We'd have absolutely no idea where to look. That's assuming, of course, there's something to look for."

"I'm tired of all this, George," Nan moaned. "I'm tired of skeletons, I'm tired of explosions, and I'm tired of people stomping around in our gardens in ways that are generally intended to screw us. Why can't people just leave us alone?"

George and Nan moved their chairs next to each other and Nan laid her head on George's shoulder as he pulled her closer to him, then drifted off into a quick, turbulent dream about the hybrid tea roses sprouting stovepipe hats that she was busily spray painting red.

A couple of male goldfinches, their feathers impossibly yellow, landed on the top perches of the tubular feeder. A red-bellied woodpecker landed on the suet feeder and began to peck violently at the rectangular suet-and-peanut-butter cake. George caught a whiff of something on the breeze. The subtle grape of the clematis? Or was it the wild honeysuckle that grew at the edge of the woods? A motion above the variegated dogwoods caught his attention. Another monarch butterfly!

A car pulled up along the Payne Avenue curb, interrupting their brief reverie. A door slammed shut. Another car pulled up. Another door shut, this one less violently. George looked over to see Shirelle and an older woman scampering up the pea gravel steps. George soon recognized the older woman as Dr. Hilda Brockheimer.

"You know what you just said about being left alone?" whispered George to the stirring Nan, who lifted her head off his shoulder and rubbed her eyes. "Maybe you'd better hold that thought."

28

Plague

"I brought along a cassette recorder," said Dr. Brockheimer. "I hope you don't mind my recording your plant talking. I'll need an auditory record of this to establish it as a field of credible study. Once we do that, we can do some kind of electrical hookup to some of your most voluble flowers to see if there's any sort of energy surge. That way, we can find out how they're reacting to your verbal cues."

"Verbal cues?"

"Verbal cues. You know, like telling them you're going to water or fertilize them. Praising them for their appearance and growth. Scolding them for not putting out enough blooms. Threatening to lop them off mid-stem. That sort of thing."

Shirelle looked away, trying desperately to avoid eye contact with Nan.

"I would never threaten my plants in such a manner," Nan said. "Well, just once with the Dusty Miller, but that's all forgiven. And speaking of forgiveness, my flowers would never forgive me if I threatened to cut them off. It's one thing to deadhead spent blooms, or to make cuttings. Flowers know when their blooms are done and should be removed to promote healthy growth. They're also willing to make a sacrifice in the name of beauty. But malevolent cutting, just to destroy, is an entirely different matter."

Dr. Brockheimer smiled, but on her, a smile looked more like a poorly executed sneer. The penitent and pitiful version of Dr. Brockheimer from FremontFest had apparently given way to her arrogant and authoritative doppelgänger.

"No need to lecture me, Mrs. Fremont. I'm the holder of three advanced degrees in my field. I understand everything you've said and so much more, I can assure you."

Nan grimaced and looked over at Shirelle, who blushed.

"Say," said Nan. "Did you know your soon-to-be-ex-husband was here just minutes ago?" She figured this would be just the time to introduce what she hoped would be an unpleasant topic for Dr. Brockheimer.

"Eh?" said Dr. Brockheimer, registering neither shock nor an elevated level of curiosity. "He was? Whatever could that be for? Well, who cares, at least as long as he's not horning in on my territory. And I doubt that. Ferd can't tell a rose from a ponderosa pine. Ha-ha! I haven't even spoken to the bastard in months. Now, Shirelle, if you'll be so good . . ."

"Dr. Brockheimer wants to inspect the new front yard," Shirelle said shyly.

"Well, what Dr. Brockheimer wants, Dr. Brockheimer gets, I guess," said Nan, standing up to lead the way around the north end of the house. "C'mon."

"I love your Russian sage," said Dr. Brockheimer as she gazed into the catmint.

"That's not Russian sage," said Nan. "That's Walker's Low catmint."

"I could swear that's Russian sage. In fact, I'm sure of it. I've been around flowers all my life, Mrs. Fremont. I know what I'm talking about."

Nan was speechless. She didn't want to keep going around in circles with someone whose professional ego would never allow her to admit to an error. But, my gosh, couldn't she tell the difference between Russian sage and Walker's Low catmint?

"Mrs. Fremont is right—it's Walker's Low catmint."

Dr. Brockheimer turned, stunned, to look at Shirelle.

"How dare you contradict me!" Dr. Brockheimer croaked. "I am your mentor and your teacher. I was immersing myself in plants when you were running around in soiled diapers chasing chickens. And you dare to tell me what my business is?"

"I do. This is Walker's Low catmint. I should know. I studied it specifically and included it in my plans for the front yard gardens. I picked it out at Burdick's personally. The little identification tags stuck in the soil next to each seedling said Walker's Low catmint. Look at any of your photographs of Walker's Low catmint and you will find them to be identical in appearance to these specimens here. Look up Russian sage, and you will find that while they look similar, they are certainly not identical. You are wrong, Dr. Brockheimer."

Dr. Brockheimer blinked rapidly, then turned to address Nan as if Shirelle didn't exist.

"Well, okay, let's get going."

"What is it you want to learn? What do you want me to do?"

"Start talking. Get down really close, and I'll have this microphone positioned right next to your mouth and the particular flower you're talking to. How about the hybrid teas up there on top? Do you talk to them?"

"*Talk* is not really the word."

"What is it then?"

"Oh, communicate, I guess. I don't know how to put it. Sometimes, yes, I actually do talk to them and then listen. But that's more for my benefit, sort of like talking to your pet, though please don't let them ever hear me calling them my pets. But you're not going to hear actual words coming out of them.

It's all part of the sensation. And, yes, they all do have different characteristics."

"I want to learn how to do it."

"I'm not sure it's something you really learn. You have to have sort of a natural knack for it. At some point, you just find yourself doing it. What they're feeling and thinking fills you up, sort of like a jolt of energy going in one direction or another. Or lots of jolts of energy going in lots of different directions that you have to sort out."

"I need to learn the language of plants," Dr. Brockheimer said. "I can learn anything I put my mind to. Just show me how."

"I doubt that you will ever be able to do this, Dr. Brockheimer. Why waste our time here?" Shirelle looked stricken.

"Oh," she moaned. "Mrs. Fremont." She gazed at Nan with sad, pleading eyes.

"Can we just go up to the hybrid teas and try?" pleaded Dr. Brockheimer, whose tone suddenly took on the characteristic of the supplicant, losing its hard-edged arrogance. "Look, Mrs. Fremont, I'll be frank with you. I've not been doing very well lately as a professor of floriculture. Nothing published in two years. I hate teaching undergraduates. I'm sure Shirelle can attest to that." Shirelle forced a wan smile. "And I've fallen behind most of my colleagues on the track to becoming a full professor. When Shirelle told me about your gardens and their unworldly opulence, I didn't believe her at first. But I wanted to see for myself. Now that I've seen, I believe. There's something amazing going on here. Something that no years of stored knowledge or chemical analysis can explain. I want to tap into that. Not just for myself, though that is, I'll admit, a big part of it. But for others, too. Maybe others can capture lightning in a bottle and make the world so much more beautiful. Please help me tap into that."

Aha, thought Nan, we're back to the helpless and humble

Dr. Brockheimer. And how long will that last? Never had she seen someone go through such a character transformation so quickly and convincingly. Except maybe for the Mikkelsons, those timid souls who a couple glasses of Sagelands two years ago at this very spot had turned into fire-breathing louts.

Who knows? thought Nan. Maybe it's the flowers.

"Well, I suppose we could give it a try," she said. "George, after all, learned, though he's still kind of stuck at the beginner's level. If George figured it out, maybe even you can. Now, what exactly is it you want me to do?"

"Can we do it with the tape recorder, please, if for nothing else, to prove that the ordinary ways of collecting data won't really work here?"

"Okay, who knows—maybe they'll surprise me. Try to leave your holier-than-thou academic attitude behind, please, Dr. Brockheimer. They won't respond to that. If anything, they'll clam up just to spite you. Understand that this is the longest of long shots. Also, the hybrids are haughty and full of themselves and they know it. But, maybe they'll respond to a like-minded creature."

Nan winked, and Dr. Brockheimer couldn't help but smile in a self-effacing way she wasn't accustomed to.

"I'll do my best," she said.

Soon, Nan was lying prone on the grass bordering the hybrid tea rose bed, her mouth within a sneeze of the stalk of their most resplendent Full Sail hybrid. She fought off the urge to laugh, which she realized might be somewhat startling and off-putting as far as the hybrids were concerned. Dr. Brockheimer, also lying on the grass, thrust the microphone into the few inches separating Nan's lips from the rose.

"Tape's running," she whispered.

"You really don't have to whisper," Nan said. "Okay, this is kind of awkward, doing it sort of on demand here. It won't seem as natural, but here goes.

"Hello, my beautiful Full Sail rose. How lovely you look today. You have made me so proud. Oh, that fragrance. You fill up my senses. Sun's out nice and hot. You like that, don't you? More of that tomorrow, they say. We'll give you more water tomorrow. And special rose fertilizer's coming on Friday . . . uh . . . right, Shirelle?" Nan twisted her head to the left to look up at Shirelle, who nodded. "Your friend Shirelle says yes, yummy fertilizer to make you even more beautiful. Okay, that's it."

"Now, we just wait?" asked Dr. Brockheimer.

"I don't know; I've never done this before."

Dr. Brockheimer snorted. One minute passed. Then, two. Three. The rose's leaves rustled.

"A message?" wondered Dr. Brockheimer.

"The wind," said Nan. Two more minutes passed in absolute silence. Not one car rumbled by on Sumac Street. Not one jogger, noisily leashed dogs leading the way, tromped down the sidewalk. Shirelle barely moved. Suddenly:

"Beat it, lady, you're interrupting my sunbathing!"

Nan jerked away from the hybrid tea and Dr. Brockheimer dropped her microphone.

"Jesus!" cried Shirelle. "Ha-ha. Ha-ha."

Nan looked up to see George leaning over them, laughing. He gave her a hand to help her up, then offered one to Dr. Brockheimer, who declined.

"Damn it, George," Nan cried. "We had a scientific inquiry going on, and you go and spoil it, you goof!"

Dr. Brockheimer self-consciously brushed some blades of mown grass off her shirt and slacks.

"Well, at least you gave us a little chuckle, Mr. Fremont," she said icily. "I'm not really sure the exercise was going to give us much in the way of quantifiable information."

"Heck, I could have told you that," said George, who from the looks of things, had refreshed his wineglass a couple of times. "It has to come from the heart, Dr. Brockheimer, and it has to be genuine. You think, what, the delphinium over there is going to sing out, 'Hey, Dr. Brockheimer, give me a drink; I'm parched'? Heavens no. It's not actual human conversation. It's . . . it's . . ."

"George, dear, how about a pitcher of ice-cold water for the three of us? Dr. Brockheimer and I have some things to discuss."

"Okay," said George. "But here's something to think about: I'm picking up bad vibes from some of the guys. Started about fifteen minutes ago, and it's powerful."

"I think that's the merlot, George," said Nan. Shirelle and Dr. Brockheimer tittered nervously. "Now, water, please! And for you, too."

George disappeared behind the north end of the house, mumbling something about nervous Nelly plants.

"Okay," said Nan. "Where were we before being so rudely interrupted? You know, Dr. Brockheimer, I was actually starting to feel something as I was lying there. Probably not anything you could pick up with your cassette recorder or some electric impulse sensors. But something. Hmmm."

"Mrs. Fremont!" said Shirelle. "Mrs. Fremont! I'm feeling something, too. Wow!"

"What is it?" said Dr. Brockheimer, fumbling with her recorder and trying to jot down notes in her steno pad at the same time. "What is it, Shirelle? Can you hear anything?"

"She doesn't really *hear* anything, Dr. Brockheimer," said Nan. "She feels it. I'm feeling the same thing right now. Wow! It just started."

"What is it? What is it you're feeling?" Dr. Brockheimer dropped her pen and steno pad and stuck her microphone in Nan's face.

"Please, Dr. Brockheimer," said Nan, gently guiding Dr. Brockheimer's microphone hand away from her. "For lack of a better definition, it's what I guess you would call a dissonance in the life force. Something is turning the smooth sort of hum vibration of growing and flourishing into a sort of bumpy, staticky sound track, though there isn't any sound in the conventional sense. It's like you suddenly pushed the wrong button on your remote and got something weird on your TV screen. But in this case you can't actually hear anything. I really don't know how to describe it, because it's not like anything else you'll ever experience."

"That's just what it's like, Mrs. Fremont," said Shirelle.

Nan smiled. "You should be very happy that you feel it, too, Shirelle. You are blessed."

Dr. Brockheimer gazed around disconsolately.

"Why can't I feel it?" she said. "I want to feel it, too."

"I'm not sure you want to feel what I'm feeling now, Dr. Brockheimer," said Nan, ominously. Hundreds of little energy impulses were shooting through her like blinking lights of varying duration and intensity.

"What?" said Dr. Brockheimer. "What!"

"I don't know what. Just something bad. But there's nothing in the forecast that even hints of violent weather. And look at the sky. Just a few puffy fair-weather cumulus clouds. A little purpling at their bases, but that means nothing."

"Oooh, gross!" cried Shirelle. Nan and Dr. Brockheimer turned to look at her. "There's a slug on one of the delphiniums, Mrs. Fremont. Ecccch! A slimy slug."

Nan rushed over to inspect the offending pest, a tiny, concentrated blob of gray mucus distinctly visible on one of the leaves.

"My gosh," she said, flicking it off. "I've never seen a slug in these gardens. Never. And look here at the leaf. It's got holes where the slug's been chowing down. I hope and pray this isn't the sign of an infestation."

As Nan turned, she noticed another slug on a neighboring

delphinium. Then, another. She counted six on yet a fourth. Shirelle grabbed her by the arm.

"Mrs. Fremont, we have to act now," she said. "Beer. Do you have beer?"

"No, Shirelle, we're wine and gin drinkers; you know that. And I'm not sure this is the time—"

"That's okay; I have some beer at home. I'm going to go get it. You'll need to get all the shallow containers you can find. We need to bury them in the ground so they're flush with the surface. Saucers for your clay flower pots should work. But no drainage holes. Then, we'll fill 'em with beer. It's the yeast that does the trick. They climb into the beer to get at the yeast scent and drown. I'm outta here. Be back in a jiff. Oh, Dr. Brockheimer, grab a shovel from out of the shed. We'll need some holes to put the beer basins in. Just a couple of inches, and flattened bottoms."

"Oh. Okay, Shirelle."

"That way, Dr. B," Nan said, pointing to the shed, just visible behind the northwest corner of the house. "Pretty sure it's unlocked. I'm headed to the garage for clay saucers."

Suddenly, there was Mary, just arrived home from work and standing next to her.

"Hey, Mom, what's everyone running around for? And what's with Shirelle? She just peeled out of the driveway as I was pulling in. Almost hit me."

"Well, don't just stand there, girl," Nan barked. "We've got a serious infestation problem here. Slugs." Nan gave Mary her instructions and sent her running off to the backyard to find George.

Dr. Brockheimer rummaged around in the shed for a few minutes before finding the shovels, then spent a few more minutes weighing whether to take the triangular-pointed spade, the rounded transplanting shovel, or the square-edged shovel. When she returned with the square-edged shovel, she stopped and stared, stunned, at what lay before her eyes. The front yard gardens had taken on the appearance of one big, crawling organism, and emitted a low sort of crackling noise. It was the sound of tens of thousands of insects eating and digesting stems, leaves, buds, and blooms.

"Ah!" she cried, dropping the shovel.

Nan was already laying out her clay saucers. George and Mary grabbed quick handfuls and ran past Dr. Brockheimer and toward the backyard, without saying a word. Announced by a couple of short beeps, Shirelle pulled into the driveway, jumped out of the car, and popped open the trunk.

"That was quick!" shouted Nan.

"Didn't go home," Shirelle shouted back as she climbed the slope lugging two cases of Tippy Toes microbrew. "Went straight to the liquor store. Got any bug juice?"

"Just the ant stuff and yellow jacket spray. Will that work?"

"Probably not."

"I can run to the hardware store."

"That'll take too long the way things are going. Hmmm . . . Okay, there's one thing that might work. Mrs. Fremont, do you have some liquid dishwashing detergent?"

"Of course. At least I think so. We eat on paper plates a lot."

"Do you have one of those Miracle-Gro thingeys you attach to your garden hose?"

"Yes. Definitely . . . Ah, I think I know what you're getting at."

"Put about two cupfuls of detergent in it, attach it to the hose, and we'll wash everything down."

"And that'll work?"

"There's a chance. That's all I can promise. I'm hoping the sun's low enough in the sky. Otherwise, everything we wash is gonna get cooked. That's because the detergent magnifies the rays . . . Good Lord!"

They both looked at the hybrid teas, which were crawling with so many insects they looked like little twitching scarecrow beings. They walked up for a closer look.

"My God!" moaned Nan. "The aphids are here, too. Japanese beetles. What kind of plague *is* this?"

"No time for talk," said Shirelle. "Let's get a move on."

"Yes, ma'am," Nan said, mimicking a salute.

"Hey, over there! Doc!" Shirelle yelled at Dr. Brockheimer, who was standing transfixed, in awe of the devastation that was being unleased on the Fremonts' gardens. "Get crackin'. Dig holes where the saucers are laid out, and make sure they're in, flush with the ground. C'mon, now." Shirelle reached down to tear open the case of Tippy Toes, and pulled out a can.

"Pretty pricey stuff for a bunch of slugs," she said, popping the tab and taking a big glug. "Ahhhh. You're letting me expense account this, I assume."

"But of course," said Nan with a wan smile. "If a slug's gonna drown in beer, it might as well be the best. Gives us all some good karma."

29

Counter-Plague

By nightfall, nothing else could be done. Every garden plot, front and back, had been sprayed, covering everything with soapsuds. Thirty-seven beer-filled saucers placed at various locations were filled with drowned slugs. But still they kept coming in such numbers that you could actually hear them eating and digesting flowers, leaves, and stems. George, Nan, Mary, Shirelle, and Dr. Brockheimer sat on the front landing, drinking what was left of the Tippy Toes microbrew.

"If I hadn't seen it, I never would have believed it," said Dr. Brockheimer, after taking a long swig of her beer. "What I have witnessed today defies all the canons of horticultural knowledge."

"Yes, well, after this, I'm afraid our gardening days are through," said Nan. "We can't continue to fight whatever these forces are that keep assaulting our gardens. It's just not worth it. George already has his job. Now, I guess I'll have to go out and get one myself. . . . By the way, where the heck are those boys? They could have helped."

"You forget, Nan-bee, they've got the evening shifts," George said. "Back by ten-thirty at the earliest. And after that, they're probably off to hang out with friends. Besides, what good would they have been?" Mary snorted.

"Ain't that the truth," she said.

"Don't be making any rash decisions about your future right now, Mrs. Fremont," Shirelle said. "Remember last year? It was like magic, Dr. Brockheimer. I mean, their gardens sprang right back. In August! After being destroyed by a freak hailstorm!"

"Yes, so you've said, Shirelle," Dr. Brockheimer said. "And I have read your report and the news clipping you included with it. It's just that I never believed it. Until now."

"And don't forget that note you found when we were out looking for fairies," Mary said. "Someone wants to help. Maybe it's that same someone who helped last year."

"Looking for fairies?" said Dr. Brockheimer, her eyes wide open in amazement. "I'm not even going to ask."

"What was *that?*" said Mary, bolting straight up out of her slouch.

"I heard it, too," said Shirelle. Within seconds, everyone could hear a cacophony of croaks and chirrups. Then, the front yard was alive with them, frogs and toads by the hundreds, the thousands. In the dimming light, the gardens looked like one huge trampoline for bouncing amphibians.

"They're eating the bugs!" Mary cried.

"Of course they are," said Dr. Brockheimer. "The bugs must have attracted them from the lake, and maybe from miles around. They may save your gardens yet."

In fifteen minutes it was all over. The frogs and toads had melted away, though to exactly where was unclear.

"My God!" cried Dr. Brockheimer. "They just disappeared. Where did they go?"

"Don't ask," said Nan resignedly. "Because there's no an-swer that will make any sense at all. Well, I'm shot. I don't

know about the rest of you, but I've had enough excitement
for one day. We'll survey the damage tomorrow. Maybe we can
salvage something. But, to tell you the truth, I'm not sure I
care that much anymore."

"Me neither," said George, more bemused than shocked at
what had happened over the past couple of hours. "But I will
say one thing: This beer is dy-no-mite."

As they walked down the driveway toward their cars,
Shirelle noticed that Dr. Brockheimer was treading carefully
and watching her feet.

"Don't worry, Dr. Brockheimer," she said. "You won't step
on any frogs or toads."

Dr. Brockheimer, flushed with excitement, chuckled.

"How can I ever possibly write this up?" she said. "No
academic journal would ever accept it. There's no proof. No
scientific evidence."

"Who says you have to write it up?" said Shirelle.

"No one," replied Dr. Brockheimer. "No one at all."

The devastation the Fremonts beheld the next morning,
while certainly severe, fell short of utter destruction. Entire
swaths of the backyard remained untouched for some reason.
The front yard was a patchwork. Many of the flowers and
grasses had been damaged, some horribly. Others appeared to
have survived the infestation with only minor injuries or none
at all.

"This could have been so much worse, Mr. and Mrs. Fremont," said Dr. Brockheimer, who returned with Shirelle to
survey the damage. "You've lost some things, sure. But I think
a lot of these will bounce back. Maybe not this year. Next
year's the true test." Nan nodded meekly as George examined
the hybrid tea roses close up.

"These guys got chewed up pretty good," he said. "As delicate as they are, I'm not sure they can ever come back."

"I can almost hear them moaning," said Nan. "The poor things."

"Yeah," said Shirelle. "I think the hybrid teas are goners. The delphinium took quite a hit, too. The daylilies are fine; they're almost immortal. The ornamental grasses were hardly touched. And, this is amazing: The Walker's Low catmint looks like it's in pretty good shape—a little chewed up, but not too bad. Next year, we'll just need to re-plant a few things, and we'll be back in business. Anyone take a look at the backyard?"

All except George, who was running late for work, walked around the north end of the house to the backyard. Nan was prepared for the worst, and, initially, that's what she got.

"These new beds are toast," she said as she walked the northern, woods-bordered perimeter of the gardens, then worked her way along the fence line before veering into the heart of the backyard. "A lot of other things hurt."

Even on the south side of the split-rail fence, there was plenty of damage.

"My blue hydrangea!" Nan gasped. "Eaten alive!"

Shirelle could feel tears began to pool in her eyes.

"And the spirea! And the . . . well, the Asiatic lilies and the purple coneflowers look a bit roughed up, but not too much the worse for the wear. Same with the monarda and balloon flowers."

"Mom!" Mary cried. "Look down here!"

Nan was level with the north edge of the patio now, and it seemed she'd entered a completely different world.

"This is *so* weird," Mary said. "It's as if the bugs never got to anything between the patio and the street. The climbing roses and clematis are fine. The phlox and alyssum untouched. You could almost draw a line across the backyard to separate what got nailed and what didn't."

"How strange," said Nan. "Hmmm, here's a visitor who might be able to shed some light on our situation for us."

Marta Poppendauber was examining the yard as she slowly negotiated the pea gravel steps to the patio.

"My goodness," she said, stepping onto the patio. "Well, at least we were able to save part of it."

"*We?*" said Nan. Marta glanced nervously at the group clustered around her. "Go ahead, Marta. This is our daughter, Mary, our intern, Shirelle Eadkins, and Dr. Hilda Brockheimer from the university. You can speak freely. Nothing will surprise them at this point."

"Edith and I. We knew Dr. Sproot was up to no good and came over here the other night to stop her."

"Let me guess—Dr. Sproot figured out some way to make our flowers bait for every garden pest within a ten-mile radius. I won't even ask how."

"That's pretty much it," said the shamefaced Marta. "We were able to scare her off before she finished the job, and Edith had something up her sleeve."

"That being the frogs and toads?"

"That being the frogs and toads. She had been communing with them for some time in the course of doing her small-pet séances, you know. It wasn't all that hard for her to figure out how to call them forth, en masse as it were."

Dr. Brockheimer gasped.

"I don't believe what I'm hearing!" she cried. "This is . . . this is . . . wonderful!"

Nan turned to Dr. Brockheimer and scowled.

"Easy for you to say, Miss PhD expert and all. You don't have to deal with these things in real life, do you? For you, this is all just grist for your academic mill. Do you even *have* a garden, Dr. Brockheimer? A personal garden?"

"Yes, yes, I do have a garden," said Dr. Brockheimer, clenching her jaw tightly and thrusting out her chin defiantly. "I grow vegetables. Organic vegetables."

A gasp went up from the group. Shirelle looked away. Mary blushed. Nan looked as if she had just been slapped across the face with a gauntlet, and was mulling over her choice of weapons for a duel. Then, a look of intense pity crossed her face. The poor, misguided dear, she thought. She thinks growing vegetables is gardening. Ha!

"We're all about beauty here, Dr. Brockheimer. Not eating. Not *farming*. Agriculture is all well and good, but you are among flower growers here. George dabbled a while back with some radishes and one or two leafy things, but that was George. My goodness, if Dr. Sproot were here, even she'd be absolutely aghast."

"That's right, she would be," said Marta.

"Ah, well, *vive la différence,* as the French would say," said Nan, suddenly perky and forgiving, as she always was on seeing that she had said something hurtful. "So, Marta, is it safe to say that Dr. Sproot didn't accomplish all she wanted to, that being the utter destruction of our gardens?"

"Yes," said Marta. "That's partly because Edith and I were there, and partly because Dr. Sproot is a novice at this sort of thing, and not very good at it yet. That's why you're seeing patches of places where your flowers are doing fine or are just slightly damaged."

"So . . . the blue fairy light."

"Yep," Marta said proudly. "That was us. You can keep the candle, by the way."

"What happens when Dr. Sproot fully develops her powers?"

"A night in the pokey and some long overdue psychiatric evaluation might cure her of any need for further action on that front. Edith intends to watch her, too. She said she's seen some ominous signs that Dr. Sproot's powers are growing. As you can probably guess, she isn't the kind of person who'd let a few scruples get in the way of her evil ambitions. We're a little worried. Let's just hope the authorities keep her under lock and key for a while."

Marta went on to explain how Dr. Sproot was now Edith's landlord and had threatened to foreclose on both her stores unless she served as her witchcraft tutor. Nan gasped. Dr. Brockheimer listened, stunned, her mouth agape.

"She missed a few payments," Marta said. "I think I can loan her enough to get her over the hump. She can pay me back when she and Felix land back on their feet. I've told the Rose Maidens about it. They're trying to work out a no-interest loan to pay off all Edith's debts to Dr. Sproot. They'd do almost anything to make sure she gets foiled in her evil designs."

"Is there anything I can do to help?"

Everyone looked at Dr. Brockheimer as if she were a four-year-old offering to replace the roof, fix the furnace, and install a central-air-conditioning unit, all in the same day.

"Uh, no," said an embarrassed Shirelle. Nan smiled consolingly and took Dr. Brockheimer's hand.

"There's no need for you to get caught up in our little weirdness here," she said. "Let's you and I stick to our cross-cultural communications project . . . because I have every intention of teaching you how to talk to plants."

Shirelle was working the front yard, and Nan the backyard that afternoon when George pulled into the garage. He soon appeared at the patio table carrying a bottle of Sagelands and two wineglasses.

"Kind of early for you to be getting off, isn't it?" said a sweaty Nan, pulling off her gloves and depositing her hand tools in their woven-wood tool basket. "Not too early for a glass of the nectar of the gods, however." George placed a half-filled wineglass in front of her as she plopped down into one of the patio chairs.

"I certainly need this," she said. "So many dead things to dig out and toss in the compost, to say nothing of all the wounded who need to be watered and fertilized. It's like a battleground, George. And Shirelle is having to dig out all the hybrid teas and most of the delphinium. Awful! Mary's at work, of course."

George nodded morosely as Nan drained her glass of Sagelands.

"Uh, George, is it too delicate of me to ask what you're doing home so early, and why you look so downtrodden? Oh, and why you've barely touched your Sagelands?"

"I got fired."

"Ah," said Nan, uncharacteristically refilling her own glass, and spilling a few drops in the process. "Oh, clumsy me. George, I'm going to leave all the refilling to you from now on. Fired, huh? As in you can never go back to work there and earn a paycheck?"

"That's generally what getting fired means, yes."

"Why? I thought you were tearing it up with sales, advice, and all that. A regular bird-stuff entrepreneur."

"I was. But there was apparently one little problem."

A sudden, shocking thought occurred to Nan.

"George, you weren't dipping into the till, were you?"

"Most certainly not! What do you take me for, Nan-bee? I'm not a thief. I am, however, as you well know, a bit of a tippler."

"I do know that. But I also know that there are loads of tipplers out there who manage to keep their jobs, tippling being quite harmless when kept in its proper place. . . . George, you got caught drinking on the job!"

"I did, yes. But it's not what you think. I had organized a little wine break for the staff. Instead of a coffee break mid-afternoon, we'd have a wine break. I took our own bottles of Sagelands, so no company funds were involved. The rest of the staff seemed to like the idea, so, at three o'clock, out came the wineglasses. The customers didn't seem to mind. Well, perhaps one or two did, because today we got a surprise visit from the owner, who, shall we say, caught us in the act. We were interrogated; I was fingered as the instigator and fired on the spot."

Nan frowned and drummed her fingertips on the tabletop.

"Well, the good thing is you'll be back out here doing what you love with me. And I know the flowers miss you, even more so now that they've been ravaged. There's so much work to do. Mary and Shirelle are talking about replanting this year, but it's so late. Of course, all of this is rendered moot since we won't have any money. Am I correct to assume there are lots more second-mortgage payments to be made?"

George nodded.

"About a hundred and fifteen or so."

"What!"

"Ten-year mortgage. I've made five payments. You can do the math."

"Oh, George," Nan moaned. "And there's no contest to save us this time!"

"No," said George, finally taking a sip of his wine. "But there is something else."

"Don't tell me about another one of your flippin' idiot inventions. This is not the time for that kind of nonsense."

"Nan-bee, it's staring you right in the face. We've got two things here that others want very badly. Badly enough to pay for them."

"Of course! Our buried treasure! But what's the other thing?"

"Your cross-cultural communications. Plant talking. I bet that Dr. Brockheimer would do just about anything to be a plant whisperer, as you might call it."

"I told her I would do that, but, heavens, I can't charge for it. That's a sacred endeavor. I wouldn't dream of making someone pay me to do that. Maybe what *you* can do is go out and find another job."

"That's probably a non-starter, Nan-bee. I'm guessing the market for employees who got fired for drinking on the job before they'd even gotten through their first month is somewhat constricted."

"Hmmm."

"So let's get back to the treasure thing, then. I'm guessing you don't have any scruples about charging Miss Price and that Dr. . . . uh . . ."

"Lick."

"Yeah, that Dr. Lick. I'm guessing you will have absolutely no objection to squeezing those two for whatever we can get in return for mauling our already damaged and fragile backyard."

"None whatsoever," said Nan.

Another half-glass of Sagelands clarified matters somewhat. They would demand, as property owners, one-half of the value of whatever "treasure" was found, plus an additional $30,000 for the rights to dig on their land. And if someone wanted all the credit for a find of great historical significance, then that was just peachy with them. They figured both Dr. Lick and Miss Price would jump at the offer, not wanting to risk the Fremonts digging it up on their own while they went through eminent domain proceedings that could drag on for months, maybe even years.

"And don't forget our lawsuit," Nan said.

"That's right. Weren't there a couple of clauses seeking restitution for mental and spiritual anguish suffered by the plaintiffs?"

"That there were, George. And, considering what we've been through, that's gotta be good for a few million in damages."

30

Livia Unearthed

Dr. Lick and Miss Price did, in fact, jump at the offer, and drove over to the Fremonts' the next Saturday with the necessary paperwork for them to sign.

"I'm so glad you were willing to listen to reason," said Dr. Lick. "Though I had to do a little arm twisting to free up the $30,000. You folks drive a hard bargain. Still, I'm convinced this will be an amazing find."

"Of course it will be an amazing find," said Miss Price, who had waved off the celebratory merlot everyone else was drinking in favor of the Fremonts' other house beverage, the exquisite Bombay Sapphire gin. "Only you have to find it first. Where do you think it might be?"

Dr. Lick scratched his head.

"No idea," he confessed. "But we can sweep the entire yard."

"The entire yard has already been swept," said George. "A year ago. And by someone who knows what he's doing. I don't think Jim missed a single square inch of our property, because, at that point, all our flowers were pretty much gone, wrecked by a hailstorm. We had nothing to lose by letting him tromp around in our flower beds."

Dr. Lick twisted around in his chair to take in the full panorama of the backyard gardens, or at least what was left of them.

"Speaking of which," said Miss Price. "It appears that your gardens have suffered another mishap of rather gigantic proportions. My goodness gracious! What happened?"

George and Nan looked at each other.

"Uh . . . blight," said Nan haltingly. "A new blight that hasn't been named yet. It strikes swiftly and devastatingly as you can see. But it is somewhat selective."

George nodded.

"Hmmm," said Dr. Lick.

"My condolences," said Miss Price. "At least I see that your birches and crab apples in your lovely arbor are still flourishing. It appears nothing disturbed that. Though I'll always remember that old locust that used to be there. I do wish you hadn't cut that down. That was a stately old beacon, that tree."

George shot up suddenly from his seat, startling everyone at the table.

"What did you just say, Miss Price?"

"Uh, the old locust tree and how I wish you wouldn't have cut it down, and what a stately old beacon it was."

"Eureka!" shouted George, thrusting his hands skyward.

"Eureka what, dear?" wondered Nan calmly.

"Isn't it obvious to everyone?" George said. "That's the other tree planted back in the old days on this property. And what did they plant the first tree for, the white oak, Miss Price?"

Miss Price's eyes suddenly lit up.

"As a marker. Of course! As a burial marker!"

"Right! The two skeletons you found all bound up in the roots. That means the second tree could also be a marker. For something else buried. Say, a treasure perhaps."

"Of course!" cried Dr. Lick. "But why wouldn't your friend have detected it when he did the scan?"

"Well, the site's covered with flagstones, and, beneath them, several inches of sand and gravel and concrete. Would that make detection more difficult?"

"Perhaps," said Dr. Lick. "Either your friend didn't hear any signals when he scanned the site, or he assumed he wouldn't find anything anyway with all that stuff in the way."

"Or," said Nan, "maybe he knew how precious our arbor is to us and didn't want to disturb it."

A quick call to Jim established that he had, indeed, neglected to sweep the arbor. Within minutes, he was trudging up the backyard slope, TreasureTrove XB 255 slung over his shoulder.

"Nice piece of equipment you got there, fella," said Dr. Lick. "Find much with it?"

"Up to this point, no," said Jim, gazing at the trees ringing the arbor. "Some spare change, a few old trinkets. I'm hoping my luck will change today. But are you guys sure you want to mess up the arbor? That's a beautiful spot."

"Yes, we're sure," said Nan. "And we appreciate your sensitivity, we really do. But things have changed and sacrifices must be made. I suppose we should take out the flagstones first, shouldn't we? I mean, just to be sure."

"That might help," said Jim. "The less there is between your detector and the metal you're looking for the better!"

Dr. Lick jumped up from his chair.

"Well, great! I just happen to have a pick and a couple of shovels in the trunk of my car," he said. "What say we leave the graduate students behind on this and do a little excavating ourselves?"

"Hear, hear!" chimed in Miss Price, holding her gin and tonic aloft. "And I shall watch and cheer you on. Uh, Mr. Fremont, my drink is getting a bit low and diluted. Would you be so good as to freshen this up a bit?"

"Hang on, everybody," said Nan. "That's a fair-sized area you're talking about there. Are you guys ready to dig up a hole the size of a bomb crater? How do we know exactly where it is? When we cut the tree down we had the stump ground up."

"That's easy," said Miss Price. "Remember me talking about that clothesline we had, and how it was ninety feet from one tree to the other? Measure a little bit less to account for the loops around each of the hooks. Measure it from where the edge of that white oak once stood, angle it halfway—forty-five degrees—between due west and due south, and, presto, you've got where the old locust was. It's two hundred twenty-five points on the compass, if anyone has one handy."

"How on earth do you know that?" Nan wondered.

"Math class," Miss Price replied. "One of our exercises was figuring out angles at home. Mine was determining the angle of the clothesline from one of the cardinal points of the compass. For some reason, that stuck with me. Lord knows nothing else about math did."

"I remember that locust being pretty much right in the middle of where we put the arbor," George said.

"Well, okay, let's get moving," said Nan. "What's everyone waiting for?"

An hour and a half later, all the flagstones had been dug out of the center of the arbor, the concrete broken up, and the sand and gravel removed. George and Dr. Lick, stripped down to the waist and covered with sweat and panting, threw down their shovels. George signaled to Jim, who was sitting on the patio, nursing his second gin and tonic, and apparently in no hurry to go anywhere.

"Get over here, metal detector man!" he shouted. "It's time to earn your pay." Jim got up slowly, clumsily gathered together his gear, and ambled over to the shallow depression that was once the heart of the arbor. It was a sobering sight, and Jim could feel the tears welling up.

"This was such a placid, restful place," he moaned. "I hate to see it torn up like this."

"We promise to put it all back when we're finished," said George. "Now, quit your whining and let's get detecting."

Jim moved the metal detector's search coil over the spot, feathering it one way and then the other. It was only a matter of seconds before it started beeping to beat the band.

"*Hot!* It is *hot!*"

Miss Price downed a long slug of gin and tonic she had directed George to make especially strong for her.

"Sheesh!" said Jim. "There's definitely something down there. And it's something of substance. And it's not all that deep. A couple feet more maybe."

"Okay, everyone stand back," said Dr. Lick, who arced the big pick back and brought it down unsteadily with a thud, sinking it six inches into the ground.

"Uh, what about gas lines, power lines, et cetera?" said George. "Seeing as how we had a rather nasty experience with a gas line next door a little while ago."

"For this part of the yard, you're good," said Dr. Lick. "I took the liberty of checking. That means we've just got some roots to worry about, but I can rip right through them with this bad boy."

Caught up in Dr. Lick's enthusiasm, George grabbed a shovel and began to dig, his field of action being somewhat impaired by Dr. Lick's imitation of a drunk day laborer.

Dr. Lick could barely contain himself. He pushed muscles he never knew existed to the limit, his lungs ready to burst, his body drenched in glistening sweat. It was to be the find of a lifetime. Why would anyone faced with such a discovery want to hold back? The way Miss Price had described it, what they'd find was proof that Europeans had traveled through the middle of the continent and even settled there more than three hundred years before Columbus. That in and of itself would be immensely gratifying. What's more, it corroborated the theories he had held all along, but which the archaeological community had dismissed as Eurocentric pseudo-history. This was to be his sweet redemption! And it would catapult him to the highest ranks of his discipline.

The tale Miss Price had woven to Dr. Lick was of a great chest fashioned almost a millennium ago that contained a historic secret with vast implications. Inside, she said, were inscriptions in Latin and Welsh etched into soft stone and leather that had identified the Fremont property as the home of the followers of Madoc, a Welsh prince banished from his home for some unknown crime or political misstep. Madoc and his followers had set sail west for Cathay and the Spice Islands and wound up in a new continent whose existence he would never be able to make manifest. The chest would contain written proof that Madoc's village of Welsh expatriates lay right under them.

Once these buried writings were translated, they would prove to be a historical record of a race that, after two hundred years of roaming the continent, warring and cooperating with Indians, and seeking to carve out its special niche in the wilderness, was beginning to lose its identify. They would speak of a tribe of Welsh that had already been decimated by wars with surrounding tribes and were seeking alliances with other, friendlier ones.

"Think of it!" the excited and quaking Miss Price had said. "Europeans here in the upper Midwest, colonizing and flourishing, at least for a while, centuries before Columbus! It's bigger than Jamestown or St. Augustine! It's bigger than the Plymouth Bay Colony! It's bigger than Roanoke Island! My gracious, it's bigger than all those rolled into one! It boggles the mind! Just think, as many as one hundred Welsh lived here, all of them born in the New World. When this village gave out, there were people living here whose families had been in this country for six, seven generations. The chest we're searching for is the record they left of this village before they scattered to whatever fate awaited them. It will probably wind up in the Smithsonian, and they will pay well. They will pay well. And they will want any of the artifacts within for display purposes. Goodness, you'll be set up for life!"

There was something else. What would likely interest him and the Fremonts more than her, she said, was that the remnants of Madoc's fortune in gold and gemstones might well lay within.

And she had the two artifacts to prove it: rune stones inscribed with Celtic characters excavated from the site of the current house when the old one was torn down and a foundation dug for the existing one. No one had been able to precisely date them, but where else could they have come from? And Miss Price had done so much study, and had such conviction! Was there some doubt? Of course, there's always doubt. But those who become prisoners to doubt never move forward to accomplish anything.

Besides, and Dr. Lick would tell this to no one, the night before he had had a dream like no other. An ancient bard had come to him in his sleep with a crudely feathered arrow protruding from his chest. He held a half-finished tin of Chicken of the Sea tuna fish in one hand and an old Duncan Imperial yo-yo in the other. What could they possibly symbolize? Dr. Lick dismissed the can of tuna fish and yo-yo as items of no consequence that often cluttered up dreams. But the bard! And the arrow! Only a blind man—or one who didn't put much faith in dreams as portents—could fail to understand the significance. A clash of cultures from one hell of a long time ago.

"Dig!" he yelled. "Dig!" By now, Mary and Shirelle had come around from the front to see what all the fuss was about.

"Oh, my God!" cried Shirelle. "That beautiful arbor! Those beautiful flagstones!"

"Need our help?" asked Mary. "C'mon, Shirelle; this is a treasure hunt, and my tuition and room and board could be buried down there."

Twenty minutes later, Shirelle and Mary were sitting on the grass exhausted, urging on George and Dr. Lick, who had markedly slackened their efforts. An hour and a half and two shift changes later, George felt the tip of the pick hit something and vibrate through the handle so violently that he dropped it.

"Bingo!" he shouted. "Got something!"

"Sure hope it's not another gas line!" yelled Nan from the patio.

He and Dr. Lick, who had been slacking off big-time over the past half hour, began to dig with a fresh enthusiasm, concentrating now on probing to the edges of the object they were unearthing. That object seemed to be about a foot wide and deep, and two feet long. George swung as lustily as his flagging strength enabled. He finally managed to get the tip of the pick under the object and start prying it loose.

Fifteen minutes later, they had it yanked out of the hole and set on the ground. It was a wood-and-metal chest of some sort, its hinges and clasp rusted almost beyond recognition, and with the outlines of a pattern etched deeply into the top, but now caked with mud.

Miss Price let out a cheer and raised her gin and tonic in salute.

"*Iechyd da!*"

"Pardon?" said Nan.

"*Iechyd da,*" said Miss Price. "It's Welsh. It means to your very good health."

"Likewise, I'm sure," Nan said, raising her own glass. "Way to go, guys. Can you drag it over here?"

"I can't say for sure," said Jim, who had run over to the site to help George and Dr. Lick extract the chest. "But that looks to me to be rather old."

"If Miss Price is right, then it is *very* old," Dr. Lick said. "Many hundreds of years old."

"A treasure?" wondered Jim.

"Of sorts," said Dr. Lick, smiling through a mask of perspiration. "We'll soon see."

There were no handles on the ends of the chest, so George and Jim picked it up from the bottom and lugged it over toward the table, over which Nan had now spread two layers of drop cloths.

"Maybe it's too heavy for the table," she said. "How about setting it right on the cement?"

"No problem for the table," George said. "It's not nearly as heavy as I thought it'd be. In fact, it seems kind of light to be holding such a heavy load."

Miss Price stared at the chest for a moment, then ran her trembling hand over it.

"This is very nice work. It was made in Wales, of course. There is no lock on the clasp, as you see. It's very rusted, though. Perhaps a screwdriver and hammer and some oil could loosen it."

Once the rust was flaked off with the screwdriver and a few taps of the hammer, and some oil was sprayed on it, the clasp proved easy to pry open.

"Now, to open this chest," said Miss Price. "And, goodness me, I find that, after all these years, I lack the nerve."

"You should be the one who opens it," George said.

"Yes," said Nan. "You must do the honor. It wouldn't be right for any of the rest of us to do it."

"Then get me another good, stiff drink to steady my hands." Miss Price knocked down most of her gin and tonic in one minute as George and Nan watched her in admiration, and

Jim, the euphoria of the find proving only fleeting, wondered whether Alicia had already sold his baseball card collection.

"Okay," Miss Price said. "Here goes."

"Stop!" said Nan, raising her hand suddenly, palm outward. "Just a moment. Listen."

"Stop?" said Miss Price. "Listen to what? I just hear birds."

"Precisely," said George. "Listen to the birds." Ten seconds later, an urgent, shrill trilling shattered the stillness, modulating higher, then lower, in a crazy series of pitches and dynamics. It stopped, then started all over again.

"There it is." George pointed to one of the fence posts, on which perched a squat, fidgety, long-beaked brown bird. It warbled again, then lifted off and disappeared into the small hole in the birdhouse under the eaves.

"Everything's all right now, no matter what happens," said Nan, beaming. "Our house wrens are back."

After a short pause during which everyone listened, or pretended to listen, to the song of the house wren, Miss Price raised her glass.

"Back to the business at hand," she said in a hoarse, croaking whisper. "This is what those whose only concerns are of a pecuniary nature would call the lost treasure of Livia." As they all sat or stood there gathered around the object, visions of debts paid, glory gained, an expensive college education, a startup landscaping business, and lots of new pairs of shoes danced in their heads. Yet Miss Price seemed strangely reluctant.

"Before I open this," she finally said, after having drained her gin and tonic with one last, noisy glug, "I must tell Dr. Lick I'm sorry. As the Lord God Almighty and my dear ancestors are my witnesses, I am truly sorry." Dr. Lick almost choked on the merlot sloshing around in his mouth.

"Sorry for what?" he gurgled.

"I'm going to tell you I have deceived you, just as I have

deceived everyone here today. But please look and listen before you vent your ire on an obsessed woman who's been on the quest of a lifetime for so many long years."

"Open it!" cried Nan and George.

"Open it!" cried the others.

The hinges creaked and squealed as Miss Price with some effort pushed open the top of the chest. Inside and taking up most of the space was what looked like a large and deep covered stoneware baking dish. The top was held on tight by tied and knotted leather straps, which George cut through with the loppers from the toolshed. Miss Price bent over, raised the baking dish out of the chest with more effort than appeared to be necessary, and placed it on the table. Standing up straight, she sucked in a deep breath, then noisily exhaled. She then removed the top, peered inside, and began rummaging among the contents. Everyone crowded around her.

"Please," she said, stretching her arms out. "Give me some space." After doing some more poking around she stopped and smiled a beatific smile the likes of which no one there had ever seen light up her face.

"It's all here!" she cried. "It's all here! Now I have proof!" She collapsed back into her chair, suddenly exhausted and fragile. "I must tell you the *real* truth of what is gathered here in this chest. This will be the complete, unvarnished truth, with no equivocation, no embellishment, and no little half-lies. So help me, God!"

George, Nan, and Dr. Lick bent over to see what was inside the dish and frowned. There was an ancient photograph—an old, sepia-toned, and cracked daguerreotype, tintype, or ambrotype; they didn't know which—several cracked and discolored leather-bound journals, a few crinkled documents, a crucifix and a chalice, a small, ring-shaped metallic object bisected by a pin, and what looked like a hunk of scrawled-on undistinguished-looking rock. Nothing more.

"Sit down," said Miss Price, chuckling softly. "There's another story coming, and you must hear it. It is of immense importance to me, but perhaps little to you. I have lied to you, Dr. Lick, and I even lied to the dolts I hired to help me find this chest. As for Mr. and Mrs. Fremont, I've done you an even greater disservice from the very beginning by hiding the truth from you and resorting to subterfuge and quasi-criminal acts to make sure it remained hidden. You purchased the property legally, and by all rights everything should have been yours, though we now have our agreement and you might not be so enthusiastic about it once you see what we've *really* unearthed. All this is an injustice and I shall take it to the grave with me. But I had no choice. How else could I have gotten anyone else interested but me? Now, just listen . . ."

31

The Story of Livia

Miss Price, deliberately and with an apparent reverence that calmed and quieted her perplexed listeners, now began the tale of two Welsh brothers, Caradoc and Llywelyn Morgan.

The Morgan brothers, she said, sailed to the New World during the mid-1800s. Not content to stay in the thriving metropolises of the East, they pushed westward, following the frontier to the grassland where Livia now stands.

At first, they lived together, trading with the Indians for furs, hunting, and doing a little scratch farming and fishing. At some point, there was an argument, and the two brothers broke up, Caradoc building his sod cabin on the bare rise overlooking Bluegill Pond, and which had been used by the Indians for their camp sometime before that, and Llywelyn moving a few miles southeast, still within the confines of present-day Livia, but in an area next to the Big Turkey River that was more mixed prairie and woods. The two brothers eventually reconciled and, though they continued to live apart, together built a store stocking the most basic of goods.

"That store was on this very rise, maybe thirty yards from Caradoc's cabin."

Miss Price stopped and gulped. Tears glistened in her eyes. She smiled apologetically and continued.

Both brothers became well versed in Indian languages and customs, though Caradoc, much more than Llywelyn, took to a primitive lifestyle. Within a couple of years, he fell in love with the daughter of an important Indian, either a warrior, a medicine man, or a chief, and married her, both in the Indian way and the Christian way, as he had not neglected his Methodist upbringing whatever the changes the wilderness had wrought upon him. At that point, settlers were filtering into the area and the Indians began to recede farther to the west and north. What had seemed perfectly natural to Caradoc, now the father of a son and a daughter, did not seem so to his neighbors, who became hostile to a family whose mixed blood marked them as outcasts. Caradoc and his wife were shunned. Even Llywelyn turned his back on them. He sold his half interest in the store to Caradoc, who eventually shut it down when business dried up. Still, he stayed on. He replaced the crude cabin with a house of hauled-in timber, turned more land, and made a poor living as a farmer.

Miss Price stopped again, and trembled.

"This part is very moving to me," she said. "Another gin and tonic would be most helpful."

"We're cutting you off, Miss Price," Nan said. "You have taken advantage of our hospitality by deceiving us and playing us for fools for your own devious and selfish purposes. We offer you no more now than just to hear your story out and decide for ourselves whether to believe it or not. Now, keep going."

"Well, I'll try." Miss Price stifled a sob, then delivered a sudden, stinging slap to her right cheek. "There," she said. "That helps."

One night, someone set fire to Caradoc's home and the

store, which Caradoc had just closed for business and was still half-stocked with goods. Caradoc and his wife died in the fire. Who did it? Settlers? Indians? Renegades white or red? Who knows? No one ever found out, and, even if so, no one told. Their two mixed-blood children, aged fourteen and twelve, escaped, shivering and scared, into the night. Llywelyn, who had seen the flames far off in the distance and ridden over, found them. At heart he was a good man, and was able to lay aside his prejudices and take pity on them. He buried Caradoc and his Indian wife, and raised their children as his own.

"Llywelyn wrote these things down in his own diary, as well as a number of other things." Miss Price said. "That went missing for decades. I was finally able to find it some thirty years ago in the attic of a distant relative, who was loath to give it up. I persuaded her with a check for $1,000. That diary is where most of my clues came from. Of course, you know about the remains of two skeletons all tangled up in the roots of the white oak we cut down."

Nan gasped.

"Caradoc and his wife!" she cried.

"Yes. Though I wasn't quite sure that's what we would find when we cut down the tree. I was actually thinking the chest would be under there. But I should have known, especially the way the tree was acting. They wanted to be found and their story to be told. Isn't it obvious?"

"Hmmm," said George.

"No!" barked Nan. "It's not obvious at all. That tree didn't die because a couple of dead people willed it to. I'm sorry, Miss Price, but that's a little too weird for me."

"Well," said Miss Price. "Think about all the strange things, both bad and good, that have happened on your property, Mrs. Fremont. And I am quite familiar from the press account with what happened to you last year. These things don't happen by mere chance. And you're hearing that from a trained historian.

Anyway, as you know, I had forgotten about the other tree. And thank you, Mr. Fremont, for remembering my clothesline reminiscence."

George nodded.

"That's all well and good," he said. "Now, please continue with your story, Miss Price."

The Morgan brothers shared a big secret, Miss Price said. They were both direct descendants of Welsh nobility of the highest order. Indeed, they claimed to trace their ancestry all the way back to Hywel Dda, the first great king of the Welsh. But the ensuing centuries of hardship and misfortune and the changing tenor of the times had leveled the family and made them common. By the time Caradoc and Llywelyn were born, the Morgans were farmers of only modest means.

So, the brothers, being ambitious sorts, were ready for a new beginning. But they did not neglect to bring certain things with them. Each brother was given a chest of belongings by their aging parents as a legacy to take with them to America. Onto the top of each chest was carved a red-painted dragon— *Y Ddraig Goch*. That is, "the Red Dragon," or the Welsh, who (or so the prophecy went) would drive "the White Dragon"— that being the invading Saxons—back into the sea.

"You can see the outlines of the dragon here," said Miss Price, closing the chest. "The paint has all chipped off and faded away, but this is it, the Red Dragon."

In each chest, Miss Price continued, were a few small, run-of-the-mill belongings. But there were other things as well. In Llywelyn's chest was the silver of kings, passed down through the generations and stamped especially to mark it as the coin of the realm, legal tender for the rich and the nobility. In Caradoc's chest were a chalice, a brooch, a large, flat piece of rock into which an inscription was etched, and a cross. They had belonged originally to Hywel Dda, who used the brooch to fasten his cloak. The inscribed rock was Welsh bluestone, now often used as paving stones for pathways and patios. So great was the pride of lineage that no one over the many years had ever attempted to use even the silver to restore some measure of prosperity to the family.

They traveled armed and guarded the chests closely on their passage to America. Once here, they kept their chests in broad view in their cabins, adding little valuables and mementoes as acquired; and, in the case of Caradoc, the photograph—it was actually a daguerreotype—and important documents as well as his own logs and journals. With the passage of time, both brothers grew fearful of the pilfering of Indians and the wild, lawless white men who roamed the land. They buried their chests. And there they remained.

"Llywelyn was driven off his land suddenly, and we don't know exactly why," Miss Price said. "But he had to leave with the two children very quickly. What happened next is lost in the mists of time. The two children—Rhys and Gwyneth—grew up and married, and found their way back to Livia, which was no longer frontier. It might have been the lure of their birthplace that drew them back, or maybe they had somehow heard about the two chests. Could Llywelyn have told them? Whatever the reason, they came back. After a few years, the acreage on the rise overlooking Bluegill Pond, where we are sitting right now, became available, and Rhys and his wife bought it. Gwyneth and her husband were able to find Llywelyn's old plot, which was not very good farmland, and which they acquired for a good price. Rhys, of course, was my great-grandfather. Anyway, they must have looked and looked and looked for the chests. Or maybe they didn't. Maybe they didn't even care. Both chests remained hidden underground, at least until today. The other one, the one with the silver coins, remains buried elsewhere. I think I know where it is, but I'm not telling. It is southeast of here. Let's leave it at that."

"So there *is* a lost treasure of Livia!" George said.

"Yes, I suppose there is. But it is not a matter of concern to me. This is the one that matters most to me."

"Why?" said Nan.

"Why?" said Miss Price, patting the chest tenderly. "Isn't that obvious? What I've believed with all my heart for so many years has only been surmise, based on flimsy evidence gathered over many decades. Now I have the proof!"

"Proof?" wondered George coldly. "Proof of what?"

"Proof of who my great-great-grandparents are. The daguerreotype is of Caradoc and his wife. There is a document from the circuit preacher who married them. There are also journals and logbooks that should establish that Caradoc and Llywelyn were the first European inhabitants of Livia. That means I beat out Marvelle Olson. Marvelle Olson is, according to the current accepted history, descended from the Norwegian Olsons, Livia's original inhabitants. And, oh, how she flaunts it! Now, Livian history will have to be rewritten, and my family will get the credit! Mine! And I am descended from the great Hywel Dda! This chalice touched his lips. This crucifix graced Hywel Dda's altar. The inscribed bluestone bears words in Latin scrawled into the rock by hardworking monk-artisans. It either broke off by itself or was broken off a flagstone that was either inside or outside of the chapel and should hold the proof that all this is true. I believe it can be dated by the proper authorities. The penannular brooch fastened Hywel's tunic. And it's not just Hywel Dda I am descended from, but also from a line of great Indians, or, I suppose we should say Native Americans! Chiefs. Medicine men who had magnificent dreams and visions. Brave and accomplished warriors honored with many ceremonial feathers. That would make me nobility from both sides of the ocean! Isn't that great? Isn't that wonderful? Thank you, God! Thank you!"

"What a waste of time," huffed Dr. Lick. "All this for a little family history one hundred and seventy-five years old at best. You could certainly make up for leading me on a wild goose chase, Miss Price, by pointing the way to the other chest. At least the Fremonts here and I could get something out of *that*."

"I told you, Dr. Lick, I don't really know where it is. I have an inkling, but I intend to take that inkling to the grave with me. I'll have no big dustup over my inheritance."

"I believe there's some legal action I can take here," Dr. Lick said. "Defrauding an academic institution in the furtherance of research and education. I fully intend to explore every avenue."

"Uh, don't forget, Dr. Lick," said Nan. "You and the university owe us $30,000 for ripping up our arbor over there."

"We'll just see about that," he said. "I consider this contract null and void since I'm the victim of a fraud." With that, he stormed off down the steps, kicking Nan's precious pea gravel all over the surrounding gardens and lawn.

Nan and George stared at Miss Price, trying to sort out whether to honor her for her quest or shun her for her duplicity.

"One thing?" Nan said.

"Yes?"

"You never told us the name of your great-great-grandmother."

"Well, her Indian name has been lost. After years and years of looking, I haven't been able to find it. Her white name, the one she took upon marrying my great-great-grandfather, why, isn't that obvious? It's Livia!"

Grudgingly, but without complaint, the Fremonts carried the chest down to Miss Price's car, and fit it snugly in the trunk.

"Don't forget that you owe us one-half of the value of what you have," said George as he slammed the lid of the trunk.

"Yes, that's right," said Nan. "It's in the contract."

Miss Price smiled.

"Don't you worry about that, Mr. and Mrs. Fremont. I intend to fulfill my obligation. Just remember, you've already been rewarded for your stewardship of the land. Whatever good fortune you've gained from this property is due to them. Call it spirituality. Call it whatever you like. I really do believe that."

"Well, there has been a fair amount of bad fortune, too," George said. "Are they responsible for *that?*"

Miss Price shrugged.

"You may come out ahead yet, Mr. Fremont," she said. "Never underestimate the power of beneficent spirits to make things right, especially for good people."

"Ba-loney," Nan said. "What about the other chest?"

"Not covered in the contract. And as I said, I'm not even sure where it is."

"A little bit of uncertainty didn't stop you from digging here, did it?" said Nan.

"This is true," said Miss Price. "And you've both been very indulgent with me, I must say. And what a nuisance we've been to you! But there are secrets one must keep to one's self."

George and Nan watched silently as Miss Price drove off.

"Jerk!" said Nan as she polished off the last of her Sagelands. "Why is the world so full of lying, malicious jerks?"

"I'm sure you can sue her," said Mary, who, with Shirelle, had been silent bystanders to the climax and denouement of the treasure hunt.

"We're already suing her," said George. "And her henchmen. Those Scroggit brothers."

"Well, you can add this to the lawsuit," said Mary. "Shirelle, what's wrong?"

"This yard," said Shirelle, choking back sobs, her face twitching in agony. "All that's happened to it over the past few days. And all the pain you can feel coming from the flowers. It's like one vast moan out there. There's no joy, no energy, no motivation to recharge and recover. And now the arbor's all torn up, and for *what?*"

Nan reached across to pat her hand.

"Thank you, Shirelle," she said. "But it's not so bad. Who knows? We might still have a comeback. Stranger things have certainly happened. Last year, for instance. But, if not, we'll just roll up our sleeves and try again next year."

Three weeks later, the Fremonts bid Shirelle adieu and best of luck in her new job with a major landscaping company in a neighboring state. The Burdick's sign had been taken down, either by predetermined design, or in acknowledgment of the very obvious fact that there was little to look at anymore. In a few weeks, Ellis and Cullen would be leaving for college, and Mary would lug her trombone to the first marching band practice of her freshman year at Stanford.

32

Battle Royal

The Fremonts loitered on the patio later than usual on a hot, muggy August night that seemed more suited to a six-pack of cold beer than a bottle of tepid Sagelands. Still, after three glasses each of '07 vintage, George and Nan were able to lapse into the sort of listless comfort that turns a blind eye to the streams of salty liquid soaking your shirt, blurring your vision, and making your underarms scream out for a thick coat of Right Guard.

Since the plague of insects and unearthing Miss Price's genealogical treasure, they'd been mired in a state of downtrodden ennui. This last assault on their gardens and the enervating treasure hunt debacle left them winded and apathetic, and there was no Shirelle to buck them up with her relentless enthusiasm. There had been no effort to replace their broken and destroyed flowers, or to even maintain what had survived undamaged. Mary's focus was now entirely on her approaching freshman year and a boy named Bertram she'd met at work.

A week before, all plant communications shut down.

The citronella candles still burned in their effort to drive off a population of mosquitoes already greatly diminished from its early-July peak. The moon rose through the trees big and butterscotch and a couple of slivers short of full. They barely noticed it. George poured them each a refill, but he did so mechanically. He wasn't even giving the bottle that little quarter-twist when he poured out the wine. A few drops spattered onto the tabletop.

"George, dear, I have the terrible feeling that we have misspent a sizable chunk of our adult lives."

George nodded.

"Yes."

"Tomorrow, we shift gears. Either both of us get working like normal people, or find hobbies that won't keep putting us through this hell-and-heaven cycle every year. Our gardening days are over. Maybe whatever money we make out of this lawsuit can get us off to a good start in another direction. Hey, maybe we can start traveling again."

"Hmmm."

"That's it from you? You're just going to be Mr. Monosyllable from now on?"

"No."

"Okay, then, it's settled. Starting tomorrow, or I guess today if you want to be technical about it, the Fremonts move on to a new, more productive stage of life. That means putting our heads together to resolve this mortgage debacle. It also means job searches. All-day job searches. And yours could be a long one, since there's that wine-break blot on your employment history. So, no more wine for you, mister. Or me either, for that matter. Our tippling days are over. First thing tomorrow, I head to the grocery store to load up on our new beverage of choice . . . herbal tea."

"Guess that makes us *tea*-totalers now," said George without a trace of humor coloring his voice.

"George!" Nan whispered urgently. "George! We have to go outside! We have to go outside *now*."

"I know," said George, who was already sitting up in bed. "I need to take my bat."

"Yes, and I need to take the butcher knife."

Without question or having to stifle so much as a yawn, George and Nan got out of bed, driven by some purpose they didn't understand and didn't bother to question. George reached under the bed for his Smokestack Gaines batting practice bat, stroked its smooth, polished barrel and the rougher surface on the knob of the handle, where the chip had gotten knocked off, and lifted it to batting stance position. Already having made her way into the kitchen, Nan retrieved the butcher knife from the knife holder block and practiced her thrusts and parries.

"Time to go," said George, tapping the barrel of the bat into his palm like a billy club.

"I know," said Nan. "But, George dear, isn't this kind of weird? I mean—"

George raised his hand for her to stop.

"Of course it's weird, Nan-bee. Life is weird. But we've received our summons and we have to go. It was only a matter of time. We knew this would come, sooner or later."

"I know. But couldn't I at least get dressed?"

"No need."

"No need? I don't want anybody seeing me in this baggy thing. I look like I've been living off cream puffs, Sugar Smacks, and heavily salted potato chips."

"You think I want to go prancing around like this, in my pjs, with a baseball bat? At least I've got the Gordon plaid bottom and the Jethro Tull *Warchild* top on. Smart of me to put those on last night. What if I'd just been wearing my underwear, huh? Slippers on?"

"Umm-hmmm. You?"

"Yep. That should be enough. Let's go. Time's a-wastin'."

The backyard, bathed in moonlight, seemed so much larger

to them now, stretching out for acres upon acres. The bordering stretch of woods to the north appeared as a distant, impenetrable forest that was . . . shaking?

"Who is THAT?" George said, pointing to a form approaching rapidly from an opening in the trees. "Whoa! It's a
woman and she's stark-naked!"

"Shhh! George, please temper your voyeuristic enthusiasm
a little."

Nan squinted. The woman didn't appear to be quite naked.
Nan thought she could see a few strategically located weeds
held in place by some unknown force, or maybe it was just
sticky pine sap she was using. She had planted herself, firm and
motionless, on the ground, long legs splayed out, and her spindly
body perched precariously on tiptoes. It looked like she was
holding a rod of some sort in her right hand. There was a muffled racket coming from somewhere in the forest behind her
that was goopy- and crunchy-sounding at the same time. The
closest George could come to describing it was by imagining a
couple thousand buckets of Klinghopper's Homestyle Cole-
slaw on the move.

"That is Dr. Phyllis Sproot," Nan said calmly. "She has either just leaped off the edge that separates the criminally in-
sane from the only annoyingly so, or is really running behind
in her laundry. Who the heck made the decision to let her out
of the loony bin? I'd say we better get ready to defend ourselves."

Nan thrust out her butcher knife, which she was happy to
recall had just been sharpened by Curman's for free with her
purchase of two pounds of tilapia fillets. George scrunched
down, raised the bat up and pulled it behind his head, then
wiggled it in the manner of Smokestack Gaines.

Dr. Sproot was now manipulating the rod and pointing it
at them.

"George, look out!" shouted Nan. "She's got a gun." There

was a muffled pop and something clinked against the butcher knife and knocked it out of her hand. "George!"

George quickly jumped in front of Nan and pointed his bat directly at Dr. Sproot and her gun. There was another pop. George swung. Contact. The invisible BB pinged off the wood. Then another. Soon, George was swinging as fast as he could, dozens of tiny BBs pocking the white-ash smoothness of the bat. There was a short lull in the action as Dr. Sproot stopped to reload. Nan had retrieved her butcher knife, and, for a moment, gloried in the way the moonlight flashed off its blade. I can throw this thing if I have to, she thought; any target within ten yards I can hit and sink the blade in deep.

The racket, which had subsided for a while, now resumed and grew even louder as Dr. Sproot raised her arm then brought it down, pointing a withered, trembling finger straight at the Fremonts. Nan, as a great, moving mass that looked like an ocean tide coming in emerged from the forest, now recognized all the noise as a guttural sort of plant speech, though far more primitive than anything she was accustomed to.

"Gracious, George, those are plants making that noise. Bad plants. Weeds of all kinds. There must be thousands of them. Crabgrass. Dandelions. Cockleburs. Creeping bellflowers. Canadian thistles. And, better look out here, George. Sow thistles! Big damn sow thistles!"

George flinched. In the moonlight, Nan could see the veins tighten in his neck.

"Steel yourself, George, because what we're facing here is Dr. Sproot in a state of dishabille as the anti–Mother Nature, leading hundreds upon hundreds of weeds she has insulted, poisoned, dug out, crushed, and basically treated like vermin. And, if I'm picking up the vibes correctly, they can't wait to get their sticky appendages all over us."

"Eccch!"

"That's right," came a voice close enough to startle the bejesus out of them. "Dr. Sproot has carried her powers to a new height. Somehow, she's been able to call forth all the dead plants she's weeded out of her gardens, and turn them into little plant people with really bad attitudes."

"Marta! Marta Poppendauber! What in heaven's name are you doing here in our dream or crusade or whatever it is? What are any of us doing here, for that matter?"

"Good question," said Marta. "If I were to guess, I'd say Livia's forces of horticultural good are here arrayed against the forces of horticultural bad in one huge battle to decide the fate of gardening in Livia. But, hey, what do I know? That's just a guess."

"I'll say one thing," said another voice. "The girl's got talent. Never expected her to make it this far."

"Edith!" cried Nan. "Or is it Sarah the Witch? What the heck is it you're calling yourself these days? Ah, hey, thanks for doing that frog-and-toad thing, and what was apparently a pretty dang good fairy impersonation. I must say, though, Edith, that you should have known better than throwing in with Dr. Sproot in the first place. And all for a little extra pocket change."

Edith lowered her head and blushed in shame, though no one could see that in the milky darkness.

"You're right, Mrs. Fremont," she moaned woefully. "I should have known she'd get carried away once she got a little witch power under her belt. I should have seen it and nipped it in the bud last year when we first met at the Hi-Lo. You heard, of course, that the mental health folks did an initial evaluation, gave her some drugs, and told her to go see a shrink. Then, they sprang her to the custody of one of her many local relatives, which is as good as no custody at all."

"I figured that," said Nan. "Otherwise, why would she be here marshaling all her forces to turn us into bone meal for her stupid coreopsis-salvia-hollyhock blend and yuccas?"

"Edith is now a helper for the good," Marta said solemnly. "It's important that you know that. She helped you quite a bit last year, too, though we don't need to go into that here."

"Yeah?" said George. "It seems as though you said some pretty nice things about Dr. Sproot, too, Marta. That sort of calls your judgment of character into question."

"So, Edith," said Nan. "If you're with us, what is it you're bringing to the party?"

"Look behind you."

George and Nan turned to see that rank upon rank of flowers had moved into position behind them, and were seething with excitement and the sweet perfume of moral purpose.

"Our little soldiers!" Nan cried.

"This is Edith's doing," said Marta. "With some help from the rest of us, that being mostly you, even though you don't realize it. But it's all we could muster. I'm afraid we're going to be outnumbered."

"Hey!" yelled George, waving, once he picked out the coleuses. "Whaddup, y'all!" He winked and gave them a thumbs-up. Nan poked him.

"This is no time for either joking or favoritism, George. We've got serious work ahead of us. . . . Hey, what's that big wooden door with the transom on top doing over there in the middle of nowhere?"

"Don't go there," Marta warned. "That's freshman-year chemistry and you haven't been to a single class all year."

George felt his pajama bottoms suddenly slip to a pile around his feet, leaving him naked from the waist down. No one seemed to notice. Blushing from shame, George bent over to pull them back up again. The drawstrings around the waist tightened them up without his having to touch them, then knotted themselves up into a neat bow.

A BB tore into the petal of one of the petunias.

"First casualty!" George cried. "Dr. Sproot draws the first

blood. Now, it's our turn. No quarter! No quarter for villains!"
He raised his bat above his head and swung it around as a rally-
ing device. Another BB ripped into the pink-and-white striated
leaf of a coleus. It slumped, then rose back up, triumphantly.

"Only a flesh wound!" cried George. "Hurrah! Hurrah for
the coleus!"

Nan patted his shoulder.

"George, let's tone down the lust-for-blood warrior stuff,
can we? And get that bat going again, please."

George flicked the bat right and left, then up and down,
sending the incoming BBs scattering in all directions.

"What I want to know is this," he said. "Isn't there some
sort of shadowy acquaintance from your past that shows up at
times like these to whisper in your ear that you're dreaming?
When's that going to happen is what I want to know."

"You're not dreaming," Marta said.

Edith nodded.

"It may seem like a dream but it's not," she said. "Dreams
keep trying to muscle in on our territory, though."

"Hey!" Marta shouted at a couple of creepy caped figures
loitering around on the fringes of the woods. "Go away. You're
in the wrong subconscious." She looked at the illuminated dial
on her wristwatch, which squiggled like an amoeba under a
microscope. "Don't forget; only three hours till your blood-
sucking night's done."

"Mom! Daddy!"

"Mr. and Mrs. Fremont!"

George and Nan turned to see that Mary and Shirelle had
joined them. They were carrying something that smelled both
wonderful and dangerous.

"Yikes!" cried George. "Angel's trumpets! What'd you
bring those along for? Shouldn't those guys be on the other
side?"

"No, Daddy. They're flowers, too, and they're here to help.

We'll use them to shoot mind-altering pollen right out of the flower. Watch!" Mary pointed her angel's trumpet at the approaching horde, which was inching closer to them. A little puff of dust arced into the moonlight then landed on top of a cocklebur, which proceeded to sway drunkenly from side to side, then collapse, writhing, onto the ground.

"See?"

"Well, okay then."

"I really don't think you girls should be here," Nan said. "And you, Shirelle, don't you need to get up early tomorrow and commute to work?" Shirelle's answer was interrupted by a howl and the slow, sweeping movement of plants in motion.

"Everyone get ready!" cried Marta. "Here they come!"

Within seconds, the two sides collided, rather softly as there were no metal parts involved. Dr. Sproot was taking down one flower after another with her BB gun. George was swinging in short compact strokes, demolishing dandelions by the score as they tried to wrap their long roots around his legs and arms, and blind him with their flying, fluffy seed down.

Nan waded into a carpet of creeping Charlie with her butcher knife, carving away and turning one weed after another into rank salad fixin's. Marta had brought pruning shears along with her, and tore a swath of destruction through the ranks of the Canadian thistle. Mary and Shirelle were doing good service with the angel's trumpets, brandishing them like machine guns, and creating huge pockets of clueless, stumbling weeds plagued by visions of paisley-colored cows chomping on them with boulder-sized pink molars.

But it wasn't an even fight. It was clear that Dr. Sproot's supernatural powers now far outstripped Edith's, which were mitigated somewhat by her guilt at once having used them for nefarious purposes. So, while Edith, with some help from the potent vibes of Shirelle and the Fremonts, did manage to summon forth hundreds of flowers—mostly annuals, of course—

that had once lent their glory to the Fremonts' gardens, Dr.
Sproot was able to call up tens of thousands of weeds that not
only she, but all of Livia's gardeners, had committed to garbage,
compost, or the slow death by a Weed-B-Gon or Roundup
dousing.

Still, the battle seesawed back and forth for what seemed
like hours. When George spotted the biggest sow thistle on
the battlefield he made for it with a vengeance, bashing his
way through the wall of enemy weeds with a whir of bat motion no human eye could detect. As he stood, face-to-vascular
tissue, with the offending monster weed, Nan called out to
him.

"Don't let its hairs touch you, George," she yelled. "Remember what happened the last time you touched one of
those. You got that infected rash that lasted for months. And
this one's ten times bigger."

Suddenly, the sow thistle lurched toward him, then started
stumbling around blindly, as if it had imbibed too much dan-
delion wine. It finally tripped over its roots, which were trailing behind it, as ungainly as a bridal train. George saw his
chance. Charging forward, he swung his bat as he'd never swung
it before, going for downtown rather than just contact. Big,
juicy chunks of stem flew everywhere, forcing George to bob
and weave to dodge the bristles.

In the time it takes an August yellow jacket to find an
open can of soda pop, it was over. The sow thistle lay torn in
shreds on the ground, its pulpy innards exposed, its leaves
crumpled up into balls of rapidly decomposing matter. The
other weeds pulled back, stunned and cowering.

"That was easier than I thought," said George, raising his
arms in triumph.

"Easy on the hail-the-conquering-hero stuff, dear," said
Nan, now at his side and keeping the weed masses at bay by
holding her butcher knife straight out toward them and swing-

ing it slowly back and forth along ninety-degree arc. "Especially when you had some help from another quarter."

"Yeah, Daddy," said Mary, who along with Shirelle had crowded in next to him with their angel's trumpets spitting out pollen puffs with a machine-gun rapidity. "That's because we psychedelicized it with a few well-placed seed shots. That guy was in no shape to take on you and your bat. Now, let's back up a little before these yard-blight scumbags start charging again."

George stared forlornly at his bat. Two more chips, one of those from the tip of the barrel, had been knocked off, and the whole thing, from end to end, was stained with gooey weed guts.

"Now, I'm really mad!" shouted George, figuring he had just lost a good $800 in value off that bat.

"George, we have to move," said Nan. "We can't hold 'em off here forever."

The weeds, recovered from the shock of seeing their champion vanquished, were moving toward them again, reinforced by ten thousand clumps of crabgrass just called up by Dr. Sproot once she had managed to tear a couple dozen lobelia off her legs.

"Fall back!" shouted Nan. "Fall back!"

The weight of numbers was beginning to tell despite the best efforts of Edith to add potency to her witch spells. Soon, there was nothing left of their flower allies but a few tiny alyssum, a badly battered core of elite hybrid tea roses, the angel's trumpets, and a smattering of petunias.

Then came a sound from out of the adjoining woods the likes of which no one had ever heard before. It was the battle cry of women who refuse to be dominated, whether by city hall, exploitative men, or a gaggle of puny-assed weeds on the brink of world domination. In an instant, a mob of them armed with rakes, shovels, and loppers passed through the piti-

ful remains of the allied flower ranks, formed a "flying V" attack column, and tore into the surrounding weeds, which fell
back from them in some disarray.

"It's the Rose Maidens!" shouted Marta. "The Rose Maidens have been summoned to save us!"

How come everyone else got to get dressed up? Nan wondered, looking at the Rose Maidens' stylish pantsuits, dresses,
and blouses, then down sulkily at her baggy, billowing, peasant-
style nightgown.

"And, look, up in the sky!" someone shouted.

"Lightning bugs?" wondered George.

"No, Mr. Fremont," cried Shirelle. "It's fairies. They glow
blue, see? And, if you look closely, you can see little gossamer
wings!"

"Fairies!" shouted Mary. "Yippee!"

The fairies swooped in like so many pint-sized Dauntless
dive bombers, dropping their clumped loads of fairy dust
timed to break up and disperse just above the attacking weed
hordes, then veering off sharply before the weeds could throw
out their stems and leaves to catch them. Dr. Sproot worked
the lever of her BB gun, aimed, and a fairy came spiraling out
of the sky. She shot down another, then another.

"Ha-ha!" she chortled. "Ha-ha! Whoever said fairies were
immortal?"

A fourth fairy, taking advantage of Dr. Sproot's temporary
distraction, managed to find the bull's-eye, and a concentrated
wad of powder exploded over the top of Dr. Sproot's head,
covering her face with a glittering white. Her allergies acti-
vated and with none of the antihistamines she normally carried in her purse handy, Dr. Sproot sneezed so loudly it rang
out over the cacophony of the battle.

But, apart from that, the fairy dive bombers appeared to be
doing little damage to her or her plant hordes. They were,

however, having quite the effect on the dwindling forces of good, who were breathing in enough fairy dust fumes to fuel a dozen cable TV comedy shows. George and Nan found themselves laughing uncontrollably. Mary and Shirelle, too. The Rose Maidens dropped their tools, joined hands, and began dancing in a ring-around-the-rosie circle as the weeds closed in and began to ensnare them.

"I think there's been a slight miscalculation," Marta said between guffaws. "The fairies' happy powder works fine on us. I'm just tickled pink now, ha-ha. Tee-hee-hee. No go on Dr. Sproot and her weeds, though. Ha-ha. Isn't that a hoot?"

Edith was bent over, convulsed with laughter after hearing one of Nan's knock-knock jokes, and fell down kicking and waving her arms. The remaining, battle-ravaged flowers were expanding and contracting like accordion bellows, which is what flowers sometimes do when they're having a rattling good time. Even George found himself laughing at one of Nan's dumb riddles.

Meanwhile, one fairy after another was being shot down out of the sky by Dr. Sproot or ensnared by the weeds. What remained of them were now beating a hasty retreat, bobbing their way off the field like tiny blue will-o'-the-wisps.

"I sure hope they're going for reinforcements," said Nan, chuckling. "Hey, how many liatrises does it take to screw in a lightbulb? Ha-ha! Ha-ha!"

Slowly, the weeds surrounded them. Then, Dr. Sproot, her face and body smeared with plant guts and caked, streaky fairy dust, her BB gun at the ready, forced her way through the packed, groaning masses, and confronted the small clot of humans and flowers that formed the only barrier left between her and total plant domination.

"Gee, Doc Phil, don't you think you could put some clothes on?" said Marta. "At least cover up those saggy boobs!

Ha-ha. And in front of all these weeds! Goodness! I guess people just don't have standards anymore. Hey, can I take my clothes off, too?"

Dr. Sproot sneered.

"Thank goodness, little Marta, I'll never have to tell you not to call me Doc Phil again. And you will keep your clothes on. I'm happy to see you've all been rendered complete idiots by your little fairy helpers. What a bunch of screwups! Ha-ha!"

Everyone else laughed along with Dr. Sproot because they couldn't help it.

"How do you manage to keep so trim, Sproot?" wondered Nan admiringly. "But up top? A little mascara and rouge would do you wonders."

"Silence!" Dr. Sproot snapped. "Now who's the first one to be sacrificed to the weed feeding frenzy?"

"Plants don't eat meat, you dodo," corrected Shirelle. "Except maybe Venus flytraps and one or two other fly eaters, but I don't see any of them here."

"I said shut up! Well, if they don't eat you, they can certainly smother you, or gross you out, or, Mr. Fremont . . ."

"George."

"George, give you a rash to end all rashes."

George shuddered with suppressed laughter tempered by paralyzing fear now that the fairy dust was starting to wear off.

"Down on your knees, wimps. This is your last chance to say your prayers. Then, you can watch as your little flower friends get torn apart, petal by petal. Ha-ha! Ha-ha!"

That last chuckle froze in Dr. Sproot's mouth. A small tornado of mist whirled up in front of her, then spewed out two ghostly forms that looked like actual people, only made out of puttyish cloud matter.

"What the blue blazes do *you* want?" sneered Dr. Sproot, who, though unafraid, was wondering how someone—presumably Edith—had managed to summon two humans—a guy and a gal from the looks of it—back from the dead. "No fair, Edith. You've really crossed the line by channeling the spirits of dead *people*."

"No need to blame Edith," said the guy ghost, who had a European accent nobody there could quite place. "We're here of our own accord. And we're here to take you away, Phyllis Sproot. You have transgressed the laws of nature and acted the part of destroyer. We despise destroyers."

"You've disturbed our home for the last time," said the gal ghost, rather serenely, everyone thought. "Your evil thoughts and evil deeds have done enough harm, to say nothing of disturbing our sleep one time too many."

Nan shook her head, trying to stifle a laugh and wondering how dead people could speak in such well-organized and grammatically correct sentences, especially seeing as how this was probably a dream.

"Yes," said the guy ghost. "We're light sleepers. We'd really like to get that eternal repose we keep hearing about, but you keep messing things up for us."

"Hey," whispered George to Nan. "It's the spirits of that Welsh guy and his Indian wife, huh? I hope they turn that Dr. Sproot-the-Weed-Queen into earthworm slime."

"Shhhh!" everyone went. The two ghosts looked over their shoulders at George and frowned.

"Could you let us please handle this, George?" said the guy ghost.

George gaped at the ghost, unable to turn away.

"Yessir."

"That goes for you, too, Nan, or may I call you Nan-bee?" said the gal ghost.

"Yes, ma'am," croaked Nan hoarsely. "You can call me whatever you want."

All this time, Dr. Sproot was calculating her odds. Let's see, she thought, I've got about a million weed ghosts against, what, about a dozen humans, a few beaten-up flowers, and a couple of human ghosts. I like my chances.

"Attack!" she shouted. "Attack!" But nothing happened. Dr. Sproot looked around, and discovered she was alone. Not a single weed from the horde that had just moments ago covered the field remained. A meek vulnerability overcame her. She dropped her BB gun and her hands struggled to better cover her private areas, which she now felt she had no business exposing to all these people and plants, either alive or dead.

"Do you by any chance happen to have a wrap?" she asked. "I guess even a moderately-sized bath towel would do."

"Time to come along," said the gal ghost, gently extending her hand. "We have an exciting new destination in store for you."

"Is it hell?" gasped Dr. Sproot, shivering uncontrollably in the chill of the night. "Are you sending me to hell? That's a little extreme, don't you think? I'll be a good girl from now on, I promise."

"It's not hell," the guy ghost said. "It is, however, a place far away. It's a place in need of your special talents, where your peculiar tastes and obsessions can best be put to use. To destroy and rebuild consistently and with a certain gaudy grandeur, yes, but with no concern for the accepted conventions of behavior and beauty."

"It's a place called Las Vegas," said the gal ghost. A gasp went up from the humans in the crowd. "Honestly, folks, we'd never heard of it up to now. Must be kinda new."

"Gee, I was kind of hoping for hell," said Nan to George, followed by cries of "Hush," "We're trying to listen," "Keep it down, please," and another stern look from the gal ghost. Dr. Sproot's eyes brightened as the gal ghost threw her a robe that didn't work so well because it was just as translucent and gauzy as the ghosts.

"Kind of thin material, don't you think?" Dr. Sproot said. "So, it's Vegas, is it? Well, that sounds like it just might work. What are we waiting for, spooks? There's no time like the present. Let's get a move on. Later, gators."

"After a while, crocodile," chirped Edith, who was still feeling the effects of the fairy dust.

With that the ghosts began rotating, faster and faster, until they became one whirling vortex of mist. With a "whoop!" Dr. Sproot was sucked in, and the mini-tornado lifted off the ground, angled off over the tops of the trees, and disappeared.

"Say," said George. "Isn't that northeast? If my geography is correct, Las Vegas is off to the southwest."

"Maybe they just said that to make it easier," said Nan. "My guess? She's going to hell." As George and Nan looked around, they saw there was no sign of the legions of plants and flowers that had been tromping around only minutes earlier. In fact, there was no sign of any other living thing. The brightening in the east signaled that dawn wasn't far off.

"Where are the girls?"

"Where are Edith and Marta?"

"Where are the Rose Maidens?"

"Well, gosh, you'd have thought they'd all stick around to give high fives or say good-bye after all we've been through here. They just vanished!"

"That means this must be a dream," Nan said.

"But if it was a dream you wouldn't be saying that. People don't say, 'This must be a dream' in the middle of their dreams. That's a known fact."

"Okay, look, if this is a dream, then we should stay here and just sort of poof into awakeness like everyone else apparently did. If this is for real, this whole landscape will shrink back to its normal size, and the house will be right over there. . . . Hmmm, there's the house. And it looks plenty real. Well, forget that part. I guarantee you that, tomorrow, everything will

be just the same as it always was. In a few more weeks, you'll
forget this all happened . . . or *didn't* happen, I guess I should say."

"Mmm-hmmm, whatever you say, Nan-bee."

It was late afternoon the next day. George and Nan were
sitting at the patio table, unenthusiastically slurping herbal tea,
and scanning the newspaper classifieds and Nan's laptop for
jobs.

"I could walk people's dogs," said Nan, a false perkiness
coloring her voice. "I hear there's a big market for that."

"You could no doubt learn to talk to them," said George.
"I'm trying to cook up another invention. Something I can
turn quickly. I'm thinking right now of a remote-control
model plane that can shoot down yellow jacket nests."

Nan shook her head.

"You're aiming way too low. How about bagging the invention thing and applying for some kind of superhero job? I
mean, you're telling me that you vanquished evil last night.
How about sprucing up your résumé with that, ha-ha? You
could write under your 'Qualifications' heading: 'Able to destroy anything bad.' There's quite the demand for that these
days."

"You make fun of that, Nan-bee, as if you don't think it
happened."

"It didn't. It didn't happen, you kook. I mean, c'mon—
flower soldiers and demons and Dr. Sproot all tarted up like an
avenging bad angel from hell. Pul-eeze!"

"I'm telling you, it happened."

"And I'm telling you you're delusional."

"Well, what about the part where the *dream* world tried to
take over, but couldn't? Like the vampires showing up. And my
pj bottoms falling down and no one noticing. And the door to
a classroom you or I hadn't been in all semester? Whaddaya

make of that, huh? Dreams trying to intrude on the reality in some kind of new dimension. That's what I make of it."

Nan snorted.

"What I do find kind of disturbing is your little middle-aged soft-porn dream featuring a naked Dr. Sproot. Good grief, George, can't your subconscious come up with something more titillating than that?"

"There's the proof!" cried George. "How could I possibly fantasize about an old hag like Dr. Sproot? It has to have been real."

"Ba-loney," Nan said.

"Okay, think about the here and now," George said. "That's where the evidence is. What's delusional about two new chunks torn out of my bat and green stains on it that won't come out, huh? And how about your butcher knife? Where'd all those nicks come from, eh?"

"It's all about the power of suggestion, George. Those things were already there. They're tiny. In the case of the bat, I'll bet they're nothing but miniscule chips. You just didn't notice them before. Now, of course, you're looking for evidence and you will find it, come hell or high water."

"Uh-oh, visitor."

A new Volvo pulled up to the curb, and they watched a distinguished-looking man with a florid complexion and carrying a briefcase get out of the car, spot them, and begin walking toward the patio.

"And, no, Nan-bee, that's not a Rolls-Royce."

As the man approached, they could see that he was older but not elderly, bald, and sporting a little clipped mustache. He was dressed in a starched white shirt, immaculate charcoal suit, and gray tie. A red handkerchief protruded from the breast pocket of his suit coat. To Nan and George, he looked British. Both concluded independently that here was someone at last who meant to conduct his business in a straightforward way, without trying to fleece or mislead them. This fellow was treading carefully on the pea gravel, which earned him extra points with Nan. He was also looking down at his feet, a welcome display of either shyness or humility considering some of the boisterous characters who'd come bounding up those steps over the past few months.

"Mr. and Mrs. Fremont?" said the man as he stepped onto the patio and offered them a thin but genuine-looking smile. George and Nan nodded.

"My name is Jones. Arthur Jones, of the Jones, Jones, Markham, and Jones law firm. I represent the estate of one Gwendolyn Price. I have some news about Miss Price's holdings and recent acquisitions that she wanted you to know about. I think I might safely say it will alter your lives somewhat."

33

A Spring Well-Sprung

It was April, the great transition month. The winter had been another hard one, with six feet of snow and forty-six nights of subzero readings.

Nan wondered what the ajuga would look like, protected as it was by such a thick layer of snow. But, of course, the ajuga wouldn't be there anymore.

Another good thing about a bad winter was that it took a toll on the pests that ravage gardens during the summer. That meant there should be a drop in the rabbit population. As an added bonus, fewer squirrels would have been stripping the bark of the burning bush. But that was of no matter now, except in her imaginings.

The snow cover lingered until late March, and the ice in the smaller suburban lakes hadn't cleared until a couple of weeks ago. A few stray snows still leaked out of the leaden skies. Some accumulated, even as the Muskies attempted to play their opening home series against the hated Millers and Deerticks. There were a few cancellations. Those games would be tacked on to others sometime in the summer as doubleheaders. Despite these last rear-guard actions, winter in Livia was clearly in full retreat. As the end of the month approached in its slowpoke way, the mercury finally topped 60 degrees and by a healthy margin. A new spring sky appeared with its warmer, wetter look of darker and more sudden clouds. The soil begun its thaw. Burdick's PlantWorld was jammed with gardeners preparing for the season. The new shed Jerry built for the Fremonts was crowded with the usual tools, fertilizers, and potting soils.

As they strolled around their new property in the southeastern quadrant of the city, George and Nan wondered how they would be able to fill up one and a half acres in a way that could match what they had before.

"And this time it's all us and our green thumbs," said George. "No good spells to help us out now. And no handy spirits to make sure everything flourishes. Though who knows what might be buried under *here* somewhere."

"Oh, George, you don't believe in all that bosh, do you?"

"No. Of course not."

"It's all through the grace of God. We've been blessed with some natural talent, and a dedication and work ethic few others can boast. We did it before and there is no reason on earth why we can't do it again."

As George gazed upon their extensive grounds, which were still to be prepped for gardening, his muscles and joints began to twitch, as they always did when he was faced with the prospect of a large, physically demanding project.

Nan, eyeing every swell in the land, mentally mapped out where the big roots would be, and imagined leaves where the buds were sprouting to form a pattern of where the light and shade would fall in the summer and at what time of day.

"This will be a whole-yard job," she said. "And it can command our undivided attention. We no longer have to even pretend we're looking for day jobs."

"Maybe, one of these days, I'll dash off a little doggerel or come up with an invention, just to keep my hand in," said George, snaking his arm around Nan's waist.

Their new yard seemed to go on forever. It left them with conflicted feelings.

"I miss . . . *home,*" Nan said, her eyes tearing up.

"Me too. Let's drive by and see how things are going in the old 'hood."

As they approached the intersection of Payne and Sumac, they passed a big sign that read ROAD CLOSED—NO THRU TRAFFIC. Several of the lots adjoining their own had also been bought by the city and vacated. A few of the homes, including theirs, had already been torn down. They pulled up alongside what bore only a topographical and geographical resemblance to their old lot and got out to inspect a site transformed. Much of it had been cordoned off, and energetic, purposeful workers swarmed around the site. A backhoe and bulldozer were parked in their driveway, or what used to be their driveway. Much of the concrete had been pulled up.

All this had been Miss Price's doing. Shortly after the Fremonts unearthed the dragon-emblazoned chest of her ancestors and stuffed it in the trunk of her car, she had instructed her attorney to try again to buy the property, and to offer the Fremonts $400,000 this time. It would then be transferred to the city to be turned into a historical park, honoring the true founders of Livia. Miss Price was donating Livia another $400,000 from her apparently rather substantial fortune. That was to buy up one or two of the surrounding properties, raze them and the Fremonts' house, and do the proper work of restoring the lot to its natural state. Also to perhaps reconstruct Caradoc's and Livia's cabin and store, which were described in full detail in Caradoc's journals. Maybe there could be water fountains, walking paths, and nice benches on top of the rise for visitors to take in that view of Bluegill Pond.

Miss Price's attorney also drew up papers transferring owner-ship of the chest, with all its contents, to the Fremonts. Miss Price figured the chalice and cross, accounting for their antiquity, their rarity, and their connection to a seminal figure in the history of Wales, to say nothing of the fact that they were fashioned of solid gold, would go for at least $1 million at auction and probably much more. The chest might fetch a few hundred thousand. The clasp and inscribed stone, well, that would probably be substantially less. There was a proviso: The Fremonts would make a full presentation of the contents to the appropriate authorities, allowing them to take whatever documents and journals they might want to preserve and display for the public, and make sure the record was set straight. Finally, Miss Price offered the Fremonts $300,000 to settle their lawsuit. It was an offer they couldn't refuse.

And Miss Price had not forgotten Dr. Lick, who hadn't carried through on his threat to sue her, but *had* made good on paying his $30,000 debt to the Fremonts. Miss Price covered the debt, and gave him $100,000 for whatever pecuniary interest he might have had in the chest's contents. To further comfort him, Miss Price began to call on Dr. Lick at his office. Dr. Lick enjoyed her visits. He found Miss Price to be a kindred spirit similarly interested in the early, undocumented exploration of America by Welsh, Portuguese, Viking, and even Chinese navigators whose names had been lost to the mists of time.

"I almost expect to walk up my steps and see bleeding hearts and hosta and columbine poking up through the ground," Nan said wistfully. "Now, it's nothing but dirt, and the steps aren't there anymore."

George smiled and nodded. It was still hard to believe they were looking at their old property with no new life ready to burst forth from a hundred different points.

"Hey, Fremonts."

George and Nan turned to shake hands with Roland Ready, their favorite newshound and editor of the *St. Anthony Gardener*. He had strolled up behind them from Payne Avenue, a press badge clipped to the lapel of his sport coat, and a pen and pad in hand. He looked to be bursting with new information that would have to be disgorged before causing internal injuries.

"Why, Mr. Ready," said Nan. "It was almost exactly at this spot a year ago last August that we were talking about that other news story involving us. Remember?"

"How could I forget?" Roland said. "Quite a different story this year, isn't it?"

It was Roland who had trumpeted to the St. Anthony metro and Des Plaines region news of the discovery with a story in the St. Anthony *Inquirer*. That was, in part, the Fremonts' doing. When it appeared as though the contents of the chest would become a finding of some local significance, and the Livia city folks had delicately suggested contacts with the press, George and Nan agreed, though with one stipulation.

"We know a guy who can handle the story right," George said. "He's been good to us in the past. We want him to be able to break the story, or, at least, get first crack at it."

So, Roland got the call. Though he no longer worked at the *Inquirer,* his old boss liked the sound of the story he proposed, and let him freelance it. The other editors were so enthusiastic about it, that they ran it on 1A, top of the fold, Sunday.

George and Nan were scrupulous about giving credit to Miss Price and they steered Roland to her and Jim, whom they decided to recognize for his part in the discovery with 20 percent of the take from the sale of the chest and its contents, and for whom all the attention and the significance of the discovery served as a semi-permanent salve to balm his wounded heart.

Coverage of the historical find under the Fremonts' back-yard didn't stop at the *Inquirer*. The interracial love story that matched Indian and European, the tragic deaths, and the life-long crusade of Miss Price to set the historical record straight, to say nothing of the excavated chest chock full of personal treasures, was an irresistible yarn, and it struck a chord. Reporters came from all over the country to tell the tale of Livia and Caradoc Morgan, and their great-great-granddaughter, Gwendolyn Price.

Miss Price basked in the attention and the opportunity to tell the world that she was probably the only person alive able to trace her lineage all the way back to Hywel Dda and God knows how far back into the dim beginnings of a great Indian nation.

Her purpose having been served, Miss Price disappeared from public view after the first big burst of publicity subsided. The state Historical Society, which had by now taken over the project, was happy to oblige her in her wish to inter Caradoc's and Livia's remains, which she had not, as it turned out, disposed of at all, on the site, and even placed a special marker at the new burial site.

The Fremonts wondered if the Scroggit brothers would show up for the dedication, set for a year from June.

The Scroggits, it turned out, had wound up in court—in several courts, in fact—after officers responding to the gas line rupture called up their outstanding warrants.

Then, there had been a stunning reversal of fortune. Guilty pleas and shows of great contrition apparently got them off with no prison time, but hefty fines, which they had managed to pay. They had also settled with their creditors and paid all their back taxes.

Somehow, the resources had become available for the Scroggits to close their two failing local stores and donate them to a couple of local charities, then open a state-of-the-art "Scroggit Brothers Artifacts" store in the heart of Civil War country itself—Spotsylvania County, Virginia.

"Did you hear, they're probably going to name the new visitor center after Miss Price?" Roland said.

"Visitor center?" cried Nan. "They're going to have a visitor center?"

"Yes, it's on the drawing boards. And a parking lot. Probably even a concessions building. It's history that's been rewritten right here in Livia. The state's going to pony up matching money for the development and maybe more. Private foundations are chipping in, too. It'll turn into a bigger deal than Miss Price would have ever guessed. They're going to buy up some more homes, you know."

"Yes, we had heard something to that effect. Some of our old neighbors aren't talking to us anymore. We felt badly about that. But that was completely out of our hands. We had no idea it was going to be this big. We've been sort of out of the loop here, Mr. Ready. We're got an entire new property to deal with, and more than an acre of gardens to map out and plant."

"They were talking about taking some of the properties under eminent domain."

"That's too bad!" said George.

"No, it's not. As it turned out, they might not have to, and I'm guessing you'll be back on speaking terms with your former neighbors before long. They're offering to pay top dollar for the properties, not to mention moving costs and relocation help. They might have willing sellers. Besides, Miss Price owned the property next to you anyway and donated it. That saved them some money right there. The idea here is to have a ten-acre site, at minimum."

"Wow!" said George and Nan.

"Oh, Mr. Ready," blurted Nan. "I wanted to tell you about a book I have in the works, a book about cross-cultural communication with plants."

"Ah."

"I've been working on it with Dr. Hilda Brockheimer of the horticultural department over at the university. We're looking for a publisher even as we speak."

"Just let me know. One thing I almost forgot—the state architects want to construct an arbor just like the one you guys had. Same spot. The crab apples and paper birches are still there."

"Gosh!" Nan cried. "I would have thought all our digging would have damaged their roots beyond repair."

"Excellent idea," said George. "For those tourists who need a little time to contemplate."

"And they're naming it after you. 'The George and Nan Fremont Arbor.'"

"With that in mind, we'll probably have to come over here and sit some, won't we, Nan-bee?" said George.

"Yes, and absorb some more magical powers," said Nan, winking at Roland. "Lord only knows what we might be capable of after a few such meditations."

"You probably won't mind checking in on you know who, would you, George?"

"I'm way ahead of you, Nan-bee," said George, who was already on a route that would take them to the Breckwood neighborhood. Nan's smartphone went off. She had just made this concession to twenty-first-century technology, and already it seemed magnetically attached to her ear and thumbs. George, who was still holding out against the smartphone onslaught, grimaced; he hated that faux-wind-chime tone.

"It's Shirelle!" chirped Nan after she hung up. "She's doing fine in her new job and wants to come by and stay with us for a few days next month. Maybe even check out the new grounds.

Maybe even help out planning some gardens." Off went the sickening approximation of that sublime tinkling again.

"That's Mary. She's at Mertons'. Wants to know how many more bottles of Sagelands we need. So?"

"We don't need any. We've got scads of them. Even for us, it'd take years to get through our current stock."

"I know, but we've made a new convert in Edith. She said no one could have conjured up anything as delectable as our 2007 vintage merlot. We need to help her spread the gospel. We also need to give her all the customer support we can so she won't have to take out any more loans our resident lending predator can gobble up. Wasn't it wonderful that she was able to take care of all her payments last summer with that one big lump sum? What an angel Marta was, lending her all that money, interest-free, and with all the Rose Maidens chipping in. I can't believe Dr. Sproot was charging her twenty-five percent interest! Why, that's usury!"

"I can believe it. And speaking of which." George slowed to a crawl, pulled over to the curb, and craned his neck to see if Dr. Sproot was lurking anywhere in her front yard.

"Careful, George," said Nan. "Remember what Marta said. Dr. Sproot owns a fully loaded BB gun, and she's not afraid to use it. She also said no one's seen her for ages. It's as if she fell off the edge of the earth."

"Mmm–hmm," said George.

There was no sign of Dr. Sproot. Neither was there any sign of her ruthless gardening energy, which should have been in evidence by now. Normally, she'd be amending the soil and fertilizing like nobody's business around this time of year.

"Maybe she's finally gotten the message," said Nan. "A few months in the loony bin must have straightened her out. My gosh, George, look!" As George inched his way along the curb, they came up to a FOR SALE sign hammered into the ground.

"Well, that should solve that problem," Nan said. "Unless she just picked up and moved somewhere else in Livia."

"She did *not* spend several months in the loony bin. She got sprung the next day. Remember? And Miss Price's ancestors whisked her off to either Las Vegas or hell, we couldn't figure out which. How could you forget?"

"Nonsense. George, are you still on that flower Armageddon kick? I might have to have *you* committed if you keep this up."

"Just keep your eyes on the weeds this year. I bet we don't have any. The sales of weed killer at Burdick's will drop to zero. That's because we vanquished the weeds from Livia just like Saint Patrick vanquished the snakes from Ireland."

"Yes, well, we'll get the scoop on the good doctor when Marta comes over. My gosh, it *has* been ages since we've seen her. Where does the time go? It's that hard winter we had. Kept people indoors and out of sight. And maybe you'll want to put a lid on all this good-versus-evil talk, if you don't mind, please, George. Ah, speak of the devil." Off went the wind chimes again. Nan stared intently at the text message on her smartphone, then put her thumbs in motion.

"Marta wonders when the best time to come would be," said Nan. "I told her around three."

The chimes jangled again.

"Good grief, who is it now?" said George.

"It's Jim. He can't make it. And guess what else?"

"He wants to do a sweep of our new yard before we start planting."

"Of course."

Back at the new place, George inched the Avalon into the spacious garage, next to where Cullen's new Honda Accord and Ellis's new Chevy Malibu would also be parked when the boys were home from college. They'd gone back for the last quarter a few weeks ago, after spring break ended.

Mary, still out running her errands, was home for the weekend after driving over the night before from Sap City. Having matriculated at Stanford, she soon discovered that her heart was in neither the marching band nor Palo Alto; she'd transferred to Headwaters State, intending to be the first student there to major in both jazz trombone and floriculture.

George was a little abashed at the size of the five-car garage. That would have been an almost unthinkable extravagance at the old place, in a neighborhood dominated by one-car tuck-unders and two-car detached garages. Nan had convinced him that they should splurge, but he had held out for a house size of no more than 2,700 square feet, the same size as the old place. She had countered by coming up with a wish list that specified new kitchen, walk-in closets, formal dining room, mudroom, and at least one bathroom with a Jacuzzi, to go along with the garage. She hadn't had to do much arm twisting to get George to agree. To accommodate all that, the house size had to expand to 4,500 square feet. They were lucky to find a home also furnished with a wine cellar big enough to accommodate their one thousand bottles of 2005, 2007, and now, 2010 Sagelands merlot.

Nan had not forsaken the out of doors. She had already bought a new set of furniture for a patio that came equipped with a built-in brick fireplace, bilevel deck, and even a built-in grill recessed into a freestanding brick column. George was happy to see that she had bought the furniture set on sale, and for 50 percent off, no less!

"We've got quite a job ahead of us, dear," said Nan, as they waited for their guests. George filled her glass to the brim, then gave the bottle that no-spill little wrist turn he could do as deftly as any maître d' worth his salt in a four-star restaurant.

"Wouldn't mind if you cranked up some Tull, dear. Can't beat that *Songs from the Wood*." George retreated inside the deck's sliding French doors, and seconds later, the waterproof speakers mounted under the roof eaves were booming "The Whistler."

"Not that loud!" shouted Nan over Martin Barre's guitar and Ian Anderson's penny whistle. "Turn it down!" The volume adjusted to an acceptable level, George returned to his chair with that stealthy quickness that was so characteristic of him.

"Look at this yard. Why, it's all grass and trees. What were they thinking? Oh, and we need to get all the bird feeders up today. And the wren houses. They'll be scouting out locations in a few weeks, you know."

"Will do," said George. "Don't you worry, Nan-bee, I'm sure we'll be up to the task."

Nan gazed disdainfully at the stump carving of Miguel de Cervantes, which, against her wishes, George had dug out of its spot in the old backyard and placed far too close to the deck, to Nan's way of thinking. A car pulled into the spacious driveway.

"First guest," said Nan. "Look sharp there with the Sagelands, George."

"Never a problem, Nan-bee." Dr. Brockheimer was bounding down the sidewalk looking radiant and happy. She climbed up the wooden steps to the first level of the deck and plopped down in one of the Fremonts' new chairs, designed and manufactured by Scandinavians for the optimum in ergonomic comfort and well-being.

"Wow, Hilda! You look happy," said Nan. "Glass of merlot?"

"Of course! Of course! And, George and Nan, refill yours, because we're going to have a couple of toasts." George filled all their glasses and they lifted them up.

"And here's to . . ." began George.

"The first toast is for Ferd. He's off on a tremendous research project to determine once and for all which explorers got here before Columbus. China, Wales, England, France, Portugal, Scandinavia. World-class accommodations. It's a two-year project, for heaven's sake. He's in hog heaven." The three of them clinked their glasses.

"Wonderful that the university will let him do this," said Nan.

"University nothing," said Dr. Brockheimer. "He's not getting any grant money either. It's all coming from some private investor who apparently has unlimited resources and an obsessive interest in the same subject."

"We're so happy that you and Dr. Lick have reconciled," Nan chirped. "Are you going along?"

Dr. Brockheimer laughed.

"Oh, no," she said. "Our divorce went through. It was quite amicable. And Ferd has a new friend. It's his investor. He calls her his 'sugar mama.' She's going along with him as his research partner. A woman, I'm told, who's been frequenting his office lately. Rumor has it she's come into a great deal of money recently. Inheritance, I suppose."

George and Nan looked at each other and smiled.

"Well, there's the last of our mysteries unraveled," said Nan.

"Pardon?" wondered Dr. Brockheimer.

"Oh, nothing, Hilda," Nan said. "We're just glad to have all this buried-treasure business over and done with. And to be sitting here in this beautiful new location with full wineglasses in front of us and a vast palette of wonderful new gardening possibilities spread out before us."

"Hear, hear," said Dr. Brockheimer, raising her glass.

"And there's another?" wondered George.

"Sure is!" gushed Dr. Brockheimer. "Here's to having a best-seller. We just sold the plant-whispering book."

"Didn't!" cried Nan.

"Did!" said Dr. Brockheimer. "The editor who bought it thinks it'll be *huge*. They're going to call it, *Talking to Your Plants: The George and Nan Fremont Way*." Glasses clinked again.

"Oh, boy," said George. "Another shot at fame. Just what we need."

Acknowledgments

Thanks to all the folks at Kensington for making me look good as an author. I'll single out editor Martin Biro especially for his judicious and insightful edits and suggestions. Martin is a shining example of how every author needs a good editor. The fact that he's unfailingly polite and patient has served to raise him even more in my esteem.

Literary agent Peter Rubie at FinePrint Literary Management has offered me sound advice on carving out a career as an author, and helps steer me on the right course of action when necessary.

In terms of research, a farcical novel such as *Front Yard* allows you by its very nature to treat accuracy with a blithe disregard much of the time. Still, I do like to get my gardening facts straight. For that, I lean on my friend and former colleague Mary Jane Smetanka, who brings the expertise of a master gardener to her perusal of my manuscripts. I will also mention a few others who helped by looking over sections of *Front Yard,* mostly to make sure I didn't write something that strayed too far from the realm of fictional possibility. They are: Sam Draper, whose experience as a tree company employee

Acknowledgments

proved invaluable; Neil Anderson, professor of flower breeding and genetics at the University of Minnesota, Twin Cities; Shaun David McGuinness, a PhD student in Welsh history at Bangor University, in Wales; and Paul Stone, assistant professor of history at the University of Minnesota's Humphrey School of Public Affairs. To them, I offer my thanks. In the case of Mr. McGuinness, I say, *Diolch yn fawr.*

Special thanks, as always, to my family—wife Jennifer and sons Sam and Ed.